RACHEL'S SED

Cattleman's Club 3

Jenny Penn

MENAGE EVERLASTING

Siren Publishing, Inc.
www.SirenPublishing.com

A SIREN PUBLISHING BOOK
IMPRINT: Ménage Everlasting

RACHEL'S SEDUCTION
Copyright © 2011 by Jenny Penn

ISBN-10: 1-61034-232-1
ISBN-13: 978-1-61034-232-2

First Printing: January 2011

Cover design by *Les Byerley*
All art and logo copyright © 2011 by Siren Publishing, Inc.

Printed in the U.S.A.

PUBLISHER
Siren Publishing, Inc.
www.SirenPublishing.com

DEDICATION

To Max.

RACHEL'S SEDUCTION

Cattleman's Club 3

JENNY PENN
Copyright © 2011

Prelude

Wednesday, February 20th

"Did your pussy put you in a better mood?"

"*Excuse me?*"

Killian's head popped up at the incredulous sound of a female gasp. *Not Bryant.* When he'd heard the person enter into the lobby, Killian had assumed it was his fellow deputy returning from his late lunch. It was a safe assumption given the storm raging outside. The downpour had kept the public at bay all day.

A safe assumption, but not a right one. Dropping his feet from the counter, he immediately straightened up on his stool. Killian did his best to school his features into a sincere look of apology as he hastily tucked the magazine full of tattooed women under the counter.

"I'm sorry, ma'am. I thought you were somebody else."

"Well, I should hope so." The little miss might be in her thirties, but her retort carried the full measure of little-old-lady disdain. With her tight bun and cover-every-inch outfit, she had more than just a matronly tone. Even the way she snapped the water off her umbrella before folding it into the stand had a certain old-grumpy-person feel to it.

Or a strict school teacher that likes to whack errant little boys. Given her scowl as she marched stiffly toward the counter, he didn't feel silly in checking her hands for a ruler. Not finding one kind of disappointed him. Killian never had been spanked. He bet that was the only thing he and Miss Proper had in common.

"I am here to see the sheriff." The petite woman managed to look down her nose while having to look up at him. "I have an appointment."

Killian bet she did. It would be too perfect for Miss Straight-Laced to end up with Mr. By-The-Book. They could have perfect, church-going little angels. Then one day Killian's little juvenile delinquent could seduce boss's goody-two-shoes daughter. *Teach her all the right ways to praise God.*

Killian could already imagine just how many sorts of pissed off the sheriff would be with him then. *Wouldn't that be some fun?* Alex might deserve it, but Killian didn't plan on having any kids. An affair, though, with the soon-to-be Mrs. Stuck-Up would certainly be a tale worth telling. That's if she didn't freeze off any important parts of his anatomy in the process.

Killian liked his women warm, sultry, even, and definitely—

"Deputy?"

Clearing his throat and ignoring his slight lapse, Killian answered with the correct amount of professional politeness. "I'm sorry, ma'am, but the sheriff's not here right now."

Like an owl, she blinked at him, those massive hazel eyes gazing out with amusing incomprehension. "But we have an appointment."

He shouldn't say anything, just nod and stay silent before he dug himself a bigger ditch for the sheriff to bury him in when he got back to the station house. The problem was Killian wasn't the type to keep his thoughts to himself. She did tempt him, too, with that flustered look. He'd bet she wore a similar look of shock when she came. *If she ever does.* Killian thought not given how stiff the little lady was.

"He's supposed to be here."

Definitely one to repeat the 'oh, God' mantra of disbelief when she orgasms. "I guess it wasn't that important to the sheriff, because he didn't mention it."

"But I made the appointment yesterday."

This was when he should shut up, but he never had matured to that level. "But it's today."

"Excuse me?"

"It's seems to me like you're a day late," Killian retorted, intentionally misunderstanding just to watch that blush grow until it touched the tips of her ears. "I mean, seriously, lady, if you make an appointment for yesterday, you really can't expect the sheriff to be waiting on you today."

The little brunette actually growled, and, damn, if that wasn't the sexiest sound he'd heard all day. Killian could see her muscles tensing for the pounce. Hell, if he was any kind of lucky, she'd launch herself right over the counter. Instead, all that energy got wasted on a stupid vexing motion. She slapped the folder she'd held clutched between her hands down onto the counter like a gauntlet...*Whatever the hell that is.*

Killian didn't know, but he bet no knight had ever looked as tempting as the mad-as-hell lady leaning across the counter to put him in his place. He gave her points for audacity, given she didn't have the least bit of height to intimidate him with. She did, however, have the harpish tone down.

"Listen. I'm Rachel Allen, reporter for the *Pittsview Press*, and I am supposed to interview the sheriff. Today. Now. About the budget. I have an appointment."

Killian studied the stubborn tilt of Miss Allen's chin and considered he might be dealing with a closet wildcat. He could see the flash of passion in the green bolts lighting up her hazel eyes and considered they just might go all green when she came. Hell, for all the grit the little miss showed in openly challenging him, she probably would give a man one hell of a ride.

Maybe it wouldn't be such a hardship to break the sheriff's future darlin' in first. Well, maybe a little bit of a pain, but in all the right ways because Killian bet little Miss Allen was a screamer, possibly even a scratcher, and, if he was very lucky, she might even bite him.

Killian took a breath and thought about draining out the sewer line until his cock stopped trying to outgrow his pants. It was a battle of control Killian enjoyed and couldn't help but indulge in.

"That's all well and good, little lady," Killian drawled out condescendingly. Starting off with the good ol' boy smirk, he rose back to his feet and showed her how intimidation was done. "But the sheriff ain't in right now, and all your tantrums ain't gonna change that fact."

Rachel's eyes rounded wide with shock, and he half expected her to either smack him or breakdown and cuss. A true Southern lady, she visibly managed to control the urge. It took a lot of effort, though, and made Killian wonder just how much provocation it would take to get her to say something dirty. *Like demanding that I lick her pussy...probably have to shave the darlin' first.*

"Well, then, I guess I'll have to interview you."

Lost in his own thoughts, Killian hadn't been prepared for that response. It threw him for a moment, and he stumbled. "But I...don't know about budgets."

"But you do know what this place needs, right?" Rachel whipped a notebook out of the folder.

Her pen clicked open. The sound echoed in Killian's ears as he stared down at the woman, completely uncertain of what the hell he was supposed to do with her now. His confusion didn't stop her from waiting, pointedly silent, with that damn pen pressed and ready against her notebook. Killian didn't like to fail a challenge, and he damn well knew when one was being issued.

After giving him the moment to feel completely humiliated at being caught off guard, Rachel pitied him with a smile. "I'm sorry,

Deputy. I assumed you could do the math. You got five bulletproof vests and eight officers. You need three more. That kind of thing."

Click. Like the bell going off at the end of the boxing round, Rachel's pen rang out with her victory. Tucking it back into her notebook, she just couldn't leave without giving him one last good kick.

"That's all right, Deputy. I can wait until somebody returns who *can* do it."

Killian blinked, staring down at the girl who had dared to insult him. What was she? All of five foot three and maybe a hundred and thirty pounds, all ass and tits. Yeah, Killian had noticed, but he'd been respecting the drab wallflower outfit Rachel had on. That was the kind of man he was.

His mama had raised him right and taught him to treat a lady like a lady. He'd learned all on his own how to treat a vixen. They deserved the flat of his palm against their asses to make them heel. It was quite clear to him which group little Miss Rachel Allen fell into, evident by the fact that she couldn't control herself and do the wise thing—quit and run.

"I guess I shouldn't even bother to wait," Rachel commented, as if they were actually having some kind of conversation. "Budgets make such boring press. *You*, on the other hand, will make quite an interesting story."

The damn woman chuckled at her own words, making the heat flare back into Killian's ears. "I think people would be riveted to learn how deputies in this city greet unescorted ladies when they enter the station. Why, I think there is an obvious need for the budget to include some funds for sensitivity training. After all, it's apparent—"

"Fine," Killian cut her off, needing to hear no more. If little Miss Rachel Allen wanted to play hardball, he'd teach her how the game was played. "Obviously, Miss Allen, the police department is here to serve the public, and, as you are a member of said group, I would be happy to show you our facility and discuss the current needs of our department.

"If you would step this way." Killian gestured to the little wooden gate dividing the large room into a small lobby and a barely sufficient-sized work space.

Rachel hesitated, intelligent enough to distrust him. Killian smiled pleasantly back at her in spite of her hard look, betting she wouldn't be able to retreat from not only the challenge but the curiosity to find out what he intended to do with her. If only she knew, Rachel wouldn't have been giving him such a sour look as she collected her folder.

Nope, she'd have been running screaming from the building instead of issuing her own warning. "Very well, but I'm still not convinced the budget would make better press."

"I thought your job was about informing the masses," Killian retorted, watching as her hip pressed into the gate, "not entertaining them. Do watch the step."

He'd offered that warning knowing it was too late. Head held high, Rachel took one step forward and went flat on her face. Holding back the chuckles as she slapped into the linoleum floor, Killian played the dutifully concerned man and rushed to her side. "Are you all right, darlin'?"

"Don't call me that," Rachel growled out, shoving herself up to her knees.

The plan had been to be helpful, to go to his knees and stack her papers and show the little spitfire he could be polite. He hadn't factored in the captivating, and very distracting, view of looking right down her shirt. The V neckline of her blouse dipped lower as she bent forward, revealing a pink lacy bra holding her plump breasts close together. The soft mounds pressed against each other, leaving a shadowed cleavage absolutely perfect for fucking a hard dick through. Killian's swelled at the very idea of feeling all that soft flesh caressing him.

Oh, yeah, and she'd be looking up at me with those big eyes all fogged with passion, her cheeks all flushed, and she'd be begging, begging for my fucking.

Killian bet Rachel would be tight, too. By the way she carried herself, he knew she hadn't gotten a lot of action over the years. Sure as shit, she'd never known a lover like him but soon enough would.

"Do I need to slap you?" Rachel's demand brought Killian blinking back to the moment. Glaring at the obvious tent forming in his slacks, she rose to her feet, wisely out of reach. "Because I'm feeling the need to slap you."

Killian smirked. He'd like to see her try. "Assaulting a police officer is a very serious offense, Miss Allen."

"Yeah?" All full of spice and sass now, Rachel shed her prissy demeanor to give Killian a glimpse of the very woman who would soon be sweating up his bed sheets. "And I'm sure being accused of peeping down women's blouses would do loads of good for your career."

"Kind of hard to cry foul when you like the attention, honey." Pointedly, Killian's gaze dropped to the puckered nipples making their own tent in her blouse. The sight whipped to the right as the woman actually did smack him.

"Ah!" Killian rolled his jaw, working out the burn. "Damn, that hurt!"

"Good," Rachel spat, turning to storm out in high dudgeon. "And you can bet the story in tomorrow's paper is going to pain you even more!"

"Whoa! Where do you think you're going?" Killian latched on to her arm, spinning her back around before she cleared the gate. He'd give her points for trying, but all the struggles she could muster didn't save her from being pinned against the counter. "You keep on squirming, darlin', because it feels pretty damn good on this side."

Leaning into her until her breasts flattened out against his chest, Killian growled right into her wide eyes. "Feels better naked, and if you don't settle down, that's where this will end. See, you hit me, and now I can arrest you. I could take you back into the private booking area and start processing you. That begins with a search of your person. I'm going to have to pat down this sexy little body and make sure you're not hiding anything…paying special attention to all the places you might have something forbidden tucked into you."

He let his hand define the threat by slipping down over her ass to press her up against the hard grind of his cock. Even as her breath shortened to sexy little pants, Killian could smell her heat thickening in the air.

"You wouldn't dare," she whispered out of her like a prayer.

Too bad Killian thrilled at playing the devil. "Honey, there isn't anything I wouldn't dare."

Obviously not a quitter, Rachel swallowed. This time, her voice came out with a little sound to it, even if it did tremble. "I'll write a story."

"About what?" Killian smirked. "About how you got so wet you needed a cock and it didn't matter to you that we were screwing on the sheriff's desk?"

"Deputy, listen to me very carefully." Her voice had gone all soft, husky with the desire he could smell thickening in the air. "If you don't let me go right now, I'll make sure the only place willing to give you a badge is the mall in Dothan."

"Threaten all you want." Killian ground himself against the small rubbing motions Rachel's hips had started to make. Her body was dancing now, trying to lure him in closer. "I know what you want."

"And isn't that every rapist's excuse?"

"What the hell?" Just the use of that word had Killian jerking back with a scowl as he stared at the woman in horrified shock. "I ain't forcing here, lady. I'm seducing."

"I fail to see the difference when I'm being held against my will," Rachel snapped back.

"Not against your will," Killian retorted, but his indignant steam ran out as he tried to follow his own reasoning. "Just against your permission."

She snorted at that, backing up toward the gate as if he might attack her. The nervous motion pissed him off all the more because he knew for a fact that he had her wet already. That was the problem with stick-up-their-asses types.

Fine, she wants to do this proper-like, I'll play it nice…right up until I have her ass tied to my bed. Then it'll be game on.

"I have *never* in all my life—"

"I have no doubt, Miss Adams," Killian cut her off. If he wanted to come out the victor, he needed to start using some of that charm his mother always warned women about. "I offer you my sincerest apologies and can only express to you how overcome I was by your—"

"Don't make fun of me." Rachel stiffened straight up. "I am not here to be the butt of your jokes just because you're having a boring day, Deputy."

"I'm not joking," Killian grunted, feeling a little insulted that she dared to reject his apology. "I'm saying I'm attracted, and I let—"

"To what?"

He really hated to be interrupted. "To you."

"Are you saying you're attracted to me?"

Her incredulousness irritated Killian. "Yes, to you. Why the hell is that so hard to believe?"

"Everything out of your mouth is hard to believe, Deputy," Rachel snapped. "You're obviously so full of shit, only a half-wit would take you seriously. It seems more likely to me that you're a bored asshole looking for somebody to fuck with because you've gotten tired of playing with yourself.

"Trust me, *honey*, you haven't got nothing that I find even the slightest bit entertaining." Her eyes dropped down to what Killian knew to be an impressive bulge. Hell, his dick was putting on the full-course strut for her, and all she did was snicker. "Well, maybe a *tiny* bit amusing."

Oh, the hell she didn't. Killian's outraged shock held him still as she swept back through the lobby and almost escaped. That wouldn't be happening. Not until he had her on her knees, begging. Then he'd leave her wanting. *She's going to ache for the rest of her life.*

Rachel Allen would never see it coming because Killian knew how to get his revenge. Latching on to her hand as it reached for her coat on the rack, he played it like he was actually sorry, like she'd taught him his lesson.

"Listen, Miss Allen, why don't we start all over."

"I'm sure you'd like to, but I don't see much point," Rachel snarled, yanking her hand free. "I have things to accomplish today, none of which include putting up with you."

"Well, what about having me bend over backwards for you?" Killian offered, taking her dark glower as a positive sign. She had stopped to glare at him, so he pressed in his best pleading tone. "I'm serious. Give me a half hour to show you the station and my best side. Then you can decide if you want to rip me a new one in tomorrow's paper or have dinner with me."

"But all of your charm will be fake, right?"

"Oh, absolutely." Killian nodded. "But I'm really good at fake charm. Now will you allow me to escort you, my lady?"

Rachel hesitated, obviously torn. Clearly, he annoyed the crap out of her, but Killian suspected he also excited her in that same strange way she was exciting him. He felt kind of like a cat that had discovered a mouse to play with. Rachel probably thought she was the cat.

She sure gave him the arrogant grin of one as she finally rested her hand on the arm he'd offered. "The 'my lady' is a bit much. Don't you think, Deputy?"

Chapter 1

Friday, March 28th

Adam Whendon stared up at the stars and wondered if Cole Jackson had gotten himself killed yet. They hadn't gotten a call on the radio, but the Davis brothers had been smart enough to hide the body. It would be a matter of waiting to see if the cocky son of a bitch ever showed back up in town.

Dumbass. There appeared to be a lot of those running around lately. Unfortunately, Adam happened to be tied to one by a lifelong friendship that that left him little choice but to put up with Killian's stupid ideas. Cole had lost his head over Patton Jones. Alex had lost his head over Sweetness.

Killian had thought it would be fun to seduce the sheriff's latest addiction away from him. Well, the cocky son of a bitch wasn't laughing now.

"I cannot believe we're stuck on patrol duty," Killian complained, kicking a rock over the uneven ground. "This sucks."

"I told you Alex would find a way to make us suffer for luring Sweetness away from him," Adam retorted without thought. They'd had this conversation about a hundred times *before* they'd gone ahead and done the dumb thing. So Killian's constant whining lacked a certain amount of honesty.

"Yeah, well, she was sweet," Killian muttered, appearing to concentrate on kicking his second stone farther than Adam. He came up short with a sigh. "Still, it isn't right. I mean, we're supposed to share. That's sort of the motto of the club, and Alex punishing us for having a little fun with his plaything goes against the grain."

"Hey." Killian straightened up with a sudden burst of energy, turning on Adam as if he'd just gotten struck by the smart fairy. "You don't think Alex actually liked the girl?"

Adam snorted, casting Killian a concerned look. "Liked?"

"Like *liked* the girl?"

"You mean as in loved her? Alex? Are you insane?"

Reality deflated Killian's momentary happiness and he slumped back into a slouch. "Yeah. Well, it's just…" Killian waved to the darkened fields stretching in all directions. "I mean this is a little extreme, being banned from the party to do patrol work is one thing, but he has us on real patrol tomorrow night and that's when the most fun is. Think about it, man. We're going to miss the auction."

"All that prime female flesh." Adam nodded, not really caring. The auction tomorrow, the orgy tonight, none of it mattered much to Adam. He'd spent all his life surrounded by the wrong type of women, even from birth.

The women at the club were great, nice and a hell of a lot fun, but they never could give Adam the one thing he'd always truly lusted after—comfort. While the beautiful, well-trained pets corralled in the club might be a world apart from his own drunken bitch of a mother, they all had one thing in common. They didn't care a lick about him beyond what he could do for them in the moment.

It kind of wore him out on the one hand. On the other hand, good girls didn't go in for the kind of fun Adam enjoyed between the sheets. At least he didn't think they would. He didn't really know because he'd never really gone trolling for a decent woman. It just seemed to him by definition that the type of woman who would settle down wouldn't be interested in a man who wanted to share her for happily ever after.

"Fresh flesh." There was something almost desperate sounding in Killian's voice.

That tone had been squeaking into Killian's words more and more lately. At first Adam had thought it was because of Adam's own comments about looking more for a relationship than quick a service by the latest honey at the club. Given Killian's sworn bachelor mentality, it made sense his friend would be getting jumpy.

What didn't make sense was the strange fixation Killian had developed for a particular brunette. It'd taken Adam a while to put the pieces together. Not that hadn't been kind of obvious.

Killian had developed a sudden habit of wanting to eat almost every meal at the Bread Box. Then when they'd get there, Killian would get all pissed and go all silent, just watching the brunette like a cat watched a mole.

Adam didn't know her name, but she appeared to be good friends with Heather Lawson, the owner of the diner. They hung out at the bar, mostly chatting, while Killian tended to position himself in a booth so he could glare at the prissy looking brunette. Not that she ever once looked his way.

It was actually kind of pathetic, a trait Killian had never been accused of. Especially not over such a homely looking thing. The woman wrapped herself in layers of oversized, dowdy clothes and did absolutely nothing with her hair but pin it into a bun.

A good girl, definitely. One who would undoubtedly be having a big family and a picket fence. Adam doubted, though, that she'd be rounding out the image with two husbands. From what he could tell of her by her appearance, the brunette was a just-one type.

That made Killian's fixation all the more strange and, consequently, more concerning. Killian's ego couldn't accept a rejection. So, of course, he had to go and prove himself with some overly outlandish action, like seducing the sheriff's personal pet.

Given the choice of a reckless partner or one who moped around like a lovesick schoolboy, Adam had picked reckless and signed onto Killian's less-than-intelligent plan. Not that any of Killian's plans were ever good, and this one had been no different.

Now, the sheriff was pissed at them, and Killian was still dragging Adam to the Bread Box every damn day. *Like a damn dog with his bone, but that woman sure ain't going to be playing with it.*

Poor Killian. He just had to live with disappointment all around. Adam tried to soften the blow for his partner.

"I don't know. Somebody's got to work. The whole station can't take the night off. Besides, the party will still be going when we get off." Meaning there would still be plenty of pussy to go around.

Killian didn't bother to respond. Instead, he returned to his silent brooding, leaving Adam to his. Only he couldn't concentrate on anything with that noise flittering in and out on the night breeze. Going still, he strained to hear the distant, sporadic scratch in the night's normal harmony. His feet shifted, following the direction of the noise as he tried to figure out what it was.

"It's late enough to call off this patrol." Killian followed after him, not even appearing aware that Adam was actually doing something. "Maybe we could still salvage something of the night."

"Give it another half hour," Adam responded absentmindedly as the gasping scratch started to gather into an identifiable sound.

"Oh, come on," Killian groaned. "All the teenagers that normally try have tried. They're probably three sheets to the wind right now, having their own party."

Pausing to cast Killian a smirk, Adam asked, "You think?"

"Yeah."

"Then what's that?"

"What?" Killian looked around.

"Shh. Listen," Adam whispered.

Killian stilled, appearing to concentrate for a moment. *There*, cutting through the soft hum of insects and the deep-throated croaks of frogs and the silence, the noise came again. An engine blended into the soft murmur of the night. It whined upward through the gears in a protest that told Adam the car was either stuck or trying to tow something way too heavy.

"Shit." Killian groaned out the word, and Adam knew he was silently hoping they could let it slide. Not in this lifetime. Terrorizing some teenagers sounded like more fun to him than watching a drunken orgy.

"Come on." Adam started off for the vehicle. "Let's go scare some sense into some sixteen-year-olds."

Killian muttered and cussed but followed Adam as he traced the sound all the way back to the road, a decent distance from the party. Adam guessed the kids were on their way out and probably got stuck in the drainage ditch running along the road. One to ten they're drunk, Adam bet himself as the outline of a small compact started to cut its way through the shadows.

The engine sounds had died out. The kids must have given up hope of driving themselves out of trouble. A wise decision from what Adam could see. The little car was close to vertical with its ass buried in the ditch. They'd left somebody to sit on the car. Literally, the kid had stretched out right on the hood.

The runt of the group from what he could tell at the distance. Adam had dealt with enough teenagers to know they'd probably left the most timid and defenseless one to guard the car until they could come back with one of their daddy's stolen pick-ups to haul Mommy's car out of the ditch.

"This should be fun." Killian barely breathed the words out, coming to a stop right behind Adam. They lurked in the deep shadows of the closest cluster of trees, watching the kid stretch out on the hood.

"Bet he's asleep."

Meaning they could get the drop on the boy and give him the start of a lifetime. "You go left."

* * * *

Rachel gave up the battle. The back tires were stuck. As in not coming out.

Everything. Everything up to this moment—perfect.

It figured, though, that her luck wouldn't hold out. Nothing in her life ever did. She should have known that Hailey's too-convenient phone call telling her about the Cattleman's party and Tim's actually being home to lend her his camera, completely set up to take night pictures, were both jinxes. If she didn't have to work hard for something then inevitably it all fell apart.

Like getting herself stuck in a ditch and having left her cell phone at home and Pittsview being way too long of a walk away for her, those kind of things tended to be all her fault for failing to take the time and do things properly.

God, I'm channeling my mom now.

If only her mother could see her, she'd be horrified, and not because Rachel had gotten her car stuck. No, her mother would turn a new shade of red, probably go all the way to purple, if she knew what kind of orgy Rachel had not only spied on but actually taken more than one picture of. Thankfully, her mother probably couldn't fathom the kind of things the local politicians had been doing to the women dressed in nothing but shoes and collars.

There had been women on leashes, women getting spanked, whipped, fucked in every position Rachel knew and many she hadn't, but then again she'd never even dreamed of doing more than one man at once. Not at all shocked by what she'd witnessed, Rachel's outrage had come a little late and resulted in her fleeing with such speed she'd gotten her car stuck.

What woman wouldn't run for her life when she realized that she was getting...*turned on? No, that's not the word for it.* It was more like she'd gone into heat. Her body still hummed, actually, but Rachel chose to ignore it and focus instead on the article that she never would write.

The idea had been to come out here and take pictures to help fill an article that would jumpstart her career and give her life some kind of zip. There was only one problem with her plan. It wasn't wise to live in a small Southern town when after publishing pictures of the mayor riding some woman's ass and the president of the city council getting his dick sucked by the same woman and, worse, at the same time.

There could be no publishing the article, no matter how much fun it might be to watch the city explode. The problem with explosions was people tended to get hurt. Her one article could wreck not only individual lives, marriages, families, but the whole damn town.

But it's supposed to be my ticket out. Her ticket to something more than Fridays wasted with frozen dinners and her knitting needles. After watching all those women have true, honest-to-God orgasms, Rachel really wanted her ticket to take her there. Maybe a good fuck would get rid of this restless itchiness that had invaded her body ever since she realized her thirtieth birthday was approaching way too fast.

It wasn't fair. She deserved an orgasm, and she shouldn't have to lower herself to going out with the likes of Killian Kregor to get one. Just at the thought of the large deputy, Rachel twitched. Despite having lived in Pittsview her whole life without ever having a run-in with Killian Kregor, it seemed lately she couldn't escape him.

Everywhere she went, she saw him. Every time, it reminded her of how big a coward she actually was. He'd been a complete ass when she'd first met him, but, true to his word, Killian's fake charm had been all but devastating. No matter that she knew he'd been putting on a show for her benefit, Rachel had found herself captivated by the arrogant man.

He had a right to his cockiness. With looks that could make an archangel jealous and a life spent traveling to all sorts of exotic locations and having all kinds of adventures, he was everything she wasn't. Nobody would ever accuse the man of being boring, and a woman only had to take a second look to know he was worth all the aggravation.

Inhaling a single breath of his musky scent flooded a woman's brain with images of sweaty bodies, of callused fingers biting into her ass while he pumped her hard and fast against his grinding pelvis and raced her toward a true, hot-blooded climax…

"Hey."

"Ahhhh!"

Rachel screeched at the sudden sound of a deep masculine voice. She started so hard she fell right off the hood and went crashing into the uneven ground. With the momentum of her fall, she rolled down the small embankment she'd gotten her car stuck in and came to a stop as a heap of limbs. Pain shot up her ankle, and the screech turned into a scream of pain.

"Oh, damn."

That voice came from right over her head, but the hands that appeared to help get her back on her feet came straight from the right. They were disembodied, and for a moment, she didn't care. She didn't intend on going anywhere. It just hurt too damn much.

"Will you look what you did?"

"I didn't mean to scare her like that."

"What the hell did you think was going to happen?"

"Oh, yeah. I planned this whole thing, Adam." An oversized set of hands cupped her cheeks gently, brushing the hair out of her face so she could see as he tilted her head up to meet his. "Are you all right, sweetheart?"

Oh, crap. Killian. This really wasn't her lucky night. How could a man look so devastating in the cloak of the night's shadows? The darkness clung to the hard planes of his features, carving them out like elegant stonework. Even the bright glow of the full moon made his amazing eyes devastating. She remembered the color, blue-green. They were light, multifaceted, like crystalline orbs designed to entrance and mesmerize any woman stupid enough to directly look into their mysterious depths.

"Did you hit your head?"

He might as well have been speaking French because the only thing Rachel understood was that he had the gentlest of touches. Big hands with slightly callused fingertips traced around the edge of her hair line in an almost ticklish caress. She definitely tingled from the sensation.

That tingle merged with the warmth of her previous musings. A flash sparked over the volatile mix of hormones in her body. His touch ignited her brimming imagination, and scenes, those dirty, dark, erotic images of woman as bitch and man as beast, snapped through her mind as still-life possibilities of Killian and her.

"She hurt her ankle, moron. Can't you see it's swelling already?"

"Doesn't mean she couldn't have hurt her head. If you hadn't noticed, she isn't speaking."

Say something before you look like a moron, or more of one.

Before she could get all the parts in her body to work together on that plan, another set of hands tilted her face in the opposite direction.

Oh. Double damn.

Rachel swore she'd never have thought the kind of dirty things that popped into her mind at the sight of Killian's buddy if it hadn't been for all the perverts up at the Cattleman's club. They'd filled her head with all sorts of naughty ideas, like how the perfect complement to Killian's black-haired, light-eyed bad-boy look was this hunk of chocolate goodness. From the mocha locks to the dark gaze trying to enthrall her, the man had the kind of soulfulness that made a woman know he'd spread her legs wide and hold her gaze while he drove her insane with his kiss.

"I don't think she hurt her head. Her eyes don't look dilated."

That statement followed his thumb and finger wrenching open her lids as he held her head straight up into the moonlight. Instinctively, she jerked her head back and glared. Handsome or not, that had been rude.

"Maybe she's drunk," Killian offered.

"I am not drunk." Finally, she said something, and it felt good to come out of her stupor.

"Oh, look. She speaks."

"Yes, I speak, and it is extremely rude of you talk about me as if I can't hear you, *Killian*."

Rachel turned her head back toward the guy with starlight in his eyes. To avoid being distracted by his mesmerizing gaze, she kept her eyes planted on his chest, his wide, hard, muscular-looking chest. His T-shirt looked so soft. It molded perfectly to the smooth planes and cut ridges of every single one of his mouthwatering muscles.

"Rachel?" She could hear the confusion in his tone. It irked her. He didn't have to sound so shocked. "Rachel Allen?"

I recognized him. You think he could recognize me. It's only been a month, after all.

"Rachel Allen?" The other one repeated slowly. "Why does that name sound so familiar?"

"Because you see it in the paper every Sunday. She's a reporter for the *Pittsview Press*."

Uh-oh.

She could feel the tension thicken in the air as they all recognized the ramifications of that statement. Hopefully before they could come to the conclusion that she had been doing just what she'd been doing, Rachel grabbed for her ankle to create a desperate distraction.

"Ow! My ankle hurts. Are either one of you going to help me with this?"

"Not until you tell us what you are doing out here." He might have the eyes of a sweetheart, but Killian's friend also had the bark of a pit bull. Rachel was really not liking him any more than she had Killian.

Irritated that neither man appeared the least bit concerned or sympathetic to her injury, Rachel moaned and groaned with more zest this time. "Oh, but it hurts. I don't think I can stand the pain."

"Your ankle is fine."

Deputy Kregor was really the most annoying man alive with all his attitude. "It is not! I twisted it. It's already swelling. It could be broken. This is all your fault."

Rachel really enjoyed the way that made Killian growl. "My fault?"

The man looked indignant, like the idea had never occurred to him. Rachel wouldn't dignify his response with an answer but pushed ahead with her plan to irritate him as much as he did her. "You broke my ankle."

"It's not broken."

"Oh?" Rachel didn't like being tag-teamed by Killian's friend. "Like you know anything."

His chin up, he studied her in a way that made Rachel worry. He was considering something, and her gut told her she wouldn't like whatever thoughts ran through his mind. "I know about broken bones."

"What? Are you a doctor?" She should just shut up, but her mouth kept forming words without authorization.

"I spent twelve years in the Marine Corps. I've seen enough broken bones to know one."

"You can't tell a broken bone by looking."

"Sometimes you can."

"Yeah, if it's sticking out!"

"You don't have any bones sticking out, do you?"

"That doesn't mean my ankle isn't broken."

"It's not broken."

"It is broken if I say it is. It's my goddamn bone, and I know when it's broken. Not you. I don't care how many years you spent in the

Marines. I wasn't there. You haven't seen my ankle before. So you don't know anything about it!"

"Enough! I swear, woman."

Rachel just loved the way Killian bit out that "woman," so full of frustration and masculine pique that she couldn't help but smile. The small gesture only lasted a second as he continued on, bitching and ruining her moment.

"You have a mouth on you that just makes a man want to—"

"—make you purr."

Rachel's eyes rounded on Killian's friend. She knew in an instant that she was in very deep trouble. Whatever thoughts had clouded his gaze a moment before, they'd cleared up and hardened over into a look that could only be described as predatory.

"I'm betting she doesn't purr."

Killian's offhanded response felt like one line too many had just been crossed, and she snapped at him without thought. "Maybe that's because you haven't got the skills to make me purr."

It was both an invitation and a challenge, neither of which should ever be issued to a man like Killian. In a moment of frozen horror, Rachel tried to fathom what kind of response she had coming to her. Wet, sweaty, hot…God did she want to be punished.

"Definitely a biter," Adam commented.

"Would you just *shut up*?" Rachel didn't even spare a look at Killian's amused buddy, still too concerned with anticipating Killian's response.

"I bet she even snarls and cusses, making all sorts of demands."

"I do not!"

"Be kind of hot if you did."

Rachel clenched her jaw and held back on her need to give back for that one. It wouldn't do her any good. They were playing with her. The fact that Killian didn't have her hauled up to her feet for her last reckless shot went to prove they weren't taking a single thing seriously, least of all her.

She would not be toyed with. Nor would she be held hostage by these two jugheads' bad sense of humor. Intentionally dramatizing the moment, Rachel let out a wail and clutched at her ankle before threatening Killian with the only weapon she had.

"My ankle is killing me, and if you don't start doing something about that now, I swear I'm going to have a private word with the sheriff about your sexist, insensitive, and outright insulting ways, Deputy Kregor."

"Go on and tell him, honey," Killian encouraged her. "That way the bastard will know we were actually out here on patrol like he told us to be."

"And did he tell you to go around assaulting defenseless women?"

There went Killian's cheeks, flushed red in under a second. She'd gotten him good with that one. Then again, he had the advantage of having a friend to help him harass her. "Yeah and how is that ankle? Still broken?"

"I am in pain."

"If that's true, you can see the wisdom in answering my questions promptly. If you would rather waste time and delay medical treatment, please, continue on with your tantrum."

"I am not having a tantrum. Why do men always say that? I am annoyed and in pain, and I am allowed to—"

"What are you doing here?"

"What are you doing here?" Rachel shot back instantly, not about to take any crap from this man.

Towering over her, he tried to intimidate her by speaking in sharp, short words. "Answer my question."

"I'm not going to be bullied by you. I don't have to answer anything. I'm the one who has been wronged in all this. I'm the one who was out here minding my own business when you two assaulted me. I don't—"

"Assaulted you?" Killian choked on that one. "You fell off your own car all by yourself, sweetheart."

Intentionally tossing her hair over her shoulder and right into his face, Rachel felt nothing but satisfaction when he cussed and shoved up to his feet. That's right, he'd better back off or she'd pull the lowest stunt she could think of. Hell, she might as well give him a little smile and threaten him with it. It would be fun to watch him squirm for a change.

"Who is to say what happened?"

"I am. I'm a cop, unless you forgot."

"Cops go bad all the time."

"I can go bad."

Killian lowered not only his voice, but his face. When they were nose-to-nose and she could feel the warm brush of his breath, smell the intoxicating scent of man and soap, and see all of her erotic fantasies promised in the wicked depths of his eyes, he growled again.

"You want to see how bad, Rachel?"

Oh, God, yes.

Chapter 2

Rachel wisely kept her answer to herself and counted it as a victory. Later on, she'd worry about being disgraced by her desires, or maybe she wouldn't. As long as nobody knew about them and nothing was acted on, having a few wild fantasies about Killian and his bedroom-eyes buddy wouldn't hurt.

"You don't scare me, Deputy. Do your worst."

Instead of throwing himself on her and ravishing her like Fantasy Killian would have, the dumb lug just glared at her and wimped out. "Answer Adam's question. What are you doing here?"

Well, shit. Rachel blinked. It took her all of a second to consider the changed circumstances and come up with a big, obnoxious, fake smile. "I was going down the road when a deer ran out. I lost control trying to avoid the poor thing and ended up in the ditch."

"What do you think, Adam?"

What a wuss. Silently, Rachel booed Killian's performance. Shifting her gaze toward the more civilized-looking man, she wondered if perhaps he'd be her hero.

"That must have been one hell of a spin out."

Nope. "Are you doubting me?"

"I'm just saying." The man shrugged, appearing completely unaware of her antagonizing tone. "Given the way your car is in the ditch, it doesn't really look like it spun into it."

"And you would know that?"

Being questioned got to him, though she gave him points for keeping his calm. It must have been hard given the threat that narrowed his gaze for too long a second. "Considering the number of traffic accidents I've investigated, yeah. I would know that."

"Oh, you're a cop, too." She really should have seen that coming.

"That's right, sweetheart," Killian gloated. "Rachel Adams, let me introduce you to Deputy Adam Whendon. Now why don't you start over your tale and let's try hearing the truth this time."

They already knew the truth, and making her say it was just being petty. Rachel wouldn't give them the satisfaction. "Just because you're cops and don't believe what I say doesn't mean I'm lying. What happened to innocent until proven guilty?"

"Given your car is pointing out of the ditch, like it drove through it matching the tracks, and not pointed into the ditch, as it would be with the non-existent tracks you left in your imaginary spin out, it's a scientific fact that you are lying."

Adam had spent some time in court, apparently. "Fine. I didn't spin out, but that doesn't mean you have to treat me like a criminal. I was out here to...look at the stars. Got to get away from the city lights and all that, you know?"

"City lights and all that?" Adam raised an eyebrow as he repeated her own lame words back to her. Pittsview didn't have city lights. Hell, most of the town didn't even have street lights. "I take it that's why you are dressed all in black, because you're afraid bright-colored clothes would interfere with your viewing."

"Oh, shut up."

"Does that mean you're tapped out?" Killian almost sounded amused now. "We're not moving on to lie number four?"

Defeated, that's what she was. Why Rachel had bothered to try and play along with the deputies, she didn't know. All she'd accomplished was amusing them. That burned, but not nearly as much as waking up alone would if she actually did the dumbest thing ever and got into their bed tonight.

Rachel had no doubt that no matter how this night ended, tomorrow would be guaranteed to begin only one way—depressed.

Given the way her life always went, tonight would probably end with another "I'm so horny" hand therapy session in the shower. That certainly appeared much more likely than either rascally deputy choosing to go home with her plump butt instead of hightailing it back to their party full of lipo-sucked tummies and silicone-plumped boobies.

"Rachel?"

The humor in Killian's voice annoyed her. Feeling like the butt of some joke only added to her foul mood. But she wasn't so addled she couldn't remember the question. "I like wearing black."

There, she'd remembered. Killian had wanted her to lie. She just couldn't do it fast enough to keep the deputy from snickering. "All black?"

"I'm grieving."

"Grieving?"

"Yes, that's why I came out here. I was hoping for some peace and solitude during my time of sadness." Rachel lifted her chin and silently dared him to tell her she didn't know any dead people.

"Uh-huh. You're not too good at lying, you know that?"

"I'm not lying." Despite the absurdity of her claim, Rachel managed to make it sound indignant.

"That's all right, sweetheart." Killian waved away the performance. "I think I know what this is all about."

"Really?" *Deputy Difficult.* Rachel remembered that smile and braced herself to be insulted in some horrible fashion.

"I don't know if I mentioned this to you, Adam," Killian began as he looked up toward his partner. "Rachel came by the station a few weeks back to do an interview with the Chief. He wasn't there, so I did her a favor."

What? Was that how he described the disaster of their first meeting? The only thing that could be said for that day was that it had gone better than this night.

"I showed her around and even took her out to lunch to answer her questions." Not fooled by his conversational tone, Rachel waited for the bait, swearing she wouldn't jump. "It soon became obvious that she had kind of a crush on me."

It took clenching every single muscle in her body to keep from leaping up at his absurd claim. He'd been the one all over her, and he damn well knew it. Hell, he'd been the one to suggest going out for a late lunch and then asking if she might like to go out for a dinner sometime.

Rachel had turned him down. She'd regretted it every minute since until now.

"I tried to be as nice as I could when she asked me out." Killian overplayed his hand with a sigh, making it just that much easier for her to hold her peace and not give the arrogant bastard the satisfaction of even dignifying his absurd claims with a response. "I let her down as easy as possible, but I got to tell you she was quite upset. I'm afraid she really has it bad for me."

Of all the—

"Listen, honey." Killian turned to her, looking as concerned as an angel. "You got to let it go. You can't continue to pursue me with this obsessive infatuation. I don't want to be rude, but you're leaving me no option here. I'm sorry. I'm just not that into you."

She couldn't hold it in anymore. Rachel burst with the need to defend herself, snarling at him as her annoyance released itself in the single sound. "I don't like you right now, either."

"Oh, come on," Killian cajoled with smirky smugness carved into every inch of his smile. "We both know you came out here tonight to try and find me."

Rachel snorted at that bit of bullshit. "I didn't even know you were going to be out here."

"Please, this is getting embarrassing." Killian gave her a look to make her feel so pitiable for a moment Rachel actually forgot she wasn't guilty of what he accused.

"Oh, give it a rest."

She shook her head, remembering herself a second later. Hell, she wasn't the one who kept showing up everywhere. Maybe she should complain to the sheriff that his deputy was stalking her. The accusation rested on the edge of her lips before sanity kicked in.

No. She would not play his game but would hold her chin up high and respond in a bored, unconcerned tone. "How could I even know you were here? This is the middle of nowhere."

"Obviously you followed me, which is really pathetic."

That did it. Sanity be damned, something deserved to be said. "I'll tell you what is pathetic. It's you thinking any woman would take enough notice to even bother being aware that you were in the same room as her."

"It's time to stop lying, Rachel. You need to confront your sickness."

"My sickness? I'm not the one following you around town like a lovesick puppy dog."

Oh, that did it. Even in the dim light of the moon Rachel could see Killian's face turn a whole different color. Dark and pissed, she rushed out more words in an attempt to drown out the ones that should never have been said.

"Like I could even follow you!" Hollering to cut off any attempt by Killian to interrupt with the storm clouds he had brewing on his brow, she really got into her tirade, fake as it was. "I couldn't even hope to get through the gates up there at the front of the club, and how was I supposed to know you were one of the jackasses working surveillance on that little kingdom of kink? I couldn't—"

"Kingdom of kink?" Adam arched a brow at her. "And just how do you know about our kinks, Rachel? You ever—"

"Like I want a man who is so pathetic and insecure that he has play perverted little games just to jack up his ego enough to screw."

Damnit. She really had to stop issuing invitations like that because sooner or later one of them might accept.

"You are so going to eat those words."

Yeah, probably. Why the hell did that excite her? Why did any of this? As annoyed and irritated as she felt, Rachel could also feel the low hum of energy fueling her emotions. It snapped and sparked, driving her to be reckless at a time when caution would have been more appropriate.

Her worry must have shown through because Killian managed a smirk, relaxing slightly as if he'd claimed a silent victory. "I think we have a feminist on our hands."

"You know what that means."

"She ain't never had a good fucking."

There, that was the Killian who deserved a good smacking a day. No man, not even the sleazy drunk who hung outside the gas station, had ever talked to her in such a way. Every prim, uptight molecule of her being roared with the need for revenge over such treatment. Without thought, her hand reared back and went swinging for the arrogant ass's face only to come up short when her wrist got caught by something hard and painfully tight.

Everything was moving so fast, Rachel didn't have time to process what had happened. The world spun around her. The rough surface of dirt and pebbles bit into her cheek as both her arms were wrenched behind her back. The clear sensation of metal bands snapping around her wrists brought it all into focus.

"Uncuff me, you deviant little turds!" Rachel shrieked, fighting the unbreakable bonds of the handcuffs.

All her struggles amounted to squat. Unable to escape, the best thing Rachel could manage was to roll onto her back and heave curses at them. Neither man stopped her from railing at them and everything in the world as she went on a long overdue tirade.

Slowly, the fire fueling her anger waned down to a simmer, reducing the cold reality of how screwed she was. The oppressive truth that she had absolutely no control of the situation left her glaring at the sky. The stars appeared to giggle back down at her, all giddy and happy to be way up there.

Killian, though, appeared quite pleased to be right where he was. Grinning like the cocky son of a bitch he'd been when she'd first met him, he loomed over to gloat. "That would be assaulting an officer."

He doesn't have to sound so damn cheery about that fact. Killian had taken to the safety of his feet when she'd gone into wildcat mode. Now he was braving the possibility of serious injury to lean down and latch on to her arm. With a careless jerk that spoke to his greater strength, he yanked her right onto her feet. Annoyed at his power, Rachel jerked back in reflexive rebellion.

"Will you look at that? The ankle held." That wise observation came from Adam.

So I'm caught. I did it. I trespassed, took pictures of some kinky party with most of the male citizens of Pittsview in attendance. I still have the power. Pictures or not, they can't make me un-know what I already know. That leaves a lot of room for negotiations.

Rachel found her well of power and grinned, unabashedly assured of her ultimate victory. "Amazing, isn't it?"

Holding Adam's glare, she refused to back down even an inch. She wouldn't be subdued by a little bit of intimidation. If the man wanted her tame, he'd better bring a whip. The instant the thought occurred to Rachel, she wished it, and the vivid memories of the orgy, away. *No. No whipping.*

"Ready to admit to what you are doing out here, Rachel?"

"No."

"Damn," Adam snickered, "that's the shortest answer we've gotten all night."

"The most honest, too," Killian added. It had really begun to irritate her the way they talked liked she wasn't standing right there. "You think she's finally starting to worry?"

"Worry?" Rachel smiled, letting them see who held the power now. "What should I be worried about? I didn't do anything wrong.

You're the supposed protector of the citizens who apparently, in his free time, likes to scare and bully women. I'll tell you who should be worried—"

"You," Killian stated.

"Yes. You!"

"So you are not worried?"

Rachel would have crossed her arms over her chest if she could have. Instead, she had to settle for a defiant chin lift and narrowed glare. "No. Why would I be?"

"Because you are cuffed and charged with assaulting an officer of the law?"

"I didn't assault you, you big baby."

"You were going to smack me."

Rachel snorted at that. "You deserve a good smack."

"And you deserve a good spanking, but you don't see me bending you over."

*Oh, the images...*Rachel tried not to focus on them, but everywhere her mind turned, it saw the same reflection—her, naked, trapped between these two men. Their callused hands felt rough against her body, rough and controlling. Killian held her tight with his hold on her waist while Adam forced her head downward with a firm grip in her hair. They bent her over, Adam bringing her lips to brush against the hard denim covering his bulging erection. With dark intent, Killian's hands smoothed over her ass in a gentle imitation of what was about to come. The soft hiss of a zipper being lowered had her tensing as...

"Not yet."

Killian couldn't know where her dirty thoughts had been leading her.

"You are going to be punished, Rachel. Have no doubt of that, but first we're going to reveal all your sins."

Punished? "Excuse me? Do I look like an eight-year-old child to you?" Rachel asked but didn't give either of the oversized

Neanderthals trying to intimidate her a chance to answer. "Let me tell you something, buddy, I'm not some little kid for you to deliver a spanking to. Nor am I some cheap-ass floozy who bends over for the right price.

"Don't even look at me like that," Rachel snapped at Killian. "You don't think I don't know what *you're* doing out here? Oh, I know what you're up to. You're one of those sick bastards that has to prove his manhood by paying some woman to play puppet to all his little commands. Let me tell you something. I'm no puppet, and you'd best watch your ass before it gets chewed by these fangs, baby."

"You know, you are awfully mouthy," Killian commented, apparently unimpressed by her passionate tirade.

"Yet another sign she is in need of a good fucking."

Rachel twirled on Adam. "Would you shut up about that?"

"So much negativity and tension." Adam waved a hand over her as if feeling for some kind of aura. "I really think if you just got laid you'd be a much happier, and nicer, person."

"I am a happy person," Rachel growled.

"With that disposition, I imagine you frighten off most volunteers. I could—"

"Don't say it."

"Why not?" Adam smirked. "You've already thought about it."

"Not once."

"You really are a bad liar." Adam's grin took a wicked turn, and Rachel instinctively shifted away from the predatory intent she could feel tensing his muscles. "I could prove it to you."

Don't provoke the lion.

"Only if you are prepared to suffer a humiliating defeat."

Ah, shit.

Adam came at Rachel then, taking the step that closed the distance between them. She went back, desperate to regain her private space. Instead of freedom, she found herself trapped with Killian at her back and Adam pushing in from the front.

They surrounded her with strength and warmth, a siren's call of security and comfort. It felt so good to be imprisoned in a cage of heated male muscles. Like a symphony, the air filled with layers of scents—male musk, soap, and earth, with subtle after-tones of cinnamon and mint. Rachel melted beneath the liquid heat of the hot, humid night. Her muscles were drugged into relaxing as the scent of lust thickened around her. Naturally, her body shifted, molding into the hard press of male ridges.

It felt amazing to be pressed between them, molded into them, almost as good as the lips on her neck. A firm, warm caress, Killian's lips flirted across her skin in sweet, almost ticklish kisses until they rested against the very beat of her pulse. He toyed with the wild beat, nibbling on the taut stretch of skin. The provocative kiss revved her heart into a pounding race.

"The taste of victory is so very sweet," Killian growled.

Chapter 3

Rachel didn't have a chance to respond to Killian's murmured gloat before his kiss consumed any protest she might have made. It would have been a lie, anyway. Her whole body craved this moment with such desperation that it had run her mouth off in a blatant taunting.

She'd begged to be captured, and Adam trapped her, holding her captive with her own lust. He fueled her need with the slow, seductive delight of being truly tasted. Drugged by the wicked teasing of his tongue, Rachel felt the fight fueling her blood flush downward so fast that she collapsed against the hard wall of Adam's chest.

Instantly, his heated scent invaded her lungs, fogging her thoughts until the need burning between her legs began to drive her actions. Everything spun so fast around her that she panicked. Feeling rushed and overheated, her mind lassoed Killian's last comment, repeating it over and over again until the mantra beat back the rising tide of her arousal.

She couldn't give in. This was just a game to them. They'd played her perfectly, getting her riled up, not jumping at her bait and duping her into thinking there really would be no consequences to playing. There would be, though. Tomorrow, Rachel would pay by waking up with the memories of not only witnessing an orgy but participating in one with these two deputies.

Rachel could live with having sex, even dirty, raunchy fucking. If only the pleasure they gave her were skin deep. Being there with them, caught between them, Rachel hadn't felt this alive in so long that she didn't want the moment to end.

A smart woman would use Killian and Adam for all the pleasure they could give her. Only an idiot would want for more. Rachel tended to pride herself on not being stupid, but everybody had their weaknesses. For some odd reason, these two deputies had turned out to be hers.

By giving in a little, she just might be able to get out of this situation without any real damage done. Unless, of course, Rachel didn't count having to endure the ache of unsatisfied wanton lust. Which she didn't, no matter the need already slickening the top of her thighs. God, she hoped they couldn't smell that. Though if they did, it wouldn't hurt her plan one bit.

Bending her arms, Rachel brought her hands up enough to cup the large bulge of Killian's cock that had been pressing into the small of her back. The position forced her to arch away from him, and she discovered another hard dick pressing into her stomach. Perfect, they were where Rachel wanted them.

Though she'd never done something so bold or forward as to make a move on a man, Rachel threw herself full force into Adam's kiss, fighting off his tongue as she invaded his mouth and forced him into taking action. The kiss changed from a delicate tasting to a hungry mating of mouths that matched the ever-increasing rhythm of her hands molding, stroking over Killian's hard length.

With every squeeze, she lured Killian into their frenzy, delighting when he tensed then shuddered before muttering a curse and arching into her touch. The motion emboldened her, giving her the confidence to roll her hips and let her stomach begin to move over the solid width of Adam's erection.

Adam responded just as Killian had. He tensed, flexed his hips, and then with a growled obscenity, his hands locked on her waist and jerked her up. A thick thigh parted her legs, and she found herself suddenly straddling Adam's hard-muscled thigh. He treated her to the same torment she visited on them, rubbing his thickness right up between her legs and making her cunt clench and cream with the need to be skin-to-skin.

Rachel could feel herself fading, getting lost in the power of the moment. As her body clamored forward into the storm, it unwound her control and sent sheer, manic fear shafting through her. The chaotic feeling stirred a revolution in her mind, igniting an alarm that had her jerking back from Adam's kiss, gasping for breath, for some relief from the lust drugging her senses.

Rachel couldn't lose it now. If she did, then all her options would disappear right along with her control. Then what would happen? The answer took less than a second to come to her in a full, vivid fantasy. Then reality would shift and pleasure as she knew it would be altered forever. Soon enough, they'd slink back off to their playthings and she'd be left with a dating population that thought five minutes of rubbing her clit sufficed as foreplay.

No. Rachel wouldn't let that happen. Looking up through her lashes, she met Adam's intense gaze. "I want you."

The truth, so easy to give, made Adam's features relax slightly. "You can have anything you want."

That promise, murmured between the little butterfly kisses he rained down her jaw and over the ridge to her neck, had her eyes fluttering closed again. Rachel tried, really tried, to amass her resistance and keep her mind on her goal.

"Not here." It came out jagged. The words cut roughly from her panting breaths. "I want a bed."

"Something soft and comfortable, where we can spend hours enjoying that sweet little body," Killian whispered against the curve of her ear.

Hours? Rachel had never once been with a man who could do hours, though she had met some who had promised. Not that she'd ever believed any of them. Rachel believed Killian, and it made her almost pant with anticipation.

Hours of being trapped between these men, being totally at their mercy, letting them use her in the way they wanted…she'd get lost. When they were done, they would return to their normal lives, and she'd end up a piece of broken wreckage in their wake.

"We could take you home, strip you bare, and feast on your naked flesh," Adam murmured into the curve of her neck before scraping his teeth over her sensitive skin. Rachel started slightly at the minor assault, but his words lured her, seduced her in ways that she had no defenses against.

"Would you like that?"

"Yes." Rachel breathed out the word with no thought left to the consequences. If they were beside a bed now, there would be no more hesitation.

"First, you need to tell us what you were doing out here."

Adam's words, no matter how softly whispered, brought back the grim truth of her situation better than anything could.

Now who is being played? Rachel had underestimated them, just as they had underestimated her. Perhaps, though, it was time to do away with the pretenses, to reveal the truth that they were not the only people with power in this situation. Rachel smiled at thought.

Opening her eyes, she met Adam's dark gaze head on. "You already know the answer to that, don't you?"

"Say it."

Rachel smiled, liking the feel of the moment. "I'm out here investigating the rumors that the Cattleman's Club is more than a place where men go to gamble and drink whiskey."

Adam's gaze skipped over her shoulder, going toward Killian, who leaned in to breathe his dark, forbidden response into her ear. "And did you enjoy seeing what we do in our free time, Rachel? Did you get all hot and wet as you watched all those women being used, punished, and pleasured? Did you imagine yourself as one of them? Wish that you were?"

She wanted to say no but couldn't.

"You broke the law, Rachel." Adam pressed into her, trapping her in their vise of heat and muscle. "By rights, we should take you down to the station and process you." Adam's hand boldly came up to palm her breast. Teasingly, he rolled and pinched her nipple. Involuntarily, she groaned and arched into his touch. "We could see to your punishment ourselves."

Oh, crap. Oh, crap. He's suggesting... Rachel sucked in a breath as arousal flooded her body, heating up places that shouldn't have been excited by the word punishment. Lust tried to twist her reason, searching for any way to convince her stubborn pride to accept his terms.

More than anything, Rachel wanted to know what it was like to be naked and vulnerable, trapped between two hard, unforgiving male bodies. Trapped between Adam and Killian while they unleashed their dirty imagination on her body, there was a fantasy she'd be having for many nights to come.

"What do you say, Rachel? You want a firsthand experience for your story?" Killian teased.

"Don't you know that's how all the great journalists work? They go as soldiers into the battlefield, as gang members into the streets, as inmates into the prisons."

As lovers into bed with the perverts. "Yes."

No. No! What the hell did I just say? Rachel couldn't believe her own ears. She'd heard what she'd heard, her voice, soft and breathless, whispering out her acceptance to a fantasy she couldn't indulge in. Rachel couldn't do this. She could barely have sex with one man.

Actually, she'd only ever had sex with one man—the same man for seven years. It might have started out with some excitement, but it had quickly grown into monotony. The same man, the same positions, the same formula—kiss, lick, suck, fuck. Even in those comfortable confines, she'd always been nervous. Nervous about her body, about her performance, about the positions, about every damn detail. So nervous that she'd never actually had the room to orgasm.

How embarrassing would it be to have to go through that with two men as witnesses?

Rachel couldn't do it, but her agreement had given her plan a chance. It seemed to back down Adam and Killian's aggression, giving her a little room to breathe but not nearly enough to escape, especially not with her wrists cuffed. She'd get them off. All she had to do was hold on to her sanity long enough.

And continue to play a very dangerous game with two men totally out of my league.

Rachel took a deep breath and then the plunge. "I accept the terms of your condition."

"I want to make sure I got this right. You agree to spend the whole night allowing Adam and I to punish you in any way we see fit, up to and including sex."

"In exchange for all charges being dropped."

Rachel could imagine what kind of headlines that story would get her. Cops willing to exchange sexual favors for the law. If only she had the balls to write it. *Balls? More like a suicidal tendency.* Even if Rachel was brazen enough to submit such an article, launching an attack like that on Killian and Adam would earn her a response she would have no capability of controlling.

"What do you think, Killian?" Rachel could hear the sudden uncertainty in Adam's voice. At least one of them had some sense.

"I think we're going to have to take her to our place."

"Are you sure?"

"Yeah, I'm sure all the cabins at the club will be filled by now, but we have enough stuff at home to keep the night interesting."

"I didn't mean that. I meant this whole insane idea."

"You don't think it's insane. Do you, Rachel?"

"No." Rachel smiled at Killian, sensing his weakness. She might not be Venus, but he was obviously horny. *Horny and stupid.* "But I don't want to go to your place. If I'm going to do this, I want to do it in the comfort of my own home."

He appeared to consider that for a moment. "Okay, but we're going to have to pick up some things from our house."

"And I want my car out of the ditch."

"We'll get it tomorrow."

"No. Tonight," Rachel insisted. This was the pinnacle of her plan. "I don't want to wake up tomorrow and be dependent on you. I'm sure you don't want to wake up tomorrow and be stuck with me."

"Fine. We'll get it out now."

"How?" Adam asked. "My truck could probably tow it out, but it's five miles back to the lodge. Are you going to sit here with her while I go get it?"

"And waste time on that? It's a little compact," Killian retorted, clearly impatient. "We could lift it out and drive it back to the truck."

"I can't lift it on my own. Neither can you."

"So?"

"So if we're both lifting, who is going to be driving?"

They both looked at her. Rachel fought to keep her expression bland. This was like a gift from fate because she'd been trying to figure out how to get out of the damn cuffs. Whining and complaining would probably have been undignified, but it was all she'd come up with. This worked a lot better.

"Rachel—"

"You can't put her in the driver's seat," Adam snapped, proving again that he was the brains of their partnership. "We're blackmailing her for sex for Christ's sake, Killian."

"We're not blackmailing her." Killian needed a dictionary and perhaps a dose of modesty because he really thought he had her under his thrall. "She wants to have sex with us, don't you, sweetheart?"

Oh, hell yeah. Dirty, sweaty, all-night-long sex with both of you.

"I want it." Rachel didn't lie, even if she didn't plan to fulfill the unspoken promise those words made.

"You're not going to run off now, are you?"

Rachel tilted her head to meet Killian's gaze. She smiled at him, hoping that she didn't give any of her true intentions away. "I wouldn't want to miss out on my personal exposé, would I?"

"I don't know about this," Adam muttered, drawing her eyes to him.

"Don't you want me?"

That question, asked in her little-girl-lost voice, stilled him. Rachel could see the answer so clearly in his eyes. Adam wanted her, but there was something else there, something she didn't understand, an intensity that worried her. Head bent, his lips whispered across hers. The kiss was no more than a slight brush of lips, so quick but so intense it held Rachel captive. So did the intensity in his eyes as his head lifted.

"I'll take the cuffs off."

* * * *

Rachel would bolt the first chance she got. Of that, Adam had no doubt. What he couldn't figure out was how he could be so wrong about the woman. At a distance, she looked way too uptight and prissy to be the kind of woman who dressed up like a ninja to go spy on an orgy.

Adam didn't buy her excuse that it was for some article. If he knew damn good and well that Carl would never run such smut in his paper, then Rachel had to know it, too. Besides, there was certainly nothing in her job description that said she had to tempt and taunt her way into his bed.

That's exactly where she'd be headed, too, even if she did run. If not tonight then some other because Adam wouldn't accept any other outcome. Hell, one night wouldn't even suffice. Not with as hard as she'd gotten him. It would take quite a while to burn off this itch, but one thing was for sure—he wouldn't be following her all around town making puppy eyes.

No, sir. He liked the chase, the hunt, especially when the prey was delicately sweet. With her lips all swollen and plumped with his kiss and her eyes shining with such lustful innocence, Rachel looked ripe to be picked and perverted. The need to be the one to educate her on the ways of all things wicked and delightful filled him with such force, he felt something he never had before—fear.

This could all be just an illusion. Hadn't she been nothing more than that all those days he'd watched Killian staring at her? In the bright light of day, there could be no hiding that she was a good girl. One who didn't flirt with all the men or show off any hint of her curves, and certainly one who didn't spend all night sexing up two men at once.

What would happen when dawn broke? Would she turn back into some untouchable lady whom they had no right to even look at? And how in the world could a woman have a mouth that pouted like that and have no idea of the way it affected a man. Maybe that's why she dressed like Humpty Dumpty, because she didn't want men worshiping her over all those Greek goddess curves.

Maybe she really didn't want them to chase her but just honestly wanted to escape. The very idea depressed Adam. It also made him fit the key to the cuff's lock. He'd never force himself on a woman, no matter how bad he wanted her…or she wanted him.

Under the lust keeping her cheeks flushed, Adam could read the hint of fear in her gaze, sense the tension and hesitation in her movement. Rachel didn't belong in this game. No matter how much she might try to play along, in the end, she belonged at home with a balding husband and three little angel-faced babies all tucked into bed.

A decent man would leave her to her fate. Adam considered that he could change that image. It might take time and every seductive skill he had, but he could pervert Rachel to his ways. He would just have to move slow and easy, and soon enough the ten inches of hard dick begging to go skinny dipping in Rachel's cunt would get to go swimming anytime he wanted.

He couldn't tackle her like a barbarian the second she bolted, no matter how much fun it would be. She really did deserve the gentleman, and Adam felt the peculiar need to at least try to be one in some aspect when she smiled up at him. Tentative and sweet, the small gesture undid him.

"Thanks." Rachel seemed to give him her first honest response of the night as she rubbed the sting of the cuffs from her wrists.

"Don't be thanking him yet, darlin'," Killian growled over her shoulder, reminding Adam that there still was one barbarian on the loose.

Killian acted the role of berserker well when he lifted Rachel by the waist with one hand. She looked like a tiny doll in comparison to the broad, hard muscles Killian flattened her against as he pinned her in his embrace.

"You're going to be wearing those cuffs later," Killian warned her.

Killian's palm wasn't big enough to hold the generous bounty of her breast as he tormented Rachel with his rough touch. She moaned, arching into the fingers that pulled and twisted her nipple as her body followed the motion until she danced the sensual sway of a woman in need.

Nothing had felt as good as having her twist against him, and Adam couldn't wait to feel that rhythm skin-to-skin.

"Promise?"

Rachel's husky purr drew Adam's gaze from the hypnotic sight of her body to catch the flash of her teeth as she turned her head and bit Killian on the neck. Like a kitten teasing a lion, she had no idea how dangerous her game was. Killian couldn't be toyed with like that.

His best friend couldn't be started and then stopped on a moment of fear. Adam worried about what would happen when Rachel tried. It was time to stop this before she pushed his partner too far. Latching on to her arm, he pulled her free of Killian, who would soon stop caring about Rachel's request for a bed.

"I thought you wanted to have this party at home," Adam pointedly reminded her. She might not know it, but Rachel was just a few minutes away from being screwed up against her car's bumper right there in the ditch.

She blinked, the fog clearing out of her chocolate gaze to let the green swizzle through. Regaining herself with a smile, Rachel proved she hadn't learned her lesson when she pressed up against him to whisper. "And I thought you were so strong the two of you were going to get my car out of the ditch?"

Oh, she is going down. And Adam meant to her knees.

Chapter 4

"I knew she was going to do that."

Killian grinned as he watched Rachel's little compact fishtail onto the pavement then roar off. She spun the engine so fast through its gears the poor thing whined painfully. In less than a minute, the taillights disappeared. Killian figured Rachel would consider any damage done well worth the cost as she long as she escaped him.

"You were the one who said to put her in the driver's seat," Adam complained without any real heat.

Yes, Killian had. He'd also warned Adam she'd fly out of here at first chance, but that hadn't stopped his friend from undoing her cuffs. Why should it when both of them appreciated the hunt? Especially with prey as delectable as Rachel Adams.

Killian had been carrying around a hard-on for the girl since he met her over a month ago. That's as long as he'd ever gone without the satisfaction of taking what he wanted, and he wasn't going to wait another night. There was absolutely no need to in Killian's mind.

He'd figured out her game. It might be a little more confused and convoluted than the games the girls played back at the club, but that didn't mean he couldn't master it and her at the same time. A Cattleman was always ready for a challenge, and that's just what Rachel Adams was.

With her prim ways and sassy ass, he might have labeled her cute, but cute didn't keep him dreaming of her every night. No, it was that damn caustic tongue of hers, always throwing out the quick comebacks that made him burn.

Her sharp words could have earned her the designation of a bitch, but Killian could read the desperation in her tone. Along with the hungry glow in her gaze, he understood that she just couldn't bring herself to ask for what she needed. All those proper values kept her from being able to admit to the desires he had fired in her pussy.

Killian didn't doubt that little cunt clenched for him. The tantalizing scent of her arousal along with the sexy way she ground her plump ass into his erection made it quite clear that the woman was in heat. Hell, that's probably what drove her to be so difficult.

As Rachel herself would no doubt point out, it was Killian's job to service those in need. He'd taken a vow to put the needs of others before his own. So if the little miss needed to tease and taunt him into hunting her ass down and giving her the fucking she craved, Killian would just man up and fulfill his responsibility.

The fact that she couldn't appreciate his willingness to help only meant he didn't have to be as nice about it. *No reason to feel any kind of mercy.*

"I just wanted to see if she'd actually do it." Killian shrugged, turning to start the long trek back to the party and his truck.

"Do it?" Adam jogged up to his side. "She did it. Now what are we supposed to do?"

"Go find her." Killian snorted, considering the answer obvious.

He guessed Adam had to think it over, because Adam always had to think everything over. Not worried about what conclusion his partner might come to, Killian didn't even pay him any attention when Adam stalled out.

Adam had always wanted to pervert a good girl, so he could hardly complain about Killian finding him a candidate. Truthfully, Killian knew Adam's motives for wanting to find a woman to settle down with went a lot deeper than some kinky need to dirty the innocent. Killian just didn't like to wade into those troubled waters.

The way he figured it, Adam's mother must have screwed him up pretty good because his friend couldn't see that he had it better than most suckers. The two deputies had hot women whenever they wanted, however they wanted, and didn't have to do much more than pay their dues to the club and dole out good orgasms to keep the tap flowing.

Simple, uncomplicated, and most of all, never boring, that's how Killian liked his momentary pleasures. He could figure out that training Rachel wouldn't be simple or uncomplicated, but it definitely wouldn't be boring, either. It had been ages since he'd felt this kind of excitement.

Every single inch of his body throbbed with anticipation, and that made Rachel the perfect compromise, even if Killian knew it couldn't last. The very fact that his blood boiled so hot testified that no matter what kind of woman Rachel Adams was, this would not be a long-term thing. This would be a fuck, fuck, and fuck some more until three straight weeks of sex had passed and the urgency finally burned out.

About then, they'd look at each other and wonder what the hell they were supposed to say. Hopefully by then, Adam would be soured on the idea of tying themselves to some wanna-be housewife. Hell, this could work out great all around. Rachel could go back to being her pleasant, goody-to-shoes self. Adam could finally realize that they didn't need a permanent woman to have a happy life, and Killian could finally get a night's sleep without Rachel starring in some pornographic fantasy.

Sex, that would cure everything. "You coming?"

"Yeah." Adam sighed and started shuffling his feet forward. "But I want to go on the record that this is not a smart idea…and don't give me that look. You know what I'm talking about."

Killian smirked at the annoyance in Adam's tone. "Relax. It's all good."

"You're going to go chasing after her," Adam stated, following in step beside Killian.

"Yep."

"And when you catch her, you're going to have to restrain her."

"I certainly hope so."

"Given she probably ran home, you're going to have to break into her house."

"Probably."

"Then you're going to have sex with her."

"Eventually." But not before he had some fun—a concept apparently alien to Adam at that moment.

"You know what they call that?"

Killian sighed, knowing what Adam would. "Let's see, stalking, kidnapping, breaking and entering, rape, and you might as well throw in assault, because I plan on paddling Miss Allen's lush behind. I'm thinking bent over the edge of the bed, maybe with her legs—"

"You really aren't worried?" Adam asked, not bothering with the argument.

"Look." Killian came to a stop to face Adam and his worries directly. "You know me. Now, I'll give you breaking and entering, but I ain't going to hurt Rachel Allen. I'm not gonna make her do anything she doesn't want, but I am going to convince her she wants what I do, and I don't expect it to be very hard. Couldn't you smell that pussy? It was hot, wet, and ready. Can't let that go to waste."

Adam scowled, not appearing pacified in the slightest. "So you'll leave her a happy woman by sunrise, but doing it this way might mean she won't be calling for another round."

"So?"

Killian had tried the civilized route last time. He'd been all sorts of charming, taking her to lunch and even asking her out for a proper date. All that effort for what? So she could pretend like he didn't exist for the last month. Well, he was not doing that again.

"It's a bird in the hand, man. Who's to say you'll get a second chance if you don't tap the honey while it's creaming?"

"I'm just saying, Rachel's not the type—"

"Like you know," Killian cut Adam's bullshit off before he could be irritated by it. "You don't know anything. I'm the one who spent a few hours with the girl. If anybody here knows her better, it's me."

"Yeah? And why don't you tell me about those few hours?" Adam shot back, getting all huffy for no reason Killian could see.

"Not much to tell." Killian shrugged. "She came in to interview the sheriff, ended up having to interview me, and we hit it off."

"Oh, you did?" Adam cocked a brow at Killian, making him itch to pound the smug look off Adam's face. "And that's why you've been mooning after her—"

"I do not moon over any woman."

"—these past few weeks, making a fool of your—"

"Who are you calling a fool?"

"—self, following her around like a love-sick puppy—"

"I'm not a damn puppy!"

"—and for what? So you can be stuck banging all those Rachel look-alikes at the club?"

"They were not Rachel look-alikes," Killian snarled, stepping toward Adam.

"You made the last brunette dress up like a dirty librarian."

Killian couldn't deny that, and he really didn't have a defense, given he never had asked for a pet to role play before. It had been fun, though not nearly as much fun as it would be when he made Rachel play.

"I know you, Killian. You want this girl."

"And you don't?" Killian wouldn't believe him if he said yes. They'd been screwing women together for over a decade, and he knew the difference from when Adam itched to when he burned. "I would have thought she fit with your own little fantasy."

Adam didn't deny it, but he did step back and give Killian one of those thoughtful looks that always ended in him annoying Killian with some stupid-assed revelation. True to form, Adam stiffened up, his features hardening into a glare as he flung an accusation at Killian.

"Is that why you didn't tell me about her? Because you're afraid she might be the one?"

"See, now that's just stupid." Killian rolled his eyes at the very idea of "the one." Life should be more plentiful than that.

"No, it isn't." On a tear, Adam stepped forward with each allegation, his fingers curling into a tight enough fist for Killian to decide to step back. "You've been burning so hard for this girl that you've made a complete ass out of yourself over the past month, and that just scares the shit out of you, doesn't it?"

Killian growled at that, truly insulted. "I'm not afraid of any woman."

"And you've been worrying that if you did anything about it, then I'd be tagging along and what? Realize that there might actually be a decent woman out there willing to settle down with me *and* my best friend?"

"Don't you think you're jumping the gun here?" Killian retorted with total exasperation. His whole life, Killian had been listening to people say how practical and down-to-earth Adam was just because he tended to be quiet. None of them knew what kind of crazy Adam hid beneath his cool exterior.

"Or is it that you didn't intend to have me tag along?"

"See, now that's just paranoid delusions on your part," Killian retorted. "I didn't even consider you tagging or not tagging along given I wasn't even thinking about banging the honey until she agreed to let us punish her, which she is waiting on. So if you're done, I got a meeting to make."

Knowing Adam could carry on for hours, Killian turned and left him there to berate himself. He meant it when he said he had other things to do, and he didn't intend to let Rachel go cold while Adam got himself all hot.

"Damn it, Killian! We're not done arguing about this."

"Sure we are," Killian shouted back without looking over his shoulder. "I'll do what I want. You do what you want."

"*Shit!*"

Killian held back his laugher at Adam's heartfelt curse. Killian could talk all he wanted, but they both knew what Adam's ultimate answer would be.

"Well, wait up for me."

* * * *

Rachel checked all the doors and windows to make sure they were locked. Then she checked them again. She knew she was being silly, but she couldn't get over the feeling of being hunted.

As if.

Only extreme stupidity or vanity could explain any woman thinking she counted enough to actually motivate Killian or Adam to chase after her. They had a whole field full of better looking, more willing women to pick from. Not to mention that all those women at the bonfire were already naked with legs spread.

Safe and alone in her house, Rachel tried to remember exactly why she wasn't one of those women. In all of her nearly thirty years, she'd had exactly one lover and no orgasms. Well, at least none he'd given her.

From that perspective, it had been sheer stupidity to turn down the opportunity to triple the number of her bed partners and actually start getting the big *O*s column filled in.

Oh, but no. I have too much dignity to have any fun.

Well, she had a little fun. Actually, the whole night had ranked as a rip-roaring good time, and the only thing she couldn't determine was if spying on the orgy had gotten her hotter than messing with the two deputies. It was actually kind of a toss-up, given she had pictures of the orgy to keep her squirming in her seat.

Oh, but she really wanted to know what it would be like to be the woman in those pictures. It wasn't that she needed to be in love and all that, but she couldn't enjoy sex without relaxing. She couldn't relax if she didn't trust the man. In order to trust him, Rachel would have to care about him.

At least that's how the theory had gone for the longest time. Sitting at her computer, going through the images, Rachel wondered if she didn't have it all wrong. She could have a fling, a dirty and erotic fling filled with passionate moans and the sweaty slap of bodies...*Oh, God.*

Got to stop looking at these pictures. They fueled the wicked fantasies playing out in her mind, reducing her inhibitions and letting her explore all the erotic images without fear. The want to actually touch, taste, feel what it was like to be pinned between two of the most delicious men she'd ever met made her burn for a release.

Damn, she needed to be touched, to find some release from the need that could be denied no more. Rachel didn't have a man, but if she wanted an actual orgasm, a man would only get in the way. There were some things a woman was just better at—like setting the mood.

It took her ten minutes to get her romantic bath for one ready, but finally she sank into the heated bubbles. With a sigh, she closed her eyes and pretended she wasn't alone. Instead of being brash and offensive in every possible manner, Dream Killian knelt at the ready beside the bathtub, a glass of wine in one hand and a soft rag in the other. Or maybe it would be more realistic for it to be Adam.

The bathtub isn't big enough for both of them. One of them will just have to watch. That idea gave her a thrill. Somehow, the idea of being watched, of having one of their heated gazes trained on her every action, her every reaction, made her feel so dirty and so damn hot it amazed her that the bubbles didn't boil away. *Killian.*

He'd be the one to watch, to watch and suffer, because surely a man of action would feel punished when left to do nothing more than observe. It would be difficult for him. He'd have to battle every instinct, every urge to come forth and force his participation. That struggle would have his muscles flexing and bulging with physical restraint. Even as he fought for control, the fight would feed his aggression, sharpening his need and making those brilliant eyes sparkle with the promise of revenge.

What a sweet revenge it would be. Rachel had earned it. Making sure Adam went slowly, starting with his hands on her body, she'd drag out the moment, teasing Killian with every sensuous second, even as she prolonged her own agony. Agony would be just what it was to endure Adam's big, callused hands massaging their way down her shoulders.

He'd be behind her, cushioning her with that hard body even as he kept her captured and displayed. She wouldn't care. With those warm palms pressing into her muscles, working out every kink and knot as they explored the contours of her back and the graceful crease of her spine, she'd be putty in his hands.

Their steady progression wouldn't pause until he reached the sensitive skin of her lower back. A few fingers would splay out to tease the crease that divided her ass cheeks, a dark hint at things to come later. The very promise had her shivering with fear and excitement.

It would come, she knew it, but first would come the pleasure, the body-numbing, mind-shattering pleasure. She'd be so drenched in it that by the time it came to that, she'd be so drunk on ecstasy she'd be incapable of feeling any pain.

It wouldn't be a long road to that ecstasy, not with Adam's hands warming up her body. They were sliding around her waist now, tickling her sides with their gentle touch and making her squirm enough to draw his notice back there. Big and callused, his hands lingered there as he let his thumbs twirl out ripples of pure electricity. Rachel's breath caught, her body stilling and tensing with anticipation. His touch was so soft, nothing more than a sensual promise of the pleasure to come.

Rachel's eyes, already at half mast, drifted the rest of the way closed. It felt so good to luxuriate in the glow of things to come. The anticipation built in her, weighing her down until her body relaxed and melted into the moment.

Only then did his hands shift, encircling her stomach. He liked it, soft and smooth. The roundness bespoke of a healthy body, one with curves to cushion all his hardness. Again, his thumbs went exploring, traveling the bottom slope of her breasts even as the rest of his fingers followed along.

In one smooth, sensual motion, Adam's hands glided up to fully cup her aching globes. His thumbs stretched out to pin her tender nipples beneath them. Slowly gaining speed, he used the rough, callused pad to roll them tighter and tighter, sending out electric ripples that had her back arching as she lifted her breast up into his touch.

More, she wanted more. Her body hummed with the need for it, slowly taking to motion as her hips rolled and flexed in the timeless rhythm of a female in heat. She became more and more aware of her pussy, of how empty it was, how desperate it was to be filled. It begged for attention, and she pleaded softly, whimpering out her need.

It fed Killian's dark desires, and she could see him tensing, clamping down the need to respond to her siren's call. He was vulnerable to it, vulnerable to a woman's desire for her master's attention. He'd give her everything she begged for, give it to her hard and fast, but it was Adam who held her, Adam who tormented her.

Adam would not be rushed or pressured by begging. Instead of testing his strength, her sensual demands only fed his restraint. He wanted her to beg, to beg him for her pleasure, to know he was the one who could give it to her and only when he decided.

Adam was all about the tease. Even as one hand dipped low to slide over her stomach and into the damp curls covering her mound, Rachel knew release was a far distance off. He intended to torment her in the worst possible way, and she welcomed it. Lifting one leg right up over the edge of the tub, she rested it on the curved rim to open herself up completely to his touch.

The vulnerability of the moment fueled her desires, making her rage with such lust that she moaned in welcome at the first soft glide of fingers over her folds. She couldn't bear his controlled restraint. Instead, gluttonous need ruled, and she covered his hand with her own, forcing his fingers to find the sensitive little bud no longer hidden in her folds. Swollen and alight with pleasure, her clit blossomed under her touch.

With a sigh of contentment, Rachel relaxed back into the tub, letting the warm water and the slow swirl of her finger over her clit melt her body. Toying with her ultra-sensitive bud, she twirled it over and over again, going faster and faster until she could feel her cunt sucking in great gulps of water in a desperate cry to be filled.

One quick thrust of fingers, one tempting taste of pressure, and her whole body quivered on the edge of oblivion. Just as she started to feel every nerve ending coming alive in celebration, Rachel backed off and let her hand fall down into the crease between her thighs. For several heart pounding seconds, her body quivered on the edge of release before it tumbled back into a fit of disappointment and urgent demands.

This had to be the best part. Well, maybe not the best, but she couldn't bring herself to go there. Not yet. If she did, then it would be over. She'd be left tired and sleepy. That would be a great moment, but Rachel often preferred to prolong it and her pleasure.

Gluttonous, Rachel enjoyed drawing out her releases, bringing herself to the edge of climax several times before she finally gave in to temptation. It was rare that she got to enjoy a climax, so she savored them with greedy delight.

Tonight, though, was even more special because she finally had a face and a name to put to her mystery lover. Normally, she fantasized about some generic hunk, but not this time. This time, she had a very specific image of who she wanted, and it wasn't just one man.

That made this occasion special, kinkier and hotter. It felt like it deserved more than the normal bathtub routine. Rachel's mind went to the small box she had hidden in her closet. Maybe not so much as hidden but ignored. When Hailey had given her the very skimpy set of lingerie, it had been more of a joke than for practical use. It was a good thing because Rachel had never once had an occasion to put the outrageous garments to use.

It was the type of thing the women at the Cattleman's Club wore. The type of thing a woman wore for men like Killian and Adam. Rachel had never worn anything so risqué before, but it felt right. Even if it was just a fantasy, she wanted to wear it for her dream lovers.

Panties like that require things to be shaved that have never been shaved.

She'd regret doing it in the morning. It would itch coming back in. Going through the day, knowing what she had done would embarrass her, but it would also make her feel sexy and wanton. It would be a silent, private reminder to her that she wasn't such a good girl. She could have a wild side, too.

Chapter 5

Thirty minutes later, freshly shaved and wearing the ridiculous outfit Hailey had given her, Rachel stepped in front of the old, rounded full-length mirror she'd salvaged from a yard sale. Her hands twitched at the belt of her robe, uncertain whether to unleash the terry knot or pull the strings tighter.

She knew what lay beneath but wasn't so sure she was ready to confront it with her own eyes. Her hormones had relented some over the past hour, relaxing back from the desperate need for release into the continuous hum of arousal. They still wanted their due, but for the moment her hormones were content to linger in the moment, waiting with anticipation for the next fantasy to begin.

This time it would be Killian doing and Adam watching. It seemed appropriate, given the outfit. A man like Killian would know what to do to a woman dressed as she was. He wouldn't accept any hesitation but would step up close behind her. Following the pass of her belt, his big hands would settle over the knot to slowly loosen the ties.

With his fingers curled under the edges of her robe, he'd follow the part up toward her shoulders, letting the backs of his fingers tease over her quivering stomach muscles and over the rise of her breasts. Her nipples, lifted and put on display by the cupless bra, would pucker and tingle under the pass of his fingers. Then they would be revealed to the cool night air and the exploding gaze of Killian's brilliant eyes.

They'd glow with prowling aggression, full of feral hunger as he surveyed the prey caught within his grasp. She would tremble under the impact of all the promises in his eyes, and when they lifted to finally meet hers in the reflection, the tension would snap around them.

Killian wouldn't be the slow, tender lover riling her body to the peak of ecstasy the way Adam had. No, Killian would plunge her into the deepest pits of rapture with a speed and force that would overwhelm any doubts or reservations she had.

His hands would be rough and unrelenting as he palmed her breasts, circling her tits with intense aggression. He would pull and pinch her tender tips, bringing pain to the party. The slight twinges and dark forewarnings fed her excitement into a fever pitch. Then he'd cup one breast, lift it up, and demand that she suck it for him. He wanted to watch her pink little tongue slip out to trace over the creases, flick over her nipple, and tease its very tip before her lips sucked it in.

Ah, shit.

The ripples of pleasure spreading out from her breasts felt more like tidal waves, flooding her pussy in a torrential downpour of heated cream, the strength of which couldn't be contained. Her hips flexed, slowly rotating in a sensual humping dance that called out and lured men in. The motion had her clit blossoming to life as it rubbed against the satiny material of her panties.

Even as she continued the assault on her own breast, his hand dropped down to the string edge over her underwear. A little pull and tug and the tiny triangle that barely covered her crotch disappeared into a line of fabric that slipped between the edges of her swollen lips to press harder, more intensely against her clit. Again and again, the material see-sawed over her sensitive bud until she released her breast with a pop to moan out her pleasure.

He wanted her to touch herself, to watch her come by her very own hand, and she didn't have the willpower to deny him. She lifted a trembling hand to her breast, doing as he had done, tormenting her nipple with a roughness that had her aching for the feel of his hands on her body.

That wouldn't happen, not until she gave him what he wanted, her pleasure on display for his. He wanted her vulnerable and weak, so when he attacked, she would be unable to offer any resistance to his darker, more perverse commands. The very idea excited her and spurred her to overcome the last of her reservations.

Rachel didn't hesitate or tease herself with any preliminary strokes. Her need was too great for that now. Like a race horse chomping at the bit, her body demanded satisfaction and her hand obeyed, slipping around the balled-up material of her little G-string to hone in on the swollen bud of her desire.

One finger, that's all it took, one single finger swirling over her clit to make her eyes roll back in her head. Faster and tighter, she rounded that sweet little bud. All the while, he watched, his eyes flashing in the mirror with the promise of what would come, what he intended to do to her very shortly. First, though, he wanted to see her do it to herself.

Rachel gave herself over to the excitement of her own touch, to the illusion of Killian watching her as her whole body tightened. Tremors quaked through her muscles as the first cracks in reality began to snap around her. Sharp shards of rapture cut through her, lacerating her body with such intense pleasure that she jerked and writhed under the impact.

Her body lost its ability to hold her weight, and she slouched forward into the mirror, blindly banging her forehead into the cool surface even as her free hand abandoned her breast to clutch at the rounded top of its frame.

Oh, God, she needed to be filled, stretched.

Cock. I need a cock.

His cock would be wonderful, but all she had were her fingers. Her scrawny little fingers didn't go deep enough or stretch her wide enough, but they were all she had, and she used them as well as she could. Years of training made her especially good, and in minutes she had herself panting, pressing into the mirror as her orgasm hit her.

Even as she splintered apart from the impact of slamming into Utopia, he made his move. Oversized and warm, his hand slid beneath the edge of her panties to cover hers like a glove. Molding itself to every finger, his hand widened her cunt as he forced her to fuck herself even deeper, harder, faster.

"It's my turn now."

Rachel didn't have the energy or even the focus to object to her fantasy lover's sudden appearance. Rachel barely managed to open her eyes to meet the dark, feral eyes of the man staring back at her— Adam, not Killian. She recognized him a moment before a second, more deadly explosion rocketed through her body.

Fireworks heralded her ascent into the heavens, and she flew with the stars twinkling all around her. How long she stayed suspended in the warm cocoon of release, she didn't know. Too soon, the world ordered itself, fitting back in piece-by-piece to solidify the image around her that had her crashing back to Earth.

Rachel blinked and met her fantasy lover's gaze in the mirror. Not sparkling bright, but dark and hungry. *Adam.*

Adam stood behind her with Killian leaning against the doorframe in the background. Her two dream lovers had come to life to haunt her with the embarrassment and humiliation of having been caught doing something Rachel would never have admitted to anybody she did. The flush in her cheeks did not come wholly from the afterglow of release.

What now?

What could she say after what just happened? Was there anything really to say? They'd intruded on her most intimate and private of moments, but did it matter? From the look in their eyes and the pounding of her own heart, there could be no denying that things were about to get a lot more intimate between the three of them.

* * * *

Adam didn't know if he could hold on for another second. It had been a struggle for the last five minutes ever since he'd walked into the room and found Rachel wearing an outfit he'd never have thought she'd even own. That shock had been minimal compared to what she had been doing.

He'd known the second her hands had slid her robe off her shoulders that she would be giving him a show that would test his control like it had never been tested before. It had been a fantasy come true, but for one detail. She hadn't watched. She'd kept her eyes closed when he knew she would have enjoyed it more with them open.

Adam would rectify that. Next time, he would make sure she kept her eyes open, and there would be a next time—many next times— because he would need it. Even now, the memory of her lifting her own breast to her mouth, of watching those full, pink lips part over her furrowed tip, had his balls drawing up in painful demand.

God, but he wanted to watch it all again, even as he wanted to be the one tasting her luscious tits. It would only be the beginning. He'd taste every inch of her, spread her out on the bed and feast on her, but first he had to get the burning distraction out of his cock. It would give him no rest until it had fucked itself to exhaustion in the sweet heat of the pussy he could already smell dripping with cream.

Oh, yeah. She'd been hot and tight around his fingers. Tight enough to have his dick swelling at the very idea of having that little cunt suck his full length into the vise of her molten muscles. Adam's cock swelled, threatening to explode before it even got a chance to bathe in Rachel's heat. He would have erupted over her then, taking what he needed with as much finesse as a caveman if she hadn't surprised him by moving.

Not away from, but toward him. She turned and pressed her flushed curves into him, surprising him with her boldness. He wouldn't have expected her to embrace the moment, but then again, he wouldn't have expected her to start it with such a magnificent display, either. Rachel might have come off as prim and proper, but within her lay the heart of a vixen.

The contradiction had him mesmerized, which was why he didn't respond at first when she stretched up to press a sweet kiss against his lips. Her quick little tongue licked at his before she nipped his lower lip, sending a sudden flash of violent lust through him. Adam's control nearly snapped, unleashing the aroused aggression pounding through his blood, but Rachel's gaze caught his and held it.

The dark orbs glinted with the dangerous combination of feminine mystery and mirth. Adam swallowed, paralyzed by the volatile mix of anticipation and excitement as her eyes slowly drifted further away from him and she went to her knees. He could see the promise in her eyes. She intended to torment him, and there was nothing he could do to stop her. Nothing he would do but stand there tense, each muscle locked and loaded.

She could have this moment. Soon, though, very soon, he would have his. The little minx might think she had the upper hand, but once she drained every inch of his cock of its stiffness, he would show her who really held the power.

Adam couldn't relax enough to smile, but he wanted to. His little temptress, Rachel, had the spirit of a vixen but the sweet soul of an angel. The way she fumbled with his belt and tugged at the zipper of his jeans told him that this would be a first for her. Instead of diminishing her power as a seductress, the underlying innocence he could sense in her made her more attractive to him.

He forgot to breathe. She'd gotten his jeans undone. The moment his hardened shaft was unleashed, it sprung forward to find a warm welcome in her cupped hands. So light, so gentle, the first tentative strokes of her palm along his cock had him shuddering with the struggle to restrain himself from taking control.

He'd never been touched like this before. Slowly, with a reverence that made him feel like she was worshipping him, Rachel explored every crease, every wrinkle of his dick. Adam clenched his jaw and endured her curious little caresses.

With each one, she filled his mind with the static of his own rampaging lust until all he could hear was the hum of tension binding down on him. With a crackle and pop, it snapped at the cool, silky feel of her tongue tracing the vein running the length of his cock. She used the tip of her tongue for that first electrifying lick. Right beneath the ridge of his swollen head, her tongue dipped and slid back downward.

At first, her mouth didn't move and the rest of her tongue snaked out, curling around his thickness until the velvety heaven cupped him and pulled her lips down toward his balls. Adam flinched and gasped when her explorations continued lower. Her lips closed over his tender sack. She sucked, and he moaned.

Oh, shit! He'd come right now if she did that again. Holding himself tense and ready for another devastating blow, he sucked in a huge breath when her tongue skipped back up his cock. The quick, flirty motion gave him a second to regain some precious needed control, but only a second. Licking around the curved edge of his head, she delivered another sharp lash of rapture to his body when she tasted the very tip of his dick.

Flaring her lips a little, she settled her mouth down around the head of his cock in a painfully unfulfilling move. So close to what he wanted, it about killed him when she didn't suck. She did go exploring, allowing her tongue to trace down the slit toward the unseeing eye in the center of his head.

That soft, velvety toying motion was followed by the sharp scrape of teeth over his sensitive skin. Adam cursed and jerked under the assault. Almost instantly, his objection turned to approval as she soothed the injury with a gentle suck. The teasing little motion had his hips jerking back toward her as a groan escaped from him.

The little tease.

She knew what she was doing to him. That truth glimmered in her eyes, eyes that had not once wavered from his. That look alone would have hardened his dick. In combination with what her wicked mouth was doing to him, the effect was almost lethal. It might not have killed him, but it did rip away the veneer of domestication he normally wore.

The primitive male inside him demanded that the woman kneeling before him finish what she'd started. He would tolerate no more games or hesitation. Her time of power had come to an end. Adam regained control by wrapping a fist through her hair. Rachel didn't mutter a single protest or utter a word of complaint when he dragged her head back, forcing her face to tilt up.

"You want to play, Rachel, but you don't know the rules to this game."

Her lips twisted up ever so slightly in a barely-there, smug little smile. Adam growled. She had challenged him. Adam never backed down from a challenge and never lost to a woman. Pushing her head back down until her lips brushed over his cock once again, Adam snarled out an order.

"Suck it."

He hadn't asked, and he hadn't left her any room to deny him, even if she had wanted to. With his hold in her hair, he forced her head lower, and her lips broke wide over his length. She rebelled for a moment, refusing to suck even as she took his dick all the way into the warm, moist haven of her mouth. Only when his head bounced against the back of her throat and she'd settled over as much of his thick shaft as she could take did she move.

With a quickness he couldn't defend against, her hand shot up to palm his balls. At the exact same instant, she jerked back against his hold, clamping her lips down and pulling her mouth back up over his cock. Adam cursed again, jerking under the sudden onslaught of pleasure that didn't stop.

She didn't stop. She sucked his cock with a speed and fierceness that had him teetering on the edge of the most explosive climax he'd ever approached. His hand kept her head bobbing up and down his cock at an ever-increasing speed until she swallowed and took his aching dick that much deeper into paradise.

The dam broke, and he couldn't contain his roar of satisfaction any more than he could stop the burning seed from erupting out of his balls in a volcanic outpouring. Nothing ever compared to the pure pleasure of a release, but this time he soared to heights he didn't know men were capable of attaining. It was almost poetic but for the savagery of the rapture that held him in its grip.

It burned straight through his flesh to brand his soul with the permanence of Utopia known. He would need this again, would need to feel like this often. That sobering reality ripped him from the ecstasy embracing him and tumbled him back to Earth, where Rachel still knelt before him and the promise of another trip to paradise still kept his dick hard.

Hard as an eighteen-year-old with the ability to go many, many rounds in one night. It had been a while since that had happened— years, in fact. Adam was normally good for two, maybe three rounds in one night. Now he suddenly had the stamina to go two or three rounds in the next hour, all thanks to the woman whose lips glistened with the proof of his last release.

Poor girl. She has no idea what is in store for her. Adam couldn't wait to show her. She'd done a good job of swallowing everything he'd blasted her with. His cock still felt sticky from his recent explosion. Tightening the hold that had gone slack when he'd come, he knotted her hair around his fist and forced her gaze back to his dick.

"Time to clean up your mess, honey. Lick it."

Lick it she did. Rachel licked, teased, and brought him back to the need to have her suck him again. Adam had played right into her hands because she didn't need him to command her. Opening her mouth wide, she clamped her lips down over his cock and worked him back to the edge of ecstasy. This time she set the rhythm. She took control, and he didn't have the strength to fight it.

Too. Damn. Good. A part of him wanted to rally and fight for dominance of this moment, but his muscles refused to respond, too wrapped up in the pleasure of the best blow job Adam had ever had. He could have relaxed and sailed right over the horizon into another atomic explosion, but this time he fought it. *Damn me. I'm not going to waste this load on her throat.*

He'd deliver it, burying it deep inside her, right after he reamed her pussy hard and good. That's exactly what Adam would do once he put a stop to this insanity. That was his last thought before the rapture consuming him burned away all rational thoughts.

Adam would have gone down under the sucking pump of Rachel's lips if her moan hadn't ripped through the rhythm. Thrown for just a second from the pulsating beat, Adam's eyes lifted, catching sight of Killian.

His friend had gone to the floor behind Rachel, and his big, tanned hands held her thighs wide, leaving Adam's captor vulnerable and exposed. Adam could only imagine how pretty Rachel's little pussy must look, all swollen and glistening with cream, naked in a way that lured a man in to take a little taste.

He watched as Killian's head dipped to do just that. Rachel jerked and skipped a beat. Another moan reverberated down his cock, and Adam smiled. Things were about to get good.

Chapter 6

Too good. It was as if a slice of heaven had speared through Rachel, straight up from her pussy to incinerate her spine in a shower of pure, white-hot rapture. Another bolt shot through her as the devilish tongue made another pass straight through her swollen lips. It pressed slightly over the opening of her cunt, a quick, shallow thrust that had her moaning and arching in a plea for more.

With another thrust into her aching pussy, Killian fed her desires before sliding free of her clinging muscles. Licking straight up, he toyed with the little bud that held the mystery of the female orgasm within its web of nerve endings.

"Oh, God, yes!"

Rachel didn't know if she'd said it or thought it. She didn't care. All she cared about was arching backward, pressing into the tongue swirling over her tender little clit and making her whole body tremble as the screws to her release tightened down all around her. She tried to rear and buck into the open mouth tormenting her pussy, but the firm, almost painful, grip of fingers dug into her hips and held her still.

Her head reared back off the cock filling her mouth. She barely got out a squeak, not near the demand she intended, before the hand in her hair slammed her head back down. Rachel didn't have the mind left to focus on any rhythm but the tongue that swirled over and over her clit.

Mindless of anything other than the orgasm building to a head inside her, she gave herself over completely to their control, to their authority. Being made vulnerable heightened the erotic experience, defining each second with a dark thrill that had her twisting as the bright light of ecstasy dawned over the horizon of her soul.

Three thick fingers, slick with her own cream, penetrated her ass, blasting her out into the ether as Killian's husky promise chased after her. "So damn tight. I'm going to fuck this ass."

Her world broke apart at the seams. She screamed as Adam pulled his cock from her mouth. She'd have been lost if it hadn't been for the pressure filling her ass, grounding her to the world. Killian fucked his fingers into her, widening her, stretching her, preparing her for something a great deal thicker and longer than his fingers. And all the while, his words haunted her, a tender caress across the flaming folds of her pussy.

"I'm going to take you right here, so hard and deep, with Adam filling out that tight little pussy of yours. You want that, don't you? You want both of us fucking you at the same time. Filling you like you've never been filled and making you explode with pleasure like no other man ever has. Feel it, baby."

Suddenly, he lifted, bringing his hips to mold around hers. His thick thighs pushed hers open even wider, forcing her to rest her weight on his as his thick shaft parted her folds with the tempting promise of penetration. It didn't come. Instead, he teased her with the feel of him, letting his actions and words work her into a frenzy of need.

"You like that, baby? You want it? You want to feel my dick stretching you wide? You gonna beg me for it?"

The deep, dark words floated through her mind, making her whimper with her own need. God, she wanted it, wanted the thick, hard cock sawing through her pussy lips and teasing her clit with its non-stop stroking motion to plunge deep inside her, fill her, and then pound her hard and fast into oblivion.

"I am going stretch this little cunt wide, fill it with more cock than it's ever had. I'm going to fuck you harder and deeper than any man has ever fucked you, and you're going to love it. Every sweaty, dirty second of it. You're going to be begging for more."

Oh, God, please. Now. That's just what she ached for.

"Then I'm going to pull it out and slam it into this ass." He leaned back, forcing his cock even tighter against her cunt as his hands palmed her butt. "This tight, plush, virgin ass. It is a virgin, isn't it, baby? You ain't never taken a man here before, have you?"

Rachel didn't have the ability to form words. Her voice had been stolen from her long minutes ago. The reasoning needed to form coherent thoughts had been eaten away by the primal instincts Killian called forth with his hands. Those primitive responses ruled now. They bowed her back lower, arching her hips up to rub back against his bold touch.

"Was that a yes?" He flexed his hips, dragging his dick back until it lodged against the edge of her cunt. With expert precision, he pressed forward so subtly that not even the full, rounded head of his cock pressed into her. Instead, it hovered, barely inside, more a promise than a fulfillment.

"Answer me, Rachel. Do you want me to fuck you?"

"Oh, God, *yes!*"

Her acceptance curled from a moaning pant into an outright scream as he embedded his full length deep into her. Just as she'd fantasized, there was no hesitation in Killian, no persuasive subtly or teasing slowness. He slammed into her with the feral hunger of a primitive man focused on one single goal—mating his woman.

He pounded into her so hard and fast that she'd have flown forward if not for the fingers biting into her shoulders. With a hard grip, he held her prisoner for his fucking. Not that she'd have tried to escape. She'd already melted into the floor, boneless and limp under the aggressive assault of pleasure overwhelming every facet of her reality. Her entire world had narrowed down to the primitive beat of ecstatic drums sounding off with each spearing thrust of Killian's cock deep into her.

It took him a matter of seconds to shred her world into tattered fragments. So thick and hot, his cock hammered in one explosion after another as rapture began to mushroom through her, racing toward one final, soul-shattering detonation. Then he pulled free and, for a second, she wavered on the very edge of either eternal bliss or total ruin.

A heartbeat later, he forged back into her with a speed and skill that had her eyes bulging. Killian didn't stop until he had embedded every rock-hard inch of his cock in her ass. The unusual pressure cracked the whip over her release and sent her soul hurtling out of her body.

She shot straight up under the impact of ecstasy's pure, raw waves and crashed back into Killian. They both tumbled back onto the floor, but Rachel didn't notice. The pain darkening the edges of her pleasure only served to deepen the depths of her lust.

Trapped within a magical, mystical sphere, Rachel writhed in Killian's embrace, completely unaware that her own instinctive motions kept the steady hum of pleasure coursing through her. Even as the brutal waves of her release began to subside, the frothy delight still lapped over her body, keeping her from truly crashing down.

She did, though, become aware of a few simple facts. The most unavoidable was that Killian's dick felt like a piece of silk-covered, heated iron, burning her ass from the inside out. He still had her imprisoned in his arms. His thighs still forced her legs open wide, but now she lay stretched across him, open and vulnerable to Adam's gaze.

Rachel's breath caught as her gaze locked with his. In some distant part of her mind, a voice cried out that this couldn't be real. It had to be a dream, a wonderfully dirty dream that excited her to the point of madness.

Insanity. That was the only explanation for the vision playing out before her very eyes. She'd lost her mind. She was not being held captive in Killian's embrace, impaled on his cock from behind, with Adam's head slowly lowering over her open, weeping cunt.

This couldn't be real, but it was. The dark look of hunger in Adam's gaze grounded her as nothing else could. He kept his eyes locked on hers, keeping her aware of the details when all she wanted to do was drown in the moment.

Then she was lost to the hot wash of breath over the sensitive folds of her pussy. Already tormented by Killian's own feasting and harsh fucking, she didn't know if she could take another round. Even as Adam's tongue tickled its way up her split slit, she flinched.

Pleasure to the point of pain came at her from both sides. Every teasing lick Adam made over her cunt had her squirming to escape the piercing shards of rapture that cut through her. The edges melted as her motions jarred the dick impaling her ass and made it burn so brightly with its own form of pleasure that no other sensation survived the inferno.

After a pause and a whispered breath, Adam repeated the cycle of torturous delight. With expert skill, he wound her back up the mountain until she was moaning out, "Please" and begging him to put an end to the game and fuck her. That's what she wanted. They'd reduced her to a thing of wild need that had one desire—to be filled, fucked, and ridden hard…from both sides.

"Please, Adam."

She couldn't take any more. She wanted to tell him that, but the rest of the words got choked off when he slid two fingers deep into her. He pressed down, back against the cock filling out her rear. She bucked up, unable to contain the bolt of wild pleasure that whirled through her. So delicious, she wanted—needed—another taste.

Arching her head over Killian's shoulder, she began to thrust in time with those amazing fingers fucking into her. The ecstasy sparkling through her body had a reverse echo, for every thrust down onto the fingers pulled her up the thick shaft buried behind her. Up became down and down became up until the sensations blurred and she no longer had control of her motions.

She was barely aware of Killian's hands biting into her hips, exaggerating her motions. All she could do was twist and shudder as the mushroom cloud returned, billowing outward as it began to rush toward total annihilation.

"Oh, God," Rachel screamed. "I'm going to come!"

In an instant, all motion stopped.

"No!"

She snarled and bucked, fighting to find some way to save the ethereal bubble of pleasure from collapsing down all around her. Beneath her, Killian cursed and clamped his arms round her stomach. Like steel manacles, they tightened down until she could barely breathe, let alone struggle.

"Don't worry, my wild one," Killian growled in her ear, making shivers run down her neck and race across her spine. "You're going to get everything you want, all the dick you can take. We're going to pack this tight little body so full of cock you won't be able to breathe without feeling us. We're going to screw you like you ain't never been screwed, right here on the floor, just like the wild thing you are.

"That's it baby. Go on and twist. You like the feel of that? You like teasing yourself on my cock? You like having your ass crammed full of meat, don't you?"

"Killian." That was all she could manage to whimper. The dark, forbidden suggestions made her burn more hotly than ever.

"I think she's ready. Don't you, Adam?"

"Hmm, she certainly is wet and squirmy enough for a good fucking."

"But..."

"But it's kind of fun to tease her."

Rachel shrieked and jerked under the sudden lick of Adam's tongue. He went straight up, pausing long enough to tickle her clit and make her jerk again.

"Definitely fun."

"You should feel it from this end," Killian groaned.

Oh, God. They're talking about me again.

This time, the arrogant presumption of their attitudes didn't irritate her. Instead, it colored the lines around the waves of lust swamping her with a tingly, foamy sensation. She had no control in this moment, no ability to protect herself from these men and their lascivious designs. That very fact thrilled her.

"That good, huh?"

"Baby girl's got such a tight ass I feel like the top of my dick is going to pop off. You better hurry and mount up because I can't hold on much longer."

Mount up? The very crudeness of Killian's words made the perverseness of the situation hit her. For a single, shining second, reason managed to infiltrate the splendor she'd been floating in. It lobbied her to object, to lash out in outrage, and rebel against their domination.

Before the seed of those thoughts could bloom into any action, her world altered around her. It was happening. Her breath caught in the back of her throat as she felt the thick, rounded length of a second cock pressing into her body.

Her eyes watered, and the sight of Adam's chiseled features pulled tight with grim determination wavered. All she could focus on was the intensity in his dark eyes. Those deep, chocolate orbs became her anchor as the pain and pressure of being overfilled began to splinter the great waves of pleasure into sharp fragments that rained down over her. The fine little cuts sent prickles of pure, undiluted rapture trickling out.

The ripples of pleasure froze as even her heart stopped. Adam had seated his full length inside her. Now came the question, would she explode? If one of them so much as breathed too harshly, Rachel feared she might.

Hot breath washed over her face and those amazing eyes were barely inches from hers. She was not only overstuffed but crushed between two impossibly hard and unforgiving bodies. It was too much. She was suffering from sensory overload and needed a moment to get her bearings.

"How do you want it, baby girl?" Adam's whisper chased her eyes closed. "Slow and easy or hard and fast?"

"Fuck slow," Killian growled out as his hands bit into her hips.

Even as his hips flexed backward, he lifted her, forcing her to take that little bit more of Adam's cock. She moaned out under the impact of the mini-stroke. A second later and everything shifted in the opposite direction.

They began with easy, shallow strokes that quickly escalated out of control. Reality ceased to exist, thinned down to the feel of the twin steel-hard cocks fucking into her with increasing speed and ferocity. Killian's hands kept her hips swaying in perfect rhythm, matching both men stroke for stroke.

Rachel screamed as the volatile mixture of rapture and pain detonated, casting out a million tiny fireballs exploding across her body. Still, Killian and Adam continued to fuck her with deep, hard, pounding strokes.

They grunted and sweated over her, racing her through the plumes of Utopia's dawning haze and straight into the horizon. The smoldering embers of her first release collapsed in on each other and grew into a raging inferno. Her body tensed, anticipating the second, more powerful explosion to come as the edge of her orgasm's end came rushing forward.

Killian and Adam fucked her right over it, tumbling her straight into the fiery abyss. Distantly, she heard masculine shouts calling out triumphantly as she felt the warm flood of her lovers' releases filling her body. Rachel didn't care. She floated in the glorious embrace of ecstasy's warmth, sighing even as the lights started to dim and oblivion began to creep in around her.

"Hey, baby girl, you all right?"

Killian's voice, warm with concern and tinged with sleep, floated through her mind. Now that had to be a dream. At least it was a pleasant one.

* * * *

Killian didn't get any more of a response from Rachel than a muttered groan, a guttural sound made only by a woman well satiated. He'd only begun to lay his claim, and if Rachel thought she could escape the rest of his plans by passing out...well, he had ways of handling a naughty woman.

First, Adam had to move. "Get off, man."

Shoving at his friend's shoulder, he pushed Adam to the side, making both Rachel and Adam groan as their bodies separated. Instantly, Rachel managed to form a word as she shifted and shuddered in his lap.

"Cold." He knew that wasn't all she felt. It wasn't anywhere near what he'd felt snuggled tight in her ass. Hot, hard, and wanting to go another couple of rounds, Killian felt a whole bunch of things but not cold. Her word gave him an idea, and it was nasty and mean, the best type of punishment for his little Rachel.

First, though, he'd have to risk the night air and leave the velvet sheath keeping his cock very happy. *Punishment all around.* Killian sighed as he lifted Rachel by the waist back to her feet. At least it felt good to get off the floor. Not that Rachel gave him a moment to enjoy stretching his muscles out. She tilted toward the bed, and he could see her going down, bent on a full-face smash into the mattress.

"Ah." He caught her around the waist. "No you don't, darlin'."

Sleepy as she was, the scowl that crossed her features looked more cute than intimidating as Rachel smacked her lips and squinted her eyes at him. "Don't be a butthead, Killian."

The insult annoyed him because she could at least have the decency to act soft and submissive now. He and Adam had put in a good showing, and for a few minutes there, Rachel had been bent to their wills. Instead of thanking them for what he was sure was her first real orgasm, the woman had gotten grumpy with him.

Obviously, Rachel would need a much sterner hand to train her right. Lucky for her, Killian's hands held steady for the task. He even had a bag of tricks to help him. Releasing Rachel to flop onto the bed, Killian didn't have to ask Adam to break out the duffle bag they'd brought with them. Adam might hem and haw all around the bend, but when the time came, Killian knew he could rely on his partner.

While Rachel dragged her blanket over her and curled up for a good night's rest, Adam began laying out all the things Killian had packed for them. Not wanting to be caught unprepared, they'd brought nearly their entire war chest. Everything from clamps and butterflies to feathers and whips filled the bag. Still, the best props couldn't be packed in a bag.

Nothing beat the bathroom Killian had just discovered. Connected by a walk-through closet, the old bathroom remained trapped in time with its ancient pink and black tile. Sadly, it was the most modern thing in the rather large room. From the old square-cut lavatory to the toilet with its water tank affixed high above the bowl, the room needed a serious update.

There was just one thing Killian wouldn't have changed. The large, cast-iron tub jutted out of the wall to take up nearly the entire middle of the room. As he walked around the enormous tub, he tested the wraparound shower rod, seeing how strong it was.

Very strong, indeed. Now all I need is a bit of rope.

Chapter 7

Sleep had never beckoned Rachel more seductively than it did that night. Then again, she'd never once felt so relaxed, so melted, almost like she was one with the big fluffy comforter. It didn't even bother her when one of her lovers started tugging on her. Assuming they were pushing her into a more appropriate sleeping position, Rachel didn't even open her eyes. She knew the moment they stopped, sweet bliss would welcome her into the land of oblivion.

A nippy air-conditioned breeze and the world spinning around her was what actually greeted Rachel. If she could have mustered the energy for a screech, she'd have given it to whatever man had swooped her off the bed. All that really came out was a garbled protest because she was too damn tired to form words. Hell, she couldn't even open her eyes.

"Relax, darlin'," Adam soothed her as he carried her away from the bed. "We got to get you cleaned up. No need to get all grumpy."

So said him. Rachel sighed. Maybe he was right. Waking up sticky in the morning wouldn't be a joy. Besides, Adam's arms felt nearly as good as her bed. Snuggling her chin into his neck, Rachel breathed his sexy, masculine scent deep and let it drug her back, bringing her back to the land of the mellow. This could so work. Rachel had fantasized more than once about taking a hot shower with an even hotter man bathing her.

To finally experience such a decadent pleasure, Rachel could stand a minute on her own two wobbly feet. She could even endure the frigid chill of the cast iron tub beneath her toes. With the expectation of hot water and a warm male body joining her any second, it took Rachel's groggy mind a moment to identify the feel of two hands working on her wrists.

By the time she realized what was going on, Adam and Killian had secured her with some kind of rope. A second later, it went taut, pulling her arms straight up until her fingers could touch the shower curtain. Yet the real problem, as Rachel saw it, was that she couldn't see. Her eyes were wide open and everything stayed pitched black. They'd blindfolded her, and that was definitely not part of the fantasy.

"What the hell are you—*ahhhhhhh!*"

Rachel's question ripped into a scream as a hard pulse of ice-cold water blasted over her mound. Somebody was having too much fun with the hand-held showerhead. She danced away from it screeching, testing how far her binds would let her go. Not far enough.

Cursing at her tormenters, Rachel put her whole strength into breaking the ties around her wrists, but all she accomplished was cutting off her circulation. There was no escape. Cornered in the back of the tub, Rachel pressed her thighs together, trying to block the pounding spray.

Thankfully, it abated, and Killian revealed himself as the bastard picking on her. "You ready to behave?"

"Go fuck your—"

This time, Rachel literally choked on her words as the cold blast returned, pounding into her unprotected rear. Although it was not unpleasant, the sensation caused the sort of instant humiliation that sent her running toward the other end of the tub. However they'd tied her, she could slide the binds down the rods, but she couldn't turn them, and the dastardly spray followed her.

"Stop! Stop!" God, but if he didn't listen to her—

"Are you ready to behave?"

It stopped, leaving her raging to cuss at Killian in response. Not about to make that mistake twice, Rachel tried to glower at him through her blindfold. Adam's heated breath washing over her shoulder warned her of the first rule of the game.

"You better answer him, darlin'. Slaves ignore their masters at their peril."

The very use of the word slave sent Rachel's heart skipping as realization dawned on her too late. They weren't playing, and she wasn't half as disgusted as she should be. Bravely raising her chin didn't stop her voice from wavering as it came out.

"I'm not a slave."

"You sure about that, darlin'?" Adam asked, the broad expanse of his hand suddenly warming the right side of her ass. It didn't dawdle but slid straight down. Smoothing between her thighs, his ticklish touch made her muscles quiver before parting, letting his fingers curl right over the lips of her pussy.

Oh, now that feels good. Rachel panted, bending forward ever so slightly to give Adam all the access he needed to make her cream right down her leg. The wetness had little to do with their previous loving and everything to do with the molten response of her cunt to the thick fingers forging into it.

Oh, glory, did Adam know how to stroke those magical digits over the walls of her cunt, tickling the magic spot that make her sparkle with delight.

"Because you sure look like a slave," Adam growled as she mewed, paying his words very little attention. "I guess I could be wrong, and if I am, all you have to do is say 'red light.' Say it and this all stops. We pack up our goodies and go home. That's all you have to do."

And why in the hell would she do that? Rachel smiled as the pleasure rolling through her began to layer over itself, building an unstable wall of rapture. Soon enough, it would cave and leave her decimated by the explosion.

"Rachel?"

It wasn't until Adam's fingers stilled that she bothered to respond. Even then, she could only muster the simplest of syllables. "Hmm?"

"What are you?"

"Really fucking turned on." The honest answer popped out of her, but apparently it failed to satisfy Adam. Either he didn't want her hot, or she'd failed to understand his question. Either way, he retreated from her needy flesh, leaving her to moan and pout over the abandonment.

"Do you remember the safe word?"

"Safe word?"

Adam sighed, having the audacity to be clearly annoyed with her lack of attention. "Do you remember the word that makes us stop?"

It took Rachel a second, and even then she answered with a question. "Red light?"

"And you understand that once you say that there is no going back? There are no time-outs, Rachel."

"So says the man who is taking the time-out?" Rachel grumbled. "Now if you are done with the lectures, can we get back to the pleasantries?"

A snort rolling into laughter gave away Killian's position. "You're sassy for a slave."

"I object to that title."

"Oh, you do, do you?" Killian's voice came closer. She instinctively shied away, bumping her calf into the tub and her shoulder into Adam. "How about 'prisoner'? You have a problem with that one?"

"And that makes you what? My guard?" Rachel didn't need to see to know how Killian must love that idea. As long as she didn't have to call him master, Rachel would let him have the thrill. It cost her, though, when she heard the cockiness in his tone.

"Yes, indeed, it does, and it certainly fits because I am here to mete out punishment for your misdeeds."

The sheer joy in Killian's tone made it very hard to take him seriously. Rachel probably should have, but no worry or fear came to guide her actions. So she blurted out the first thing she thought.

"My misdeeds? That's rich coming from the cop who broke into my house and then proceeded—"

A finger, pressing her lips together, smothered the words until Rachel finally gave up. She could feel Killian now. His heat warmed her skin, leaving her anticipating a brush that never came.

"First warning, my little captive, you speak when spoken to. 'Yes, guard,' or something really dirty like 'fuck my pussy,' or you can go with thanking your maker. I accept any number of compliments."

Rachel nipped his finger to gain her release and pointedly flaunted his authority. "And when do I get my thanks for putting up with this childish game?"

"Oh, you've done it now." Adam didn't sound sad at all about that fact, just the contrary.

Chuckling, he corralled her to the middle of the tub. While Adam tended to her right arm, Killian tended to her left. They made quick work of the ropes, using them to pull her arms straight out until she bent at the waist. The realization of how much more vulnerable her position had become had Rachel shuffling forward.

Holding her steady, their hands quickly moved to her legs and slid down to her ankles. They were good with those ropes, downright ingenious. Rachel had to give them that as she found her feet all but locked into position. It was not only impressive but quite intimidating how quickly they managed to secure her bent over with legs spread.

It made Rachel wonder where they'd gotten their training. "Do they teach you a rope tying course at the Cattleman's Club, or do you deviants come by this behavior naturally?"

Killian answered her honest question with a crack of his palm over her bare ass. The searing heat almost bugged Rachel's eyes out of her head as she reeled with the revelation that he'd not only spanked her but that it felt good. *Very good, actually.*

Savoring the moment, she panted through the aftershocks as the pain vibrated through the honeyed pleasure and made it bloom in the most interesting of ways. Such a delightful punishment only tempted her to misbehave even more.

"You're smiling. I don't like 'captive.'" Adam's silky growl cut off into an annoyed comment. "It doesn't feel right."

"Well, you're not calling me 'slave.'" *Oh, yeah.* Rachel breathed in deep, anticipating the sharp smack to her ass.

"*Silence, wench!*" Killian snapped, only to respond to Adam in a perfectly civil tone in the next breath. "Oh, I like that."

"Wench?"

"It fits, doesn't it? All sour mouthed and bent over for our use."

"Not that you're getting the job done or anything," Rachel muttered intentionally loud enough to earn another spanking. It didn't come, and it left her a little frustrated. She'd climbed out on this limb, and now they were dawdling.

"Is that a complaint from the peanut gallery?" Adam asked.

"You do know, wench," Killian said, clearly enjoying the title, "you already owe us quite a debt, and adding to it will delay what you really want."

"So what, you're going to leave me like this?" That could get kind of tiresome.

They ignored her question, going so silent Rachel started at the whisper of Adam's breath over her cheek. He must have squatted down beside the tub because his voice came right at ear level. "Listen up. I'm only going to go through this once."

"You already said that."

"Don't interrupt, or we really will gag you."

"We probably should do that anyway." Killian snorted from some distance. "This being her first time and all."

"Nah." A finger followed the sigh right across her lips. "I got plans for this mouth."

Rachel nipped his finger, enjoying the grunt it earned her. Unfortunately, no spanking followed, just more of Adam's boring speech. "Now, this is punishment. That means no orgasms allowed.

You are to do as told, no hesitations. Hesitating, arguing, doing anything other than what you have been given permission to do will result in more punishments."

Rachel rolled her eyes. *Whatever.* It seemed like a lot of ceremony with very little substance to her. Even if the Cattleman had taught Killian and Adam how to tie a woman up, they had obviously failed to educate on what to do next.

"From now on, you'll refer to us as 'sir.' Understood, wench?" Adam really relished calling her that, which only provoked Rachel into being obnoxious.

"Aye, aye, captain, sir," she gleefully cheered, being intentionally disrespectful.

"And for that, you will now be punished." When Adam sighed and shifted away, the warning he left in his place gained another hidden eye roll from Rachel.

"But I put the 'sir' on it," Rachel complained, holding back the laughter. Feeling completely assured that whatever silly thing they'd come up with would lack any real follow through, Rachel waited worry-free.

* * * *

Killian could tell Rachel didn't fear anything. The relaxed muscles and the little smirk were signs of how comfortable she was in her binds and all of them told him they'd done their job right. Despite Adam's reiteration of rules, the real point of the last ten minutes had been to get Rachel at ease in her binds.

A good master gentled his way into a wench's trust. They had earned it. Now came the moment when they used it. Approaching the honey he intended to make a treat out of, Killian rested his hand on her back, following the graceful swoop of her spine all the way to her lush rump.

God, but does she have an ass on her. He'd been the first man to tap it. What a joy that had been. Killian savored the memory as he palmed her rear. Really, it was an honor and a privilege. He'd claimed not only a piece of Rachel's body but a piece of her history. Forever, he'd be the man who introduced her to the pleasures of ménage, the joys of punishment, and the thrill of letting a man ride her ass.

It might be a thrill for the night, but Killian planned to addict Rachel to the feel of him fucking her sweet rear until she craved it every night of the week. Binding Rachel in the invisible ties of lust would start with dipping his fingers downward. Slick with lotion, they prepared her for the toy to come. The invasion earned him a guttural groan as Rachel shifted away, becoming slightly mouthy.

"What are you trying to do? Embarrass me to death? *Oh!*"

Rachel gasped on the answer Adam fed her. Lining up the dildo, he slowly pressed it, bit by bit, deeper into her, chasing her babbling murmurs of, "I can't…" with another thick inch. Whatever it was that Rachel couldn't, she didn't get it out before Adam managed to seat the full length of the plastic cock in her ass.

Penetrated, she strained in her binds, stretching forward as she panted for breath. Adam left Killian to cool her down as he went to collect necessary items. Rachel would need the moments to get herself ready for what came. Maybe more, Killian thought, listening to her mew. She really did make the sexiest little sounds. They drove him wild, making him itch for the moment when all the games came to an end and he was wrapped back up in the tight fist of her body.

The insanity had started that first day at the station. He'd been dreaming of this moment since then. Now came the time for his revenge for making him wait this long and work this hard.

It started with rubbing soothing circles into her back as he checked on the little darling. "You doing all right?"

"Am I drooling?" Rachel managed to retort between pants.

Her tart response brought a grin to Killian's face. She really was sassy, and that delighted him to no end as it gave him an excuse to forget all about mercy. The warm honey greeting the fingers he slid down over her ass to dip into the heated well of her cunt told Killian Rachel didn't have a clue as to what was coming.

It tickled him to keep her there, squirming on his fingers as he rolled her little clit until her cunt spasmed and clenched down on the fingers he'd fucked into her. With a moan she arched, and Killian could see that sweet ass clench with the motion, making her groan tip upward into a near squeal.

"I think you're drooling now," Killian growled, smirking over her easy response. Rachel's hands had curled around the ropes holding her in position, clenching them with white knuckles as her ass lifted, parting her legs slightly to give him more access. She strained, panting and purring as her body trembled and tensed, ready for the orgasm his fingers pumped her toward.

Over the glisten of sweat building along her back, Killian caught Adam's heated look. Yeah, Rachel was a sight—a sight to be shared and pleasure to be enjoyed by more than one. Adam and Killian had worked together, taming and training women for nearly six years now. Words had become an unnecessary complication.

Now all Killian needed to do was nod, understanding perfectly what Adam intended to do with the thin chains in his hand. Adam held off, though, waiting for Killian to work Rachel's pussy into a frenzied moment when her mouth rounded and her body stilled for barely half a second. That's all Killian needed to pull back, leaving Rachel hanging there on the edge of her climax.

Adam struck then, snapping a clamp over one tender tit and sending her into a writhing fit that tested the strength of both the knots and the bolts holding the shower rod to the ceiling. They held as Adam used the second clamp to leash her other nipple to her first before his hands dipped. Snuggling his fingers into her pussy to trap her clit, Adam had to struggle against Rachel when she tried to fight back.

Clearly having figured out what came next, she started to gulp air in, shifting to close her legs on Adam. Not about to let her get away with any more misbehavior, Killian lent his strength to Adam and held her soft thighs apart while his buddy spread her pussy wide, leaving her pink clit vulnerable to the dark clamp in Adam's fingers.

"No," Rachel whined, stretching as far as she could to get away. She didn't even move an inch, turning her panic into begging. "*Please*, Adam, I can't…can't—*ahhhhhh!*"

Killian moved back, mimicking Adam, as Rachel went tearing into a screaming frenzy as she thrashed in her binds. The tantrum gave Adam and him enough time to get ready in their positions, but they hesitated until she calmed down enough to breathe with at least some regularity.

"You all right, darlin'?" Killian called out, waiting to see if she could actually form a word.

Rachel gave him the yellow light when she managed to roll a groan into an actual syllable. "No."

"But you feel good, right?" That was all Killian really cared about.

Even if she couldn't form the word "yes," Rachel didn't tell Killian "no" either, and he knew damn well and good she could have. Killian also had the eye sight to see the thick sheen of arousal on the inside of her thighs, not to mention the ability to smell the sex rolling out of her body. Whether she would admit it or not, Rachel was right where they wanted her. Nodding to Adam, he unleashed his partner to start.

"Listen up, wench," Adam grunted, not the least bit compassionate sounding. "You've been rude, disobedient, and difficult at every turn. For all of that, you will be punished."

"P…pu…punished?" Rachel stammered out, her head lifting with the obvious sense of panic.

Killian answered with a crack of the whip in his hands. The flat side of the velvet tassels slapped over her thigh, making her start with a scream as her own motion set all the chains jingling. Before the red marks had even started to fade, Adam matched Killian's mark with his own, bringing his tassels down hard over her ass and sending the little wench into a fit.

Chapter 8

Pain and pleasure blurred beneath the intense vibrations radiating throughout Rachel's body. Her ass burned as the whips licked up over her rump, each slap unleashing a lash of fiery sparkles. The searing sensation danced over her skin in shuddering ripples. The motion made the clamps pinch even harder, sending back their own searing bolts of pleasure through her muscles.

Trapped in an endless cycle of pain and pleasure, Rachel could only cling to the hope that a climax would come and release her. She needed it now, before the pressure killed her, but no amount of crying, pleading, or begging worked on Adam or Killian. They showed themselves to be merciless in a way she'd have never conceived. They drove her further and further into the heart of passion's madness until she became a feral thing of naked need.

As the tide of lashes receded, Rachel could still feel its echo rippling spastic waves of delight through her. She'd have willingly said or done anything they had wanted right then. If only they'd give her a taste of the ecstasy barely out of reach, she'd have pledged them her soul.

A broad hand brushed back the hair sticking to her sweaty cheek, and she turned into the touch, trying to find the sound in her ragged breathing to beg. Raw from screaming, her throat could only issue broken squeaks that ranged into heavy pants.

"Now don't you come yet, wench," Adam warned in a hard voice, thrilling Rachel even more. Oh, but she wanted to defy him. "Or you'll earn more punishment."

The threat didn't change anything. Rachel would have endured any repercussions for stealing an orgasm right then. A little more punishment meant nothing in comparison. All they had to do was give her a chance to defy them. Adam did so a second later.

When the first clamp popped free of her nipple, Rachel thought she'd been shot in the chest. Pure, liquid heat shot straight through her body, igniting every cell in its wake until her entire body hummed with undiluted pleasure. So close, every muscle strained and stretched to reach the promised land of release. At the tugging on her other nipple, Rachel braced, readying herself to get swept over the edge.

The second wave of rapture to crash over her body wasn't enough. As her chest throbbed out a primitive beat of need that echoed down to her cunt, all Rachel could do was twist in her binds and beg.

"*Please.*" Scraping over sore vocal cords, the word almost hurt to form. Her neck strained painfully as Rachel tried to beg for them to have mercy.

"Not yet, baby girl." Killian's murmured assurance didn't help the rigidness seizing her muscles as Rachel braced, feeling Adams finger brushing over her mound.

One more clamp. Rachel's eyes rolled back in her head with the thought as Adam's thick fingers began pressing her pussy lips wide. The sizzling streaks of delight whipped up her spine as he started tugging on her sensitive bud. Her clit blossomed with full scale rivers of rapture the second Adam released it. Blood rushed into the tiny nub making it pulse, setting the tempo for the constant rush of lust crashing over her body.

The need left its mark on her face. Overwrought, Rachel gave in to the emotion, letting tears leak right down her cheek. A warm, rough set of fingers brushed the moist tracks away as they curled around to lift her cheek. The soothing touch turned heated as Killian rubbed his thumb over her lips and growled down, "You have the prettiest mouth."

"And the best fucking suck, man."

Rachel could easily imagine them sharing a grin over Adam's lewd comment, but it didn't bother her. Not with the sound of Adam's voice coming right from behind her. He was there. She could hear him stepping into the tub, feel the brush of his jean-clad thigh against the back of hers.

"Yeah? It seems unfair you know that and I don't." Killian's complaint couldn't cover up the sound of a zipper. Through the din of lust, Rachel found a smile and the ability to form words, even if they came out in broken whispers.

"Is punishment over? Sex now?"

Adam laughed, sending a wallop of gasping out of her with a smack of his hand over her still-throbbing ass. The slap jostled the dildo, stretching her wide, making her clench and groan over the spasms the motion caused.

"You'd like that, wouldn't you, wench?" Adam rubbed the sting out of her tender flesh, his other hand coming to mimic the motion and slowly start to pull her into position—an inch back, right over the bulge of his thighs. Her knees bent, widening as he took responsibility for some of her weight.

At the first press of his blunt, swollen cock head against her slit, Rachel moaned, "*Yes.*" That's what she wanted and she let Adam know it, arching her hips and rubbing her wet pussy all down his rigid length.

The teasing invitation earned her another spank as Adam ordered, "Don't be demanding, wench. You get what you're given."

What he wanted to give her, Rachel silently corrected. It didn't take a genius to figure out just what Adam had in mind. The hard press of his swollen cock spoke for itself. All she had to do was stay quiet and surely he wouldn't deny himself.

* * * *

Adam shared a smile with Killian over Rachel's back. She'd never make a good slave. Even after everything, she still didn't grasp the concept of rules. Not out of hardness or rebellion, Rachel's misbehavior stemmed from a childlike giddiness, anticipating the pleasures to come. It clearly showed she hadn't been taking the right men to her bed.

Well, now she had him. Adam knew without question that she belonged to him. Running a palm over the soft, glowing globe of her ass, he couldn't deny they fit perfectly together. Always a lover of a beautiful ass, Adam could have easily lost himself in Rachel's, but the slick, honeyed glide of her pussy was a temptation he couldn't pass up.

He never would be able to deny himself this. The only thing that would keep Adam from the heaven waiting for him in Rachel's cunt would be Killian in his way. Right now, though, Killian had a different obsession, leaving Adam to press himself against the soft, wet entrance to Rachel's pussy. Nodding to Killian, he watched his partner's hand thread into Rachel's dark tresses as he lifted her head up.

As one they invaded. Slow and easy, savoring every fucking inch, Adam sank himself into Rachel's welcoming heat. Her tight cunt sucked him deep, squeezing and spasming all along his length. *Mine.* The word steeled over his will with a strong possessiveness that bordered on barbaric.

Adam didn't fight the emotion as it swept through him. Instead, he wallowed in it, keeping his hips swaying with a shallow, easy rhythm meant to drive Rachel nuts. With each drag of her head up, her body shifted. The tight vise of her cunt pulled the taut skin of his dick tight until Killian thrust her head back down his cock and pushed her little pussy back down on Adam's.

Keeping her trapped between them, they rode her slow and easy until the wench started to buck in protest. Twisting her hips, Rachel tried to break Adam's hold, his control, over her. Feisty as ever, her motions proved too much for Adam's willpower. Loosening the leash, he let the little darling run free. Instantly, she took advantage, pumping fast against him as she went wild.

It took her less than thirty seconds to rob Adam of the last vestiges of his control, reducing him to her level, hungry and free. Driven by a thirst that felt insatiable, Adam slammed furiously into Rachel, pounding out the ferocious need tearing through him.

So tight, so wet, so good. Adam growled, giving voice to the feral rapture that exploded through him as her cunt gripped his cock in greedy, sucking spasms. Embedding himself full-length into her clinging sheath, Adam broke over the edge of his orgasm, drowning under the relentless, inexorable flood of emotions.

Even as he surged into Rachel, he could feel her soaking into him, filling every corner of his mind and heart and laying claim to him. Her pleasure became his, inundating him with pure ecstasy as her climax swept down her pussy and lured him into a world of flames. Never before had Adam come twice within a minute, but the boiling rush of the second tide swept down his cock.

The second release sheared him completely from the physical world. Only the painful need for air slowly returned him to the sweaty, tired body that heaved for breath. He'd collapsed over the woman trembling in her binds, still buried deep inside her.

Rachel.

She'd not simply weakened his hold over his control but ripped away his legendary grip. Finally, Adam knew what it was like to be the slave. His lips quivered upward at the thought, but Adam couldn't deny it.

The women who came to the club found pleasure beyond measure when they gave over their will. All the toys, all the moves, all the showmanship meant nothing if the woman wouldn't let go. Now, thanks to Rachel, Adam could know the other side of the token and keep his pride and dignity.

For that gift, he'd forgive her for coming without permission. Even with a mouthful of cock, the wench needed to learn the rules were always obeyed. *Some other night.* Adam sighed, straightening up. Still not soft, his cock really didn't want to leave its warm glove, but Rachel had to be tended to. Bracing himself, Adam slid free, matching Rachel's murmured protest with his own soft groan.

"You all right, darlin'?" Killian had already tucked himself back into his jeans and now squatted at the head of the tub, brushing the hair out of his way to examine the woman they'd used so well.

"It'd be nice to be untied," Rachel retorted, showing her true spirit, even if her voice barely rose above a whisper, though she still managed to tack on a "sir" after a slight hesitation.

Killian shot him a smirk. "*Now* she remembers the rules."

"And here I didn't think the wench was listening at all." Adam snorted, stepping over the tub to start the work on the ropes. It took a minute before Rachel had free movement. She used it to immediately pull the dildo free. Adam brushed her hands away, taking over the task as he soothed her murmured protest.

"Shh, darlin'." Adam pressed a kiss to her cheek, nuzzling his way into her neck. "Let us take care of you now."

"Are you going to bathe me?" A tenor of hope quivered in her question. "Because I've always had a fantasy about that."

"Really?" Adam swept a hand down her back to rub a gentle reminder of what fantasies were all about over the still-heated curve of her ass. "You sure you're up to a fantasy?"

Blindly turning her head into his shoulder, Rachel admitted, "Maybe not."

Working to clear the ropes completely out of the way, Killian paused to smirk up at them. "A little sore, baby?"

"Mmm-hmm," Rachel sighed into Adam's neck, not bothering to lift her head as Killian pulled the blindfold free. "And tired."

"Were we too hard on our wench?" Adam asked, not bothering to hide his gloating in a soothing tone like Killian. Neither did he wrap his arm around Rachel as she so clearly wanted. Instead, he worked on getting out of his jeans without shifting the shoulder holding up his woman.

Another sigh, another murmur, there could be no hiding Rachel's contentment. "Yes, thank you."

"Well, you're very welcome," Adam retorted, kicking his jeans down his knees and across the floor. Stepping into the tub, he slid an arm around Rachel's waist and snuggled her back into his chest.

"Come on." Turning with her required a lot of little steps in the narrow tub, but Adam got them facing toward the showerhead, Rachel in front. "Now, there we are. All you have to do is relax."

* * * *

Relaxing wasn't hard to do. Staying awake, or at least aware enough not to melt into the tub like a puddle, was much harder to do. Thanks to the hot water, the soap-scented steam, and the big hands rubbing all the tension out of her, Rachel had never felt so safe and protected. Better than an orgasm, this felt like love.

Even if only for the night, Rachel would never regret sharing this with them. Letting the world blur, she lost sense of actuality as Adam held her for Killian's cleaning. It surprised her, in a delightful way, that it would be Killian who went to his knees before her and washed her feet so gently.

She would never have expected such tenderness from Killian, but then she would never have imagined how brutal Adam could be during sex. *A very gentle man with the heart of a warrior, and a warrior with a very gentle heart.*

That's what they were. Surely tomorrow, Rachel would laugh at her fanciful thoughts, but it did feel kind of like a fairy tale when Adam scooped her up in his arms. Only, it was a perversely delightful tale with two knights in shining armor to tend to drying her off and snuggling her back into bed.

At least one of her knights had something else to snuggle into her back. Killian muttered and shifted, obviously not able to get comfortable with the fully hard dick pinned between them. How the hell could he still be hard? Not that Rachel would call herself an expert at blow jobs, but he'd had his moment, his second one of the night. It seemed to her a man his age should be good and done by now.

Rachel certainly was. Apparently, that didn't count for anything. With another mutter, Killian gripped her thigh and shoved it forward, forcing her to bend her knee over Adam's. Popping open her eyes, she found herself staring right up into Adam's soft smile as Killian fitted the bulbous head of his cock against the undefended opening of her pussy. Without even asking if she was awake, he surged into her.

"I…" Rachel gasped, intent on complaining, but the words got lost in the smooth sway of Killian's cock through her cunt. Not full strokes but an easy tide that seduced the honey back out of her body.

"What, baby?" Tucking a stray lock behind her ear, Adam gazed down on her with such tenderness. "Hmm?"

Rachel couldn't answer, not with Adam's lips brushing over hers. Whispering kisses across her mouth, he kept her from protesting as Killian slowly pumped the tension, the need, back into her body. A moan parted her lips, and Adam drank the sound from her mouth as he sealed the rest of her cries behind his kiss. Lazily, mimicking the unhurried motions of Killian's loving, Adam's tongue slid into her mouth and seduce the will right out of her.

Giving herself over to her lovers' demands, Rachel wrapped her arms around Adam's neck and clung to him as Killian thrust himself ever-faster into her. Grunting with each thrust, Killian put all his strength into pounding into her, pumping her stomach right against Adam's swelling cock. *Oh, God, it won't ever end.*

The fear of losing herself again so completely, so quickly, to them spiked enough panic in her to make her tear away from Adam's mind-numbing kiss to gasp for fresh air. Like an antidote, it washed through her chest, fighting back the rising tide of lust for barely a second. The oxygen flooding her system lent fuel to her need, making her own body betray her by flexing back into Killian's hard rhythm.

"Adam, I...please...can't..." Barely capable of speaking, she fumbled over the order of the words, distracted by the chaotic battle of reason versus want.

"Ignore him," Adam murmured, as if that was even an option. As soft as his words were, as gentle as his look was, it was Adam's hand clenching into her thigh and dragging her leg higher up over his hip to leave her completely vulnerable to his partner's pillaging.

"But...I..." Rachel gave up, her head collapsing onto Adam's shoulder. Worn out, her body felt too weary for another trip to heaven, but that wasn't stopping either of them from forcing her onto the flight.

"Is he going too fast for you, darlin'?" That was only part of the problem, but unable to vocalize the rest, Rachel nodded against Adam's chest. "Then let me help."

"Help" must have meant "make it worse" in Adam's dictionary because that's what he did. Gripping her waist, it took him barely a second to pull her off Killian's cock and slide her down on his. One slow stroke bled into another, making her back arch as her body twisted under the reset tempo. Her head rolled back on her neck with the motion, falling back onto Killian's shoulder.

"Well, if you get that, then I get this." Killian's cryptic grunt explained itself as his hands cupped her breasts. With a warning stroke of his thumbs over her nipples, Killian's chin nudged her head to the side so he could taste her lips, licking the groan from her mouth. Killian didn't know how to kiss with the sweet hesitancy Adam mesmerized her with. Instead, he unloaded all his hunger, all his need, into her, devouring her will with his own until she didn't care anymore that the two friends passed her back and forth.

The pleasure of being so wantonly shared made it irrelevant which man filled her in the moment. Rachel didn't care who fucked her, who kissed her. All she knew was the cock thrusting into her had become a leash, holding her back with its slow and steady rhythm. Bit by bit, they peeled away her layers of humanity until all that remained was a wild thing of wanton need. Rising up, the primitive need took command of her body, making her hips arch and flex until she fucked her lover, riding him hard and fast right into ecstasy's blinding horizon.

Rachel didn't know whose cock delivered her there, and she didn't care as the glorious rapture reached out and wrapped her in its wicked embrace. Whoever it was, he would be the last because the whirl of pleasure around her whipped her tired body straight into the peaceful abyss of total oblivion.

Chapter 9

Saturday, March 29th

Despite the long night, Adam woke up when the first rays of sunlight managed to stretch all the way across the floor and flood over the bed. By rights, he should have just turned over and snuggled back into the warmth and comfort of the soft body cuddled along his side, but the very fact that he woke to such a delight kept him in the realm of the conscious.

The sheer white curtains softened the powerful waves of sunlight, letting them stream out in gentle bands that made the pink princess room glow with a soft, girly hue. This was a sweetheart room, decorated and cleaned by the type of woman who planted flowers around her mailbox and talked to her kitty cat. The kind of woman Adam had always dreamed of waking up beside.

Though he never would have admitted it aloud for fear of being laughed at, Adam longed to know what it felt like to be loved, to be kept safe and comforted within a woman's soft warmth. With the big, flowery comforter keeping him tucked in and the subtle scents of gentle woman and hard sex filling his head, this felt like his fantasy come true.

Given the tensions in his own home life as a child, this moment had long seemed like a myth, something only pansies and sissies believed in. Now that he knew this was no illusion, it seemed he'd been too hard and cynical.

Right here in this bed, with Rachel's satiny skin rubbing against him in all the right places, this was where he belonged. The thought tightened his arm around her waist, pulling her protectively closer out of the fear that something, anything, might take her away. Instantly, she grumbled, shifting and wiggling until he loosened her.

Rachel's natural reaction to being bound breathed a concern into his happy cocoon. What if she didn't want to be held by him? Despite last night's festivities, Adam could see clearly what kind of woman Rachel was in the bright light of the morning sun. It showed in the pink and floral theme decorating her room.

Weathered stuffed animals sat alongside cute little porcelain on the shelf across from the bed. They smiled down on him, knowing as Adam did that he probably wouldn't get to wake up any other mornings under their noses. This was a good girl's room, and good girls didn't run with wild boys like him but for a night, maybe two.

Not that Adam knew what the hell to do to keep a lady like Rachel happy in the long run. Not a damn thing. All his mother had ever cared about was her booze and beating on him when she didn't have any.

She certainly hadn't taught Adam what a decent woman would expect from a man, though he was pretty sure it wasn't running out on the family like his father had. That pedigree alone would probably make Rachel think twice before hitching her wagon to him. It certainly made him think twice about how the hell he was going to hold on to her.

The obvious answer would be sex. His abilities had always made women cling unnecessarily to him. With her obviously limited knowledge and passionate spirit, Rachel would fold easily under his mastery. The question was, would she stay there and for how long?

He'd need more than that. Keeping her busy with kink could only last so long, and then he'd better have some other skills to fall back on. He could already guess at a few things he could try, but they'd be new to him.

If he wanted to make this last, Adam would have to make some changes. Killian would never change. He'd made himself perfectly clear every time Adam brought up the subject of looking for something a little more serious than suck-and-fuck games out at the club.

Killian enjoyed the excess and had no desire to wake up next to anybody. Actually, he'd gone as far as to argue that no woman would want to sleep with him because he snored. Well, Rachel didn't seem to mind.

Her backside might have been curved into Adam's hips, but her head was firmly planted on Killian's shoulder despite the noise that ruffled through the tresses at the top of her head. For all his talk, Killian didn't seem to mind, either. He actually had Rachel's hand clenched in his own, holding it up near his heart.

The small gesture gave Adam hope. He already knew Rachel held Killian fascinated with her grit and sass. As for the sex, he'd never seen Killian go so long or come so often. Maybe he could be persuaded to lighten up on some of his more dramatic tendencies.

And if he can't? Adam didn't want to deal with that question because he honestly didn't know the answer. Having to choose between Killian and Rachel would be devastating. For all the promise Rachel represented, Killian matched her with the loyalty of years past.

All the happiness Adam had ever known in his life had been experienced with Killian. As kids they'd been best buddies, giving Adam entrance into Killian's privileged family life. The bastard had it all. The father who played catch, the mother who baked the most amazing pies, even the kid sister who drove him nuts with her pushy, nosey, ratting-him-out ways.

It had been Killian's family that had seeded Adam's desperate need for one of his own. Sure as shit, he hadn't been born into one, so he had little choice but to build one. He'd always sworn he'd do whatever it took, and looking down into Rachel's angelic features, Adam renewed that promise.

She really was too cute while she slept, looking all vulnerable and defenseless. Maybe a decent man would suffer alone, but Adam had never claimed to have much decency. He'd make some changes, but if this relationship was going to work out, she'd have to make a few allowances for his randy nature.

His hands had already started to shift when the shrill ring of his cell phone saved the wench from her morning duties. *Later.*

With that promise to his cock, Adam rolled over and forced himself to sit up. Kicking over the clothes littering the floor, he waded through the homage they'd left to their frenzied fucking. It had been a long and glorious night, and, hopefully, tonight would be, too. That is, if the sheriff let them have any time off.

Glancing at the clock, he could guess who was calling. On the phone, Alex wasn't very happy with either Adam or Killian right then, but Adam bore more of Alex's displeasure than Killian. It didn't matter if it had been his partner's idea to seduce Sweetness out from under the sheriff. Everybody at the club knew when it came to Killian and Adam, Adam was the brains of the operation.

Apparently, that sin earned him a surprise double shift. With a glance back, he glared at Killian. The lucky bastard got to sleep later with Rachel. His friend would definitely owe him.

* * * *

Killian blinked, taking in the strange ceiling and trying to understand how it fit with the strangely sweet scent tickling his nose. This was not his bedroom and sure as shit not his bed. He didn't need his eyes or nose to tell him that truth.

The warm woman draped over him with her plump breast smashed against his chest told him all he needed to know because he did not allow for any sleepovers in his bed, no exceptions. That was the rule.

Then again, he had a rule about spending a whole night in a woman's bed. Waking up next to a man tended to make a woman think she had a right to cling. His slip up would have worried Killian but for the fact that he felt too damn good to be bothered.

No more dirty dreams for him. He'd finally gotten to fulfill a few now that he'd caught Rachel. Of course, he had more. Actually, Killian had a very long and sordid list. Good for him, he also had a very naked and totally vulnerable Rachel tucked against his chest. The little wench might be asleep, but she was also wet.

The sultry kiss of her cunt against his thigh was all the permission he needed to bury his wood inside her right then. He'd wake her up with a good and proper morning fucking. Hell, given Rachel's appetites, he could probably make her beg for an improper one.

Who would have thought the woman he'd been dreaming of perverting had such a sweet naughty streak? Not that he'd been following her around or giving her any longing looks, but maybe he had positioned himself to stare at her. Who could blame him when he had a naked, horny version of her running wild in his dreams every night?

At least he'd had the sense to know that had just been a fantasy. No woman had ever lived up to his imagination. All it should have taken to put his itches to rest was a good dose of reality, but Rachel had to go and mess everything up by taking him beyond his pitiful definition of a release.

That wasn't the morning wood thumping against her rounded belly but an itch that actually surpassed the one he'd started with last night. *That's sure as shit the wrong direction to be going in.*

That strange warmth curling around his heart wasn't lust. It was something deeper and more insidious. Something that said holding her close while she slept would be just as satisfying as sex. The very concept froze Killian's good mood until it dripped with icicles.

This was comfort, which led a man down a very dangerous road. Killian didn't have time to take the trip. He had a shift he had to go work but first he'd have to go home and get cleaned up and dressed for patrol. If he was late, the sheriff might curse him with a double shift, and no bit of snuggling would be worth that.

As Killian shoved the blanket back and rolled quickly from the tempting press of Rachel's body, he told himself that it wasn't fear driving him from her bed. No, it was outright panic that had him rushing through getting dressed.

More like terror, Killian corrected as his breath started to leave him. No amount of heaving and panting would draw it back in. Definitely afraid now, Killian fumbled with his buckle as he rushed for the front door. Slamming through it with shoes in hand, he collapsed against the smooth wood surface as the fresh air filled him.

He could breathe now, think now, and he felt kind of like a fool standing barefoot on Rachel's stoop with his shirt half-buttoned. Probably not the image she wanted to present to her neighbors as they went about their cheery Saturday afternoon. Shaking off his weird moment, Killian he fixed his clothes.

Dressed and with his cool returned, Killian could admit to a few things. He really did have a soft spot for Rachel Adams, and he really didn't want to know where that led. She was cute and sweet and beyond hot to fuck but that alone told him how all of this ended. Things that burned brightly burned out.

There is nothing to fear here. With that solemn swear echoing in his head, he shut the door on Rachel's house and fled. This time, he really did haul ass for worry over being late. Speeding home and rushing through his shower didn't save Killian. He still showed up nearly a half hour late for his shift.

A fact clearly being felt by the whole station house. That was evident by the sour looks Killian received from the other deputies as he pushed in through the lobby door. It took him no more than one step to run into the tension and the dark looks turning his way. Adam caught his eye as Killian swept through the little wood gate. With a pointed look at the clock hanging on the wall and a raised eyebrow, Killian glowered darkly at Adam.

The son of a bitch could have woken him up and saved him from—

"Deputy Kregor, in my office *now*."

That.

Dropping his hat on his desk, Killian ignored the looks from the other deputies as he sauntered into the sheriff's office. They all knew Killian was about to get an ass chewing, but he earned it.

"Shut the door, Deputy," Alex commanded as Killian stepped into Alex's little cinderblock-cell of an office. With no windows and the paint peeling back, it really was an oppressive little room. The sheriff had his chair, though. Big and leather, it made Alex appear more like a Mafia don than a small town sheriff as he settled into it.

Killian preferred to stand. Presenting himself right in front of Alex's desk, Killian stood at attention.

"Oh, for God's sake, Killian. This isn't the military. Sit the fuck down."

"I'd rather stand if I'm going to be fired, Sheriff." Killian knew every single one of Alex's buttons and delighted in pushing them.

"I'm not going to fire you, Deputy." Alex smirked with a twist of the lips that conveyed the very hard soul lingering behind the made-for-campaign poster face. It kind of irked Killian the way everybody always seemed to think Alex was the "good guy." They didn't know about the beast lurking beneath all those pretty boy looks.

Killian did, and that's why he kind of delighted in taunting Alex. "You sure about the firing? Because we could just make this painless and simple."

"But I don't want it to be painless." Alex shifted forward over his desk, his smile starting to glow with predatory intent. "You see, Deputy, if I fire you, then that makes you a civilian, and then I'd have to be nice to you."

"You should still be nice to me." Killian grunted, finally settling into one of the stiff metal chairs Alex's guests were stuck with. "You know I did you a favor, Alex."

"By what?" Alex blinked. "By sleeping with my slave?"

"She wasn't wearing your collar." No way in hell would Killian let that one slide. Sleeping with another man's slave could get a man kicked out of the club. At the very least, it could earn him privilege suspensions. Killian had worked hard for his rank, and he wouldn't let the sheriff knock him down.

"But you knew she was mine."

"I know you fixated on her to an unnatural degree," Killian corrected. "But that doesn't change her status from fair game. Nothing changes that but the woman herself, and you know that, Alex. Sweetness wanted to stray. I was just her convenient solution."

"I'm going to enjoy making this one hurt, Killian."

Killian didn't doubt him. "What are you going to do?"

The range of possible answers stretched long and wide. Killian would like a little preparation. Not that the sheriff would give it to him. Settling back in his seat, Alex shrugged.

"We'll see what I think of. Now, you want to tell me why you were late this afternoon?"

"Overslept." Killian matched the sheriff's shrug, though he couldn't duplicate the relaxed assurance of the man in power. "Guess I had too much fun last night."

It dawned on him a second later when the sheriff's smile widened into a toothy grin that he probably shouldn't have said that. "Fun? I thought you had patrol duty last night."

This time, the lift of Killian's shoulders felt stiff. "Went to an after party."

"Private one?"

"Very private," Killian retorted, using the words like a warning because he could already sense the direction of Alex's retribution. A woman for a woman, Rachel for Sweetness, and that was nowhere near an even trade.

"Am I to assume, then, you'd prefer not to be working a double shift tonight?"

"Who wouldn't?"

"You know, Killian, I'm a Christian man, raised to believe in mercy and forgiveness."

More like slaughter and mayhem, but Killian wouldn't argue with the sheriff. "Uh-huh."

"So, you work your half hour over, and then you can have a good night."

It took a second for Killian to follow that, and then he still had to think about it. No matter how he tried to figure it out, he couldn't understand what the hell the sheriff was up to. All these mind games really were Adam's territory. All Killian could think to do was blink and say, "Thanks, I guess."

Not about to give the sheriff a moment to change his mind, Killian rose up out of his seat. He silently accepted Alex's offer with a taut nod before heading for the door.

"And, Deputy?" Killian paused with his hand on the knob at Alex's call, but he didn't look back. "Her name was Gwen. Not Sweetness."

Breathing out deep, Killian opened the door and fled Alex's office. Adam waited outside, tapping his pencil against the file spread out on his desk and glaring at the door. Killian caught his look and gave him one back as he curved around the corner of the sheriff's office to sulk down the hall toward the locker room.

It didn't surprise Killian in the least when Adam barged into the room not seconds after him. Before Adam could see him around the row of lockers, he already started demanding answers. "Well?"

"It's Gwen, not Sweetness," Killian repeated in a high-pitched girly voice as he threw open the thin metal door to his locker. He caught the motion of Adam turning into the alley and looked up to pin his best friend with a hard look "It's a sickness."

"What?"

Snapping the keys from his belt, Killian grabbed the lock box key and shoved it into its hole, muttering to himself the whole time. "I knew it. That son of a bitch was in love with her, and I don't care what you say."

"What are you talking about?"

"Alex." Killian pulled his service piece from his safety box, looking up to catch Adam's confused scowl at he tucked the gun into its holster. "Alex is in love with Gwen."

"Who's Gwen?"

"Sweetness."

"Well, la-di-da for him." Adam rolled his eyes. "I really don't give a shit right now because I'd rather be hearing about Rachel."

"Rachel?"

Killian cleared his throat on her name. There was a subject he wanted to avoid, but somehow it kept coming up. Now he'd have to deal with what he knew would be Adam's pissed-off reaction to how Killian had left her. He barely spared Adam a glance as he snapped closed his locker door, trying to make it sound like nothing.

"Rachel is asleep. That's how Rachel is."

"You tired her out again?"

"No." Killian shook his head, trying to play it nice and easy before his best friend hit him. Adam wanted to. Killian could feel the tension building in him. "I was a gentleman and let the lady get her rest."

"But you gave her a kiss on the cheek and told her you'd call, right?"

Killian didn't want to answer that one. Simply walking away wouldn't work when Adam could—and did—easily follow him toward the sinks.

"Right?"

"I didn't want to disturb her." That was half of the truth, which was not nearly enough to cork Adam's relentless interrogation.

"So then you left a note."

It would hurt more in the long run to go this slow. Sighing, Killian gave up making Adam pull his teeth out one by one. Shaking the water from his hands, Killian met Adam's gaze even as he moved out of hitting range and toward the paper towels.

"No, I didn't leave a note, and if you'd wanted a note left, you should have written it."

Never one to let Killian get away with any bullshit, Adam held firm, keeping Killian trapped by the sink as he ripped right through Killian's lie. "You ran, didn't you? You woke up feeling too damn good and then ran out the door all afraid that you might actually like Rachel."

That was too close to home for Killian to do anything more than bristle and bluff his way through the moment. "Okay, look, man. First, I do not run for any woman, and second, as far as all this feeling shit goes, yeah, it was a hot night, and sure, I wouldn't be against going for another round, but it's just sex, Adam.

"That's all it will ever be because women like Rachel don't do ménage relationships. They just dabble." It was harsh, but it had to be said. "Trying to think that there will ever be anything more than a good fuck between you and Rachel is just not healthy."

"Not healthy?" Adam repeated tightly. "Kind of like having a fist smashed in your face?"

"Now, see." This time, Killian didn't back away as Adam paced forward but stepped up to meet his friend face-to-face. "You're acting as crazy as Alex, and yet, less than twenty-four hours ago, you were going on about how idiotic he was behaving. Like a man who thinks he's in love."

Adam didn't even try to deny it. "I don't care."

"But you haven't known her a whole day."

"And you screwed up the possibility of getting to know her for more."

"It's nothing more than lust." Killian felt desperate to get Adam to understand because he sure didn't want to have to be the one holding his friend up when he figured it out the hard way.

"Lust is what had you running out the front door?"

Adam had Killian pausing on that one. There would be no getting through to Adam if he didn't cough up some honesty himself. "I'm not saying I don't feel it. I'm just saying a little bit of rational caution is—"

"Rachel Allen belongs to me," Adam interrupted, obviously unimpressed with Killian's confession. "Whatever it takes, I'm going to make sure she knows that."

* * * *

Rachel Allen. Alex repeated the name to himself as he slowly settled the locker room door back into its frame. He'd known it. Killian had the twitch. Alex knew it well. He'd felt it the second he'd met Gwen. Like a lightning bolt shooting up his spine, pure excitement had vibrated through every part of Alex at just the sight of Gwen.

That was finished business now. Alex wouldn't be seeing anymore of Sweetness. Killian, that bastard, had it right on one level. Now Alex knew he couldn't trust Gwen. It was a shitty-ass feeling. One he wanted to share.

Rachel Allen.

"Sheriff," Dale came rushing down the hall, looking like he'd just got a call that Satan had arrived in town, "the Davis's old barn is on fire."

Chapter 10

Rachel wasn't surprised to find herself sore or alone when she woke up. What really disconcerted her was waking up when the sun was setting. Sleeping past eight in the morning was a rarity for her, but sleeping until almost eight in the evening had to be a sign of a mental breakdown.

She was sore in some strange places and, as much as she tried to fight it, a little embarrassed. Instead of wallowing in the memories of the previous night, she tried to focus on going through the normal motions of what should have been her day.

Shower, dress, food, and then maybe she'd be fortified enough to confront what had happened last night—what she'd let happen. Stepping into the tub to take her shower instantly broke her plan as all sorts of pleasurable details floated through her mind.

As her hands moved the washrag over her body, Rachel couldn't help but remember how gentle both men had been when bathing her. For as hotly as they'd made her burn, it was that sweet memory that twisted around her heart and made her ache for them to materialize and hold her again.

That's what she really longed for, to wake up in their arms, surrounded by their warm scent and protected by their hard bodies. It would never happen, and she'd known that last night. That's why she'd run. The truth was Rachel did have to feel something to let a man touch her, but only a fool would think either Killian or Adam would ever care for a woman like her.

Rachel knew what she was—normal. Killian and Adam could dine on the extraordinary every night of the week, so what did they need with a woman who spent most of her Saturday nights doing jigsaw puzzles or knitting? Not much.

She should be thankful that they'd given her one night to teach her just how much better a climax was when it was delivered by the hard thrust of a thick cock. That didn't make it any easier to accept that today was the first day of the rest of her boring life.

Her normal life felt very depressing in the shadow of the previous evening. Cleaning always helped a little when it came to putting a new shine on things, but Rachel really didn't have the energy to bother. Instead, she wandered from room to room looking for something to do.

Everything was so quiet, so perfectly still, it bothered her. Maybe she should get some cats. *No, a dog. A big, manly-sized dog to walk in the park and use as bait.* Maybe that would put the spark back in her life and give her some kind of thrill to look forward to at the end of the day. The good Lord knew she'd gotten kind of tired whiling away the hours alone.

Rachel couldn't help but breathe in the delicious scents of meat on a grill. Instantly, her stomach grumbled. Given the sounds of a party in swing, Rachel would bet it was Duncan and Bryant. The two bachelors who lived up the road traditionally liked to party, though they kept it tame enough not to disturb the family atmosphere of the neighborhood.

After all, it wouldn't be good for the sheriff to be getting complaints about two of his deputies. *Two of his deputies.* Rachel scowled as the thought sunk in. Adam and Killian were deputies. There was a party going on three doors up, and her one-night stands had probably already moved on to some bikini-clad bimbos.

She didn't have any right to feel betrayed, but that didn't stop her shoulders from slumping forward with her misery. This was exactly why she'd fled last night. She'd known it would end like this, with her entertaining stupid and totally pointless thoughts, like what she'd do if they showed back up.

It would be too easy to just smile and welcome them...*Or perhaps it wouldn't.* Remembering the way she'd behaved with the deputies out by the road side, Rachel had to admit she didn't know what had come over her. It had been the same the first time she'd met Killian.

There was something about the man. He radiated out some kind of energy that made her sparkle and itch until she found herself acting out, speaking out. With Adam in the mix the drive to tease, taunt, and outright frustrate the two of them had overwhelmed her. It had been fun but a kind of evil, mischievous excitement that probably shouldn't be enjoyed.

Perhaps they were all better off going back to their perspective worlds. Yeah, they had a pool and a big grill while all she had to eat was...*What? Nothing. Crackers and peanut butter?*

It wouldn't seem so bad when she got back in the house and away from the tantalizing smells of a meal worth eating. Going for the crackers, Rachel tried to console herself with the theory that a missed meal was good for the waistline. So was physical activity. Combine the two and Killian and Adam could have been her best diet plan ever.

Well, she'd always been a little full-figured.

"Knock, knock."

* * * *

Killian sauntered into Rachel's kitchen knowing he could very well be walking back out of it minus two balls. Adam hadn't given him any options but to take that risk.

Yes, he'd screwed up, but fixing it would be a hell of a lot easier than putting up with Adam's grumpy, complaining ass for the next few weeks. So he'd come hat in hand to make sure the little miss still had a spot reserved for them in her bed tonight.

He could have left it to Adam, but Adam had made it clear that he wanted Rachel no matter the cost, even if that meant tucking their balls between their legs and acting like a bunch of pussies to charm the girl. That had become quite clear in all of Adam's lecturing about how to handle a woman like her and how they'd have to pay attention to the little things and be thoughtful and...*Blah, blah, blah.*

No, Killian couldn't remember the rest, but he considered that a relief. Adam's behavior was embarrassing, and hopefully it would pass before any of the other guys started noticing what a wimp he'd turned into.

Killian certainly wouldn't have lowered himself to such a shameful state. He'd made that clear to Adam, right along with a few other tidbits. If Adam insisted on perusing a relationship, then Killian would go along, but that didn't mean they wouldn't be doing this right.

It would be just like Rachel to send them packing. That would be even more humiliating than being called a pussy. Every woman who had a taste of Killian had always wanted more. That was his reputation, and he wouldn't let Rachel ruin it.

Since Adam clearly didn't know crap about women, Killian had to step up and make sure everything went right. Being the one in charge of the decisions didn't happen often, so Killian had put a lot of thought into it before coming up with their game plan.

Adam's horny nature might have convinced him that sex would be the thing to bind Rachel to them, but that was just stupid. Women like Rachel needed the security and comfort of their bland sexual routines. It provided them the assurance that their men respected them and saw them as something more than a piece of ass.

In fact, if they wanted a relationship with Rachel, then breaking into her house last night and tying her up had been a major misstep. That was something only a one-night stand did, and by now, the girl had to be both embarrassed and pretty damn ticked that they'd skipped out on her.

It made him cautious as he moved through her house toward the shuffling noises coming from the kitchen. He'd been a cop long enough to know better than to underestimate a pissed-off woman.

Finding her stretched up on her tiptoes as she rooted through a cupboard let him relax a little as he settled in along the door frame. He'd play it cool, getting under her control by acting like they already had a relationship. Pure arrogance, it would work if Rachel went along with the plan.

"Knock, knock."

At least he got to enjoy startling her. Jumping into a twirl with a gasp, her big eyes rounded on him with shock that should have led straight to indignation. Should have but Rachel had to screw everything up by going all soft and rosy looking. With that blush creeping through her cheeks and the little tremble shivering over her lips, she made him ache to pervert her all over again.

God, but he did love that mouth. All pouty and naturally puckered, she looked ready to take a good suck of something, and Killian's trousers started to feel tighter by the second as his dick swelled with the enthusiasm of volunteering to be her lollipop.

"What the hell do you think you're doing?"

Ah, there is the sass. Rachel had recovered and put Killian back on track. He played his part, stepping up to envelope her in a big hug. "Coming by to see my favorite lady."

Instead of any softening, his smooth words only earned him an unladylike snort. "Don't even try that favorite lady crap with me." Rachel wagged a finger at him. "I should call the sheriff and have you arrested."

"For what?" Killian eyed her finger. He wondered what she'd do if he leaned forward and sucked it into his mouth. Then he could press her right back into the counter and push down her sweats and pull that oversized shirt right off. Killian didn't think she was wearing a bra.

"Breaking and entering." Curling into her fist, Rachel's provocative finger disappeared.

Oh, well, some other time. Killian sighed and gave Rachel his full attention. "The front door was unlocked."

"That doesn't mean you just walk into a person's house without knocking."

"I did knock. Didn't you hear me? I said, 'knock, knock.'"

"That's not knocking, especially when you do it after you already entered."

"Technicalities." Killian waved away her complaint, still hoping to get by on charm alone. "Now what is with the attitude? I'd think after last night you'd be a little more gracious and thankful."

"What? Are you Miss Manners, here to remind me to send a thank you note?" Rachel dropped the box of Saltines onto the counter. Turning her attention back to searching for whatever in the cabinet, she continued talking to him as if he weren't important and last night hadn't been absolutely fantastic. "Or are you just stopping by to ask how you did?"

She must have tacked on that last bit just to piss him off. Knowing that didn't stop the heat from flaming in his ears. His annoyance didn't show through in his tone as he responded with ease. "Don't worry about how you did, sweetheart. You did just fine as a beginner. With a little work and a lot of training, I'm sure you'll improve."

"What?"

"Of course, this attitude is not a positive start." There, that got a little green fire glowing in her eyes. Killian tried to add more fuel to her ire by giving the peanut butter jar in her hand a disgusted look. "That's not your dinner, is it?"

Rachel shot him a look before turning to yank out a drawer and fish out a butter knife. "Yes, it is. Now what do you want?"

"To save you from eating that," Killian retorted with all honesty. "Peanut butter and crackers in not enough of a dinner, Rachel."

"Don't worry," Rachel retorted with such instant ease he didn't doubt she believed what she muttered. "I have reserves."

Killian was worried. He liked his women with some curves, some softness. Rachel was very lush, and he intended to keep her that way. Crossing the distance, he snatched the butter knife she'd fished out of a drawer right out of her hand. The move earned him a scowl. Before she could object, Killian set about explaining a few things.

"Yes, you do, and they are very sweet reserves." So sweet and he was very hungry. "I would hate to see any of them waste away, which is exactly why Adam is bringing dinner."

He'd tacked the last on as an afterthought, hoping it would help her to see things his way. Not that a woman could ever be that sensible. Instead of thanking him for the foresight to see to her needs, Rachel just scowled at him.

"Adam? Adam is coming over here, too?"

"Well, duh." Killian rolled his eyes. "It's our dinner break. You're our woman—"

"I'm your what?"

"—so, of course, we're going to be eating with you." He ended with a smile that Rachel didn't return. At least she'd stopped glaring at him. Now she just stared in utter amazement.

"Does this normally work for you?"

Killian blinked, unsure of how to answer that question, mostly because he didn't know what the hell she was talking about. "Does what normally work?"

"This." Rachel gestured to the room at large, which didn't clarify anything for him. "Walking into my house like you own it, pretending we have some kind of relationship. What the hell do you think I'm going to do? Just go along with it?"

"Oh, that." Killian shrugged. "I was kind of hoping, but..." He glanced up at her hopefully, but Rachel didn't crack a smile. "Okay, no. I guess it isn't working."

"Good guess."

That was just the wrong thing to do right then. Killian didn't like being in this position, feeling all cornered and itchy. The last thing she'd make him feel right now was desperate because there was at least one thing he could just step up and do. They both knew she'd accept it. *Hell, she'll beg for it.*

"Why are you looking at me like that?" No longer smug, Rachel gazed at him with alarm starting to widen her eyes. She took a hasty step back, bringing a grin to his face. He liked it when she ran.

"Don't even think about it, Killian."

He was going to do more than think about it.

"You stay away from me."

Like that would ever happen. She didn't want it to, either. Tracking her, Killian matched each backward inch she made with a steady press forward. In a second, she'd back herself right into the counter. Then he'd have her good and trapped.

"Killian?" The slight tremor in her tone told him she was wet and ready for him to pounce.

"Thoughts of you have been a burn in my balls all night."

"That's disgusting." The husky whisper made a bald-faced lie out of her rejection.

Those pretty hazel eyes went wide as she banged into the counter. Killian had her right where he wanted her, and she wouldn't be escaping. Locking her into position with an arm caging her from either side, he dipped his head to murmur his last taunt against her trembling lips.

"Disgusting, dirty, and so much damn fun. I've got plans for tonight." He'd intended to seal that vow with a kiss, but Rachel screwed him up at the last second.

"Red light."

"What?"

"Or is it yellow?"

"It's no damn light and don't you be—"

"Those are the rules." Now she had a little bite to her tone. It really annoyed him.

"You ain't naked, so there are no rules," Killian argued, making it up as he went along. "You can't enforce any rule unless you're playing the game."

Rachel blinked, taking his retort very seriously. "This isn't a game?"

"Are you naked?"

"Aren't you planning to get me naked?"

"Am I breathing? Am I man? Of course, I plan on stripping you down for a little fun time, but that's just the nature of the beast. Trust me, when we're in church I'll still be thinking about sex. You know up there in the choir's box I could make you praise—"

"What the hell are you babbling about? What church? When are we going to church together?"

Killian scowled at Rachel for interrupting a very good fantasy. Well, maybe good wasn't the word to use, but it would be fun. He always had liked to try the most inappropriate places, like right there up against the kitchen cabinets. With the windows open, who knew who might catch the show?

"Killian?"

"Huh?"

"You're poking me," Rachel pointed out sourly, making him glance down to where his cock had deformed his slacks. "I said red light. That means you can't poke me anymore."

He'd be doing more than poking her in the next five minutes if she didn't stop being so ornery about everything. Hell, he knew a million ways to make her beg without poking.

"How about licking?" Killian murmured, leaning down to show her every reason she shouldn't say no. Tasting the delicate stretch of skin from her collarbone to her chin, he whispered kisses right in her ear. "Can I still lick you?"

The question had her sucking in a breath that thrust the generous globes of her breasts right under Killian's nose. *No bra.* With one hand right around the collar, he could shear her girly nightshirt out of the way and unleash the little vixen within. A tug and those sweats would be a puddle at her feet. If he did it right, he could take out her panties in the same move.

Then he'd have nothing but warm, naked woman to serve up right there as a feast on the counter. Killian would bet her red light would turn green then. He would just have to fudge on the yellow. He started by spearing his hands through Rachel's hair and jerking her into his kiss before she could object.

Eating the words right off her lips, his tongue chased back down into her mouth. The little witch trapped him. For a second, Killian worried as the sharp edge of her teeth settled over his vulnerable voyager. His fear melted in an instant. A ball-searing heat replaced it when the little sexpot sucked his tongue and made his dick swell to twice its size.

More than ready to play, Killian growled in warning right before he tightened his fingers in her silky tresses and jerked her head back enough to break her hold. Not about to be toyed with or teased with when he was already in such painful need, he took control of the kiss, ravaging her lips as her sweet taste intoxicated him all the more.

Without any effort, Rachel ripped away all sense of civility and domestication, leaving Killian as much a victim of his own primitive needs as she. Clenching his arms around her, he flattened her against his chest, wanting to feel all those "reserves" rubbing up against him. Soft, she made the perfect pillow, except he wouldn't be getting any rest with the tantalizing scrape of her nipples keeping his heart racing.

The spicy allure of feminine desire thickened so heavily in the air, Killian could almost taste it. The urge to take the feasting lower set his hands into motion, and they slipped down to dip under the wide edge of her nightshirt and curled over the elastic waistband of her sweats.

The brush of his fingers along the soft skin of her stomach had Rachel's muscles quivering as she pulled back from his kiss. He never should have released her. It didn't even take a whole second for the worry and fear in her gaze to unleash that damn warmth in him again. Just like that, the curls of tenderness wrapped themselves around the lust burning in him and tempered the ragged edges of his need.

"You just don't care what color the light is, do you?"

She looked so cute with her eyes all glowing and her lips all swollen, like something precious and delicate to be protected instead of mauled. Smiling even though he knew he lost the moment, Killian ignored her grumpy expression to whisper kisses over her tense mouth.

"You know what I like most about you? I like the fact that you never shut up. It provides a man with ample reason to kiss you quiet."

Rachel didn't take to his teasing. Instead, she remained somber looking and even more serious sounding. "I can't do this, Killian. You're not supposed to be here."

Killian considered her statement for a moment. It didn't make any sense. Not that telling her how silly she was being would get him anywhere, except maybe the hospital. The problem was he didn't know what else to say, so he chose to ignore her comment altogether.

"Are you wearing anything under this nightshirt?"

"That's it! Get out!" Her finger pointed the way.

"But I haven't even got in yet."

"Ah! Do you ever think about anything other than sex?" Just as her kisses deprived him of the ability to think rationally, his sense of humor appeared to do the same to Rachel. "Everything that comes out of your mouth is sick and disgusting. I don't know how your mother raised you, but I can only imagine the disappointment and shame she'd feel if she heard the way you talk to a lady."

"Not so much a lady all the time, though."

She straightened up to all of her five feet six inches with that insult, and Killian knew he'd crossed the line. "Leave. Now."

"But I don't want to and Adam is bring—"

"I didn't ask Adam to bring anything," Rachel cut him off coldly. "I didn't invite either of you over—"

"You didn't really invite us over last night," Killian pointed out. "But you sure didn't mind having us."

"Do I have to get my gun out and shoot you?"

"As long as you don't shoot anything off you'll be missing. It wouldn't be a relationship ender."

Rachel's head fell with a groan as she finally begged him. "Why? Why are you doing this to me? One-night stands do not show up the next day to harass you, but yet, here you are."

That was his cue to bring the hammer down on the little miss. "Well, that might be true, but we're not having a one-night stand. We're having a relationship."

Rachel's chin snapped up, revealing her shocked gaze peeking out at him from the locks of hair that had fallen in front of her face. He'd caught her off guard, just as he'd anticipated. Now she'd need a moment to recover. Then she'd be in his arms, all smiles again. *Perhaps she'll even show me her gratitude right up against the—*

"No."

"What?" For a moment, he wondered if he'd slipped up and suggested what he'd been thinking about doing. Rachel put the kibosh on that fantasy and all the others he'd been contemplating all day.

"No," Rachel repeated, "we're not. We're not having a relationship, Killian."

Now it was his turn to respond with shocked confusion. "What?"

"Don't 'what' me," Rachel snapped. "We both know this is not a relationship. A relationship starts with dating. You know, dinner, flowers, and not breaking into my house and tying me up in my bathtub while you try to drive me insane with sex. That's how you start a relationship."

"Well, it is if you want to have a good one." That unauthorized retort had slipped out. Killian knew, even as he spoke, his flippancy wouldn't be appreciated. His mind scrambled to connect it to something that wouldn't get him shot before he could get out the door. "I mean, I thought we had something here. We get along, and the sex is fantastic. What more is there to a relationship?"

It took her a moment to answer. "If I have to explain it to you, Killian, then it just goes to show you're not ready to have one."

"Oh, fuck that." Killian snorted. "That's stupid female logic so you can cover up the fact that you don't have an answer."

"Oh, really? And what does a relationship man do before leaving in the morning? A, he runs out the door like a complete chicken-shit, or B, he takes the time to say good-bye?"

"I didn't run," Killian lied without feeling any shame. "And I was thinking of you. Didn't want to disturb you and all. Figured I'd show a little consideration after all the activity last night."

"Right." Rachel rolled her eyes. "Do I have 'moron' tattooed on my forehead?"

Killian grinned, kind of thrilled at being called out. "Nope, and I'm not sure I'd want the relationship if you did."

"You don't even know what a relationship is."

"I know what a relationship is." And if he didn't, he'd ask his mom before he admitted anything to Rachel. "And I don't think this has anything to do with me. Why don't you just admit you're scared?"

The twisted mysteries of the female mind remained too complex by half for Killian to understand. He certainly couldn't figure out why she smiled now. He had her in the crosshairs, but she looked pleased to be there.

"Nice try, Killian. The answer is still no."

This was just why he didn't want to get involved with the contrary woman. Already, she'd started to be difficult and for no damn good reason, as far as Killian could tell. Stubborn and combative, she wouldn't go down under a direct attack. So Killian switched gears.

"Okay, then how about a fling?"

"A fling?"

It pleased him to catch her by surprise with his suggestion. He'd outwitted this fox. "Yeah, you know, like stretching a one-night stand into a few-week sexfest? Can we do that?"

"See, I told you, you weren't a relationship man."

Killian wouldn't be sidetracked. "Ah, come on, Rachel. Give me something here."

She breathed in deeply, studying him in a manner way too serious for contemplating a simple affair. "Fine. A fling, but I expect you to call before coming over and knock before coming in."

"And I expect you to beg before coming at all."

Chapter 11

"Anybody home?"

Adam's holler echoed through the living room before Rachel could give Killian the set-down his chauvinistic attitude deserved. True to form, Killian didn't give her an extra second to get a word in.

"In the kitchen."

"Hey, darling."

Rachel watched Adam saunter into her kitchen much like Killian had—as if he owned it. It spoke to how confident both men were that they could control her. For some strange reason, that both pissed Rachel off and excited her at the same time.

"Everything good?" Adam directed his loaded question at Killian, who had the audacity to smile with all arrogance.

"Just fine. Rachel and I were—"

"Agreeing that Killian is a pompous ass." Rachel shot a too-sweet grin at Killian.

"Is that so?" Adam smirked, relaxing slightly.

"Oh, you missed it, Adam." Rachel didn't intend to let this opportunity pass her by. With his obnoxious mouth, Killian deserved what she intended to give him. "Killian is such a sweetheart underneath all that toughness. He came over here so very worried that his lack of manners and grace this morning might have somehow upset me. Even though I insisted that it hadn't, he had to apologize."

"Did he?"

Rachel placed a dramatic hand over her heart. "Then he got down on one knee and begged my forgiveness. You can imagine how shocked and embarrassed I was for him, especially when he went on about what an amazing woman I am and how his life wouldn't be complete without me in it. Really, I was touched."

"Oh, you're going to be touched," Killian warned as he started forward. "Just wait until I get my hands on you."

Not about to be pinned in the corner this time, Rachel danced quickly around the island and toward freedom. "It's just a shame I had to break his poor heart by explaining I didn't really like him *that* way."

"Keep it up, wench, and I'll be showing you all the ways you like it." Killian tracked Rachel as she retreated.

She might have run, but she wasn't intimidated. "I took pity when he groveled and consented to sleep with him for the next few weeks, just until I get bored of him."

"There ain't going to be any sleeping, and trust me, you'll be well entertained."

They'd circled the counter and Adam once now, but Killian wasn't giving up his pursuit. Rachel didn't intend to go down like that. Not now, not until she'd gotten him good and riled. No point in having a dominating man in her bed if he was flaccid.

"I'm just hoping I don't end up with a stalker once this fling ends."

"Fling?" Adam repeated, interrupting Rachel and Killian's dance.

Rachel paused, not wanting to circle around and end up in a trap because Adam appeared to suddenly be in the game. Going tense with a scowl, he didn't look like he'd be on her side. Then again, having both men annoyed could lead to its own kind of fun.

"Yes," Rachel answered Adam, deciding to pay Killian no attention. Being ignored would keep him simmering and ready for action. Of course, the big oaf could do her the courtesy of catching her now. After all, she'd stopped. "Killian and I have decided to try to have one of those."

"You have?" Adam lifted a brow in Killian's direction.

For all the hard work she'd put into rousing him to the hunt, the big jerk didn't look hungry anymore. Now he appeared concerned, but not with her.

"Yeah." Killian chin's lifted, and Rachel could feel him digging in, though she doubt the real argument had anything to do with the fight he had picked. "With you playing the kinky sidekick."

"Oh, *I'm* the sidekick?"

"Did I stutter?"

The whole argument backfired on Rachel as the two men squared off, apparently having forgotten about her. She guessed it was the danger of sleeping with two men at once. Still, this would not do.

"I think you should let me decide that. Don't you?"

All she got for her indignation was a dirty look from Killian, who actually appeared insulted by her interruption. Rachel matched his glower with her own. His lips thinned, and her eyes narrowed before Adam finally called an end to their staring contest.

"Why don't we argue over that later? Time for food."

It was time for sex, but Rachel figured saying it would only make them more determined to make her wait. They were Cattlemen after all, and what did that stand for if not contrary? It also stood for stupid because if Adam thought she was cooking whatever he'd picked up at the grocery store, then he could take that conquering grin and shove it right up his—

"I brought sandwiches."

"Sandwiches?" Rachel double-checked the name on the bag just to make sure Killian hadn't driven her completely insane in the last ten minutes. "The grocery store? You bought these there? Why didn't you just buy meat, cheese, and bread?"

Pulling two more hoagies from the bag, Adam looked at her as if she were the weird one. "Why go through the effort of making it when they already have?"

"Because the lettuce is brown."

"Oh." Adam frowned. "Then I guess you won't want the salad I bought."

"A salad?"

"He isn't any good at this, is he?" Killian, of all people, had the audacity to throw that stone at Adam. Never one to lack for confidence, the big deputy braced his arms on the island, resting his hands on either side of Rachel to cage her in with his heat and hardness. "I tell you what, darlin'. Why don't you go put on something pretty, and I'll take you out to a nice dinner."

"Nice?" She could only imagine what he defined that word as. "What are you thinking? Burger King?"

"No." She could hear the smile in his voice. "I was thinking the Bread Box, or does that not pass muster?"

"That's a bunt," she said, because he knew damn well she ate there almost every day. Lately, so did he. The thought slipped right out into words before Rachel could realize she'd said them. Now both men stared at her like she'd lost her head. Killian even shifted to the right, releasing her, so he could give her a "you're a crazy woman" look. Rachel was quickly becoming familiar with that expression.

"What?"

"Nothing." Rachel slid away from Killian and his question as she offered both men a smile. "I'll go get dressed."

Not trusting either man, Rachel locked her bedroom door and the one leading to the bathroom. This time dressing took longer as she actually considered what to wear. She wanted to look sexy. After all, a fling with the two hottest cops in town required a girl step up her game a little.

A fling. She really had lost her mind. Strangely, insanity felt kind of good, sort of like a sugar high. Rachel certainly could have giggled and danced about with all the sparkly energy filling her. Silly little girls didn't have flings with hard, tough men. Neither did boring homebodies, but that wouldn't stop her.

It did keep her realistic. Whatever had driven Killian and Adam back to her house tonight, it wasn't love. It could be blinding lust, but she kind of doubted it. More than likely, they saw her as a challenge, something new to play with and conquer. Killian's offer of a relationship and talk of her being "his woman" would dry up after a few weeks. *A few weeks, try a few days. These are Cattlemen.*

If it only turned out to be a few days, then she would squeeze every bit of fun and excitement out of them. It all started with picking the perfect dress to reel both men into her bed before the night was over.

The perfect dress for a fling... And she still wasn't wearing a bra.

* * * *

Adam glared at the sandwich in his hand, still not understanding Rachel's objection. "I like these sandwiches."

"You're a putz. You know that, man?"

Glaring in the face of Killian's smirk, Adam bristled at being the butt of the joke. "You like these sandwiches."

"And I like to pee in the shower, but I'm not going to do it with Rachel standing in front of me." Killian shook his head as he lifted up the plastic box containing a salad, a little pack of croutons, dressing, and even a fork. "I mean seriously, a salad?"

"What's wrong with that?" Instead of bringing home a bachelor's dinner of pizza, he'd gone the thoughtful, healthy route and bought a damn salad. Besides, a little brown lettuce never hurt anybody. "The lettuce isn't *that* brown, and women love salads."

"Maybe." Killian flipped the carton back into the bag. "But when you buy one for a woman, that's like saying she's fat."

"It is not!" It better not be, or he was in deep trouble. That didn't seem fair to Adam. It wasn't like Rachel came with a manual. He certainly didn't have any experience to help guide him. Trying should count for something, but Adam didn't think that argument would win him Rachel's heart.

"Yeah, it kind of is." Killian laughed, making it unclear whether he was messing with Adam or really trying to help. "There you were, worrying all about how I was going to muck up this relationship and look at you now. Needing pointers."

Adam came down on the side of Killian being a jerk. "I don't need any pointers from you, and I didn't hear anything about a relationship."

"Fling." Killian shrugged. "Whatever. Same thing."

"No," Adam corrected, feeling superior. "A relationship is about love and commitment. A fling is trying to see how much sex you can cram into it before it ends."

"And that's in the dictionary?"

"Look it up."

"Don't have to. Don't care." Killian never did. He'd been barely above a D student, and that had been with cheating.

"I assume your definition of a fling means we get to indulge in all those perversions you were warning me off of earlier." Adam could very clearly see how Killian had manipulated this to get his way. "After all, no need to keep the whips in the closet if we're not having a relationship."

"Hey," Killian broke into a big grin as he nodded, "I hadn't actually thought about that, but yeah. This is turning out to be a pretty good night."

Adam didn't think so. He'd trusted Killian, and the bastard had betrayed him. "You promised me a relationship."

"Fine then," Killian snapped. "We keep the sex vanilla and continue on with our relationship plan. Doesn't matter what she calls it, soon enough Rachel will need us in her life."

Adam studied Killian's glower, not sure if his friend had sabotage on his mind. "I don't know why I'm listening to you. It's not like you know anything about being boyfriend material."

Killian snorted at that. "Whatever the definition of a relationship man is, I know I'm more of one than you. Look at the sandwiches, my friend."

It would snow in the middle of the summer in lower Alabama before Adam would admit that Killian might be right. Not that Adam knew any decent women well enough to ask them for help with wooing Rachel. There was always Killian's mom. She knew about these kinds of things.

"We'll see about that."

"Bold words, my friend. Tell me, when was your last date?"

Killian knew damn good and well that Adam had never actually gone on a traditional date. He met women at bars, at parties, at the club. If they went anywhere, it was to bed. No real stops in between, and Killian couldn't claim to be any different. "When was yours?"

"Mary Katherine Ogel." Killian sighed with a smile. "God, what a name."

"That was over ten years ago, Killian." Adam snorted. He remembered Mary Katherine. How could he not? "Besides, what we did with her wasn't dating."

"Well, it didn't end with it," Killian conceded. "But it started with my mom setting me up on a blind date."

Back then, Killian used to go at it alone. They'd been sixteen when Mary Katherine had put all of that to a stop. Even if Adam hadn't run half as wild as he did, his mother's reputation in town ensured that no "respectable" family would let their daughters near him. For some, like Mary Katherine, that had just made Adam all the more appealing.

With a preacher for a daddy and a kindergarten teacher for a mother, Mary Katherine was a step above respectable and several steps up the paragon of virtue ladder. Perhaps that's what made her rebel so hard. Whatever it was, that girl had learned some moves from two of the Davis brothers that still had Adam thanking them to this day.

"What has the two of you smiling?"

Adam blinked, taking in the fact that perhaps a whole minute had passed since Killian had spoken. He didn't know what his partner had been thinking, but Adam knew his thoughts would get him into trouble. Planning something smooth and witty to say, he turned and forgot to breathe as he spied Rachel in her little sundress.

His eyes locked on her lush-looking cleavage, and his cock instantly swelled. Now there was a feast he definitely hungered for. Adam almost groaned as the idea turned into a fantasy. One where he pressed those generous tits together and pumped himself right through her softness to feed those full lips all the meat she could take.

Adam's chin hit his chest as his head snapped forward under the force of a palm smacking him in the back. Killian sauntered past, and Adam could hear the silent taunt in Killian's smirk. So maybe he did need pointers, but Adam was willing to learn.

"We're smiling because you are such a beauty to look at." All charm, Killian took Rachel's hand and prodded her into a turn. A gallant gesture in appearance, Adam knew Killian was just trying to check out her ass. "And you just get prettier every second."

Rachel stopped him from trying to seal that overly mushy compliment with a kiss. "Food first."

Seeing his opportunity to take the spotlight, Adam forced Killian back from Rachel by simply threatening to walk through him. On his way past, Adam returned Killian's previous smack before roping an arm around Rachel's waist. "Food it is, then."

He escorted her to her car, but he had to leave her to drive herself. Adam was certain that was not proper boyfriend behavior, but she'd have to cope. They didn't have much more than a half hour left to their dinner break. It appeared to be even less time by his estimation when he pulled into the Bread Box and saw the little parking lot packed full of emergency vehicles.

Pittsview didn't get a lot of action, and he guessed all his fellow deputies and the firefighters had decided the occasion deserved pie. It also meant they would have to walk the gauntlet of hellos and speculative looks as Adam and Killian ushered Rachel through the horde camped out in the middle of the dining room. That alone shaved off nearly three whole minutes.

"It seems awfully busy for this time of day," Rachel commented once they'd gotten her past the gaggle of men.

Adam followed her right into the booth's bench seat before responding. The move smoothly forced Killian to sit alone. It also earned him another smack to the back of the head. Adam ignored it. Focusing instead on Rachel's words, he scowled when her attention stayed on the other men.

"Ignore them." Adam certainly intended to, but before he could change the conversation, he earned his first frown.

"They're all cops and firemen," Rachel leveled at him like an accusation. "Did something happen tonight?"

"Nothing much," Killian answered from behind his menu, completely oblivious to Rachel's darkening scowl. "The old barn out at the Davis ranch burned, but that's—"

"What?" Rachel's outraged gasp had Killian's gaze peeking over the plastic edge. Adam caught his eye as Rachel snapped her glare between the two of them. "When?"

"If you'd let me finish, I'd tell you," Killian shot back, his menu now forgotten.

"Well, then tell me."

"God, you're bossy."

"Tonight," Adam answered before Killian's comment could provoke an all-out argument. This was supposed to be the charming and wooing phase of the date, not the antagonizing phase. All he received for his efforts, though, was Rachel's scowl turned on him.

"Tonight? Why didn't you call me?"

Now Adam frowned. "Why would we?"

"Because I'm a reporter. Somebody from the press should have—"

"Andy was there." Killian grinned, obviously thinking he'd fixed it when a second later, Rachel blew up all over both of them.

"Andy? Andy was there? Of course he was." She nodded at her own answer. "Who else would it be? If there is some real story like a fire or something, everybody calls Andy. Now, if it's about some pastel-dyed egg hidden in the grass with a bunch of two-year-olds running around with poopy diapers, that's when my phone rings."

Settling down into a simmer, Rachel's eyes narrowed with malicious intent on the huddle of men. "They never think to call a woman because they're just a bunch of men."

"Oh, don't start that shit." Killian snapped his menu down, more than willing to rush headfirst into trouble. "It doesn't have anything to do with Andy being a man. It has to do with the fact that the old fart keeps a scanner in his house. Trust me, nobody bothered to call him."

"So he just shows up?"

As stubborn as she was cute, Rachel apparently didn't intend to let this topic go. Her intense determination on this subject started him thinking. From her continued muttering, he could tell his woman was in need, and that's just why she had him.

"He just shows up and asks questions. Why didn't I think of that?"

"Well, because you'd have to first own a police scanner," Killian retorted. "Then you'd have to be so lame as to sit around listening to it for hours on end."

"Yeah." Adam grinned, feeling victory in his grasp. "Or we could just call you."

Score one for him because Rachel's frown turned upside down into a glowing smile. "You could?"

"Sure," he agreed easily, making it seem like no big deal despite the warmth creeping into his blood as she stared so hopefully at him.

"But it would be *after* everything was under control." A sneaky little son of a bitch, Killian had tried to worm in on Adam's well-earned googly eyes.

Not about to be upstaged or forgotten, Adam upped the ante, knowing Killian wouldn't be able to keep up for long. "Hell, I bet we could even help you with some research and things like that. I mean, if you want to get into crime reporting."

"Better yet, we could probably let you know who to be interviewing, help you set all that up."

"Or you could do a heroes piece and interview some of the cops and firemen. We know all those guys."

"I could teach you to shoot a gun."

Now that one sucked, and Adam let Killian know it with a smirk. Like Rachel would want to play around—

"That's so sweet. I've always wanted to learn." Rachel's response had Adam doing a double take. Damn if she wasn't giving Killian the look that should be focused in Adam's direction. "But I'd definitely appreciate anything you could tell me about this fire."

Not about to stay down, Adam looped his arm around Rachel's shoulder and pulled her right into his side. "What do you want to know?"

Chapter 12

Saturday, April 19th

"She wants to infiltrate a prostitution ring?" Paused and with her hands full of dough, Heather gave Rachel that mom look she liked to give Taylor. Rachel didn't need a second mother or even an extra conscience, so she just shrugged before popping one of chocolate chunk bites into her mouth.

Tiny little cookies, they had pecan slices mixed in with the chocolate, making them irresistible to Rachel at any time. Heather had left a whole rack of them cooling not a whole foot from where Rachel sat perched on her stool, which went to show who the real dummy in the room was.

"And why in the hell would she want to do something like that?"

"Oh, you know Kitty Anne," Rachel retorted, her cheek chipmunked out with another cookie. "She's bored."

Kitty Anne was one of Rachel's oldest friends. She'd been born in Pittsview, but her family had moved to the big town of Dothan when she'd been twelve. That was way too late to break up a best friendship, so they'd kept it up all these years, despite the fact that they no longer bore much resemblance to the little girls who'd had so much in common.

About the only thing Rachel had left in common with Kitty Anne was a tendency to get bored. While Rachel's wild streak led her to try a new hobby, like candle making, Kitty's led to a job-of-the-year mentality and a man-of-the-week track record. Blonde and drop-dead gorgeous, Kitty could pull off that kind of lifestyle while Rachel was just thankful for the past three weeks.

"I do know Kitty, and I know she wants your help with this insane idea."

Rolling her eyes at Heather's know-it-all tone, Rachel felt cornered by what she knew would come next. "It's not so crazy."

"Which means you agreed to..." Pausing again to straighten up and fix Rachel with that no-nonsense motherly look, Heather waited to hear the answer to her implied question.

"Cover the whole thing in an exposé for the newspaper."

Heather started to nod slowly as she appeared to consider Rachel's response. "And would that exposé be on her being raped or murdered?"

"Oh, for God's sake." Rachel groaned, but Heather had already dismissed her to go back to working on her dough. "She's not going to get hurt, Heather. She's just going to make some interesting friends and explore some options and see where it all leads."

Heather laughed outright at what Rachel knew sounded like a weak excuse. "And why exactly are you going along with this? As busy as you've been lately, I wouldn't think you would be bored enough to be this stupid."

"I'm not being stupid," Rachel retorted with no real heat. That must have annoyed Heather because she came back with a low and dirty blow.

"Yeah? So Killian and Adam approve of this operation?"

She stiffened up at that accusation. "I don't need their permission, Heather."

"Are you sure about that?" Cutting through the dough log she'd formed with her hands, Heather started laying out the bread for its final rise before going into the oven. "Because you did have to check with them before agreeing to meet Kitty in the first place."

Rachel wished she could say no, but Heather knew better. She'd been standing there when Killian and Adam had given her the third degree over Kitty. "They were just curious because I never mentioned Kitty before. They weren't really giving me their permission because I sure as shit would never ask for it."

Heather snorted at that. "The very fact that they feel a need to know about every facet of your life and invade its every aspect should tell you something."

It did. It told her no matter how much she might want to label their association as a fling, Killian and Adam were just as stubbornly trying to turn it into a relationship. Any moron could see it. They were with her all the time.

They slept in her bed every night, ate meals in her house, called her during the day to check up, scheduled things for them to do, and had even started to systematically move their things, bit by bit, into her house.

That wasn't the only territory of hers they'd started to invade. When they'd first volunteered to help funnel some information to her on stories, Rachel had thought it would be a rare kind of thing, given that there was rarely any interesting crime in Pittsview. That hadn't stopped Adam or Killian from intruding right in on her career.

It had started right after she'd published her interview with Patton Jones and come up with the concept of running a Heroes and Survivor series in every Sunday paper. She'd mentioned it once, and then suddenly, Killian had a surprise for her. It had turned out to be a she, a Mrs. Abigail White, specifically. Mrs. White had been caught in a car fire after an auto accident.

Her tale had been more heartbreaking due to her long and painful recovery, which had made Killian think she'd make perfect press. He hadn't been wrong, and Rachel hadn't been dumb enough to turn down the opportunity to do the interview.

Still, the very next day when Adam had turned up retired Captain Daniel Baker, Rachel knew a problem was developing. Captain Baker had served twenty-three years with the Marines without ever getting shot, only to retire to the country and end up with two bullets in him when he'd interrupted a gas station robbery.

Like Mrs. White, Captain Baker was worth a story and it had only been the beginning. Every night now, they came home eager to tell her what new idea they'd cooked up while on shift. It just rubbed her the wrong way that Andy was finally red with envy at her front page success, and she couldn't take almost any of the real credit. While she knew both deputies meant well, they made her feel almost like a puppet.

So did Heather by brutally pointing out what Rachel would prefer to ignore for the time being. "Well, if you're going to write an article on Kitty's adventures, you'll definitely need their approval. Who knows? Maybe you can follow up the 'Heroes and Survivors' series with 'Pimps and Hoes.'"

"You're not funny."

"But I am right."

There would be no point in arguing. Heather always had to have the last word. She was technically correct. "So what if Killian and Adam previewed my articles to give me their opinions? That's what…"

"What? That's what a fling does?" Heather slapped the last tray onto the rack and began shoving the long, slender shelving system toward the other side of the kitchen. "Because to me, two men that not only give you their opinion, but also facilitate all your recent articles, not to mention assist you by bringing you ideas, are after something more than sex. That's just way too much work for some ass, and you know those boys don't have to work that hard."

Rachel did know. Killian and Adam could have almost any woman they wanted and could make any woman beg for things she'd never dreamed of wanting. Rachel was still panting over the memories of that first night herself. *That had been fun.*

Not that the past few weeks had been any less climactic, but neither man had brought out his arsenal. No whips, no clamps, no rope. If she was lucky, they might tie her to the bed with some of her old scarves, which was a very boyfriend thing to do and not so much a wild boy thing to do. Rachel sighed.

"Maybe I should make them work harder for it. They do like the chase."

That had Heather pausing as she began to pull out the trays of now cooled down chocolate chunk bites. Holding one barely inches from Rachel's nose, Heather gave her an honestly confused look. "What?"

"Huh? Oh, nothing." Rachel didn't want to have that discussion, but she did want some cookies.

"Hey." Heather swatted her hand as Rachel snatched two more off the tray. "Those aren't for you."

"They're for my party." The words came out distorted by the mouth full of chocolaty delight filling her mouth.

"They're for your guest at your party," Heather corrected before returning right back to Rachel's sore spot. "Which those two deputies planned for you, down to approving the guest list, and if that doesn't say control issues, I don't know what does."

That's why Rachel had gone out to Dothan to meet Kitty for lunch. She hadn't introduced her yet to Killian and Adam, so they hadn't included her in their surprise birthday party. When she'd explained to them her tradition of going out with Kitty on her birthday, they'd both confessed to having planned a party and immediately begun questioning her about Kitty.

It really would have helped if they'd consulted Heather when they'd thought up the idea of a party. Then, at least, Heather wouldn't have been half as put out as she so obviously was now. Neither Heather nor Kitty approved of Killian's and Adam's growing control over Rachel's life. The ladies believed the men were up to something.

Rachel knew they were, and she knew just what it was, too. "Yes, they have control issues, but really, what is that compared to great sex?"

"Sex isn't everything." So said the woman who only got laid once a year. Then again, Rachel was pretty sure that Heather knew what a climax was. Something Rachel hadn't until she'd met Killian and Adam.

"It is in a fling."

"And you're not having one of those."

"Yes, I really am." Rachel believed her words, too. It didn't matter how much Killian and Adam tried to make their situation into something more permanent. This thing between them would never work out because once they got what they wanted, they'd lose interest in it...*In me.*

It was the chase they loved, not her. They had proved that on the first night. What else explained their need to hunt her down and break into her house? It wasn't lust based on overwhelming sexual attraction. Rachel did not inspire that kind of interest in any man. *Well, they certainly didn't come running after me because of my amazing charm and seductive flirting.*

Nope. That hadn't been it. In fact, Rachel figured the only thing she'd done that had earned their notice was run away from them. Men like Killian and Adam probably didn't have a lot of experience with the word "no" when it came to women. It must have really gotten them good that she'd outright fled. That would explain why that first night had been decadent with punishment and the rest a symphony of sweetness.

Thanks to her rejection of them as relationship men, they'd gone to the other extreme, becoming playful and teasing...*And certainly not like men.* Rachel snickered at her own thoughts. Maybe she should tell them just that and enjoy their response. That would certainly give them something more entertaining to prove than that they could be counted on to put the seat down.

A more mature woman would have confronted them and discussed the issue in order to advance the relationship further. Rachel was not that woman. Instead, she preferred to overindulge in the moment and suffer the consequences later. It was sort of the same way she felt about chocolate. Besides, she reasoned that there would be consequences no matter what, because at the end of the day, no matter how hard they tried, Killian and Adam were not relationship men.

"You're dick whipped," Heather spat in utter disgust. "That's what you are, letting those men boss you around all the time, and don't think I don't know what they're like in private. They're Cattlemen, and I know just what that means."

That wasn't any lie. Heather probably knew more than Rachel, given her long term fuck-buddy status with one of the oldest members of the club. They might only get together once a year, but after ten years, that still gave Heather the greater wealth of experience. Rachel almost envied her friend's knowledge and her uncomplicated agreement.

"They're not half of what you accuse them of." Unfortunately, that was the truth.

"Look," Heather upended a large bag of flour into a mixer that rested on the floor with the bowl lip reaching her hip, "far be it for me to tell you what to do—"

Rachel snorted at that familiar phrase. Heather repeated it every time she told Rachel just what to do.

"*But*," Heather spoke unnecessarily loud to drown out Rachel's rude interruption, "you need to get your head on straight, honey. Those men have you twisted all around. If you were just using them for sex and some good times, I wouldn't be worried, but what you've got going on is a lot sicker."

Pausing with her finger on the trigger of the big mixer, Heather hesitated, turning on the loud machine to finish giving Rachel the rest of her lecture. "Now those men are playing like they're your boyfriends. Worse than letting them get away with that, you're playing along with what they want you to be. I've seen you with them, Rachel. You aren't you around them, and how long are you going to keep that up?'"

Rachel opened her mouth to answer that loaded question, only to be cut off by a high pitched whine. The piercing sound heralded in the vibrating drumbeat of the mixer's paddle whirling to life. Instead of a sharp retort, Rachel had to settle on glaring at Heather. She was being really annoying with being right about everything.

Sure, she'd bitten back on the urge to take control of her more recent project. All it would have done was cause an argument and force her to face some facts because she already knew neither Killian nor Adam would listen to her. Things were too good right now for her to risk blowing everything up over some fight that really wouldn't matter in the long run because this was a fling.

Except that going in with Kitty on this prostitution story would be kind of like frying gun powder over an open flame. If she told either of the deputies about it, they'd go into full no-way-in-hell mode, which would require her to respond with a you-don't-own-me attitude. That could only result in catastrophe.

Though they'd find out once the article was printed, so there really would be no avoiding the issue in the end. There would only be postponing it. Really, how long did she have left with Killian and Adam? A couple of weeks? A few, maybe, if she were lucky.

It would take Kitty that long just to get into the action. Kitty wouldn't be making any moves until Rachel did some research. So she could delay things a little and make sure it took as long as she needed. Her research could actually take a while, given she wouldn't be asking Killian or Adam any questions. The rest of the department would be off limits, too, what with their blue-buddy attitude.

Not that they seem very fond of the sheriff. That thought popped in her head as she spied the man through the warped plastic window in the kitchen door. Sitting in the restaurant, Sheriff Krane was talking to his companion, Konor Dale. Rachel recognized him, thanks to her research into the barn fire. He worked for the fire department, and that could very well be her best introduction.

Or it could backfire on her. Either way, it would make for a more interesting time than listening to Heather's lecture. She really should have skipped the Bread Box and gone right over to Hailey's. Hailey Mathews had called earlier to explain that Patton Jones had dropped a birthday gift off for her. Rachel needed to stop by and pick it up, given Killian and Adam had also forgotten to invite either of those women to Rachel's birthday party.

It really made her wonder who was actually coming to her party. *Doubt the sheriff will show up, though.* If she wanted to talk to him, then she needed to make her move because she really did need to stop by and see Hailey.

"You know I'm right," Heather declared the second the mixer died down. "You need to start thinking about what's best for you."

"And that's just what I'm going to do," Rachel assured her as she slid off her stool. "Starting right now."

Chapter 13

"You know you're glowing." Cole Jackson curled his lip as he studied Adam. "It's kind of disgusting."

"You should see him with his girl," Jacob, Cole's cousin, quickly chipped in. "He goes all googly-eyed, like some virgin schoolboy dreaming of his fourth-grade teacher."

Not about to be outdone by his brother, Aaron continued their laffy-taffy banter. "Let off the man, tonight is his big night. He's getting his macramé badge for all the streamers he handmade for Rachel's party."

"You're all a riot," Adam shot back at the three other Cattlemen smirking between each other at his expense. Cramped in around a slanted table on hard plastic chairs, all four men vied for elbow room and leg space as they waited for their lunch to be served.

He should have been eating at the Bread Box with Rachel instead of putting up with these three. Normally when they worked the day shift, Rachel would meet Killian and him there. The ritual felt very relationship-like to Adam, and he'd grown to depend on it.

Only today, Killian had gotten called away on a domestic right before lunch, and Rachel was off in Dothan having a mid-day birthday celebration with an old friend. *Kitty Anne. What the hell kind of name is that?*

One that was easy to remember, and if he'd ever heard Rachel mention it before the other night, Adam would have remembered. Still, out of nowhere, Rachel had this best friend she'd known forever who always took her out on her birthday. How the hell was he supposed to have known that in time to invite Kitty to the damn party if Rachel had only mentioned her two days before the thing?

It brought home a sore point for him. He didn't know any of Rachel's friends. Except for Heather at the Bread Box, she hadn't bothered to introduce them to anybody. That had to be a clear sign of what she thought of their relationship. They hadn't even gotten to the friend test.

"Grumpy." Cole's grin only widened over that word as he swirled his straw through his ice tea. "What's wrong, buddy? Getting tired of having your dick tucked between your legs?"

Yeah, a little. Adam kept that thought to himself as he growled back at his friend and challenger. "Just a little sleep deprived from having a woman in my bed *every* night."

That had Cole stiffening, his tone sharpening. "I've had a woman in my bed every night, thank you very much."

"Well, not exactly in your bed," Jacob corrected.

Cole shot him a dirty look for pointing out that technicality. "In *a* bed. Happy now?"

"Better watch out, Jacob," Aaron warned his brother with too much humor in his voice to make the threat sound real. "Or it might just be *game on*."

Adam had no idea what that referred to, but it led to an argument that turned their attention away from him. He didn't really care as long as they took after each other and left him the hell alone. Normally, he could take the teasing and banter, but he felt unsure enough about things with Rachel that the added commentary only built up more confusion.

Not that he should be worried. Killian told him that daily, like Adam ever trusted his friend to know enough about wooing women to rely on him. Killian's mom, however, could always be trusted. Adam had sought not only her assurances, but her much-needed advice on how to treat a lady.

He'd followed every one of Mums' rules. He'd cooked dinners, cleaned up after himself, and showed an active interest in Rachel's work. Adam had even followed Killian's dictates and kept his more perverted desires restrained. His friend's arguments had strangely made sense. Rachel would want a considerate and normal lover who would make her think a man cared for more than her body.

"Oh, spare me." Cole's loud and obviously insulted tone piqued Adam's attention for a second as he focused back in on the three men still arguing about whatever. "I am not afraid of any *woman*."

"And how many Hailey look-alikes have you fucked in the past week?"

"Oh, shut up, Aaron."

"Hailey who?" Adam's curiosity couldn't resist finding out who finally had Cole squirming in his seat.

"Nobody."

"Hailey Mathews," Jacob answered at the same time Cole did. Ignoring Cole's pointed glare, Jacob kept the story going without any need for Adam to prod him along. "She's Patton's friend and helped set ol' Cole here up the night of the bonfire. He felt kind of sore—"

"Try pissed," Cole corrected. Not that anybody paid him any mind.

"—about that, seeing as how he's been panting after the girl forever—"

"I do not *pant*."

"—and she can't even manage a civil word when he's around, right? So she set him up for a beat down and then the next day came walking into the Bread Box, right past Cole, like he doesn't even exist—"

"So I paddled her ass in the parking lot and told her game on." Tired of hearing a story he probably knew too well, Cole jumped to the last line and left Adam searching for something worthy to say.

"And then?"

Adam must have come up with the right response because Aaron and Jacob burst into laughter while Cole's scowl got darker. "Then...I got busy. You wouldn't believe the schedule out at the club. We're down so many men, I've been completely overbooked."

"He wimped out," Aaron translated.

"I did not."

"You know, Hailey's a friend of Rachel's," Jacob took the moment to point out, surprising Adam and making him glower all at the same time. How did he know that when Adam didn't? "Ol' puppy dog eyes over there might be able to help you out."

Being referred to that way did not help Adam's mood. He spared a moment to shoot Jacob a dirty look before turning his frown on Cole. The last thing he needed was to complicate his situation with Rachel by trying to help Cole score some revenge on one of her friends.

"You don't need any help with a woman. Do you, Cole?" That was one way to make sure he didn't end up embarrassed by this conversation.

"No," Cole grunted. "Certainly not from you, because trust me, when I get into Hailey, it's going to be her pussy wrapped around my cock and not my dick getting whipped."

"You're un-invited to the party."

"That's fine." Cole shrugged. "From what I hear, the guest list is nothing but men."

"No, it's not. There are going to be women." Rachel, Heather, and Killian's mom were all coming, which really didn't justify Adam's sore-toned response. Screwing up on the one task given to him by Mums did, especially when he'd really tried to get it right. His damn woman didn't own an address book, though, and he hadn't dared to snoop through her cell phone.

As Rachel herself had pointed out the other day when their surprise had been revealed, he could have asked Heather for some names. That would have taken some balls. Heather obviously didn't approve of them being with Rachel. Not that she ever said anything because she almost never said anything to either one of them.

The pointed distance she'd put between her and them told Adam all he needed to know, and it wasn't good. Rachel's best friend had aligned herself against them, and women always valued their friends opinions. They didn't have the kind of pointlessly juvenile relationships that men did.

"Maybe Jacob can bring you his blow-up doll collection to add a little more pussy."

Jacob's ears went red right along with the rest of his face as the rest of them burst out laughing. They all knew Jacob had ordered the dolls as a practical joke, but it had backfired and he'd been the one to look like a fool, having spent nearly three hundred dollars on an army of plastic women. He was saved, though, from the endless well of mirth the rest of the Cattlemen could find in remembering that incident by the arrival of the waitress and plates overloaded with large potato wedges and juicy burgers.

The smell of the meat made his stomach grumble with anticipation. Three weeks of eating pretty much every meal at the Bread Box had made him dream of something different. He could have simply told Rachel he wanted to go elsewhere, but he knew how close she was to Heather and wanted to show his respect for that relationship.

If eating the same fried chicken for every twenty-one meals a week kept Rachel happy, Adam would grow to like it or at least suffer in silence. A man endured for a woman he loved. Adam understood that because he'd seen firsthand what happened when a man didn't. His own father hadn't been able to take on the responsibility of his wife and child.

Instead of getting Adam's mom help and forcing her to clean up, his dad had just left his mom to wallow in her own mire. He'd left Adam right beside her. He might not have learned all the fine courting techniques Mums knew, but Adam's mom had taught him one important thing about women. They needed to be catered to.

Perhaps if his dad had made his mom's life easier, she wouldn't have needed the drink to escape. If maybe his dad had actually loved his mom, he could have made her feel it, and then she would have been happy. As happy as Rachel and Rachel was happy…wasn't she?

Everybody told him she looked it, sounded it, and acted it, but something in Adam's gut told him it was all a lie. That first night she'd been full of spit and sass, but now she was all agreeable all the time. He could have taken the credit for making her world sing on a daily basis, but even Adam wasn't that arrogant.

Killian was. Adam had always worried that Killian would intentionally screw up something when the right woman came along. That fear had turned out to be baseless because Killian had jumped right into the game of outdoing each other as they competed to be the better boyfriend. Instead of reassuring Adam, though, Killian's relaxed attitude tended to frustrate him.

Here Adam had to try so hard to be the right kind of man, and the effort wore on him, while Killian was pretty naturally a good boyfriend. It was like a constant reminder that he and Rachel didn't fit. Not really, but Adam couldn't afford to lose her.

Being with Rachel made everything in life more vibrant. Her very presence made him excited in a way that went beyond the physical. Suddenly, the air smelled sweeter, the day held more hope, and the night more interesting possibilities whenever she was near. Sometimes she'd look at him or touch him in some small way, and for a moment, Adam felt loved.

Still, a part of him sensed her pulling away. Even if nobody else saw it, Adam did. Her opinion of their relationship lay hidden in the small details, like the way she'd never gotten around to introducing them to her friends. It bugged him, keeping him silent through lunch and brooding as he said good-bye to his friends, all of whom he'd already introduced to Rachel.

With the sun out, the sky perfectly blue, and the trees and grass looking lush and full, it was too pretty of a day out to sulk. Slowly, the drive unwound some of his tension, and Adam repeated all the positive things Killian was forever pointing out.

She'd never said a word about them moving their stuff into her house. Nor had she objected to the amount of time they spent together. Despite the bland nature of their sex lives, she always came to bed eager and went to sleep satisfied. The reassurance worked, and his speed dipped as his mind wandered.

Killian and he agreed that once they had truly established themselves as Rachel's men, with no arguments from the woman in question, they'd slowly reintroduce her to their world of extremes. In fact, Killian had even said if Adam could get a collar on her, they could take her out to the club.

Being held in check for the past three weeks had given Adam ample time to develop a variety of fantasies for when that time came. They kept him entertained and made it easier to accept the current conditions. Some of them might even shock the little darlin'.

Shocked was just what Adam was to see Rachel's car parked in the Bread Box. He hadn't expected her back so soon and couldn't help but to slow down to a near crawl as he passed the deli's big windows, hoping for a chance to see his woman. Expecting to see her at the bar gossiping with Heather, Adam reacted instinctively when he saw her, clear as day, in the front window, sitting and laughing with the sheriff.

The cruiser jerked hard when he slammed the breaks. It took all of Adam's control not to jump out and go smash in Alex's face. Only the sure knowledge that walking into the Bread Box and beating the crap out of Alex would not only be bad for his career but devastating for his relationship with Rachel stopped him. *Relationship.*

Adam hated that word right then. He might have every right to make a scene, but knew Rachel would still disapprove. A boyfriend had to trust his girlfriend, not act like a paranoid lunatic. If he gave into jealousy, she'd accuse him of insulting her. Then he'd be in the hole when she should be because a taken woman didn't spend the afternoon having coffee with another man.

Especially not when that man is Alex Krane. The sheriff was a good-looking son of a bitch, known to charm any woman into just about anything. Hell, that's how he kept getting elected. Who the hell wouldn't get elected with over ninety percent of the voting females choosing him?

Worse yet, he had a bone to pick with Killian and Adam, one that involved a woman. An eye for an eye said Alex had every reason to try and seduce Rachel away from Adam. If that happened, he really would make a scene.

For now, though, he'd play the good boy and let them finish their conversation in peace. That didn't mean he had to like switching his foot to the gas pedal and continuing on to the station house.

"You worthless disgusting pig!" Mabel's slurred shout greeted Adam the moment he pulled up behind Killian. The big deputy struggled to pull the woman out of his patrol car while the woman jerked backward, kicking at him. "Don't touch me, you filthy boy. All you men want the same thing!"

Yeah, a woman who hasn't just puked. Adam kept that opinion to himself as he went to help Killian. Together, they managed to get Mabel from the car to the jail cell without causing her any injury and without getting any spit on them in the process.

They left her there to sober up a little while they started the paperwork, a task that Adam could not concentrate on. His mind had locked in on the image of Rachel and Alex together. *This is all Killian's fault.*

He'd been the one to suggest they play like good little boys, and look what happened. Staring across his desk, he watched Killian scowl at the keyboard as he searched for the letters. It took him about five minutes of muttering cusses before he glanced up and noticed Adam's glare.

"What?"

"I saw Rachel's car parked down at the Bread Box."

Adam's comment didn't draw any reaction. With a shrug, Killian turned his attention back to the keyboard. Concentrating on it really hard, his finger hovered over one key as he responded. "She's probably hanging out with Heather. You know, I really want to know who designed all keyboards to be fucked up like this. Seriously, it should be A to Z, but you've got your E right between the W and R. What kind of stupidity is that?"

"I don't know," Adam answered, referring to the Heather comment, but Killian misunderstood.

"Yeah, nobody does." Killian snorted, throwing a smirk Adam's way. "It's kind of like who the hell came up with the Dewy Decimal System?"

Mouth open to correct Killian's assumption, Adam got caught on his friend's last bit. "Dewy."

"What?"

"Dewy," Adam repeated, unable not to get distracted. "Some dude named Dewy came up with the Dewy Decimal System."

Killian gave that way too much consideration before asking. "Was that his first name or last?"

"How the hell do I know?" Adam snapped, more annoyed with himself for letting Killian so thoroughly sidetrack him. "And that's not the point. The point is that Rachel wasn't hanging out with Heather. I saw her sitting with the sheriff."

Killian perked all the way up. "The sheriff?"

"At his table and laughing," Adam leaned in to whisper.

He knew every dark thought that should have gone through Killian's mind, but the damn fool grinned instead of getting mad like he should have. "Oh, look at you. You're all paranoid. Sitting at his table and laughing and what? You think she's back in his bed moaning right now?"

No. Maybe. Hell, Adam didn't know. "Well, I certainly don't think it is anything to laugh at."

"Actually, your expression is kind of funny." Killian leaned over his desk, dropping his voice though the only other deputy in the office was Duncan, half asleep at the counter. "Look, I know you haven't run around with any nice girls before, but trust me—they don't cheat. So stop worrying. There is nobody else in this world more important to her than us, except maybe her family. Just relax."

Adam wished he could, but he didn't come by trust very easily. Still, he gave a five-minute effort while Killian went back to typing. It didn't last. His concerns couldn't be contained. "What do you think they have to talk about?"

Killian groaned, turning to bang his head onto his table before lifting a pleading gaze in Adam's direction. "Please don't start this. We have our big birthday dinner to cook to show her how domestic we can be and then the party we organized to show that we're willing to invest our time and energy into making something special for her. Everything just as Ma said to do it, so don't be fucking nothing up now with your worrying."

"I still don't like it." Adam shook his head. "We need to take steps to make sure this situation doesn't get out of hand."

"This situation?" Killian laughed. "That is—"

Killian broke off his argument as the sheriff strutted into the lobby. All smiles and swagger, Alex greeted Duncan, who scrambled to look awake. Alex even managed a happy and all too smug hello for Adam and Killian before he disappeared into his office. The son of a bitch was gloating, and there wasn't any way Killian could miss it.

Adam waited, glaring at Killian as Killian glared at the sheriff's door. Finally, Killian turned his scowl back to Adam and conceded defeat. "I guess we better come up with a plan."

"I've got an idea." It was time to show Rachel who they really were.

Chapter 14

Killian relaxed against the bar and considered the party in front of him just didn't look so right. The pink and yellow girly decorations were spot on, thanks to his mother. The food and sweets were excellent, thanks to Heather. That meant Killian had done his half of the party right.

So the fact that they were standing around Riley's bar with a three men to one woman ratio was all Adam's fault. He'd been in charge of location and guest list. Killian had told the putz to go through Rachel's phone and call everyone in it, but the man had to have his principles about snooping through her stuff.

It wasn't like Killian had been telling him to look for some secret lover. He'd just wanted to avoid a room full of too many available men. Other than Heather and his mother, every single other woman in the bar had come as a date. Given his mother's age and Heather's mother status, that only left Rachel for the pickings.

Not that Killian worried over the gaggle of men surrounding Rachel. They wouldn't touch her because she wouldn't let them. Rachel knew who she belonged to, which was just what he remembered when Adam had started going over his crazy plan to take Rachel out to the club. The man actually wanted to use sex to force her to tell them what she had going on with Alex.

Using sex as a tool didn't bother Killian, but Rachel wouldn't appreciate it. There was only so long they could keep her doped up on lust. Eventually, she'd sober up and then have their balls for breakfast. Rachel would need to be a hell of a lot tamer before they started to introduce her to her new role as their woman.

It was kind of like gentling a filly. First, they had to get her used to their touch and having them around all the time. Then, they'd slowly rope her and train her for the riding. If they moved too fast or took her too far now, they risked her bolting.

Then she'd go wild. Killian had seen it happen, women showing up at the club all uncertain and nervous, but once they had a taste of the thrills, they couldn't get enough. *Hell, how many times did I help it along?*

Too many for him to risk taking Rachel out to the club anytime soon. Even if she had some kind of friendship with the sheriff going on, pushing her now might be the thing that pushed her right into Alex's arms. That bastard would love for Killian to shoot himself in the foot.

Besides, Killian didn't completely buy Alex's show. So he'd shared a lunch with Rachel. They'd been keeping enough tabs on that girl to know that's probably all the sheriff had shared with her. A little small talk about the weather and maybe even some conversation about Killian and Adam, that's all they had in common.

Nothing there to overreact to, no matter how much the sheriff wanted them to believe otherwise. *This party, though, that could be a problem.*

Killian had to hand it to his mother. She'd done a bang-up job of turning the dark, manly space into a somewhat cheery and almost appropriate area for a woman's birthday party. It had to have taken her over ten miles worth of streamers and whatever they called those things that looped all around the tables. Killian glared at the pink and white tissue-like paper that dressed every single hard edge in some kind of skirting.

Whatever they were, his mother would know what to call them. Having her handle all the details might have been a brilliant idea, but it also meant that they'd come to the introducing-Rachel-to-his-mother stage of the relationship. By rights, it should have terrified him because there would be no stopping his mother after this night.

His mom had made it clear. She wanted her grandkids, and given his sister preferred the company of women, that left it to Killian to step up to the plate. Or so the reasoning went, but Killian didn't buy it. Robin could have kids. She didn't need a man for that. Not that he could say that to his mom.

She'd bent over backwards to accept her children, but she'd drawn the line at grandkids. Somebody would make her a grandmom, and Killian had been chosen for the task. So he'd simply stopped bringing any dates by. It saved him having to endure the endless pressure once the woman disappeared.

His mother knew his game, and Killian could swear that she was more than partly responsible for Adam's sudden need to settle down. His mom had figured out quickly enough which boy could be pressured and already knew that Killian's sons might very well be Adam's as well. Like any good mom, she knew which boy was weaker and had started to work her motherly charm on Adam.

It would help if Adam didn't talk to her about everything. Killian knew he'd already done the stupid thing and asked her for advice about Rachel. Now that they'd actually introduced her to his mother, there would be no stopping her. He'd be lucky not to be wearing a tux and standing in front of a preacher by the end of the summer.

Oh, well. At least as my wife, I won't have to worry about her running wild. As an added bonus, she'd be obliged to see to all his needs. The very idea of how they'd be spending the honeymoon made Killian grin. It would be lewd and sweaty and all the right kinds of fun.

They wouldn't even need to waste money on some exotic resort. They could just take her to the club. Killian stiffened right up, both to his full six feet along the bar's edge and his full ten inches inside his jeans. *Now that was a moment of pure inspiration.*

He wondered if she'd let him get away with that. Instinctively searching out Rachel in the crowd, Killian made a silent bet with himself that he could get her to agree. Almost as soon as he swore to try, he completely forgot about what he'd been thinking about. Charlie was still talking to Rachel, and he didn't trust that player for anything.

Charlie was young. He had only been a deputy out in Cladsine for four years and a member of the Cattlemen for two. That kind of youth made him cocky and eager to make a name for himself, or so Killian reasoned, given that's what he'd been like at Charlie's age.

As a randy buck, Killian certainly hadn't wasted time flirting with older wallflowers, which meant Charlie shouldn't, either. Then again, he would have if he could have stolen the uncollared filly from a much older Cattleman because that would impress the ranks out at the club.

Over my dead body. Actually, more like Charlie's if he didn't stop making Rachel laugh. Not about to sit back and play the fool while some other man made his move, Killian slapped his beer down onto the bar and went to put a kibosh on ol' Charlie's plans.

It was fitting that she interrupted Charlie to greet him with a big smile and quick kiss. After all, he was her man. "Hey, baby."

"What's up, man?" Charlie nodded at him.

"Not much. Just wondering what you're saying to my girl that has her all smiling?" Killian shot back without any heat, looping an arm over Rachel's shoulders to tuck her into his side.

The possessive gesture didn't go unnoticed by Charlie, who smirked at him. He could laugh all he wanted as long as he understood just who Rachel belonged to.

"I was just telling her about the boat Duncan and I are buying." Charlie grinned wolfishly, and Killian knew what that pervert was thinking. The boat was a pleasure craft, and those two deputies intended to make the title a reality.

"He was saying he'd love to take us out sometime this summer."

Rachel explained what Killian already knew. Well, if he wanted to get Rachel into a bikini and out on the water, Charlie should be talking to Killian first. "I guess we'll see how it works out. Now—"

"Rachel?"

Killian's blood froze in his veins. Not just because a man had dared to interrupt him but because Rachel tolerated it. Turning toward the sheriff and offering him a big smile, she greeted the bastard like a welcome friend, which he knew he could not possibly be. *The dirty bastard works faster than I thought.*

"Alex?"

By his first fucking name! That didn't go over well with Killian. Neither did the slight alarm in her too happy surprise. It put Killian right on edge because it made him think Rachel wanted to hide this association from him. The rest of her greeting didn't put that worry to rest.

"I didn't expect you to show."

"Well, I can't stay long, but I did want to stop by and say 'happy birthday.' Hey, Killian, Charlie."

"What's up, sheriff?" Charlie greeted him while Killian just glared over Rachel's head.

"Nothing much. I just wanted to give this to the birthday girl."

Alex held an envelope out toward Rachel. Killian smirked to see it unaccompanied by a gift. The idiot wouldn't be wooing Killian's lady away with just a card. Not when Killian and Adam had gone all out and gotten her just what she always talked about buying—a new, big-screen monitor for her computer.

"I didn't have a chance to get to the store."

Rachel accepted that weak excuse with a gracious smile. "Oh, you didn't have to get me anything."

Killian barely paid the too-cute animal card any notice as she pulled it out. Instead, he met Alex's smirk with his own. "I didn't know you and Rachel were such good—"

"*Oh, my God!*" Rachel squealed before throwing her arms around Alex and swallowing him in a big hug. That bastard's grin went from smug to victorious.

Son of a bitch! Killian knew this game, every step, because he'd played it before. Alex was making a play for Rachel. A subtle one, because the whole point was for the woman to not recognize the come on.

The move stuck the lover, Killian, with only two choices. He could take it silently or pick a fight. If Killian started the fight, his stock would go down with Rachel. Alex, as the injured man, would have his in. *Well, fuck that.*

He wouldn't give the bastard the pleasure of falling for his tricks. Killian would figure a way out of this...*Correction, Adam will figure a way to keep Rachel protected.* Only Adam wasn't exactly thinking straight these days. God help him if he actually had to talk to his mom, but it might come to that.

"I can't believe you took the time to do this. That's just so sweet." Rachel settled back on her heels to gaze up at Alex with the googly-eyed look she should only be turning on Adam and him.

"Well..." Alex shrugged with a bashful look. "I wanted to be of some help for the famous author. Maybe you can name your sheriff after me when you write your book. Make me all smooth and good looking, you know?"

"Book?" Killian snatched the card that had led his woman astray out of Rachel's hand. Even as he began scanning to see what had gotten her all excited, he started demanding answers. "What book?"

"Oh." The sudden tension in Rachel's voice flattened out the excitement. In that instant, as she rushed to answer him, Killian knew she was lying. "It's nothing, just a little daydream kind of project I had floating in my head."

"I don't think it's nothing," Alex disagreed. "You're a great reporter with a smart enough head to be the next big name."

Whatever the hell they were talking about, it pissed Killian off. He should know about a book if she was writing one. It sure as hell wasn't "nothing" given Rachel's disproportionate response to the long list of reference books and websites Alex had given her as a gift. It was even handwritten to make it look like he'd spent a lot of time on his "thoughtful" present.

"Prostitution?" Killian lifted his glare from the notes to Rachel's too wide, too innocent gaze. "You're writing a book on prostitution?"

"Not exactly…it's just…you know, an idea." Rachel was hedging, which triggered all of Killian's instincts. Something was wrong here. *Very, very wrong.* The itch to hit Alex ate at Killian, but he held back, trying for the higher ground in front of Rachel. He could hit Alex later, when her back was turned.

"If you want to write a book, that's really cool." Killian forced a smile as he handed the card back to Rachel. "I think the sheriff's quite right. You could easily be the next biggest thing."

"Yeah." Rachel stared at him for a solid second before turning to cast a big smile at the other two men. "Thank you very much for the gift, sheriff, and it was wonderful to meet you, Charlie, but you'll have to excuse me. I need to ask Heather about…the food."

* * * *

"I told you to stay away from that man."

"No, you didn't," Rachel snapped back as she turned away from Killian's glare. "And could you at least pretend to look like you're fussing over the food."

"Well, I would have if you'd told me that you were going to be messing with the sheriff," Heather groused as she surveyed the long line of food laid out before her. "And I'm not working tonight, so consider the fact that I'm even standing by the buffet a birthday gift."

Rachel knew that stubborn tone and didn't have time to try and fight it. "Well, then can we at least stand in the kitchen?"

"Why?" Heather glanced up, finally looking ready to smile. "You've lowered yourself to hiding now?"

"I'm not hiding," she said, but she really wanted to. "I just need a moment to figure out what I'm going to say to Killian and Adam."

"Ah, got to get your story straight." Heather nodded. "You should talk to Taylor. He's a master at making up stories."

"Ha. Ha." Rachel rolled her eyes at Heather's obnoxiousness. She already knew she was acting like a juvenile. She didn't need Heather to remind her. What Rachel needed was help. "Come on, Heather, I'm in a jam here."

"Yeah, and I'm still not clear on the details." Casting her another smirky look, Heather taunted her. "You want to tell me a story?"

She shot Heather a dirty look for having fun at her expense, but Rachel didn't bother with thinking of a lie. There was no point to it, and Heather might actually have something useful to say at some point. "It's not that bad. I bumped into Alex and Konor when I was leaving the Bread Box and, you know, one thing led to another with Konor mentioning he'd heard about the party and Alex not knowing.

"So I kind of invited them." Rachel shrugged it off despite the snicker Heather so visibly held back. Heather might not be buying it and she had glossed over something, but the line sounded pretty good to her. One well worth using on Killian and Adam when that moment came.

"You invited Konor and Alex," Heather repeated it as if she needed to hear the words one more time to believe them. "I never thought you could be so dumb."

Rachel didn't think she had earned that. Not, at least, for what she'd confessed to so far. "What?"

"Seriously, Konor and Alex." Heather did that little head shake as if Rachel should be getting a clue right then.

Nothing came to mind but irritation. "What?"

"You don't know?"

"Know what?"

"I can't believe you don't know."

"Whatever." At that point, Rachel didn't believe there was anything to know. Even if there was, she wasn't going to spend the next hour repeating herself.

"Fine," Heather waved Rachel away as she turned toward the row of tiny cupcakes, "don't listen to me. Who am I, anyway? I just spend all day listening to all the gossip from all my customers."

"*What?*"

Looking up all insulted and hurt, Heather stuck her nose up into the air. "Ask nicely."

"Heather—"

"Fine. I don't know the details, but I know enough for there to be a valid reason for Konor and Alex to hold a grudge and that it's about a woman." Heather finally settled on chocolate and popped the little sweet into her mouth.

"Great," Rachel groaned. Whatever the rest of the details were, she didn't care to know. "I really stepped in it this time."

"I just can't believe you didn't know," Heather retorted with some sympathy finally softening her voice.

"Well, I knew Killian and Adam weren't all buddy-buddy with the sheriff, but I figure that was just 'cause he was their boss. Alpha dog attitude and all that, you know? But this is a lot worse."

"Why's that?" Heather asked around another cupcake. "Go with that bullshit line you gave me a moment ago. If you put a little more sincerity into it, they'll buy it and think the sheriff was just screwing with them."

"It might explain what Alex was doing here, but it won't explain this." Rachel held up the card for Heather to take a look.

It took her friend a second to shove in another mini delight before she took the card. Exactly twenty seconds after opening it up, Heather choked on her cupcake. Rachel caught the card as it fell while Heather wheeled and snatched up her beer. Half a bottle later, Heather managed to choke down the cupcake.

Glancing over her shoulder where Rachel patted her comfortingly and, hopefully, helpfully on the back, it took Heather a second of panting before she began to form her response. It started with a cough and rolled into peals of laughter that left Rachel feeling anything but sympathetic.

Even when Heather wrapped an arm around her shoulders to give her a hug, Rachel remained stiff. "Oh, God, Rachel. I don't know what I'd do if you weren't around to make me laugh so hard."

"I'm glad I amused you," Rachel snapped. "Now I really have a problem and if you could *concentrate* here, I need to come up with an explanation."

"Why don't you start with trying to explain it to me." Heather straightened up, obviously trying to put her mirth on the backburner. "And I mean the real reason. Not the lie."

"Okay." Rachel turned to keep their conversation private, even though nobody was near enough to hear over the music. "I need some help with the research for this project with Kitty Anne."

"Oh, God." Heather groaned, her head tipping backward under some invisible strain. "That's not what this is all about, is it?"

"If you'd let me finish—"

"Fine, then, go on."

Rachel hesitated, half tempted not to tell Heather. "So, I need help, but I obviously can't ask Killian and Adam."

"Obviously," Heather repeated. "They'd ask too many questions, and then your exposé would be turned into their bust."

"Yes." Rachel nodded, pleased that her friend saw it the same reasonable and logical way she had. "But they're, like, ideal to ask because their cops, so they know about these things. I could ask another deputy, but he would only tell Adam and Killian and that would make the situation worse.

"Then I see the sheriff, and it dawns on me that they don't get along too well with him, so it's unlikely they'll be talking about me at any point. I figure I have the go clear on that front, but still the man is a cop, so I can't really tell him the truth about my project."

"Of course not," Heather agreed. "So what kind of lie did you make up?"

Rachel smiled. Even if her plan had gone kaput, it had been a solid one. "That I was writing a book, which worked. The sheriff was very helpful."

"But he also saw an opportunity to needle your boyfriends, and now your beans are spilled and you have to come up with a third lie to figure your way out of the first two." Heather didn't sound so much in agreement with Rachel anymore. "You really should have consulted Taylor first. He's much better at this than you."

"Oh, will stop comparing me to your son?" Rachel had enough of that. "It was a good plan."

"It wasn't," Heather contradicted her instantly. "But I'm still curious as to why you bothered with all this. If you're having a relationship with them, then lying like this is really low. If it's just a fling, then what the hell does any of it matter?"

Rachel stared hard at Heather, considering her last words carefully. What did it matter? She could tell the same story to Killian and Adam that she had to Alex. They might even be of some help after all.

"You have that look in your eyes again," Heather commented. "You had that same look earlier today, apparently right before you went out and did something very stupid."

Other than shooting her a dirty look, Rachel didn't jump to Heather's bait. Not when she'd actually helped Rachel after all.

Chapter 15

"Then she ran off."

Killian crowded in close to Adam, obstructing his view of Rachel as she huddled near the buffet with Heather. He'd dragged Adam away from his game of darts into this dark corner to ruin what had already been a pretty grim night.

Adam had been trying very hard to assure himself that Killian was right. There was no need to worry about Rachel and Alex. They'd probably innocently bumped into her and she'd just been being polite, given Alex was their boss. All of the sheriff's posturing was nothing more than a show meant to tempt them into doing something stupid.

He'd been repeating all of Killian's reasonable arguments to himself all night long. None of them sounded half as satisfying as dragging Rachel out to the Cattleman's Club. They could use one of the observation rooms to show everybody, once and for all, who she belonged to. That had been Adam's offered solution but Killian had actually been the voice of modesty and moderation.

What the hell does he ever know? The one thing Adam could count on Killian being was wrong eight times out of ten. So he shouldn't have been shocked by Killian's story. Sadly, he wasn't. His gut had been telling him for weeks now something wasn't right. Now he knew what, and it was bad.

"I thought we didn't have anything to worry about from the all-talk-no-show sheriff." Adam flaunted Killian's earlier dismissal of his own concerns back at the now very worried looking deputy. "I thought I just had to play it cool and relaxed and not act like a…what was it?"

Like Killian would answer that. All Adam got was a dirty look and a muttered, "It doesn't matter."

"Oh, yes. I remember. A jealous, crazed Neanderthal trying to thump his chest and impressing nobody."

"Do you want to hear I was wrong?" Killian shifted backward, giving Adam a good look at the defcon level three meeting going on between Rachel and Heather. "Or do you want to focus on the problem?"

He kind of wanted to do both. Adam's mood was that sour. "A book? She hasn't mentioned anything about either a book or researching prostitution to me."

"Me neither."

"Then how the hell does that bastard know about it? And when the hell did Alex and Rachel form a strong enough friendship for her to be confiding in him?"

That's what Adam really wanted to know because it burned bad. Killian and he were supposed to be her confidantes. Best friends and lovers, Mums had sworn that's what made for the strongest relationships. Well, they couldn't be best friends if they didn't tell each other everything.

Then again, maybe Alex was the reason behind their stalemate. If he'd somehow befriended Rachel without their knowledge, the sheriff could have been feeding her all sorts of stories. They wouldn't have to be lies. Adam and Killian's past was colorful enough to be unsettling for a woman like Rachel.

Worse, those tales would confirm her opinion that they weren't suitable relationship material. If Alex got Rachel to trust him like a friend, he'd have all sort of leverage over Adam and Killian.

"This is all your fault." Adam took a certain amount of delight in blaming Killian right then. "If you hadn't started this damn competition over who could be a better boyfriend, then we wouldn't have been so distracted as to not notice Alex sneaking into the picture."

"One has nothing to do with the other," Killian shot back with clear indignation. "And all that competing has kept Rachel busy almost every spare second of her day, so it's probably slowed the bastard down."

"Is that right? Then when did he find the time to con her into telling him about her aspirations to write a damn book?"

"I don't know, but I know this isn't good." That would probably be as close to admitting he was wrong as Killian would go. "She's acting too squirrely, like she knows she did something wrong."

Which meant she probably had because good girls suffered from guilt. That's what had Rachel panicking right then as she obviously tried to seek either help or justification from her friend. Even over the distance, Adam could read the tension in her stance, the aggravation in the way her hands emphasized whatever points she made.

"She's arguing her case," Adam commented. "Building up for when she has to perform in front of us."

"What?" Killian blinked, his brow loosening into a look of confusion. "What do you mean 'perform'?"

Sometimes it really irked him how dense Killian could be. The man saw the whole world in black and white, good and bad. Nobody could ever have shades of gray and because Rachel was good, she could never be bad. Despite all they'd seen and experienced, and for all his talk, Killian was too damn trusting.

It was Adam's job to show him the truth. "I mean she knows we're going to be asking questions, and she's checking her answers right now with Heather."

Glancing from Rachel and Heather back to Adam, Killian swept that thought across the bar floor for a long moment. Still, he could have done with more time to figure out the obvious. "You think she's going to lie?"

Hello, dumbass. Adam wanted to say it, but picking a fight with Killian wouldn't help get the truth out of Rachel. So he stuck with a simple, obnoxious, "Yeah."

"I ain't going to stand for that." Killian said it like the words alone would be enough to force his will into reality. "I say we take her home and screw her until she agrees to wear our collar. Then Alex won't be able to make any more moves."

Adam rolled his eyes at that attitude. "She can just take it off whenever she wants."

Killian knew that, but the reminder had his fist clenching tight enough for Adam to worry that he might actually take a swing. Not that he could blame his friend, Adam understood. He'd been trying to figure out a way to bind Rachel to them that wouldn't allow her to escape.

Unfortunately, the only thing he knew that stuck people together for the long term was having kids. Even children didn't guarantee anything. Adam's father proved that. Besides, getting Rachel intentionally pregnant to trap her wouldn't be right.

"What about a baby?" It figured Killian would offer up the worst idea with the greatest amount of excitement. "That could really work because Rachel would marry a man for a kid, and then she'd be settled down, and we wouldn't have to worry so much about having our fun. My mom will be over the moon, and so she'll stop nagging. I mean, it might be rough at first, but things would—"

"And are you going to marry her?" The question alone should have had Killian backing up faster than a pig to the slaughter. Adam smirked that it didn't.

"Whatever." Killian shrugged the concern aside before giving his objection barely a half-hearted attempt. "I know you'd probably like to be wearing the ring, and it would probably make my life easier given all your paranoia, but we both know Rachel likes me better, so she might—"

"What?" That had Adam lifting off the edge of the bar, finally ready for that fight. "She does not."

Killian snorted. "Please, you're the idiot that thinks taking her to the club and showing her who the man is will help anything. We need to be cool about this, Adam."

"I am being cool, or Rachel wouldn't still be at this party, and she certainly wouldn't be dressed."

"It would help if you'd stop thinking with your damn dick. We have a real problem here."

"No shit?" Like Adam hadn't figured that out weeks ago. "We don't know what the hell is going on here. The sheriff certainly isn't going to tell us. That means whether you like it or not, we're going to have to put the screws to our little lady."

Killian chewed that over for a moment before finally relenting a little. "Fine, but we're doing this at home. I'm not taking her out to the club until she's wearing my collar." He turned to gaze back at where Rachel still lingered, talking to Heather. "This would be so much easier if we could just beat the crap out of the sheriff."

"Keep your leash on." Adam enjoyed turning that expression back on his partner. Appeased, if only slightly, at the loosening of his own leash, Adam needed a beer to plot everything out. He flagged Riley for a drink. A second later, Killian gave up his vigil to second Adam's request.

"I'm just saying," Killian defended himself after Riley had popped two bottles open and slid them down to their end of the bar. "It would feel awfully good to give Alex a pounding."

The idea didn't hold much appeal for Adam. Alex had a right to try and make his play. There was no loyalty between them, not like what was supposed to be between Rachel and them. That's where the real betrayal lay.

"Just one good pop." Killian savored his own words before perking up slightly. "You think he'd arrest me?"

"Yeah, and then Rachel will get cranky and accuse us of not trusting her and blowing things out of proportion, which is just what Alex wants."

"But isn't she going to accuse us of not trusting her when you do whatever it is you're planning on when we get home?" Killian reasoned, suddenly becoming logical.

"Yeah, but what I'm going to do isn't going to make her cranky." Well, maybe a little, but she'd be too desperate to do anything other than beg.

* * * *

Rachel couldn't quell the nerves in her stomach as she watched Killian and Adam strap the presents down into the back of Killian's truck. Neither of them had brought up the sheriff's unexpected appearance or his gift, but Rachel wasn't fooled. Their smiles were forced, and beneath the relaxed attitude they projected, both men seemed tense.

Social nicety would block them from making a scene. Rachel didn't let herself be fooled into thinking they weren't biding their time, waiting for the moment when they'd all be alone. That time would be in about five seconds, right after Killian's mom finished giving her a big bear hug.

"Well, I'm going to say goodnight." Karla Kregor gave Rachel a beaming smile as she stepped back. "It was so good to finally meet you, dear. I hope you'll be stopping by the house soon."

"I will. I promise."

She'd get there right now if Karla would invite her. Anything to put off what would be coming to her in the immediate future. It wasn't so much the confrontation that had her worried. It was the lying. First, she didn't do it well. Actually, she'd never succeeded in bullshitting Killian or Adam.

Then, she hadn't put much effort into it before because it didn't feel right to truly deceive them. Rachel tended to believe that people should be honest in relationships, thinking there was no point to lying when a person could just leave instead. It sounded good and proper in theory.

Things in life would be so much easier if what sounded good actually worked, because leaving Killian and Adam would be too hard to do. They'd have to leave her first. Rachel was pretty sure that would happen eventually, so what did lying really matter?

"And, you two," Karla turned on Killian and Adam, both lingering against the truck's tailgate, "it would do this old heart good to see your faces tomorrow morning in church."

That guilt trip got an instant groan from her son. "Please, you aren't that old that we have to be worrying about your heart just yet."

Karla slapped her hands on either side of Killian's face and yanked her son down for a loud smack on the cheek. "Services start at eight."

"Yes, Mom."

"And you." She turned toward Adam, who leaned down to accept his kiss. Just as she had with her son, she ended the familiar gesture with a maternal order. "And a tie would be appropriate to wear."

"Yes, Mums."

Adam had the manners to escort Karla off toward her car, leaving Rachel finally alone with one of her men. At least it was only one, and he was grinning at her like a cat who'd cornered a mouse. The dark gaze Killian sent roving down her body assured her she would be eaten.

"What?" The gesture flooded her with warmth, leaving her aroused and frustrated. A look like that should have been a promise, but all too often lately, they'd failed to deliver any real heat.

"Nothing." Killian's grin straightened out as he stiffened up. "I was just thinking."

Here it came. Rachel braced herself for whatever smartass comment Killian wanted to lead her toward and followed by asking, "About?"

"Boy, you're grumpy," Killian groused, completely ducking her question. Apparently, he wanted to drag this out because he actually managed to look a little injured. "Didn't you like your party?"

Between the lack of her friends and the drama of the sheriff's visit, her honest answer was no. Rachel kept that response to herself, recognizing she held the greater sin and shouldn't be picking any fights. "It was lovely."

"Don't be falling all over yourself to thank us or anything."

Rachel sighed, figuring she should at least attempt to play along with a little more grace. With a smile, she stepped down off the sidewalk to stretch up and give him a kiss on his cheek. "I'm sorry, Killian. It was lovely."

Wrapping an arm around her waist, he pinned her there. The possessive gesture sent a thrill through her, winding up her heartbeat as she wondered if she might have stepped into a trap. Maybe there was promise for this night after all.

"And your gift?" Killian prodded, shamelessly looking for another compliment.

"You know I love it," Rachel assured him as she settled her cheek against his chest. He was warm and hard, his scent filling her with a strange mixture of comfort and excitement. She would miss this when he was gone, just being held and feeling like nothing could hurt her here.

Like the calm before the storm, the tenderness in his hug only made her anticipate the coming break all the more. There would be a break because she'd put up with three straight weeks of vanilla sex. For as great as it all had been, this was her birthday, and they were having a fling. A fling was almost contractually obligated to deliver something sweaty, hot, and completely incapable of being discussed in front anybody ever.

"I got a lot of great gifts this year." It was wrong to be taunting him like that when she should be avoiding the subject of gifts all together, but Rachel couldn't help herself. "Your mom gave me a really cool cookbook. I can't wait to experiment on you and Adam."

"Is that right?"

"And you should have seen the jigsaw puzzle Hailey gave me." It was a pointed reminder of who hadn't been at the party. She might as well get her digs in now. If worse came to worse, she'd need a little ammunition to distract them with. "It's got over five thousand pieces."

"As long as it doesn't have any naked men on it, we're good," Killian stated as if he had any say over what kind of puzzles she put together. "Which reminds me, what did Patton give you? Something you're going to be modeling for me, hopefully."

Patton Jones designed lingerie, which explained Killian's hopeful tone. It would have been the obvious choice of a gift, but instead Hailey had passed over a CD with a note that clearly said that Killian and Adam were not to know about the disc. The overly dramatic message had made Rachel snicker at the time because Patton was known for her flair.

She was also known for causing trouble, which made Rachel hesitate. She had enough of that right then. "Just a bottle of perfume."

"You two ready to go?" Adam saved her from having to keep on with that lie. One thing Rachel knew was, Adam would never bother with lying. He didn't even bother to hide the aggression brewing in him. From his narrowed glare to his stiff stance all the way to his barked words, Adam looked ready for battle.

Perhaps she should rethink her strategy of antagonizing them into a wild frenzy of fucking. "As ready as I'll ever be."

Rachel forced herself to smile up into Adam's scowl as he took her hand and pulled her away from Killian and around the truck. With his tight grip assuring she couldn't escape, he guided her around to the passenger door. The very jerk of his motions warned Rachel that he was riled up enough, perhaps a little too much.

"You know, it really was a lovely party. I don't remember if I thanked you yet." Rachel tried to lighten his mood with a smile and a kiss right over the muscle twitching in his cheek. It didn't work as well on him as it had on Killian.

Past the point of playing any game, Adam answered her with a blunt honesty that told her not to waste her time on any more frivolous conversation. "You don't really think that's going to save you, do you?"

"It would help if you told me what has you all growly," Rachel muttered. It would help because then she could keep her explanations to a minimum, answering only what she needed to. "Then I'd at least know what my lines were supposed to be."

"In about fifteen minutes they're supposed to be, 'oh, please, oh, please, master, I can't take anymore,'" Adam explained as he held open the door for her.

If he'd meant it as a threat, he failed to scare her. All Adam's words did was send another delicious thrill racing through her as she tried to smother the response with a grumpy retort. "I got that part. It's the why I'm going to be begging you that I'm missing."

She'd hoped to get the conversation started, but apparently Adam wasn't in the mood to discuss anything right then. "Because I like to hear you beg. Now get in the truck."

An order given in that tone demanded compliance, and Rachel didn't rebel. Sliding up into the seat, she felt that special kind of flush spread over her as Adam hefted himself up beside her and sandwiched her between him and Killian.

Surrounded by the warm musk of their scent, Rachel started to feel that undeniable twitch. This was what had been missing for the past three weeks. It wasn't lost on her that the only other time they'd worked so hard to corner her and intimidate her was the last time she'd so openly defied them. Worse, the only time she felt this soul-deep awakening was when they got rough.

They needed this, all of them, but it could only end in disaster.

Just the way a fling is supposed to.

Chapter 16

Killian revved the truck's engine as he turned it over. After a series of unnecessary mechanical growls that reminded Rachel of a battle cry, he slowly eased the big vehicle out of its slot. He made her almost laugh because symbolically, that was Killian. He had a big bark but a very sweet bite.

Adam, though, remained mostly a mystery to Rachel. He could be quiet and very tender, or he could be like he was now, a hard, dark shadow infusing the air all around him with a sense of wicked danger. While a woman could guess every move Killian would make, she couldn't begin to anticipate what Adam planned.

Rachel wanted to have a clue before they actually reached home. That way she could know whether or not she needed to start begging now. A small, panicked voice in her head whispered, "Yes." It was voted down by a desire to be at Adam's mercy when he went bad and a soul-deep assurance he'd never truly hurt her.

No reason to freak out, but a definitely time to be cautious.

"We're not heading home?" Now that was alarming.

"We have to stop by our place and pick up some stuff." Rachel didn't have to wonder what Killian meant by stuff, but that didn't stop him from trying to tease her and torment her at the same time. "Don't worry about it. We just have a little surprise for you in store."

"A surprise?" Rachel really had to snicker at that.

Killian ignored the doubt in her tone to continue on smoothly. "Yeah, you know, something that's supposed to catch you off guard, like the way the sheriff brought up you writing a book. That was a surprise."

So it begins.

"Yeah, Killian mentioned something about you starting a career as an author." Adam shifted more into the corner, slanting slightly as his thigh pressed harder into hers. "Seems like a man who has warmed your bed for the past three weeks would know a thing or two about something like that."

Rachel slouched away from the implied threat in Adam's dark tone only to bump into Killian's hard shoulder. Being intimidated from both sides made it hard for her to remember her practiced answers, especially when the idea of lying weighed heavily on her conscience.

"So, why is it we haven't heard about this book?" Adam pressed. "Are you and the sheriff working on your own surprise?"

Gratefully, the dirty implication in his words had her bristling. She might be guilty of a lot of things, but not that. "I know what you mean by that, Adam, and you better watch yourself."

"Is that like watching you hug the man?" Killian's tone might have been light, but the effort strained his voice.

Rachel could see his knuckles going white and knew his words riled his own temper. Perhaps a sane woman would have tried to make a little peace right then, but not Rachel. Instead, she stiffened up and shot Killian back as an obnoxious a response as his accusation deserved.

"I hugged your mother, too, do you think something's going on between us?"

Adam didn't skip a beat as he cut right through her flippant attitude with his own perverse one. "You can hug all the women you want, darlin'. In fact, if that's the way you want to play, we know some—"

"I bet you do." Rachel didn't want to hear the rest of that. "Which just goes to show who should be the jealous bitch in the truck. Instead, I have two dumbass bastards who want to read into something as innocent as a socially polite response to a gift."

"About that gift, honey." Killian eased back into the conversation with a slow drawl that about made Rachel snarl. "When were you planning on telling us about your book idea?"

"I wasn't hiding it." Irritation and annoyance allowed her to snap that lie at him with full-on indignation. "It's just an idea I think about now and again. Hell, I didn't even mean to mention it to Alex, but—"

"Oh, it's Alex, is it?" Adam growled out from the shadows he'd buried himself in. The darkness cloaked all but the glitter in his eyes, and he looked more predatory beast than man. "That's awfully familiar."

Something fired in the distant part of her brain, roaring at her to escape—as in now. It didn't penetrate the hypnotic state Rachel found herself trapped in as her gaze locked on his. Adrenaline slammed through her, making her heart race and her breath shorten. The intoxicating thrill whipped the arousal burning in her womb into a tidal wave of heat that swamped over her body.

"Which kind of makes a man wonder." Adam's words slid smoothly through her trance, rousing her slowly back to reality as he ended them with a sharp bite to his tone. "Just how long have you and the sheriff been sharing things you didn't mean to?"

Like a cold blast, that accusation had Rachel's eyes narrowing as she considered who might get hurt if he didn't stop leveling lewd charges at her. "Don't even start with that again. I told you once, and I shouldn't have to tell you again. There isn't anything going on between me and *Alex*."

Adam's teeth flashed in moonlight as he snarled, but Killian cut in before Adam could form words to go with that sound. "Nothing but a book and I'm still waiting to hear about this project."

There was nothing more irritating than to be flanked on either side, having to conduct almost two separate arguments. It confused her on all the pat answers she'd tried to memorize. With only bits and fragments coming to mind, she had to shortcut her answers. "The book isn't anything to know about. I just ran into Konor Dale when leaving the Bread Box. He was sitting with the sheriff, and he introduced us."

As she started, the lines came back to her, and she even managed to put some attitude behind them as she warmed up to her planned tirade. "I just sat with them for a few minutes, and Konor brought up my recent success and started teasing me about moving off to New York, and I made some sharp comeback about maybe being the next great American author. There really wasn't anything to it."

"So it was just you and Konor, is that it?" Adam asked, sounding like he already knew the answer. "The sheriff wasn't part of anything and he just decided all on his own to show up and give you a list of references to research prostitution? Because that's either a seriously deranged gift or an awfully intimate one."

Rachel snorted at his choice of words. "I wouldn't say a card with some notes in it qualifies as intimate, Adam. Silk panties, see-through robes, hell, even a French maid outfit, that's intimate."

"That's sex," Adam retorted instantly as if that wasn't what they were talking about. Apparently, he wasn't. "Intimacy is trust, knowing things about each other and sharing dreams like becoming an author, so how is it you got so damn intimate with *Alex* in one accidental meeting?"

That answer threw Rachel because she really had thought he was accusing her of cheating on him. In a way, he was, but Adam didn't think she and Alex had steamed up the sheets. He thought they'd shared something. Something she'd kept from him, and in a way, she had. Guilt flushed over her features, and she squirmed, not easily finding a response.

Killian saved her from having to look too long. Bumping over the little incline to the wide driveway, they arrived at their destination. Killian and Adam shared a rather large house with four other guys. Strangely enough, it tended to be clean but still very chaotic.

Tonight was no exception, and already three cars were packed in the double-sized drive with two more eating up the left part of the yard. Lights shined from almost every window with a mixture of noise wafting out. It looked like a party, and Rachel didn't feel like another one. Apparently, Killian and Adam didn't, either.

Flashing her a wolfish grin, Killian didn't even bother to turn off the engine before he popped out, assuring he'd be back in a moment. With that, Rachel suddenly found herself alone with a very grim, brooding Adam.

"I'm still waiting on my answer."

"What's the question again?" Rachel asked, offering him a smile.

"You want to play?"

Yes, she really did. With a negligent shrug, she wisely moved into the space Killian had vacated. "I don't have any choice, since you refuse to believe the answers I give you."

"You haven't given me any reason to." That smartass answer made her forget all about who had muscle on his side, and she leaned in close to make sure he heard her clearly. "More importantly, I haven't given you any reason *not to*."

He could have at least appeared a little contrite, but the bastard smirked instead. "I guess we're going to find out, aren't we?"

"What's that supposed to mean?" The pointed reminder of how precarious her situation was had Rachel shifting back toward the door and freedom. She would have gone running down the street if she had to.

"Well, you could start with giving off a lot less attitude and answering my questions."

That sounded reasonable, even if he didn't appear to be. "I guess we could try that."

"So when did you first meet the sheriff?"

"I told you," Rachel responded coolly to his interrogation-style tone. "Today."

He shifted with obvious displeasure. The subtle movement flexed his muscles in a flaunting of how much power he could lend to his cause. "See, I'm having a difficult time with that answer, darlin'.

'Cause it doesn't seem like you to meet a man in passing who, in the same day, shows up at your birthday party uninvited with a gift."

"Well," Rachel wet her lips and swallowed as she tried to keep her tone steady, "as for that, he did have an invitation."

Still in full cop mode, Adam didn't even take a second before he punched his hole in her answer. "So you met him and five minutes later invited him?"

"No," Rachel dragged the word out, buying her the second to find the right way to explain what happened. "Konor brought up the party, and given the sheriff is your boss, I sort of felt obligated to issue an invitation. It's one of those things where you don't really expect the person to take you up on it, but..."

Rachel hesitated, hoping Adam would come up with another one of his annoying questions and fill in the void. She really couldn't explain why the sheriff had showed. At least, not without admitting she knew about what Adam and Killian had done to her. With his current mood, there would be no way Adam wouldn't accuse her of knowing that *before* she invited the man.

That reminded her that he had a sin or two to be confessed. Now was his opportunity to show her that this was something other than a fling. Adam could make this even, make this a chance to honestly talk some stuff through, but instead, he brooded silently in the shadows.

Sighing, Rachel wondered why she even gave him the chance. "If you don't believe me, ask the sheriff."

That got a strange smile from him. "And this book? How long has that silent idea been floating around in your head?"

"Only since lunch. Kitty and I were joking around, and she brought up the possibility because, you know, she works in a library. It just stuck in my head and was on my mind when I ran into Alex." Because he annoyed her with that little smirk, Rachel irked him back with the use of the sheriff's first name. It worked, flattening out the small, smug gesture.

"Is that right?" Finally, Adam straightened up, shifting out of the darkness to bring his heat and hardness pressing in close as he began to force her back against the door. "So, you're thinking about taking your writing in a new direction and what pops into mind? Prostitution. You want to explain how that one works, darlin'?"

"I don't think I have to." Cornered but not defeated, Rachel lifted her chin and held her ground. "And I'd really like to hear what it is you think I'm guilty of."

"That's the problem." This time, Adam's smile had a certain sadness to it as his gaze softened over her features. "I really don't know."

He might be a little jealous and somewhat paranoid, but Adam wasn't wrong. Silly as it might be, Rachel didn't want him to worry over it. Things would turn out the way they were supposed to. Fighting it would only ruin the time they had.

Lifting a hand to cup the hard length of his jaw, Rachel tried to soothe him. "There really isn't anything to worry about. Nothing is going on between me and the sheriff, and this book idea is just something I'm flirting with. You know if I ever take it seriously, you'll be the first to know."

That seemed to appease him slightly. The arrogant tilt came back to his grin as he reverted into his normal bossy mode. "We'll help you with the book, but I'm not sure this prostitution idea is going to work out."

Choking on a laugh, Rachel shook her head at his audacity. After putting her through the ringer, the man thought he could now take over her idea and control it. If she'd ever really intended to write a book, she'd be pissed right about now. Instead, she felt relief that he wasn't anywhere near the truth of the situation.

"Thank you very much for the offer," Rachel responded as seriously s she could. "But I think I'll just stick to writing for the paper."

She must not have succeeded because Adam reverted to scowling. "I'm being serious here, Rachel. For a book or for the paper, I don't want you getting involved in anything dangerous."

"How can I possibly get into any danger when all I'm doing is research?" The answer came back naturally. She paid for it by having to slide back across the seat as Adam jumped all over the implication.

"So you are researching prostitution?"

"No." *Damnit.* Her and her big mouth. Well, that might be the thing that saved her as she talked fast. "But if I want to, I will. You're my lover, Adam. That doesn't make you the boss of me."

"I'm your boyfriend, and that does give me certain rights." There it was, the conversation she really didn't want to have. Not then, not ever, but he must have felt her discomfort because Adam dug in. "I am your boyfriend, Rachel."

Anything she might say right then would only get her into trouble. So Rachel borrowed a page from his playbook and stayed silent, giving him a smile that would hopefully let him think whatever he needed to not pursue this subject any further. *Perhaps I should practice my smiles because none of them are working tonight.*

"Say it."

That's what she should do. It would make everything easier, but Rachel couldn't bring herself to lie to him like that. Not that she went with any sympathetic answer sure to piss him off. Instead, she chose annoyance, since that's what she felt right then.

"Why we have to put a label on it? I'm surprised that you, of all people, would even bother." His reputation earned that comment, even though it probably hit below the belt. "We have what we have. Isn't that enough?"

The second the words blasted out of her mouth, Rachel knew she should be reaching for the door handle. She had laid down one hell of a challenge but couldn't move fast enough to escape her fate. Shockingly, it didn't come from Adam, who appeared frozen in the second, but from Killian, who did her the favor of opening the door.

Only she hadn't been braced for it. The sudden loss of the solid support at her back sent her toppling blindly into Killian's hard chest. He caught her easily with an arm around her waist and held her pinned there as he glanced between the two of them.

"Am I interrupting something?"

"Rachel doesn't want to admit that we're her boyfriends," Adam answered crossly.

Not that it appeared to phase Killian one bit. "Oh, well, this ought to change her tune."

This turned out to be a black duffle bag that Killian lifted over her shoulder and shoved at Adam. He accepted it, taking its weight as he settled back into his corner with a look too smug for Rachel's comfort. She should have kept her mouth closed, but she never did listen to her own sound advice.

"What's in the bag?"

"Your birthday surprise." Killian nearly laughed out the words as he pushed her back into a sitting position. When the seat bore enough of her weight for Rachel not to fear falling, she quickly scrambled away from his hold. Happy or not, Killian was every bit as dangerous as Adam.

"I guess, technically, it's our surprise," Killian corrected himself as he slid behind the wheel. Popping the foot brake, he paused to cast her a devilish grin. "Because what's in that bag is going to help us reveal all your secrets."

"I don't have any secrets," Rachel ground out, about sick to death of going in circles. The annoyance kept her from focusing on the panic that swirled in her gut. She had a pretty good idea of what they intended to do. They probably planned to torture her with pleasure until she was too mindless with lust to remember her lies. It worried her because it could work.

"I guess we're going to find out, darlin'," Adam sang out from behind her, smugly assured their plan would work.

Chapter 17

It took all of Adam's control to sit still and wait until they got home to respond to Rachel's challenge. Not her boyfriend? After he'd bent over backward to be the ideal boyfriend, she had the audacity to say that? Well, he'd had enough.

Adam didn't care what Mums said or what Killian thought. They might be right, Rachel might be happy, but she wasn't in love. That was the only thing that could really bind her to him. That's why he couldn't let her go.

Without that, the only thing left that he could think of to tie her to him was sex. If it was good enough, hot enough, he could addict her to it and to him in the process. It was all he had left, and it was an area where Adam shined. All he had to do was wait until the cheery light that shined out over her quaint front porch came into sight, then he could relax.

Rachel didn't. Either still in a huff or, perhaps, finally starting to worry, something held her stiff and silent beside him. That wouldn't do. Surprises were best when they weren't anticipated, and it would be a testament of his skill if he could get her to relax. To that end, he draped a hand over her shoulder to slowly work the tension out of her tightly drawn muscles as Killian eased the truck down her road.

"Why so tense, darlin'?"

That earned him a sour look and a snotty retort. "Don't even bother with the sweet, innocent routine, Adam. I know what you're about."

"And what's that?" He couldn't help but grin at her, feeling like a dog that had just shaken his collar off and could now run free.

"Probably tie me up and then torment me while you ask me a bunch of stupid questions." Rachel didn't beat around the bush. Nor did she bother to hold anything back. "Given your dirty mind, I imagine we're about to fulfill some kind of twisted cop fantasy where you have the guilty vixen at your mercy."

"You're not that far off." Adam couldn't deny it, and he was tired of trying.

"I ain't ever had one of those fantasies." Killian broke the tension building between Adam and Rachel with his grunted intrusion. Like anybody had asked him, he continued on with his explanation. "I got this one, though, about a speeder. You know, I pull her over, and she's so desperate to avoid a ticket she's willing to do anything. Then I have to punish her for being so forward and trying to bribe me."

He tipped his head to the side, flashing Rachel a quick look before shrugging. "You don't really speed, though."

"And I wouldn't try to bribe you," Rachel retorted with all sourness.

"How soon they forget." Killian all but laughed out as he brought the truck to a smooth stop. "Or do I need to remind you of an incident where you promised to do anything to get out of being arrested?"

"I was playing you." Rachel turned her shoulder on Killian, trying to dismiss him with that, but Adam blocked her path.

"Not as well as we played you that night, darlin'," Adam delighted in reminding her. "Now it's time for round two, so I'd better be hearing some 'sirs' following those sassy comments, or it's going to be a long night."

She could have said something obnoxious and tried to stop them. Adam wouldn't have forced her into anything, but Rachel didn't even need to be led. Chin up, she bumped into him as she tried to force him right through the door. Adam didn't need to be nudged twice.

Getting out of the truck, he held the door open as she stormed right past and up her walkway. She marched like a trooper toward battle but had to know she could win. It felt like a good sign to Adam.

Maybe she wanted, needed things to be rough just like he did. Perhaps that's what they had in common, what could bind them together.

"Getting cold feet." Rachel's sharp prod jerked Adam back to the moment.

"I didn't hear a 'sir' at the end of that." Adam hefted the duffle bag over his shoulder before slamming the door closed. "So that's one."

* * * *

That's one, whatever. Rachel rolled her eyes and turned to mount the front steps but nearly collided with Killian instead. Before she could take a steadying step backward, his hands fitted to her waist, and suddenly the world shifted.

"Upsadaisy, darlin'."

"I'm not a sack of feed, Killian," Rachel complained as he settled her over his shoulder. The steps looked strange and far away as they passed under her nose in the opposite view she normally had walking up them herself.

"Just don't want you to take off and make me waste any energy chasing you down."

He almost cracked her head on the side of the door jamb as he juggled both her and the key. "Watch it, now. There is nothing romantic about a concussion."

"You think being tied naked to your dining room table is romantic?" Adam's voice sounded from above her as his boots came clumping into view beneath her.

"Tied to the table?" Rachel snorted. "That's what all this show is for? I thought we were going back to the tub."

"You thought *that* was romantic?"

Killian sounded honestly aghast, making her hesitate with her answer as it dawned on her that she might be a little more twisted than them. "No."

"You're lying," Killian accused her as he finally got the door open. "Hell, maybe I was wrong all along, Adam."

"Told you."

Rachel didn't know what they were talking about, but she wanted to. As the living room flashed past, she tried to lever herself up so she could at least see Adam's expression as she asked her question. "Wrong about what?"

Killian's smirk replaced Adam's smile as he lowered her onto the promised table. Straightening up, he lorded over, flexing his arms as he crossed them over his chest and letting his gaze narrow into a hard look.

"Don't you be worrying about that, wench. You should be concerned about how many 'sirs' you've been skipping. Now, if you don't want your punishment doubled, you'd better be naked in thirty seconds."

He barked at her like a damn drill sergeant, using every intimidating inch of his massive frame to assure she did as told. They'd been here once before. With them threatening and only delivering more pleasure with each one of their punishments. It had been her first time, and she'd folded too easily under the delight.

Not this time. This time, she wanted to test their control and see how long it took to break it. Deciding that words wouldn't do, Rachel put her defiance into action. With a smile, she slid closer to the edge of the table. Letting her legs go wide around Killian's thighs to capture him, she snuggled in close to his chest.

Beneath the warm softness of his cotton T-shirt, Rachel could feel the hard, heated strength that trembled ever so slightly as she ran her hands along his length. The tell-tale gesture of how much her touch alone pleased him tickled Rachel. It made Killian snarl.

"This isn't what I meant, wench, but if you want to see where it gets you, then go ahead."

Yes, Rachel did want to see. She bet he did, too, or he'd have put an end to her game right then. Keeping her smile to herself, Rachel stretched up to nuzzle a kiss into the crease of his neck. "Okay, then, we'll do this my way."

To give him a little taste of what that meant, Rachel scraped her teeth down along the corded length of the muscle strung tight beneath her lips. It jumped, quivered, and then flexed on Killian's sharp growl. This time, she didn't bother to hold back her giggle as her fingers settled over the first of his shirt buttons.

"Are you sure you're ready for this?" It was an arrogant thing to gloat so brazenly in front of Killian, but he held firm against her teasing.

"Go on, wench. You ain't going to show me anything I haven't seen before."

He had to go there and fortify her will to make damn good and sure he was the one on his knees at the end of the night. Rachel bit him again in retaliation, right over the fast-paced throb of his pulse. Killian could mouth off all he wanted, but he stayed stiff, braced for war, as that first button came free. That's how much power she had over him.

Rachel reveled in it, enjoying the way his muscles shivered under the strain of her lips raining butterfly kisses all the way down to where his shirt slid slowly open. There could be no hiding the thunderous pound of his heart when her lips drifted over the hard ridge of his chest.

She'd wanted to listen to his heart as her hands slipped over his buckle to dip down and measure the hard cock she could feel deforming the denim. Though the way he flinched when her lips brushed over his own pebbled nipple lured her into teasing him with a twirling lick that had Killian growling.

That's all Rachel needed to hear. Lingering over the kiss, she tormented him as he so often did her. Licking, sucking, she savored the taste and textures that were Killian. Musky, spicy, all male, his flavor drugged her with a wanton need that was only driven higher by the quivering of his muscles.

Pulled tight beneath the satin softness of his skin, she chased the tremors with the tip of her tongue, teasing him into shudders that ended when he growled and clenched himself tight against her tender assault. Not about to let him find refuge in the iron will that served him too well, Rachel reveled in unraveling him with the simple grind of her palm over the thick bulge of his cock.

From beneath the rough fabric of jeans, she could feel him swell and pulse at her touch. That's all the encouragement Rachel needed. Tightening her grip over his thick erection, she used the stiff, almost unbendable denim to massage his dick with long, milking motions that brought the growl back to Killian's lips.

He held fast, though. Fists clenched tightly at his sides, he let her wind him and herself higher and higher until the need to feel his fullness pounding into her once again became a pain that she could not bear. Clothes be damned, she needed one moment of relief from the heat driving through her.

Abandoning the erection straining to greet her grip, she gripped his hips in her hands to jerk the long ridge of his cock to the sodden mess she'd made of her panties. With the skirt of her dress up to her waist, she delighted herself with a full-length stroke right up the thick line of his dented jeans.

The unforgiving steel of his dick pressed the hard, ridged edge of the zipper right through the swollen folds of her pussy lips and caught the tender bud of her clit in an explosive caress. The thin barrier of her silk underwear protected her from the rough side of the grinding press, turning it into an addictive delight.

With her hands smoothing over his warm skin, testing the muscles beneath, Rachel clutched at Killian as she gave over to the frenzy. Rubbing herself against him in an escalating tempo, the rhythm matched the need whirling out of control inside of her, but it wouldn't be soothed by so little.

The gasping, empty spasms clenching her cunt tight became almost painful. She needed him. She needed him now. That thought registered barely a second before her hands dipped in an assault on his belt buckle. The move cost her.

Having to peel herself back far enough from his delicious bulge to let her hands work only made her pussy cry foul. That discomfort paled in comparison to having her wrists caught by Killian's strong hold. He brought all motion to a stop and sent ice water trickling down her spine with his even-toned question.

"And just what do you think you're doing?"

Rachel looked up into Killian's somber gaze and came to a stuttering, horrifying conclusion. He wasn't anywhere near ready to take his pants off. Her plan had failed. Worse, it had backfired. Not only did he not appear ready to ravish her, but now she'd added fuel to his determination to make her pay tonight. That would be both a joy and a torment, which reminded her that she didn't have anything to lose in this game.

"Are we moving to the tub now?" Rachel smiled, pulling back slightly as she tried to fake being something other than in desperate need for him. "Is that where Adam's disappeared to?"

"Don't you worry about what he's up to." Killian released her hands as she shifted even farther back on the table.

Against the adamant protest of every fiber of her being, she released him enough to push her dress back down. The gesture drew a narrowing of Killian's gaze and a hope in her heart that he wasn't half as cool as he pretended. He must have been straining under the pressure of his own desires, or why else would his bark be so harsh?

"Best you focus on answering my question, wench." The man definitely felt the itch. Otherwise, he wouldn't cross his arms over his chest, trying to both intimidate her and keep his hands from betraying him. "What do you think you were doing?"

Rachel shrugged, deciding the thing that might break his control would be just the right amount of sass. "You said to get naked."

"I said for you to get naked."

"Yes, for *you* to get naked." Rachel had a hard time getting that out without laughing.

Killian's hard look helped, assuring her a giggle would be a step too far over the line. She had to settle for watching his jaw clench and hearing that little growl sound he made whenever she had him riled. Still, none of that justified the arrogant and totally pompous way he held out his hand to her.

"The dress."

The outrageous way he handled his demand could only deserve an equally disobedient response. It started with leaning down to capture his thumb in her mouth. Giving the fat digit a suck, she let her tongue twirl around his callused finger and lead her kiss into an exploration of the rough textures and rigid planes of his hand.

It took over a minute for her to land on the thundering pulse of his heartbeat. Lifting off the tell-tale sign of his own desires, Rachel gave Killian the most innocent smile she could manage as she looked up from his hand.

"You'll have to help me with the zipper."

Eyes narrowed, lips thinned, he didn't even respond to that taunt as she straightened up. Ignoring his heated glare, she twisted to offer him her back. With her hair swept out of the way, Rachel waited until she figured he intended to ignore her challenge. That alone would have been a magnificent victory, but Killian ruined all the gloating prods coming to her mind by finally taking the small, metal tag in hand.

His thick knuckles brushed teasingly over her spine as he tugged on the delicate fabric, working the zipper down only as a man who didn't do ladies' zippers would. The muttered curses that floated over her shoulder as he snagged the tiny zipper on the silky fabric brought a giggle to her lips, but she kept it clamped in as he worked the tangle free.

It must have taken great care for those big fingers not to tear through the snag. The consideration he showed reminded her for a moment of just how good a heart the big, gruff deputy had buried beneath his sexist attitude.

The soft, warmth spreading through her had her forgetting all about the game they'd been playing as she released her hair. With a smile on her lips and an idea of how to reward him, Rachel started to turn back when Killian's fingers suddenly gripped the undone edges of her dress.

"What—"

Rachel's question ended in a shriek and a good amount of flailing as she tried to escape the hands shredding her dress into rags. She was neither quick enough nor strong enough to escape Killian's wrath. He had her down to nothing but panties and a bra in less than thirty seconds.

Panting over the sudden struggle, Rachel made it to the middle of the table and out of arm's reach before she turned back to glare at him. She meant to tell him that wasn't funny, that he'd be paying for that dress. The predatory intent of his hawkish gaze made her reevaluate the wisdom of prodding him any further.

It also made her reconsider the security of her position. With the clear conclusion that she wasn't far enough away, Rachel began to inch back. Killian cocked his head, finally finding the wisp of a smile as he studied her retreat.

None of that smugness showed through when he asked her very calmly, "Do you need help with your bra?"

If she hadn't been wearing one of her best and most expensive pieces of lingerie, Rachel would have given Killian the answer he deserved. Instead, prudence made her assess his threat and come to the conclusion that snapping it off and throwing it at him would serve to make her point.

It did kind of delight her that his smile faded away as a cup caught on his head and the bra dangled there, making him look about as intimidating as a clown. She also got to enjoy hearing him growl again before he snatched the thing off. Then, though, the entertainment took a more daring turn as his eyes dropped pointedly to her panties.

He didn't seem think she'd give him a face full of that, but Rachel had come too far to back down now with a pathetic whimper. Whipping them off, she snapped the sodden underwear right at his cockhead, but the bastard managed to catch them in mid-air. Her missile fell to the ground, leaving her defenseless and vulnerable with a very high-strung Cattleman staring her down.

The silence drew out long and tense as she sized him up, knowing he was ready to pounce. The second he flinched forward, Rachel hauled ass. She should have made it right off the table's opposite edge but slammed into a hard, warm mountain of muscle that shifted to bind her tightly to Adam's chest.

"And just where do you think you're going?"

Chapter 18

Stretched out on her stomach with Killian's fierce grasp dragging her ass backward, Rachel still tried for a light smile as she clung to Adam's shoulders. "I was looking for you, wondering where you went."

"Is that right?" He sounded way too indulgent, almost disbelieving.

"Where else would I be headed?" It was even harder to look nonchalant than to sound it, especially with Killian forcing her ass up. Gripping her hips, he lifted her waist up high enough that she had to crawl forward to support herself. She found herself on her knees and could only guess at the exciting possibilities of what came next.

One thing she knew for sure, it would only be better with Adam's participation. With the possibility of victory restored, Rachel turned her attention on him and ignored the sound of all the chairs being pulled out behind her. With a grinding rub that teased her nipples against the scratchy fabric of Adam's flannel shirt, she tried her own impression of Killian's famous growl.

"You do know how much I enjoy having you in the mix." The taunt didn't come out right. Her mind was too preoccupied with the pleasure of rubbing her swollen breasts against the unforgiving hardness of his chest.

Not one to let something slip, Adam latched on to her poor choice of words...and the source behind them. Smug, slightly humored, he repeated, "In the mix?"

"Uh-huh." Rachel fumbled again. This time, her weak response rolled into a moan as Adam's thick, callused fingers tickled up her side to cup her breast. Forgetting completely about conversation, she gave over to the panting mews his thumb elicited when it swirled over her tit, only to reappear in a harder twirl that made her arch into his touch.

"Is there any other place you'd like to have me in?"

Rachel's lust-fogged brain tripped over something in his tone that she couldn't place in that moment. The spontaneous worry came and fled, chased away by the circular delight of his rotating thumb. Caught in the rhythm of his touch, lost in the pleasure, her whole body started to follow his motion. Swaying in soft, needful swirls, her hips lifted and her legs slipped farther apart as her cunt began to clench in the same yearning tempo.

"I'm thinking of a place right now." Barely audible, the words came out in sharp, jagged spurts.

"It wouldn't be here, would it?"

Killian's dark growl barely penetrated the cloud of want captivating her before he emphasized his question with a sharp, hard thrust that filled her aching pussy. The deliciously thick, hard, plastic cock stretching its full length through her started to vibrate a bare second later, ringing out a beat much faster than her spasming muscles.

The clash spiked a bolt of pure, molten rapture through her as her breath raced to catch up. Turning her pants to wheezes, the delightfully wicked sensation had her eyes rounding as she clutched Adam's shoulders, needing his strength to keep everything feeling so good. He held her firm, both to her body and her breast.

Never stopping the slow, tormenting caress, he gazed down at her with a look that made her shiver with desire. They'd only begun to play, and Rachel did so love being their toy. Adam proved why with his next calm question.

"Remember what is was like to be eaten out while being fucked?"

"Oh, my." This would go down at the best birthday gift ever because she remembered that delight in detail. "Yes."

Feeling Killian force her legs wide to fit his massive shoulders between them, Rachel offered no resistance. Instead, she welcomed the warm breeze of his breath against the swollen folds of her pussy, eager for the velvety feel of his tongue against her clit.

She'd have smothered him in her desperation, but Killian kept a firm grip on her hips. With his fingers digging into her soft sides, he held her barely out of reach of the heavenly mouth she could almost feel brushing against her heated flesh.

"You want me to suck these pretty little tits while Killian loves on you?"

"Uh-huh."

Rachel would have agreed to anything right then. She wasn't even sure what she did actually agree to. Whatever, it required more conversation and too much of the wrong kind of action, like losing Adam's touch on her breast.

"Well, then, you're going to have to hold yourself up."

That smooth comment didn't jar anything, but him shrugging her hands off did. Startled, Rachel caught herself before she fell over, or at least half of her. Killian kept her ass up, and she had to brace her palms against the table to keep the rest of her in position. Her arms strained under the sudden weight, going wobbly for a moment.

The realization that the new position gave her a little leverage to fight Killian's hold put some strength back into her muscles. Not that all the wiggling did any good. The only thing her efforts accomplished was to get Adam's thumb lifting her chin up to meet his steely gaze.

"None of that, or we'll put a stop to this right now."

"No." They couldn't do that, but Rachel knew they were capable of it.

"Then behave."

"I'll be good," Rachel promised, though she meant only for the moment.

"Promise?"

"Promise."

"Okay, then." Adam released her to pull out a chair and take a seat. He scooted up close to the table's edge, right at eye level with her breasts. "Oh, and Rachel? There is no safety word tonight."

Killian didn't give her time to understand that warning before he wrenched her cunt right down into his open-mouthed kiss. Before the first high decibel of her shriek broke the air, Adam dove in to ravage the bountiful feast of her breasts. They worked together against her as Adam's hand fisted over her neglected breast and offered it up to the spontaneous swoop of his mouth.

Sharp teeth nipped before his tongue pressed down to lap at her poor abused nipple in the same fast paced twirls Killian's devilish tongue used to torment her throbbing clit. As if the splendor of being loved in perfect unison weren't enough to shatter the last visages of her control, Killian redefined the word rapture for her and reached up to latch onto the vibrating cock still making her melt from the inside out.

With no sense of mercy, he drug the long length backward, making her muscles clench in sudden despair only to rejoice in a tidal wave of splendor as he began fucking her hard and fast with the thick toy. With hands and mouth, Adam and Killian drove her relentlessly to a climax of such epic proportions she strained with every muscle quivering to reach release.

It was right there…almost…*Damnit to hell!*

* * * *

Adam knew the second Rachel began to peak. She gave herself away. Each and every time, right before she came, Rachel bit her lower lip. The tell gave her away, and when those pearly whites sank into the plump curl of her pouty mouth, Adam did what he had to.

"Okay, that's enough of that."

Barely spacing a second between that declaration and action, Adam scooped Rachel right up and dumped her over his shoulder. Killian didn't hold on but let her slide from his grasp, keeping the toy clutched in his fist.

Without a word, he rolled back off the table and onto his feet, ready to follow the couple as Adam carried Rachel off to the bedroom. Killian's acquiescence didn't strike Adam as odd, but Rachel's did. She didn't offer him any resistance…for about thirty seconds.

"You stub-cocked bastard!"

The words jarred him slightly, mostly because Rachel didn't tend to get mean about things. "Watch yourself, darlin'. Best you remember your place before I decide to pack that ass with another dildo and then spank it."

"Screw that," Killian retorted right on Adam's heels as he rounded the corner to Rachel's room. "I say we pack that ass and give that pussy a good disciplining."

Adam could get behind that. "Sounds good to me."

"Well, it doesn't to me," Rachel snapped. "Now put me down!"

"Okay."

Adam shrugged, letting Rachel topple right off his shoulder and down onto the waiting mattress. With no grace at all, she flopped around on the sheet, trying to right herself until she kneeled in front of him. Flushed with more than arousal, she appeared to not realize that her position showed off the pink folds of her pussy as they glistened in the light or that her beautiful breast swayed in tempting delight with each heaving breath she took.

If she had, she might have chosen her words with a little more caution.

"Red light?"

"What?" Killian responded in obvious confusion.

Killian might be thrown, but Adam knew what she meant. The implication had the anger stirring in him again. How could she possibly think he'd let her go now?

"Or is it yellow?" Rachel glared at Adam as if he were supposed to answer. He only had one response, and he didn't think she'd like it. All he had to do was manage to get the words through his tightly clenched jaw.

"There isn't any color."

"There sure the hell is."

That sharp retort cost Adam more than a little of his patience. Stepping up to grip her chin and hold her gaze steady, Adam made sure she understood every word he had to say by speaking very slowly. "There is only a safety word when it's a game, when it's just screwing around. When it's a man having to tend to his woman's misdeeds, then he has to do what he has to do."

Rachel flinched back, finally appearing to realize her predicament. Casting a nervous glance at Killian, who had flanked the other side of the bed to ensure she couldn't escape, she offered him a tentative smile that she turned back on Adam. "I guess you're still upset about that boyfriend comment, huh?"

The very idea that she thought she could backpedal now made Adam chuckle. "Women and their labels. Huh, Killian?"

On cue, his partner matched Adam's laugh. They had always had that perfect synchronicity to know where the other was headed and how to help get him there. "Yeah, they're an odd sex because me, personally, I'd be worried about the rope."

Rachel had bristled at their humor, defiantly switching her narrowed gaze between the both of them. At Killian's reference to the rope, though, her eyes snapped over the bed until they landed on the corded silk strung across her headboard. Adam had even fashioned mini-nooses for her wrists. They could slide up or down and even be twisted to turn her over and put her into any position they liked with no chance of escape.

Adam knew the moment Rachel realized all those facts. It was hard to miss when her jaw actually went slack. She spun around, looking both outraged and very flushed. The rosy blush from her previous bout of passion had started to fade, but now it flamed back to life, spreading from her cheeks down to her neck to consume the luscious tits beginning to sway under her labored breath.

It was like waving a red flag at a bull because Adam couldn't take his eyes off her breasts, and he certainly felt ready to pounce. The luring temptation of her puckered nipples reminded him of all the fun they had planned. He'd gotten tired of waiting.

"This isn't fair," Rachel pouted. Backing steadily up the bed and strangely toward the very ropes Adam thought she'd want to run from, she continued to try and argue with fate. "I didn't do anything wrong."

"I guess that's all a matter of what people call perception." Killian paused before shooting Adam a curious look. "Or is it subjective?"

"They both work." Adam shrugged, giving Killian his full attention and all but dismissing Rachel. They did it to toy with her, make her think that maybe things wouldn't get too rough or that Adam wasn't really half as pissed as he was. "Of course, you could have just said something like, 'Your opinion really doesn't matter because I'm the man and I decide when you need discipline.'"

"Well, yeah." Killian nodded before shooting Adam a smirk. "But I think that would just piss the little honey off."

"Got that right, butthead." Rachel emphasized her snapped retort with a pillow to the face. Only instead of going just for the butthead, she popped Adam and then dove around him, clearly trying to make it to the bathroom before he could recover his sight.

It took the pillow less than a second to slide off and plop onto the bed. Adam only needed two more to swoop her off her feet before she made it even three whole steps. Rachel didn't take to being trapped in his arms easily but put a full on show of squealing and wiggling as she fought for freedom.

Adam figured it was a waste that all her tempting curves caressed nothing but the air as she threw her tantrum. Rectifying that gave her one second to think she could run, but by the next he had her plastered back against his length. This time, he got to enjoy the sweet delight of her grinding into him.

Spanning a hand up her back, he flattened her breasts against his chest, letting her work her own nipples into hard, puckered points. His other hand slipped down to palm her scrumptious ass. Perhaps he went too far, though, when he split her damn thighs wide over his leg and offered her a helpful suggestion.

"Go on and rub yourself against that, darlin'. We'll both enjoy it." Some part of him knew she'd go still, but another part surely hated him for his loose tongue.

"You're a pig."

Adam snorted at that and had to lean back to let her see his smirk. "I ain't the one who gets to have a dozen orgasms a night. So if I'm the pig, then, honey, you're the hog."

That insult had her jaw going slack with only a squeak escaping. Speechless was not something Rachel was often, so he figured he should go ahead and press his advantage before she wasted the whole night resisting.

Despite their earlier banter, neither Killian nor Adam would take things further until she gave them some small sign of acceptance. While they liked to hold a woman captive, neither would ever force one.

"So are you ready to settle down and behave, because all this delay only adds time to the clock." He let that last bit tease her because Adam knew Rachel expected more spanking or more punishment. As he expected, her curiosity couldn't be held back for more than a few seconds.

"The clock? What clock?"

"There's only one way to find out that answer."

She didn't trust him, and Adam doubted the sight of Killian offered her any more assurance as she switched her gaze over his shoulder. Back to him, her eyes returned to consider Adam with a wariness that didn't mask the growing scent of feminine arousal perfuming the air. His little wench was having naughty thoughts, probably trying to imagine what they planned.

"I'm not agreeing that you are doing this for any of the right reasons." Rachel broke but didn't go down gracefully. "And I'm certainly not agreeing that either one of you is man enough to be the boss of me. Not even combined, boys."

Every single insulted fiber of his body tightened with wicked thoughts of retribution for that challenge. Any part of him that had felt a twinge of empathy for what they planned to put her through hardened. Adam let her see it as he lowered his head to growl right in her face.

"Let's get the wench tied up then see how mighty her words are."

Chapter 19

Rachel didn't put up a fuss as Adam dropped her back on the bed. Her ass didn't sink a whole inch into the soft mattress before the men started lassoing her wrists to the headboard. Other than rolling her eyes and giving them a dramatic sigh, Rachel didn't bother to object.

What little resistance she offered was mostly for show. When it came to ropes and whips, they could do as they pleased. Rachel trusted them that much. More importantly, she enjoyed their domination and had honestly missed the heat that had infused every second of that first night.

It was back now. She could only wish that it hadn't taken jealousy and rejection to light those flames. Wasting time on wishing wouldn't change reality. Right then her life was way too delightful to bother escaping. Tomorrow would be soon enough to make sure they understood that they might command her in the bedroom, but nobody would tell her how to live her life.

Later, Rachel promised herself as she settled back into the pillows. The ropes didn't cut into her wrists as long as she didn't tug on them. With no interest in fighting the ropes, she could take the moment to study them. The construction amazed her. They had everything set so perfectly, not only for their comfort but hers.

Even though her hands were pinned in place, the long stalk of silk stretched down so that her wrist rested on the pillow. The position kept blood flowing to her fingers and actually allowed her to enjoy her captivity. It kind of made her wonder who had taught them all these tricks.

"Do they teach some kind of 'how to tie a woman up with rope class' out at that perverts' club of yours?" Rachel glanced down to where they secured her ankles to the foot board. "Or is it some kind of dirty cop training?"

That earned her an annoyed glance from Killian, who shot his response to her taunting at Adam. "You know, I'm thinking we should amend the plan."

"Oh, yeah. The plan." Rachel rolled her eyes before giving them the biggest insult she could think of by closing them. "Aren't we supposed to be starting some kind of clock, or is the plan to accomplish nothing tonight?"

"Hey, Rachel?"

About to respond to Killian's question coming from the right, she was totally unprepared for the slap Adam delivered from her left. His broad palm lit up her pussy, sending vibrations of wicked delight cascading through her cunt and right up her spine. The words peaking over her lips contorted into a moan as her whole body lifted with joy.

About damn time. That's what she wanted to say, but even Rachel knew better. Besides, her mouth was too busy panting through the mini-explosions that followed along with the series of spanks that twisted her into a thing of wild need. They came from either direction, landing harder, faster until her breath broke into a series of pleading mews.

It felt so good. All she needed was one more expertly placed blow to snap the reins of the inferno burning through her cunt. It would consume her, release her into a world of such beauty that it figured that's when the bastards would stop. Leaving her stretched taut in her binds, Adam and Killian's touches faded into nothing more than a throbbing memory of pleasure.

She couldn't live without it, not now, but she had no choice. That message came through clearly when her gaze lifted to dance across Adam's tense features. Even with tears of frustration clouding her eyes, Rachel could read the seriousness in his.

"You like that darlin'?"

"Uh-huh." She couldn't lie. There would be no point, not when her body swayed with the need pooling so thick in her womb it spilled from her body in wave after wave of heated cream.

"You want more?"

He was teasing her, and Rachel knew it. That didn't stop the desire from blossoming into hope as she tried to sound properly submissive. "Would you, please?"

"Would you care to explain what you've been doing with the sheriff?"

That eroded some of her enjoyment. Annoyance bristled through her, dampening her arousal and bringing a scowl to her face. "You can punish me for whatever you want, Adam, but not for that."

He didn't look convinced and accepted her answer with way too much ease. "Okay, then. Killian? You want to…"

Adam's question faded out, but Rachel didn't need to hear the rest. At his words, her head had snapped to the other man shadowing her bed. Killian had reappeared, and he'd brought his favorite toy. Rachel watched the vibrator fisted in Killian's hand warily, under no misconception that he'd actually use the toy to end her anguish.

The only thing he'd do with that is ratchet up her need, probably to the point where she'd answer any of Adam's questions without hesitation. In that shining second of revelation, Rachel could see what they really planned. They wanted answers, and they meant to use everything in their power to get them.

She was doomed because there were secrets that they could learn far more frightening than what she was up to with Alex and Kitty. The kind of power that would give them had her breath halting as she watched Killian lower the thick, rounded head of cock down to the blushing mound of her pussy.

The fear and anticipation only served to heighten the erotic thrill of watching her own body being penetrated. Rachel moaned, unable to stop the glorious clench of her muscles as her cunt sucked the cock in with one long pull. Stretched over its deliciously long length, her cunt broke into a frenzy of panicking spasms when the toy slipped back.

"*Nooo...*ohhhh."

Rachel's denial turned into a groan of pure pleasure as Killian fucked the toy back into her. He kept slow and steady at first, keeping her panting out little moans as her hips lifted up in beat to his loving. The steady rhythm had her eyes closing as she gave herself over to his mastery. Killian didn't disappoint, picking up the speed as he pumped the cock harder into her.

"Yeah, that's it." Breaking into a smile that yawned wide over another series of mews, Rachel humped back against the hand beating the wild drums of lust to a fever pitch inside her pussy. It wept and raced to keep up as molten rapture began to vibrate through every cell.

"Oh, yeah. Don't stop...*son of a bitch!*" Rachel roared out the obscenity at the loss of the release she could feel only beginning to crest through her. The bedazzling sensation collapsed, as empty as her cunt, leaving her completely enraged. "If you don't—"

The threat whipped into a squeal as the bulbous head of the vibrator returned. The slick, cool head kissed her ass a second before it filled her rear. The sudden, deep penetration shot her hips as high up as her binds would allow, forcing her butt cheeks tight and clenching around the toy. Caught in the throes of a tidal wave of heated pleasure, Rachel gulped soothing, cooling air in with ragged pants.

Her ass on fire, her cunt painfully empty, she'd never felt such need. It left her clinging to the last shred of her sanity. Then Killian flicked on the damn vibrator and ripped away any semblance of domestication she had. Screaming, writhing, Rachel fought for her release with all her strength but only ended up twisting herself into a state of need so painful that tears started to seep from her eyes.

"Please, Killian." Begging was all she had left. Rachel felt no shame in the act, only the unrelenting desperation. "Please, I can't take it."

That declaration ended on a scream as her pussy exploded under another blast from his palm. The hard edge of his hand landed over her clit, trapping it and the heat of his blow beneath as he rubbed down on the tender nub and made her cry out all the louder.

"Mouthy wench." Killian growled, fucking two fingers up into her cunt as he continued to torment her swollen clit. "You know better than that. You know how to address me when you beg."

She did, if she could only remember. "Please...please..."

"Sir," Killian supplied in obvious annoyance. He made her pay for the reminder, pressing his fingers down over the thin stretch of skin separating them from the toy vibrating out liquid rapture through her ass. He rubbed, and she forgot about everything but the pleasure. "Say it, wench."

"W–what?...No! *Damnit!*"

Rachel went wild when he denied her, unable to believe he could be so difficult as to leave her not only empty but to turn off the wonderful toy. It would have been enough. Eventually, it would have worked, but thrashing within her binds certainly didn't. All the jarring motion did was to tease her with a reminder of how good that cock could feel.

There would be no getting back to that wondrous sensation without Killian and Adam's help. That thought helped her settle down, even if it only heightened the tension in her already corded muscles. Killian and Adam could do a good impersonation of merciless. Cussing at them would only make them more likely to show her that side.

"Now what do you call me?"

It would help if Killian didn't sound so damn tolerant. Rachel gritted her teeth and managed a correct answer, even if it came out somewhat sharp. "Sir."

"I'm still detecting some attitude. Aren't you, Adam?"

That question snapped her eyes open. She'd lost track of him some time ago and now felt desperate to catch up. These two worked too well together to ever forget about the one who went quiet. That was normally the man who should be feared in the moment. Only this time, she didn't find Adam waiting with a whip or some other device to drive her insane.

Instead, he slouched against the bedpost, looking relaxed as he watched the show Killian and she had just put on. Still as he might be and as easy as his smile might have come, Adam couldn't disguise the predatory intent in his gaze or the enormous bulge deforming his jeans. He could tease all he wanted, but there would only be one conclusion to this game. That gave Rachel a measure of confidence, even as Adam's response sent a new thread of irritation through her.

"I don't know. You ready to start talking about Alex, darlin'?"

Adam knew how to ruin her good mood. Rachel found herself snarling at him for being so rude. "No, and if you think that you can use sex against me—"

Rachel gulped down the rest of that threat along with a desperately needed gasp of air as she found herself suddenly stretched over a second cock. She'd been watching the wrong man again. Killian had managed to slip in on her blind side with a dildo that he used to maximum effect. Being filled from both sides left no room for her to even breathe without feeling the cascading rush of pleasure flooding up from her pelvis.

"What was that?"

The humor in Adam's question made her rash with her response. "I was just about to tell you to go fuck your—"

"Watch it now, wench." Killian's warning came with another smack to her pussy that she just didn't have the endurance to bear. The motion jarred the two toys stretching her tight, making every muscle in her channels contract with joy.

She whimpered under the effect, wishing that she'd chosen her words with more care. Antagonizing them was not wise, especially when Killian took his role of tormentor too seriously. Why else would his fingers linger to twirl her clit? Rachel didn't need the added antagonism when her whole cunt already throbbed around the long length of the toy filling her.

"Now, what were you about to say about fucking?"

Rachel didn't remember and this time kept her mouth wisely closed.

"That's what I thought." Killian rewarded her with a bare wiggle of the dildo, chuckling as her body followed the motion in a silent, desperate plea for more.

"She's still not answering my questions right."

"Right? As in what you want to hear?" Rachel tried to pin Adam with a hard look through the mist clouding her vision. It probably failed as much as her voice going all squeaky and breathless. "Why don't you just tell me the answers, Adam? Then we can stop playing this game."

"Oh, honey." Adam shook his head. "I haven't even started playing with you, but I'm about to."

The implication couldn't be clearer. Talk or play, those were her only two options. Rachel might not have the stamina to see the game to the end, but she wouldn't go out by forfeiting. If they wanted her secret, they'd have to fight for it. With that decision cemented in her mind, she lifted her chin at him.

"Do your worst."

It was a bold thing for a woman tied up naked and already packed full of cock to say. Rachel risked it with her head held as high as her position would allow. Her confidence only got a boost when Killian's calloused fingers reappeared to ruffle her clit. If this was all they had planned, she could handle it.

"Okay, then," Adam sighed, though she doubted he was half as disappointed as he appeared. Apparently, he did plan to time her.

Stepping back to lift up the big, white kitchen timer he'd laid out on her dresser, Adam started turning the dial, only to pause and shoot Killian a look. "What do you think? Fifteen?"

"Don't be insulting our woman," Killian snapped back. His fingers still circled her tender nub, sending sparkles of delight through her even as he discussed her coming demise. "Rachel thinks she's such a hard case, give her thirty. Then she'll tell you whatever you want to hear. Isn't that right, wench?"

Smiling over not only his cockiness but the pure delight twisting through her, Rachel couldn't see any downside to her current situation. His fingers, those toys, she could levitate here forever, caught in the pleasant haze of simmering arousal.

"Why not just add the two together and make it forty-five?"

That rejoinder earned her a slight bounce to the dildo filling out her pussy. Killian settled a finger over its end and gave her a few shallow, teasing pumps. It was just enough to make her mew and arch upward. That small sign of rising lust earned her an unwelcome opportunity at a reprieve.

"You sure about that, wench?" Killian sounded doubtful, but that only made Rachel more certain of her answer.

"Oh, yeah." She got the word out and managed not to drool.

"All right, then forty-five it is."

Chapter 20

Rachel had a dreamy smile curling at her lips. It matched the darkening lust turning her eyes into liquid pools of desire, which complimented the beautiful flush pinking her skin from the tips of her toes to the fine, feathered edge of her hairline. Spread out and tied up for their viewing delight, Killian relished in the sight of his woman in need.

Right now, it was a soft, gentle need that kept her hips swaying ever so slightly as she teased herself on the toys he'd fed her. Her swollen folds glistened with the same cream seeping down her thighs and moistening the sheets. Stretched wide around the black base of the dildo, he could see perfectly how the thick cock forced her little cunt wide and left the swollen nub of her clit waving up at him.

Now there was a vision he never tired of. He loved watching her take him. Feeling her pussy clench down over his flesh, sucking on him until he couldn't think anymore, the only thing he liked more than watching Rachel get fucked was fucking her himself. Every time that little bud taunted him, crying out to be petted, licked, and sucked, and he couldn't do a damn thing about it when he was balls deep inside her.

Tonight, though, he could do whatever he wanted. A thrill that he'd missed for these past few weeks because the only thing hotter than a naked Rachel was a naked Rachel tied up and at his mercy. Her taunting defiance only served to arouse him all the more, ensuring that he didn't feel the least bit charitable toward her.

If he had, he wouldn't have smiled as her face fell. The rosy glow of desire keeping her features soft faded the second he released her little clit to step back. After about five blinks, she managed to narrow her gaze on him, but Killian waited until those swollen, pouty lips parted on whatever sharp thing she planned to say.

That's when he smiled and let her see the butterfly he had tucked between his teeth. Killian had never seen Rachel go as still or her eyes widen as round as they did in that second. Almost an instant later, her head started to shake and her fear to started to babble out.

"No, Killian. You can't."

He responded to the hoarse, jagged whisper with a simple dip of his head. Going to his knees, his lips closed in over her spread folds as he turned a deaf ear to her pleading. She said he couldn't, but he proved her wrong. It took expert precision and Adam's two extra hands to hold her down as he settled the toy over her naked clit.

The poor little bud got twisted all about while he worked. The small motions sent Rachel into a spasm of squealing pleas as her body fought their hold. Her wants and needs obviously demanded more. With her sweet taste on his lips, Killian was inclined to indulge the little woman.

Absolutely delicious. He couldn't get enough of her. Licking, swirling, sucking, he even nipped the little darling with his teeth, making her scream as her body bucked under the pleasure. With so much encouragement, he had to do it again, delighted that it was him she begged for more of. Then it wasn't.

"Oh, God…Adam, no. *I can't.*"

Killian didn't even have to lift his lips to glance up the lush landscape of Rachel's body and see Adam's hands closing over her breasts. Cupping them, he offered the puckered tips to his tongue for tasting. Growling over her pussy, Killian matched his own movement to the slow roll Adam used to torment her tit. The steady rhythm had Rachel gasping, arching until she finally mewed out encouragement, demanding more, faster, harder.

They gave it all to her. Adam's hand shifted to pin her other nipple beneath the hard rotation of his thumb even as Killian lifted his palm to bounce against the flat end of the dildo and pump the toy deep inside her. With the vibrator still humming in her ass, Rachel went crazy beneath the onslaught.

They drove her through it all, toward a release that made every muscle in her body tense. In that second, Killian pulled back. He knew the feel of a breaking orgasm and wasn't about to let her steal one, no matter how addictive her pussy was.

"That's enough of that." He said it mostly for Rachel but as a subtle reminder to Adam to ease back. She wasn't near ready to start talking honestly. That truth became apparent the minute they stopped when her curses started flowing. Rachel really did turn into a potty mouth when denied, but it only went to show how spoiled they'd let her become.

It hurt to admit that Adam might be right. The gentle hand technique had backfired, and the girl had run wild anyway. While he was pretty certain that made her too crazy for Alex to have tamed, Killian wouldn't be suffering the same fate. He wouldn't be losing out for being nice.

Tonight would be a harsh reminder to Rachel of who she was dealing with. When they'd finished with her, she'd know her place. It was beside them, loyal to them, sharing everything with them, and trusting them to take care of her. Killian would not be having any more arguments on that. Rachel belonged to them. It was about damn time she realized it.

"Stop the clock, Adam." Killian nodded to the dresser but kept his gaze locked on hers. "She isn't going to run out her time by throwing a tantrum."

"I say we go ahead and start," Adam retorted, picking up the remote instead of the clock. "Let the little darlin' pitch her fit through every climax missed. And," Adam shot Rachel a look, "just in case you become bored."

He didn't finish that thought but clicked on the TV. Instantly, the room filled with the guttural groans of a woman being pleasured as she begged for more. There could be no doubt of what she wanted with the camera on a close-up image of a pussy getting pounded by an oversized cock. Killian didn't need to glance at the screen to see the action but kept his smile locked on Rachel's face as it went slack with shock.

It delighted him when it went tense with pleasure as he clicked on the little butterfly. Now she wasn't just listening, she was joining in, moaning and begging. It took every bit of willpower Killian possessed to follow Adam out of the bedroom and leave her like that. Rachel didn't help with her crying and begging for them to come back.

They wouldn't be doing that for at least thirty minutes. Neither man trusted the other to be able to deny her for that long, which was why they vacated to the dining room. Not that they had much to talk about, but there would be no watching TV while Rachel continued to wail out from the bedroom. Instead, they took up a silent game of rummy.

Each man pulled the same score sheet out of his wallet, neither trusting the other to keep an honest score. This one game had been going on for over ten years and they'd managed to accumulate a score well over thirty thousand by then. Still, they didn't call a winner, not needing one between friends.

Between lovers, that was different. Killian wanted to make damn good and sure that Rachel wouldn't be able to offer up even the slightest defense. For that reason, he let the butterfly run for a good ten minutes before using the remote to give her a reprieve, but not a long one. Keeping an ear tuned to the lowering pitch of her sounds of passion, Killian didn't let them mellow out before he clicked the toy back on and sent her back into squealing and begging as loud as she could.

He told himself she would be good. She'd do whatever they said if only they'd come back to her. That really made it hard for Killian's ass to stay seated. For as much as Rachel needed to learn this lesson, he really didn't like leaving her alone. They'd never done that before to any woman. A good master endured just as his submissive did, but Rachel was different.

Killian knew if he saw her now he'd take her. He wouldn't be able to help himself. That's how weak she made him. Strangely enough, she also made him feel stronger, like he had to be strong to keep her safe. As sweet and innocent as Rachel was, she didn't understand men or the world they'd created around her. Instead, she lived in a Disney movie, and he very much wanted to keep that idyllic spirit alive.

Tonight, they pushed her beyond that reality. Killian only hoped that when she woke up in the morning cartoon birds still greeted her cheerily. Otherwise, he feared the Ken dolls would be getting kicked out for GI Joes. There was no way he'd let Alex anywhere near Rachel. Killian would go He-Man on the sheriff's ass before that happened.

Ring...

The shrill, penetrating chime of the telephone in the kitchen made him realize he'd lost track of time. Lost in his thoughts, he'd left the butterfly on for too long and wound Rachel's cries up to near ear piercing screams. As he clicked it off, Killian borrowed a second to shoot Adam a dirty look.

The bastard really had a chip on his shoulder tonight, otherwise he'd have reminded Killian to be a little easy on the darling. After all, it wasn't like she was used to this kind of thing. Adam, though, didn't even bother to look apologetic.

Since Rachel had declared that she didn't think they were her boyfriends, Adam's gaze had held on to that dark, dangerous look. Whether Rachel knew it or not, she'd actually managed to piss Adam off. That was a feat rarely accomplished.

Ring...

Killian didn't even have to get out of his seat to catch the phone before it let out another wail. All he had to do was tip his chair onto two legs and stretch back through the opening to the kitchen to snatch it off the wall. With the long cord, he could even sit back up and go back to beating Adam's ass at rummy.

"Hello?"

"Killian?" Duncan's voice on the other end of the line had Killian's attention shifting up. The other deputy had desk duty tonight and wouldn't be dumping that into Killian's lap no matter how sick he claimed to be.

"I ain't coming in." He couldn't be clearer than that.

"I wouldn't think so, given whatever you're up to with Rachel has her neighbors calling in concerns."

Killian grimaced at Duncan's words. That went down in the big "whoops" category. It could also land them in the doghouse if Rachel ever found out about this. Something he was sure motivated Duncan's next offer.

"So either gag her, or I'm sending Bryant over there to check things out."

Killian knew Duncan would, too. With his sense of humor, Bryant would only make the situation worse. They'd be the talk of the town for weeks to come. That was how long Rachel would stay pissed at them.

"One more call, Killian."

With that warning issued, the line went dead. Killian understood the threat. If Duncan received another concerned call, Bryant would be showing up on their doorstep. Not that he knew it, but Duncan gave Killian all the cover he needed to do what he wanted to most and go see Rachel. He covered up his eagerness with a grouchy grunt as he stretched back to settle the phone into the cradle.

"What?" Adam asked of Killian's expression.

"We're making too much noise. The neighbors are calling the station house."

Finally, Adam managed to look something other than intense. He actually relaxed enough to smirk. "Well, that ain't good."

"It's about to be worse. If Duncan gets another call, Bryant will be coming over for a visit."

Adam had to consider that to come to the obvious conclusion. "I guess, then, we're going to have to cut things a little short."

"Not by much. There's only about five minutes left on the clock. Besides, I think she's sounding more cooperative."

Killian offered that assurance with a nod to the hallway and the whimpering mews floating down it. All the cursing had stopped, all the begging had faded and there only remained the guttural moans of pure, wanton need. Like the songs of a siren, they lured Killian back to where his beautiful wench awaited him.

She'd made a mess of the bed with all her thrashing about. The sheets had popped free of the mattress and bunched in a chaotic swirl under her arched body. Bowed out from where her wrists and ankles remained anchored, Rachel's body glistened with sweat, and her pearly skin flushed a deep tomato red.

Only her hair served as a cool contrast to the desire drawing her tense. It pooled across the mattress and over the only remaining pillow. Stray dark strands clung to her cheeks, trailing along the rivulets of tears seeping from her wild eyes and curling around pouty lips broken apart by ragged pants. He'd never seen a woman look so gorgeous or be so easily affected by joy at the sight of him.

"Don't leave me." She about broke him in half with that soft, pathetic plea.

It made him ache to assure her he never would as he took her in his arms. That was the kind of weak behavior that had gotten them here, so Killian forced himself to hold back. Instead of sweeping her up, he settled calmly onto the edge of the bed.

The one thing he couldn't resist was touching her. He needed to feel the softness of her skin beneath his palm, to reassure himself in this most basic of ways that she really was his. Cupping her cheek, he rubbed away the tears until they no longer brimmed over her lashes.

It took a few minutes for her to calm down. They gave her that time because they needed honest, intelligible answers. If she didn't have them to give, then they really would have to gag her and start the clock over, no matter how much Killian hated that idea.

"You're not going to leave me again?" she asked in that little girl voice. Matched with big doe eyes, Rachel made sure he didn't have the balls left to deny her.

Killian held strong but couldn't mask the husky concern in his tone. "I don't want to, honey, but that's really all up to you. Are you ready to answer some questions?"

The softness in her features shifted but not toward hardness or defiance. It looked to Killian like sadness, but he couldn't fathom why. Then she spoke, and he understood completely. She didn't want to lose.

"You really don't give up. Either of you."

"Not when it's this important." Killian offered her pride that much salve. "Now, are you ready to tell us about the sheriff?"

He feared the answer might be no when her eyes closed and her head rolled back. Her body still trembled with her need, the air thick with the scent of her desire, but Rachel fought back admirably. Killian really hadn't expected her to even offer the least bit of hesitation. She didn't offer resistance but a sort of depressed acceptance.

"I already told you. Why don't you believe me?" Her eyes opened on that question, but they focused at the foot of the bed where Adam's shadow stretched across her sheets between her splayed legs. "Do you really think I would cheat on you?"

"It's the book."

Killian could have hit Adam for his blunt answer. They needed to tread lightly here. For as bad as she'd made it sound, their punishment had obviously not broken Rachel's will. The last thing he wanted to do was get a gag. That's where they were headed, given Adam had her cussing again.

"What is your damn obsession with the book?"

Her mouth went from thin to rounded in less than a second as Killian's ears detected the soft whirl of the butterfly clicking on. He shot an annoyed look over Rachel's lifting body at his partner for picking up the remote he'd left. Adam offered him a smug smile, a silent assurance he'd get his answers.

"Please...this isn't fair...I didn't do anything."

"I want to know about the book."

"Fine...fine," she babbled as her head stared to roll across the mattress, slowly nudging the last pillow toward the edge. "It was Kitty's idea."

That bought her a moment of reprieve as Adam considered that answer. "Kitty? As in your friend from Dothan? Why is it you haven't talked about her before?"

Maybe because this Kitty was bad news. Killian shared that silent conclusion and a look with Adam.

"She's just an old friend."

That evasion cost her as Adam clicked on the butterfly. Not wanting to have to get a gag but needing to stop those high pitched shrieks, Killian decided to use his kiss to consume every bit of noise she made. It sounded wise until he sank his tongue into her mouth and forgot about every bit of the plan.

Rachel was ravenous in her enthusiasm as she drove the kiss with her ferocity. Their tongues warred, dueling and loving, until her lips closed over his tongue and sucked so hard he feared his dick would have a permanent impression of his zipper along its length.

He pulled back before he lost it and spewed in his damn jeans like some overeager teenage boy with his first girl. The sight of her bruised and swollen lips tempted him too much, making another taste irresistible.

This time, he put her in her place and showed her what the definition of hunger really was. He was hungry. Starved, in fact, and he couldn't get enough, becoming only that much more desperate for her taste, her feel. The need overwhelmed his reason. Killian started to shift, eager to mount the woman so ready for his possession. He'd have done it, too, and humped her right there through his jeans if Adam hadn't smacked him on the back of the head.

"How the hell can she answer my questions with your tongue in her mouth?"

Killian's head lifted to stare down into the eyes of the best thing he'd ever known. "You make me weak."

The thought slipped out on a whisper that should only have echoed through Killian's mind. Horror hit him the moment it floated past his ears. Rachel didn't help the sudden panic beating through him as her lips curved into a smile. Not smug or victorious, the soft gesture was much more dangerous than either of those emotions. It was satisfaction because she knew she had him wrapped around her little finger now.

Chapter 21

Rachel's words confirmed his worst fear.

"Make love to me."

"Okay, enough of that." Adam spoke loud with clear annoyance. Fisting a hand into Killian's collar, Adam whipped him off the bed and sent him stumbling across the room. "You'll get your turn, lover boy, *after* the wench answers *my* questions."

Despite Adam's attitude, Killian was grateful for his interference. That had been a bad situation getting worse, so he was more than happy to give Adam the floor while he took a moment to recover. Recover and plan, because the only way to fix this disaster would be to get a confession of his own out of Rachel. That would put them back on an even field.

"Now, I want to know how this book on prostitution connects to your friend Kitty and the sheriff." Adam lorded over the edge of the bed, blocking Killian's view of Rachel but he could imagine her expression right then. It would be grumpy. "And don't be giving me that look or I will get the nipple clamps and a gag out and we'll reset the timer for another forty-five minutes. The choice is yours."

"That's not what I'd call a choice," Rachel retorted crossly.

"Okay, guess it's time for the clamps." Lobbing the remote at Killian, Adam turned to rifle through the bag of treats Killian had packed. It gave Rachel a moment to turn her molten gaze on him. She might be bound and at their mercy, but that didn't make the little woman any less dangerous as she gave him the puppy dog eyes.

"Don't even." Killian stopped her before she could get whatever pathetic plea out. "I'm immune to your wiles now."

That only got him the pouty lip, a small gesture that packed quite a punch with his unruly cock. It pulsed out demands that had Killian growling as he retaliated by clicking on the butterfly. That got rid of her practiced seduction and sent her bucking back into a fit of wild, wanton need. With his eyes tracking the tempting rotation of her hips, his gaze remained stuck on the dildo bouncing between her flushed, spread pussy lips.

Her begging pleas didn't help matters. They filled his head and warmed his heart with all the right kinds of warmth. She pleaded, telling him how much she wanted him, needed him, would do anything for him. It was about all a man could endure. Only his earlier slip and the need to prove a point kept him from jumping on her right then and there.

Even as he could claim a victory the joy was tempered by the need to undo his zipper. Never had he been so hard or endured such pain, but the stroke of his own fist in perfect beat with her humping motions helped.

"Stub-dick idiot," Adam muttered as he brushed past Killian.

Killian smirked in the face of Adam's censure and cast a pointed look down. "That ain't no stub."

"I guess the real question is whether or not it has any balls behind it."

Adam might be bitching at him, but his jeans were horribly deformed by his own erection and his gaze stayed stuck on Rachel.

"You make me weak? We had a plan, man."

"You had a plan," Killian corrected. "I have a very lonely dick, and right now, Rachel sure does look welcoming. Doesn't she?"

That pointed comment had Adam jerking forward, finally breaking his stare to shoot Killian a dirty look. "Are you going to turn that off, or you want to make this a challenge?"

Killian's thumb didn't twitch on the remote's switch but a smirk did at the edge of his lips. "I did mine with my mouth."

"And I held her down."

"I can get behind that." Hell, Killian wanted to get in it while he was there but that fun would have to wait. Maybe he shouldn't have sounded too eager because Adam didn't jump on his offer as he circled around to the far side of the bed.

Shooting him a hard look, Adam cast a doubtful glance down Killian's body. "I'm not sure I can trust you."

That insult prompted Killian's feet into action. He'd made a mistake earlier, but he wouldn't be making any more. "I'm just ready to gag the girl if need be."

Hazel eyes clouded by lust followed him as he sauntered closer. With every step, Rachel's words grew more encouraging, more provocative. She told him she needed his touch because nothing felt as good as his hands on her body and his mouth on hers and if he would only give her a kiss she would do whatever he asked.

As Rachel's stuttered pleas babbled out, Adam's features only grew harder. It clearly irritated him to be ignored, not that he really was. The moment Adam tucked the clamp between his lips and started to lower his head, Rachel's head lashed toward the other direction as her voice spiked with panic.

"*No*, Adam. Please don't. I'll tell…whatever you want." Rachel strained as far toward Killian's side and away from Adam as she could get as she began babbling. "It was all Kitty's idea. She saw a show on prostitution and thought it would make for a good story. She was going to befriend some prostitutes and tell me the stories to write up."

The clamp popped across her belly as Adam spit it out on his roar. "*What?*"

The same pure male rage that shot Adam back to his feet also had Killian whipping off the edge of the bed. He couldn't believe his own damn ears. Rachel had broken and there was no stopping the stupidity rolling off her tongue.

"She's going to get to know them all, and I'll write up stories about all the different types of prostitution from the crack whores to the professional call girls, but I didn't know how to research it, and then I saw the sheriff and I thought if I brought it up as a book—"

"No. No. *No.*" Killian couldn't stop the word echoing in his head from being spit out as he stared down at his sweet Rachel. "Are you insane? You are not researching prostitution or letting one of your idiot friends go undercover."

"I have never in my life heard something so damn *dumb!*" Just as flabbergasted as Killian, Adam caught his gaze with a look of sheer horror on his face. Killian could feel the same emotion clenching in his gut. They'd screwed everything up.

Killian could see it so clearly now. He'd worried over driving her wild with the wicked delights of pure domination, and all the while her rebellion had been growing right under his nose. Worse, they'd fueled her craziness with all the assistance they'd given her these past few weeks.

Obviously, her head had grown too big for her tiny body. Now she thought she was all grown up and ready to take on the dangers of investigating actual crime. The very idea of what might happen to her had him trembling with pure fear.

"You were trying to shine on the sheriff." Killian pinned Rachel with a look he hoped conveyed his anger enough to keep her from getting mouthy. He couldn't take that right then.

His glare must have worked because her lids dipped and her chin dropped as she tried to shrink deeper into the mattress. "I knew you'd be distressed if I told you about the idea, so when I saw Alex sitting with Konor I thought…"

"You thought you'd cut us out of the equation all together," Adam filled in for her when she remained silent. "That's even worse than if you had fucked the sheriff."

Adam's blunt statement had her eyes shooting up to lock on his with confusion. Whatever she didn't understand, Killian couldn't help her when she shifted her gaze in his direction. He could see her worry, though, and it soothed a part of the tension in him. Rachel hadn't meant to betray him. She just didn't understand.

That only became clear as she offered up her pathetic excuse. "I didn't want to fight about it."

"I don't care," Killian answered her pleading look without flinching. "You don't lie to avoid the fight, Rachel. You argue it through, work it out, and handle the issue. Otherwise, this relationship is doomed and not because we can't handle one but because you won't let us."

He must have been right. Otherwise, she wouldn't have dropped her head in guilt. Rachel might feel bad and might not be up for round three of the night's festivities, but she still didn't fold. "I'm writing my article, any article I want."

"No, you're not," Killian corrected her, speaking slowly and clearly to make sure she heard him.

"And you will remain tied to this bed until you agree," Adam tacked on, showing a united force to do whatever it took to bring this insanity to an end.

"That's not working things out," Rachel shot back with enough grump in her voice for Killian to threaten her with the remote.

He'd clicked off the butterfly when she started talking, not wanting her distracted from her confession. Now he used it as a reminder of the lesson already learned. It worked, sort of. Rachel did settle down, but her gaze remained mutinous, showing the spirit Killian didn't truly want to rob her of. He wanted her sassy and difficult, not raped or dead.

"You're going to have to trust us, Rachel. This idea your friend has is a bad one."

Adam snorted. "Bad? Try dangerous. You're not doing this story. Period."

They both paused, waiting for the rebuttal because neither of them expected her to fold easily. Rachel could be stubborn and headstrong, but Killian would be patient, and soon enough she'd see reason. Having an adventure wasn't worth dying for.

Not when they could fill her life up with all the excitement she'd ever need. Right then and there, Killian started to re-evaluate his stance on taking her to the club. It might be worth the risk if they could divert her time and energy into other interesting investigations.

"You're right."

Killian blinked at that simple statement, trying to figure out if he'd missed some part of the conversation. Maybe she was being clever in some way he didn't get. If so, she'd have to explain it to him. "What was that?"

"You're right," Rachel repeated, adding in a small, strangely apologetic smile. "It is too dangerous, and I shouldn't have involved the sheriff. I should have been honest with you."

That sounded too much like the Fantasy Rachel in his mind to be the real one. The illusion unnerved him, making him straighten up and cast a look at Adam to see if he'd heard the same thing Killian had. From Adam's doubting look, Killian went with a yes to that question.

"She's bullshitting us." Adam narrowed his gaze on her as he offered up his suggestion. "I say we punish her with the clamps."

"I'm not bullshitting you," Rachel snapped, showing none of the fear she'd had when Adam had almost delivered on that threat. "I'm just not willing to spend the whole night tied up to this bed arguing."

"She's bullshitting us." Killian nodded.

"Now, can I get the clamps?"

* * * *

Adam really did want to put the clamps on her. Most of his urgency came from not getting to play these past three weeks, but a good share came from the worry it would be several more before he got this opportunity again.

"I swear, Adam, if you put those clamps on me, I'll…"

"Yeah?" It took a lot to hold back his laughter and get that one word out. Adam couldn't even smile, or it would ruin the routine. Not that he'd felt the urge until she'd finally confessed. The whacked-out plan she and her friend had dreamed up wouldn't be happening. He wouldn't let it, but Adam didn't buy her easy acceptance of that fact for a moment.

Still, her harebrained scheme sounded better to his ears than hearing about how nice Alex was or what a good friend he'd become. The idiot didn't stand a chance with their Rachel because she didn't respect the sheriff in the slightest. Just the opposite, she'd tried to play him for a fool. Adam couldn't wait to explain that to Alex.

"Nah." Killian's grunt interrupted Adam's thoughts. He'd wandered while waiting for Rachel's response, which apparently wouldn't be coming. That figured about as much as Killian's suggestion. "I think this is the kind of argument you have to settle into."

Adam smirked, catching Killian's drift. The bastard was horny, and he'd grown tired of waiting. It was just sad and pathetic for Killian to act so eager, but it did make Adam's life easier. This way, he didn't have to admit to the urgency testing his own control.

The only reason he hadn't started to crack like Killian was that Adam enjoyed the rush. He loved to push himself to the point where his own civility shredded away and he took what he needed with the kind of savagery that made the women at the club line up for a turn in his bed. He sure bet Rachel would enjoy it.

"Fine, but next time, we're sticking with my plan."

Adam hadn't finished agreeing before Killian started ripping off his clothes. His shirt went left, his boots went the right, and he all but launched himself out of his jeans, leaving them to puddle on the floor as he tackled Rachel. It should have been tongue in mouth, cock in pussy, but Killian didn't even waste time pulling the toys free of their woman.

Instead, he started to hump her with hard, grinding motions. As wet and spread as she was, the position had to trap her clit, which explained why she went wild. Even as Killian consumed the moans pouring out of her lips, Adam could still hear the succulent sounds of passion as their bodies slid over one another. It made it that much harder to stand there and remain fully clothed.

Not that either one of them paid him any attention. Killian appeared to be flying completely solo, taking it upon himself to reach up and loosen the ropes at her wrist. Adam knew what he wanted—to be touched, to feel those soft hands gliding over his body with such gentleness that a man actually felt cherished.

"Yes! Oh, yes, just like this, sir. Make me come."

Rachel's hands weren't stroking tenderly over any part of Killian but clenching around his shoulders, her nails biting into skin as she levered herself against his strength to grind her pelvis frantically against his.

"Oh...please, don't stop," she cried out.

Not that Adam could see any resistance left in Killian. He really didn't have any control around Rachel. Now the fool ran the risk of pumping his seed all over her stomach. He should have let him suffer that embarrassment, but Adam had tired of being forgotten.

"Excuse me."

That loud intrusion got Killian's attention and, by that virtue, Rachel's as she cried out in anguish when Killian forced her to come to a still. Adam ignored her carrying on and focused all his displeasure on his partner.

"Is that how you planned on helping?"

Killian had the good grace to look a little sheepish. "Well, not exactly. Actually," Killian paused to reach down and pluck the dildo out of Rachel's pussy before continuing, "it started like this."

With that declaration, Killian surged into her, making Rachel's back arch as she gulped for air, much like a fish out of water. Obviously, from her mewing moans, she approved of Killian's plan, but Adam still had his doubts. At least the dumbass hadn't started fucking her and eroding all of their advantage.

"Is that it?"

"No," Killian shot back with an obnoxiously annoyed tone. "If you'll undo those ankle ties and find the remote I seem to have lost, we'll get this party started."

Making sure his friend knew he doubted this new strategy, Adam reluctantly did as Killian requested. The second he loosened the ropes holding her legs in place, they flexed up, caging Killian's hips and trying to force him into some kind of motion. Adam had to give him one for not budging.

Instead, Killian settled more of his weight down on her, forcing her to remain still, if not squished, beneath him. Maybe this could work. Adam considered the likelihood of that as he picked the butterfly's remote up off the floor. He didn't hand it over but studied it before shooting Killian a hopeful look.

"Do I get to play with this now?"

"No." Killian smirked at that question. With a quick roll, he presented Adam with the lush, flushed bounty of Rachel's ass. "You get to play with this."

That certainly beat the remote he tossed to Killian. He managed to catch the little device while still holding Rachel as still on top of him as he had when she'd been below him. Closing his fist around it, he offered a helpful suggestion to Adam.

"Why don't you get the whips out?"

Chapter 22

"What?" Rachel's head snapped up as she tried to turn it far enough to see Adam. He stayed just out of her range as she began begging him not to do that.

"Don't work yourself up into another tantrum, wench." Adam followed that warning with a slap to her rear.

He made sure his palm landed squarely on the butt of the vibrator. It might have taken the impact of the blow, but he knew it also made the toy pump a little deeper into her, a little harder against Killian's thick dick. From all her squirming and moaning, Adam knew she liked it, too, and so he treated her to a few more.

On the last pass, he latched on to the toy and pulled it free, making her ass lift up in a silent expectation of the vibrator's return. Adam had something else to give her, but first he wanted to hear her beg.

"What are you waving that ass all around for, girl?" Loudly popping the button on his jeans free, Adam drawled out that question in his deepest Southern accent. He had hoped it would give her more than a little thrill, and so the giggle she tried to smother against Killian's shoulder pleased Adam. Her answer didn't because she didn't give him one.

The only response Rachel offered was a provocative lifting of her rear in a silent invitation. Killian had to match the movement of her hips to keep her from getting any distance to pump herself along his dick. It made him grumble.

"The man asked you a question, wench." Killian's own accent had thickened up, growing husky with desire. Perhaps that's why after all they'd done to her tonight, Rachel found the courage to lift her head and shoot Adam a smug smile.

"I would have thought a man with so much experience wouldn't need instructions on what to do."

Adam matched her cocky grin with one of his own as he lowered his zipper. Thicker than he'd ever been, Adam swore his dick had grown an extra inch just for her. Springing out of his jeans like an unleashed dog lunging forward certainly made her eyes widen, but they stayed large and fixated on his cock.

Because she seemed so captivated, Adam took his time stepping the rest of the way out of his jeans before shrugging off his shirt. He made sure she got a full look and emphasized his girth by stroking a fist over his dick, getting it slick and ready with the lotion.

When she licked her lips, Adam had to give himself a few extra pumps until the head swelled, bright red and angry looking. Rachel certainly wasn't laughing anymore.

"Trust me, honey," Adam assured her as he stepped up to the edge of the bed. Bringing one knee down on the mattress, he growled over the way she bit her lip and looked up at him with such want. "I know what to do with a woman like you."

Adam didn't spare any more time for teasing as he settled himself into position. As much as it might have hurt to strain her neck, Rachel kept her gaze locked on his. It was the sexiest damn thing to know she was watching him, even as he forged into her tightly clenched back channel.

The ring of muscles at her entrance squeezed down hard on the tender head of his cock, threatening to pop it before releasing him into the sultry heat of tight ass. Adam panted through the exertion, matching Rachel's ragged breaths as they shared this moment. A part of him wanted to levitate there, barely surrounded by the heaven of her body and caught in the revelation of intimacy shining in her eyes.

He'd fucked her ass many times before but never like this, never getting to watch the pleasure as his slow progression melted her gaze to a molten a molten pools of desire until she collapsed beneath him. Flattening out over Killian's chest, Rachel's lids dipped as her pants turned into tiny shrill coos that babbled with bits of encouragement.

Adam had to agree. It never had felt this good. Settling his full length into her, he couldn't resist giving her a little pump and watching as she tensed before breaking into shudders. The small motion made her muscles pulse, tightening over him for a second, long enough to tempt him into another hip roll.

"Damn, Adam, that does feel good."

Killian's grunted interruption into Adam's sensual odyssey came as an unwelcome intrusion. Part of him wished they could forget the game so he could go chasing after the little bubbles of rapture boiling out of his balls.

Not yet.

They had other matters to attend to first. At least he could look forward to winding up those sensations so tight that when they did burst, the explosion would be beyond magnificent. Then Rachel would know exactly what it was like to be ravaged and would look on them with newfound respect.

"Yeah?" Adam responded when he managed to find a suitable tone. "How does this feel?"

* * * *

It felt absolutely wonderful, but Rachel didn't get a chance to drool out that answer over Killian's shoulders, not with Adam jerking her all the way up to her knees. The motion forced her ass down hard into his lap, impaling Adam's cock another half inch into her while her cunt clung to Killian's, trying to take his dick with her.

All the tugging in the world couldn't stop him from slipping back an inch, and she groaned, attempting to seesaw between them and enjoy the best ride any woman could take. Adam held firm, keeping her hips tucked into his and freeing Killian's hands to do some damage. He had her whole body on display, and the idea of what he could do with those nimble fingers made her throb with anticipation.

There was no way he'd let Adam win this sudden competition. That could only be to her delight. Knowing it was coming didn't make her any better prepared to take the sudden vibrations tickling over her clit. That damn butterfly had become her single greatest torment. For as good as it felt, it left her only in a greater state of need, almost desperate to be licked.

This time was worse. As the butterfly feathered sparkly waves of pleasure over her tender bud, the sensations echoed out until her muscles contracted and pulsed in beat with the little toy. With their deliciously thick erections filling her out, Rachel couldn't stop the urge to shift and sway, to fuck herself along the heated lengths of cock holding too still inside her.

Even when she arched her back and put all her muscles into pulling free of Adam, she couldn't break his hold enough to fulfill her desires. The strain of trying only left her weaker, collapsing into his hold as she gave over to the shudders coursing through her. Her head fell back onto his shoulder, and she tried to whimper out a plea.

They'd taken things far enough, and now she needed them to finish it.

"I do think the wench likes that, but she's going to love this."

Adam's voice rumbled through his chest and vibrated across her back. All thick and sexy, the sound gave her hope that his control had finally broken. Now would come the ravaging. It would be like the first time, beyond orgasmic.

It all started with the curl of callused fingertips closing in over her breast. With her head back and eyes closed, she smiled at Killian, enjoying how much he liked to pet and stroke her when he was on the bottom. Her sigh of delight at the gentle touch stuttered off at the cold scrape of metal.

Whipping open, her eyes widened on the sight of Killian smiling up at her, hands behind his head. Somewhere along the line, the pleasure had so absorbed her attention she hadn't realized that Adam's arms had shifted. He'd freed her in one sense, but Rachel could feel the clamp he broke open over her tit.

"*No, wait—*"

There was no more time left to avoid her future. With a scream of raging delight, she faced the pleasure racing through her and then collapsed forward. She caught herself on arms that wobbled as her breast pulsed out tidal waves of heat that only inflamed the inferno burning in her pelvis. It demanded action, movement to ride out the tension coiled tight.

That need broke her as the second clamp snapped over her other tit. The instant streak of pain bucked her back hard onto Adam's cock. That pleasure only drove her forward onto Killian's. She couldn't stop then, no matter what the consequences.

It all felt too good. They felt too good, thick and hard and so filling she had to be fucked. Right then and there, even if she had to do it herself. With her nipples pulsing in perfect rhythm to the sway of her hips and the sweet caresses along her clit egging her on, Rachel found her tempo.

Only it needed to go faster, harder, until there was no rhythm anymore. All that remained was mindless thrusting and grunting as she raced toward the climax. The horizon shined down with glorious rapture as she felt every muscle in her body go stiff in anticipation of her oncoming release.

She hadn't been this close to the edge since they'd been in the dining room, so she should have known that's when her men would put a stop to her climax. The second four hands pinned her down flush along Killian's hard, sweaty length, Rachel went crazy.

They couldn't do this to her. It wasn't right. She wouldn't stand for it. Those convictions might have given her the spurt of strength she needed to wiggle her way back toward her release, but they couldn't overpower Adam's weight flattening her into position.

"Not yet," Adam ground out, his voice so ragged he sounded almost mad.

"Why?" Rachel didn't understand. They'd played the game, and now it was time to finish it. "What? What is it you want? Please, whatever it is, just tell me."

She'd have done anything, said anything to put a stop to her torment. All they had to do was direct her.

"We don't want you to get hurt." It was a sweet thing for Adam to say, but given he was the reason she ached right then, Rachel didn't believe him.

"Then move, please." They always made her beg. It had never bothered her before, but tonight tears gathered in her eyes as frustration overwhelmed her. "I can't take this anymore."

"I know, darlin'," Adam soothed her, rubbing his broad palms up her arms in a tender gesture that only made her over-sensitized body jolt with nearly painful sparkles of pleasure. "And I want to make it all better, but you have to promise me that you're not going to be doing anything dangerous."

"I never do." She never did. Until they'd come along, the most exciting thing she had going on was her new knitting pattern.

"And you're never going to," Killian finished for her. "Right?"

"No. Never." The last word moaned out of her as Adam rewarded her answer with the slightest of shifts in his hips. Wound as tight as she was, the small motion rolled through her like a tidal wave, making her ass clench and pulse as it tried to milk every last bit of pleasure from the ripples.

"And we're going to help you decide when something is too dangerous." Adam pressed that point home on the end of his cock pumping barely an inch into her clenched cunt.

"Oh, yes," Rachel drooled out over Killian's shoulder as her own hips matched Adam's motion, stroking herself along both cocks. Her pleasure turned to pain as Adam once again denied her, pressing enough weight down onto her lower back to bring her teasing to a still.

"Yes, what?" Adam's sharp question prompted an instant response.

"You decide."

"Good." He shifted behind her, giving her even more room to stretch and sway between them. It felt so good to be surrounded by their heat and hardness. The clamps caught on Killian's chest, tugging on her nipples until she mewed and rubbed herself harder against him.

That only had her hips bucking harder in silent demand for more space. With more room, Killian could turn off his toy and begin stroking her with his own fingers. He had such a wonderful touch, so much better than the weak teasing of the butterfly. As fast as it vibrated, it couldn't keep up with the pounding desire pumping through her. She needed more.

"So you're going to be running all your story ideas past us from now on?"

"Yes." Rachel knew how to answer Killian's question even if her mind couldn't comprehend the words. The desperation to finally be free of this game understood enough. It was rewarded for its insight when Adam shifted even further back.

She could do more than sway now. She could actually pump her hips enough to feel the scrumptious contrast of two cocks beginning to fuck her in opposite rhythms. Push and pull all in one small stroke, having both of them filling her assured Rachel that every motion would be a delight.

"You're not going to be asking *any* other man for help?" Adam settled his hands on her hips with that question. Rachel read the motion as both a threat and a promise because he could either start fucking her or bring her motions to a stop.

"Only you." Her correct answer ended on a gasp as Adam brought her hope to life. Holding her steady, he wrenched his hips back before slamming them forward until his pelvis smacked into her ass. Rachel screamed with the penetration, her whole body rioting with joy. *"Oh, yes. Again."*

Bless Adam, he did it again and again. Hard and steady, he screwed her ass until she about melted over Killian, whimpering out as her body rejoiced but couldn't be released, not without Killian. He held her hips pinned to his, forcing her to keep still on his cock. That didn't stop the smooth glide of Adam's dick from grinding down over the tender stretch of skin pulled taut by Killian's thick length.

Caught between the two hard erections, the bit of flesh dividing them pulsed out a panicked beat of rapture that washed over her but didn't pool thick enough to consume her. Instead, Rachel clung to the edge of sanity, trembling with the need to finally be swept away. It was an emotion she knew Killian shared.

There could be no disguising the soft, panted grunts blowing against her ear or the trembling in the fingers that pressed a little too hard into her hips. She made him weak. If only he'd been talking about something other than sex.

Killian was full of sweet words tonight. "You need us, baby. You need us to take care of you and keep you safe, and we always will. No matter what."

More than she wanted him to free her to move, Rachel wanted to believe him. His words stroked a different kind of warmth over her heart, making the heat impossible to contain. She cried out, giving in to at least one kind of release.

"Need you…always need you…love you…"

Everything went still with the words slipping from her throat as she wound down into a whimper, jerking hard between them in a pointed reminder of what she wanted. That need consumed her to the point where she didn't understand her confessions anymore. All she knew was that in one breath, things went from painfully quiet to raging out of control.

In an instant, their hands went everywhere. Adam's swallowed her breasts, tugging on the chains and sending a riot of pleasure tumbling down her spine. Jerking her upright, he gave Killian's fingers room to pluck the butterfly free and give her the kind of caresses she'd been dreaming about for the past hour.

All the while they fucked her. Thrusting, pulling, pushing, they filled her at the same time, leaving her empty until the strokes came too fast and hard for her keep up. She tried, bucking frantically between them, but the uneven tempo only wound her boiling lust tighter.

"Need us?" Adam growled before licking down her neck to suck another moan out as he lips settled over the dangerously fast pace of her pulse.

"Need you," Rachel repeated back, letting her head roll to the side and leaving more of her tender flesh exposed for his tasting.

"Love us?" Killian whispered into the underside of her breast.

Adam's fingers burned through her skin, holding her generous globes up for Killian's feasting. The feel of his velvety tongue soothing the tender flesh pinched by the rim of the clamps held her voice back as she tried to pant fast enough to breathe. That delay brought all motion to a painful stop for the barest of seconds. The pain of halting ripped the answer from her lips in a cry full of agonized need.

"*Love you—*"

Killian's lips closed over the clamp and popped it free. The sudden rush of blood to her tender tit sent a bubble of rapture rolling down her stomach to explode as both men drove themselves deep into her with one single motion. They didn't stop but pounded into her in unison, driving her mercilessly toward the release she'd been begging for.

She could feel every unforgiving inch of steel powering deep and hard into her pussy. The tantalizing motion was echoed back by the orgasmic pleasure of having her ass stretched wide over Adam's cock. Together, they powered into her at the exact same moment. Rachel screamed, feeling the rush of her climax beginning to consume her.

Then Killian's hungry lips shifted to her other breast and latched on to the second clamp. The slight tug whipped a decadent thrill right through the heart of the frenzy consuming her. Then the clamp snapped free and sent her hurling over the edge.

Mindless of anything other than the rapture consuming her, Rachel lost control of her body. She didn't even notice that the men followed, becoming near crazed in their fucking. Too consumed by her own climax, she could only sense the pleasure of the last few hard, grinding pumps that had her muscles tightening down, trying to suck every last bit of ecstasy out of the moment before collapsing under the exertion, right into a deep, contented sleep.

Chapter 23

Sunday, April 20th

Sunlight danced over the bed with a joyous kind of warmth that made Rachel snarl. Grumpy understated her mood the next morning. Unable to ignore the smells of coffee and bacon, she unwillingly rolled out of bed and stumbled toward the bathroom. Even the near scalding, pulsing spray of her shower couldn't rouse her from the foulness that had invaded her bones.

All it wanted was a target. Killian provided a convenient one when he sauntered into the bathroom right when she was stepping out of the shower. Glaring at his intrusion, Rachel tightened the towel she had wrapped around her.

She did not feel up to any morning hanky-panky and was getting damn tired of not having a shred of privacy in her own house. Maybe if he'd come bearing coffee, Rachel might have forgiven him. The tall glass of juice he carried with him did nothing to assuage her annoyance.

"Morning, sunshine," Killian sang out with the kind of cheeriness that left her feeling the need to curse.

Dropping a kiss on her forehead, he had the audacity to offer her the juice. Rachel didn't take it, nor did she return his greeting. Anything she'd have said would have started a fight, something she didn't have the energy for. Instead, she put all her focus into glaring at him until he finally got the silent message. The stubborn man just wouldn't listen to it.

"Now don't give me that look," Killian retorted with too much indulgence. He sounded like her damn father lecturing her. "I know you want your coffee, but that much caffeine isn't good for you first thing in the morning. So you're going to be having orange juice from now on."

The man had the arrogance to actually take her hand and fold it around the glass before ordering her to drink it. "It's good for you."

Rachel growled, a feral warning that messing with her morning rituals wasn't good for him. Killian completely ignored the sound, or maybe he didn't hear it as fast as he retreated out of the room. Either way, she had to resist the urge to lob the glass at the door closing behind him. It took a great deal of effort but she managed to set the glass down on the sink and not pitch an all-out tantrum.

Dressing, doing her hair and makeup, all the normal morning tasks she went through didn't make her feel any more ready to open the door and face the day. If it hadn't been for the seductive smells of frying meat, Rachel probably would have crawled back into bed.

No matter how miserable she was, she couldn't resist bacon. Like a siren's call, the scent lured her into the chaos of the kitchen where she nearly crashed right into Adam as he turned the corner around the island.

"Morning, darlin'."

Adam gave her the same kiss Killian had, but he matched it with an arm around her waist. Steering her with one hand toward the dining room table, he kept her obediently moving forward by waving a plate loaded down with eggs, hash, and bacon right before her nose with his other hand.

"I got your breakfast all ready, but I'm afraid we can't join you. We have to go into work this morning."

She already knew that and really didn't care. What worried Rachel were the eggs as she studied the plate Adam lowered down, and she settled into a chair.

"Why are they so white? Did you put cheese in them?" That idea perked her up, but Adam's answer sent her spiraling back into seething frustration.

"White? What, the eggs? That's just the whites."

"It's healthier that way," Killian explained, as if she didn't already know. Rachel could care less about healthy at eight in the morning. She might have been able to cope, though, if Killian hadn't delivered another damn glass of juice with his condescending comment.

"Why the hell did you make coffee if I'm not allowed to have any?"

That cranky outburst earned her two tolerant smiles from either side. Killian matched his with the kind of calm, rational answer that a parent would use on a child. "The coffee is for us because we need a little pick-me-up for work. Now you go on and drink your juice. It's good for you."

Before she could threaten Killian and show him how unhealthy taking coffee away from her was, Adam distracted her with another patronizing kiss to the head. "We have to get going, but we'll see you for lunch, darlin'."

Killian followed Adam's domesticated gesture with his own, then paused to snatch the salt shaker off the table before sauntering out of the dining room. A second later, the back door clanged shut and heavy stomps echoed down her steps.

Rachel waited until she heard them back out of her drive and take off down the road before she got up to help herself to a cup of coffee. With her mug of caffeine sweetened with sugar and fattened up with milk, she settled down to have a breakfast of coffee and bacon. It helped her mood slightly, not making her any happier but giving her mind the energy to start analyzing what was so horrible about this morning.

Staring out through the window, she couldn't deny that today her yard looked different. It looked vacant and empty, forcing her gaze into the shadows instead of the light. It felt unnecessarily grim that morning. Everything did, and Rachel began to understand why.

Things had changed last night. For the first time, Adam and Killian had used sex against her. They'd stripped away all her defenses and bent her to their will. Unlike that first night in the tub, they hadn't done it for her pleasure but their gain.

It showed how little they trusted her, how little they respected her. Worse, it had revealed how little they desired her because Rachel would never have been able to do that to them. When it came to Adam and Killian, she didn't have that kind of control. She wanted them with every fiber of her being, but they could hold back.

They could even walk away from her. Tied alone in the bedroom, enduring nothing but frustrated desire, a part of Rachel had panicked. That's what it would be like when they were gone. It would be unthinkable torture.

Knowing that didn't change the future. In fact, last night only confirmed what Rachel had felt with every moment spent with them—time was winding down. What they had couldn't last, wouldn't last because they didn't love her.

...love you...

That was the real secret she'd been trying to hide. Not from them but herself. Rachel would have done anything to keep that truth hidden. That's why she'd lied to the sheriff, to Adam and Killian. She'd known Kitty's idea would blow up her relationship with the deputies. All she'd been trying to do was buy some time.

Well, time had run out. Now she had to face all the truths. They didn't love her. This was going to hurt. She only had two real choices—speak up now and put things to an end or let them mold her until they tired of her and traded her in for a new pet. The answer should have been obvious, but love clouded her thinking, making her incapable of coming to a decision.

Her pride wouldn't back down, insisting that she face the reality of her situation. There was really only one way to do that. Given every option she had would only end in pain, this one carried the greatest unknown danger. Rachel brewed another pot and took her time refilling her mug before she made herself go to her desk and pick up Patton's gift.

Whatever Patton had put on the disk, she hadn't wanted Killian and Adam to know about it. That could only mean it pertained to them and probably not in a good way. A part of her could already guess what she'd find as she popped the CD into her computer, but knowing only made her hesitate as the file manager popped up with two massive files stored on the disk.

Their Cattleman records. She didn't want to read this. Opening those files would lead to jealousy, betrayal, and anger. She needed all three things to stiffen up her resolve.

* * * *

"Did Rachel seem a little cranky to you this morning?" Adam asked the question that had been bugging him since she'd stumbled into the kitchen, scowling at everything in her path. It seemed an odd reaction to him given how absolutely wonderful he'd felt this morning. At least, he had until she'd grouched away his good mood, but he was pretty sure that Killian bore responsibility for that.

"Eh." Killian shrugged as he slammed his locker door closed. "She probably didn't get enough sleep last night. You know how crabby she gets when she's tired."

Adam did know, but he didn't think that was it. "Or maybe she was a little annoyed with your bossy attitude."

He had to follow Killian over to the sinks to level that accusation at him. Not that Killian appeared the least bit bothered. He snorted as if Adam's description had been absurd. "Bossy? I'm just doing my job and looking after the girl. You have noticed how deplorable her eating habits are, haven't you?"

"I thought you liked her body." Adam certainly did. He wouldn't have Killian trying to change her, either.

"I do, but that doesn't mean I don't also want her alive and healthy at eighty."

"Well, perhaps you could be a little more subtle in your instructions." He'd tried to be diplomatic in his phrasing, but it still drew an annoyed scowl from Killian as he snapped paper towels out of the dispenser.

"What's with you? Why are you acting like I'm going to screw things up? Huh? Didn't Rachel say she loved us? Didn't she say it after we spent the last few weeks following my plan and not your insane idea about taking her out to the club. Now, don't be getting that look on your face. The answer is no!"

Adam shot Killian a dirty look for that high-handed attitude. He really did want to take Rachel out to the club. There was this observation room where he could not only claim her but make sure every damn man in the club saw. Then everybody would know who Rachel belonged to. They'd stay the hell away if they knew what was good for them.

It would be the final assurance that Rachel was bound to him for all time. Of course, it might be the very thing that sent her running. The club part, not the sex part, because she'd kept up well with them last night. In fact, Adam had to wonder if they couldn't have gotten her confession a week ago if they'd been playing a little more rough with the girl.

"Ah, I guess you're right." It pained Adam to admit it, but Killian had a point. "Still, given last night, I don't think we have to hold back anything at home anymore."

Home, it sounded good. Adam had never really had one before. Killian's parents' house had come close, but for all the comfort the Kregors had tried to give him, a part of Adam had always felt lonely. Killian's parents weren't his, and eventually he always had to go back to his house.

Not this time. Rachel belonged to him as much as she did to Killian. She wasn't his, but theirs, and her house, their home. He simply couldn't lose that now

...love you...

Her voice floated through his head, soothing the panic rising up in his stomach.

"I guess not." Killian shrugged his way through the locker room door. It nearly hit Adam as it swooshed back, but he caught it in time, shaking off the worry trying to creep into his mind. Killian's arrogant swagger kind of surprised Adam because of the two of them, Killian should have been the one in a panic.

More than most bachelors, Killian had built a reputation for being out the door the second a woman showed any sign of actually caring about him. Adam always figured a woman would have a better chance of holding on to his friend if she maced him instead of saying she loved him.

As it had been from nearly the beginning, Killian didn't appear the least bit spooked. He'd had a moment that first morning, but then Rachel had gotten stubborn and refused to commit. Adam figured that challenge washed out Killian's fear, making him act with the cockiness of a man who already had a ring on his lady's finger.

"In fact, I think it might be a good thing if we started being more proactive about everything. It really isn't right that we don't know her friends or what kind of craziness they're trying to get her involved in."

Adam's nose wrinkled at the indirect mention of Rachel's mysterious friend Kitty Anne. On principle, he didn't like anybody who endangered his woman's life. So as far as Adam was concerned, Rachel shouldn't be spending any more time with Kitty.

"You know, it's strange." Adam settled down at his desk before leaning forward to keep their conversation somewhat private. "I really thought that Rachel was happy with her new series. It's been getting the front page, and she's seemed so thrilled, but now it doesn't seem enough."

Killian snorted at Adam's confused admission. "Face it, Adam. Rachel's got a taste of what it's like to be the center of attention. Now, you know I love Rachel—"

Actually, Adam had figured that out, but it surprised him Killian had. More shocking, Killian had admitted to it without so much as a bead of sweat appearing anywhere on his body. The man didn't even hesitate to recognize the magnitude of his own confession.

"—but she's not the type who ever got to star in the play or lead the cheerleaders onto the field, so you have to figure that all this who-ha over her stories is probably really exciting to her. That's probably what's pushing her to up the ante and try for something even bigger."

Shaking off the weirdness of Killian's glossed-over revelation, Adam considered his partner's words and came to an upsetting conclusion. Killian had a point, a very frightening one. "Well, if it's prostitution today, what's she going to be onto tomorrow?"

"Exactly." Killian nodded. Settling back into his seat, he met Adam's gaze with a grim look. "And you know whose responsibility it is to keep her safe?"

"Ours."

Chapter 24

Thursday, May 1st

"*Ow!*"

Rachel smiled at the greeting that howled through the house as she shoved in the front door. She'd known when she'd gotten out of her car that Adam and Killian were up to something. It seemed like this past week they were always up to something, filling every spare moment of her day with surprises.

Tonight, it was apparently cooking her dinner. The mouthwatering aroma of meat being grilled had wafted down her driveway, luring her up the path. It clung to every breath she took, making her stomach rumble. As she entered the house, the scent only thickened.

That and the curses coming from the kitchen. Dropping her purse on the entry table, Rachel made her way to the back of the house to find Killian cussing at a pot of boiling oil. It snapped and hissed back, making him dance around, shaking his arms.

"*Ow!*"

With his back to her, he couldn't see her smiling at him. The man really had no clue about so many things. Not that he'd ever admit to it. Moving around behind him, Rachel snatched the splatter screen off its hook and went to save Mr. Know-It-All before he seriously burned himself.

"Here." Rachel reached across him to settle the screen over the pot.

Breaking into a big grin, Killian sidetracked her instantly with an arm wrapping around her waist. "Hey, darlin', I've been thinking about you. Say, that's pretty clever."

"Isn't it, though?" Rachel asked as she snuggled into his hold. "Makes the 'ows' all better, doesn't it?"

"No, sweetness. This is what makes the pain go away," Killian growled huskily, rubbing the callused tip of his finger against her lips.

Things had been different since her birthday. No longer did Killian and Adam seem content with the smooth, easy loving that only took place appropriately at bedtime. Their lusts had turned ravenous, feeding into the very desperation Rachel felt.

She knew this phase. She'd read their files. If this was to be the end, then she wanted it to be a glorious, gluttonous explosion that could keep her satisfied for a lifetime. That's why she didn't control the urge to tempt the heat she could feel building between them.

Unable to stop herself from teasing him back, Rachel nipped his finger with her teeth and felt the instant reaction of cock swelling into a hardened log between them.

"You really shouldn't have done that." Killian matched his threat by using his considerable bulk to back her up.

"And why not?" Rachel loved him like this, all predatory and dangerous. The hunger in his gaze left her question more of a breathy whisper than an actual sound.

"'Cause we're cooking you dinner to be all romantic and gentlemanly. Then we have to get to work, but I'm thinking now you won't be awake when we get home." With every step, his hands dipped ever lower, sinking past her waist to pull one fistful of her skirt up after another. "You'd be kind of cranky if I woke you up then, wouldn't you?"

"That's never stopped you." Rachel couldn't help the way her voice came out all breathless and ragged sounding.

He'd backed her right up against the counter and pinned her there with nothing but a little bit of lace and the rough fabric of his jeans protecting her from the hard bulge of his cock. He could make no claims to decency with his palm warming her ass, protecting it from the ridged surface of the cabinet.

"You never want me to stop," Killian growled down at her.

"I really don't know what you're talking about, officer," Rachel whispered, unable to control her smile or the way her legs slid up along his to tempt the beast a little more. "I was just saying hello."

There went her panties, torn from her body with one hard tug of his hand. "All I'm saying is dinner is about to be burned."

Rachel sucked in a deep breath as the magical feel of his hand slid down the curve her rear to nudge between her thighs, already sticky with cream. He didn't have to demand entrance. Rachel's leg lifted up along his thigh, inviting his touch with the intimate press of her knee against his denim-clad muscle.

"I guess you've been thinking about me, too."

Always, but the word didn't make it past her lips with the sigh she released. His wonderfully thick fingers slid right up along her pussy lips and parted her for the deeper touch. Head dipping back, she arched upward, expecting an invasion. She moaned when nothing but cool air caressed her heated flesh.

Forcing her lids to lift, Rachel gazed up at Killian, trying to think of what rule or tradition held her back from the want he'd so easily sparked in her. Nothing came to her in the second it took Killian to supply one. "Has my wench been missing me?"

Rachel smiled. Leaning into him, she pressed her splayed cunt tight against the bulge in his jeans and gave herself a thrill with a little rub. "Been missing something, sir."

"And what is that?"

Rolling her hips against his, Rachel whispered, "Guess."

No wise woman would taunt Killian with such open defiance, but then again, a wise woman wouldn't have as much fun with him as Rachel did. Her brazenness caused Killian's eyes to darken, narrowing with impure intent glinting in them. He was thinking punishment, and she was thinking pleasure, because that's what came when he sank to his knees with a snarl.

The sudden motion barely gave her a chance to brace herself for the wash of hot breath over her wet folds. Braced for a mauling, the quick lick of his tongue straight up her cunt shot a bolt of pleasure through her tense muscles, making her hips jerk hard in blind search of more. Her throat strangled her cry, barely letting a shriek out.

"My wench tastes like honey," Killian growled, giving her another teasing lap. "Spicy honey."

"*Sir*," Rachel ground out, barely holding back on the demand that wanted to follow.

She both hated and loved the way her men liked to tease her. Licking, nibbling, toying with her clit, he made her knees wobble and then fall down when he penetrated her with one liquid thrust of his tongue.

The velvety intruder tickled her from the inside as it discovered the magic spot that made her body boom with rapture. Gasping out shrieks, Rachel collapsed into Killian's hold. Held upright by his hands on her hips and pinned into place by his body, Rachel didn't cling to the counter but to the silky tresses covering Killian's head as she pressed his lips tight against her pussy.

Killian ate pussy like a connoisseur. Savoring and discovering, he drew out her tasting until tears trickled down her cheeks. With his lips wrapped around her clit, he milked the cream from her body with his suckling kiss. The arousal flowed from her body until his kiss dipped and his tongue came back to fuck her right to the point where her whole body clenched and she couldn't take a breath without the painful need to come.

Killian held her in a state of anticipation, letting the pleasure build in her until she would have given him anything. Everything was what he demanded from her, night after night. Rachel didn't have the stamina to deny him. Not then and not now as Adam came whistling into the kitchen with a platter of burgers.

"Hey, sweetness, I thought I heard you come in."

Rachel didn't have the voice left to respond with anything more than gasped squeaks, fighting Killian now as she tried to ride his mouth to release. Eyes glazed over and watering, the tears distorted Adam's grin as he dropped a chaste kiss on her cheek.

"Ah, man, Killian. You burned the fries," Adam complained over the clanging and banging he made by the stove.

Rachel had no idea what the hell he was doing until Adam's hands bit into her arms. Before she could begin to fathom his intent, Adam wrenched Rachel away from Killian's kiss. She found the strength to shriek in denial at the loss of a release so close. Bellowing curses as she floated off the ground, her objections came to a grunting halt when Adam dumped her over his shoulder.

Killian added his complaint, whipping straight up to confront his partner. "What the hell are you doing?"

"You burned the fries, so no dessert for you," Adam retorted, sounding more than a little annoyed. "I think you'd better get dinner together and set the table while I tend to our woman."

Apparently, that's all Adam had to say. Sauntering off toward her bedroom, he left her dangling over his shoulder, watching Killian's scowl fade in the background. Fogged with lust, her mind couldn't reason out what was happening to her beyond the loss of her pleasure. That made her very grumpy with Adam.

"You better tend to the right things, Adam," Rachel warned him as he dropped her on her bed.

She was not in the mood for one of his marathon screwing sessions. Even for what his file said about Adam's appetites, he'd been particularly rough with her lately. Pushing her harder and further, each time they came together, he appeared to be desperate for something she couldn't understand, much less satisfy.

That, more than anything, told Rachel their time would end very soon. The only thing she couldn't give Adam was the one thing his file clearly showed he needed—diversity. Rachel shied away from that thought, using the pain it caused her to fuel her anger at being denied Killian's kiss.

"You'd better be planning on finishing what Killian started, or I'll…"

Rachel didn't know what she'd do. Her brain was too drugged to reason it through to a proper threat. The need to find one, though, died when Adam's hands started pulling on his jeans' button. Grinning at the prospect of getting exactly what she wanted, what Killian probably would have delayed giving her, Rachel watched Adam struggle with the stiff denim.

The material had stretched as far as it could go under the strain of his swollen cock, making it very difficult for him to get the zipper down without doing himself damage. If she were a girlfriend, Rachel might have offered to help. At the very least, she would have waited patiently. But if Rachel wasn't the girlfriend, she would embrace her role as the temptress, a vixen. That gave her the right to bend over and suck the very tip of the cockhead peeking out at her.

It pulsed under her lips, and Adam cussed, jerking back from her. "That isn't helping."

Rachel smiled, enjoying making him twitch. The smile turned to giggles when he grunted, flinching as he caused himself some injury. Either Adam had grown tired of fighting with his zipper or aggravated by her teasing, but he gave up working on actually undoing his jeans and just started trying to shove them down.

Her giggles pealed into all-out laughter at the strange dance he did. The silliness of it all evaporated the hard edges of her lust, making the moment seem almost playful until Adam's pants finally plopped to the floor. Unleashed, he growled and launched himself at her, tumbling her backward across the bed until he had Rachel pinned beneath his weight.

Neither his heated look nor the thick thigh forcing hers apart could intimidate the smile from her lips. Wrapping her legs around his hips as he shoved her skirt out of the way, Rachel arched up in blind search of his heated length. The thick, swollen cock burned against the tender lips of her pussy before parting them to slide through the creamy folds.

Rachel bit her lip, fighting a moan as his hardness brushed over her still- tingling clit. The press and scrape of her tender bud made electric sparks of pleasure race up her spine, taunting Rachel into grinding herself against him in the mindless search for more.

Adam grunted and flexed above her, making her mew and twist beneath him as all sense of mirth became lost in the rolling wave of heat washing over her body. It mewed out of her, thinning into a wail when his thick head slipped down to push against her tender opening. With an easy stroke, he filled her, only to glide almost all the way out before pumping her full of deliciously filling hardness.

"Ah, baby, you feel so good," Adam groaned. "All tight and warm and wet and mine."

Each word flowed out on an expiration of a deep breath, punctuated by the flex of his hips in time. Panting, Rachel clung to him as Adam began riding her with a smooth easiness that quickly drove her insane.

"Do you know how much I need this?" Adam whispered, brushing kisses up her neck. His warm breath tickled over her ear before seducing her with his husky murmur. "How much I need you?"

His word curled around her heart, stroking over her soul with a tenderness that brought tears to her eyes. They might be bedroom lies, but she savored them. This was as close as she'd ever come to her fantasy, this moment. As much as she wanted to cling to it, it started to slip away, driven out by the pressure growing out of her womb.

Rachel needed Adam's force, his aggression to release her, but he held steady. Keeping her hips from tempting his into a quicker pace, his hands held her pinned to the mattress as he continued to seduce her with his velvety growls.

"You need me, too. Don't you, darlin'?"

This is what it was like every time now. He needed. She needed. It was never enough. Rachel couldn't give Adam what he wanted. She couldn't satisfy him anymore, so she didn't even try.

Instead, she threw all her effort into unwinding him. Clawing at his back, she used all her strength to break his hold and flexed her hips out of rhythm with his. Attempting to jumpstart him to a faster pace, she begged him in all the ways Rachel knew Adam liked. It got her nowhere, and quickly the frustration burned through her euphoria.

"Tell me you need me?"

Not paying his words any attention and not having any compassion for whatever desperation drove him, Rachel planted her hands on his shoulders and shoved. Adam let her roll him over till their positions were reversed. In the past week, they'd screwed in about every position Rachel's body could bend into, but not this one. Her men didn't care for the woman on top thing at all.

Tonight, though, all Adam did was scowl. "Tell me you need me."

"Enough to take what I want." Rachel gave him an answer that she hoped would keep him still. Being on bottom did not make Adam vulnerable. She knew whenever he wanted, he could take full control of the situation.

"Then take it."

Adam's simple statement held a wealth of satisfaction, leaving her to wonder if she hadn't found his magic trigger. Maybe what Adam had searched for was the one thing no woman had ever dared to give him—domination instead of submission.

Not about to let this precious moment go to waste, Rachel played into it with all the fantasies she'd ever entertained about being the one in control. With slow, hopefully seductive, motions, she undid her shirt, letting the blouse dangle on her shoulders before shrugging it off.

She should have known Adam wouldn't let her finish. He did not take to being teased but instead preferred to be the one in charge. Taking control of the moment, his hands came up to span over her stomach and creep toward where her fingers pressed on her bra's hook.

It popped open, and his warm palms were there to push the cups out of the way. Rachel didn't have enough time to slip free of the bra before Adam pulled her down.

"Come here."

Growling out his demand, he showed her where "here" was when he stretched up to capture her nipple with his lips. He sucked her back down to the mattress with him, making her moan and arch as he held her tender tip captive for the teasing torment of his tongue. As the pleasure trickled out of her breasts, it sparked a response deep down in her pussy, making her muscles contract all along his hardness.

The glorious pressure commanded friction, triggering her pussy to contract, but it wasn't enough. Slowly, her muscles began to obey the rhythm being set by the need burning in her womb. Up and down his cock, she swayed faster and faster until her ass bounced against the legs Adam bent to give her some support from behind.

So close to being consumed by her climax, Rachel strained forward, trying to ignore the pain burning in her thighs as they tried to race her into bliss's sweet embrace. It didn't work. The searing burn contrasted with the pleasure, keeping her from true fulfillment. Screaming with her frustration, Rachel twined her arms around Adam's head, pressing his face deeper into her breasts as she tried to roll him a second time.

This time, though, Adam wouldn't budge. With a twist of his head, he broke her hold, growling up at her to let Rachel know he didn't like being controlled. Her audacity unleashed the aggression she'd been hoping for minutes ago. Unfortunately, they were in the wrong position, and she was about to get stuck doing all the work.

Rachel didn't think she had the stamina left, but Adam didn't seem to care. Clamping his hands around her waist, he started forcing her up to speed. Banging her down on each forceful thrust of his hips upward, Killian proved he had more strength in his arms than she did in her whole body as he took command.

Free of any responsibility of having to put forth any effort, Rachel leaned back against his legs and gave herself over to Adam's fucking. Harder, deeper, he forced her up and down his length faster than she could ever have ridden him. It didn't take but moments before her cunt began to vibrate with the sparkly tingles of rapture.

The pleasure bloomed out from her pussy, filling her until she felt almost dizzy with the sensation. Bubbly and playful, Rachel moaned as the tide consumed her and drowned her in a sea of ecstasy. The world faded away as her whole body rejoiced with the pleasure. It left her weak and limp and very, very happy as it slowly receded.

Smiling wide, Rachel slowly opened her eyes only to find Killian's scowl glaring down at her. At some point, his thighs had replaced Adam's. Legs pressed into the mattress with knees in her lower back, Adam had forced Killian's legs wide to get that close. The position certainly explained why the cock inside her felt so filling. It might also explain why Killian growled down at her. He was the only one who had really gotten screwed.

"Dinner is cold, and we're going to be late for our shift."

Contentment clouded Rachel's mind, leading her to make a very bad mistake in that moment. Yawning out her words, it didn't even register that she shouldn't be speaking her thought aloud until Adam went tense as a coiled snake beneath her.

"Yeah, I got to get a move on it or I'll be late, too."

"Late?" Killian grunted, sounding every bit as annoyed as he looked. "To where?"

Despite his recent release, Adam didn't sound any happier either. "You didn't tell us you were going anywhere."

No, Rachel hadn't, and for a very good reason. While the sex might have become "Dear Playgirl" stories for the past week, Killian's and Adam's behavior outside the bedroom had become outright oppressive. The adjectives she'd been using lately to describe them were "bossy," "demanding," "controlling." She'd even had to use the word "interrogation" when complaining to Heather. In response, Rachel had become secretive and taken to planning around them.

"Rachel?" Killian's tone held no sign of patience, nor did the arm he used to loop around her waist and jerk her right off Adam. Setting her on legs that wobbled, he forced her to look him straight in the eye. "Where are you going?"

Not appreciating his tactics, Rachel jerked free of the thumb holding her chin up. "I'm just meeting up with Hailey and Heather."

"And how come we didn't know about this?" Killian dogged her into the bathroom, where Rachel finally felt compelled to put on a robe. Arguing with them naked gave them too many opportunities to balance the scales in their favor.

"Why would you?" She retorted behind her armor of terry cloth. "It's not like it's a big deal, either, so don't scowl at me like that."

Killian didn't take the hint and only glared harder at her. "And just where is this get together happening? The Bread Box is closed."

Rachel didn't want to answer that and hoped that if she didn't, he might get pissed enough to start harping on something else. Choosing the unwise path of ignoring him, she pretended to be absorbed with assuring the shower water wasn't too hot.

"He asked you a question, darlin', and I'm thinking you better answer it, as in now."

Great, Adam had joined them. There wouldn't be any escaping the anger in his tone. Killian could be distracted, but Adam was like a damn pit bull with a bone when he got stubborn. Taking a deep breath and turning to face the two macho men trying to cow her into obedience, Rachel offered them a smile.

"Oh, we're meeting up at Riley's."

"At Riley's?" That had Adam straightening off the doorframe. He didn't get to give her the rest of the tirade she could see building in his tensing muscles. True to his nature, Killian exploded before anybody else could.

"No. No way. A bar is not safe for a single woman. I forbid it."

Chapter 25

"He forbid you?" Heather almost laughed the question out. "Exactly how hard did you hit him for that?"

Rachel smirked at Heather's sarcastic question. "I didn't have to. They had to go to work. With the sheriff riding them lately, the last thing they could be is late."

She made light of the situation, but there had been a glower in Killian's eyes that clearly stated the argument would be picked up once he got home. By then, though, it would be too late to stop her, so Rachel was expecting a full gale when he got off his shift. Hell, she'd half been expecting them to actually show up at the bar and park themselves outside to keep an eye on her.

"How the hell do you put up with those men?"

Now it was Rachel's turn to laugh. "I guess you just have to love them."

Her quick response had Heather studying her over the lip of her cup. It was early yet, but Riley's had filled out as much as it would. Given the size of Pittsview, Riley's could be considered packed even though it was mostly empty. Several men gathered around the pool tables and the dart board tucked into the back.

"That's coming easier to you these days," Heather finally commented, drawing Rachel's attention back to her friend.

Despite the delay in the conversation, Rachel didn't bother to misunderstand the observation. "I guess I've just given up fighting it. No point, really."

"Except to them, right?"

Rachel snorted at the stupidity of Heather's question. "Oh, yeah. Every night."

"Am I supposed to take it from that cheery attitude you're still intending to crash your relationship headfirst into a dead end?"

"Hey, guys, sorry I'm—" Hailey's greeting cut off abruptly, as did her cheery tone. "What the hell is he doing here?"

"Who?" Rachel looked around, for some strange reason expecting to see Killian or Adam. She couldn't find anybody out of place. Apparently, she wasn't supposed to.

"Nobody." Hailey plunked down into her seat with enough agitation to make Heather's brow's go up. Hailey didn't take notice of the look either Rachel or Heather gave her. Instead, her focus remained tense, almost angrily staring at the pool tables in the back.

"As if it isn't horrible enough to be stuck every damn day, day after day, in a garage with that man, he has to follow me here."

Hailey must have been talking about her "nobody," but Rachel still didn't follow. "You all right, Hailey?"

"Do I look all right?" Hailey retorted, finally glancing in Rachel's direction. "No. How can I when I'm being driven steadily insane by a slimy, slithering slug that's trying to weasel his way into damn near every moment of my life."

Hard, raw emotion poured out with that complaint. Rachel wanted to empathize, but Hailey did sound a little nuts right then. "And, um, just who is the slug?"

"Kyle," Hailey's gaze bore into Rachel's, "Harding. He's such a little prick. I just wish he had one. I mean, my God, that thing is always hard. It's not like—"

"Uh, Hailey?" Heather tried unsuccessfully to bring the other woman back to their reality.

"—I want to notice, but how can you not with him strutting all around half naked." With the quickness of a mad woman, Hailey's fingers clamped around her arm, and Rachel suddenly found herself strapped to the table.

"Look at him," Hailey whispered as if they talked about the devil instead of a man. "All day, Rachel. No shirt, all sweaty muscles covered in grease, and the bastard still smells good. I just want to strap him to my bed and—"

"*Hailey!*"

Rachel's panicked interruption snapped Hailey out of whatever had possessed her. Blinking, scowling, she released Rachel to shove her chair back with a mutter. "I need a drink."

"Sounds like you need a few," Heather called out as Hailey took off for the bar. The only response she got was a one finger salute.

"Well, I guess you're not the only one having man trouble." Heather laughed. "I'm so glad I don't have a boyfriend."

"Killian and Adam are not my boyfriends."

"Rachel, honey, when two men share your bed every night, spend every free moment of their waking hours with you, and move their shit into your house, they're your boyfriends."

No, none of that made them anything to her. The fact that she loved them did, but they didn't love her back. Without that, there was no relationship. Only borrowed time, and Rachel would do anything to make her time with them last.

She didn't want to think about that tonight. "You know, it's really easy to be all-knowing when the only man telling you goodnight is Jay Leno."

"Like I stay up that late." Heather snorted. "And it is, because I'm not sunk so ass deep into the relationship quagmire that I can't help. I'm the reasonable person, unclouded by lust, here to offer my wise counsel."

"Yeah." Rachel snickered. "Isn't it mating season for you?"

That earned her a glower and a prim response. "Taylor's going to visit his grandparents in a few weeks, if that's what you're asking."

Every year when Heather's son went on his ritual summer trip, Heather got laid. She had a running tradition with her "good friend,"

GD. Rachel kept waiting for the day Heather woke up and realized that the two of them had something more going on.

Maybe it was time to help that revelation along. "Taylor's out of the house and GD's…"

"Busy," Heather filled in with no emotion in her tone. "Apparently, he's being overworked at the club."

Rachel cringed. Heather could pretend she didn't care, but it had to cut. "So you're staying in this year?"

"I don't know about that." Heather's tone lightened with her smile. "I have one week a year, and there is no reason to waste it just because GD's not available."

"Good for you." She must have responded with too much forced cheer because her positive statement only earned a dirty look from Heather.

"Thanks, but I really don't need the positive reinforcement. GD and I are nothing more than good friends. He's allowed to be busy with somebody else."

Heather could say what she wanted. Rachel knew that look in her eyes, knew, too, where it came from. They were a fine pair, loving men who would never love them back. Fortunately, they had Hailey to show them how wallowing in misery should be done.

Returning with her drink, she plunked down in her chair and without a word took up a concentrated study of Kyle Harding as he bent over the pool table. Not a bad sight, but not nearly as mesmerizing as Hailey seemed to think it was.

"Are you going to stare at that man all night long?" That drew Hailey's glower from Kyle back to Rachel. "I'll take that as a yes."

"Leave her alone." Heather waved her cup at Rachel. "Kyle's good to look at."

"But he's not looking back," Rachel retorted. "And there is a point when a look goes from interested to pathetic. Now wipe the drool off your chin, Hailey, and focus. I have a real problem here."

"I'm paying attention," Hailey groused, but sure enough it took less than a second for her eyes to go wandering back to the pool table.

Rachel rolled her eyes, catching Heather's smirk in the process. "At least I'm not that bad."

"Yeah, right." Heather glanced over Rachel's shoulder to take a peek at the Cattlemen clustered in the back. "At least Kyle's nice to look at. Better than your two deputies."

"What?" Rachel couldn't hold back her shocked indignation at that tidbit. "Are you drinking some whiskey with that Coke because Kyle's all scraggly. Adam and Killian are built like mountains, all hard and rippling with muscles."

Heather lifted up her napkin for Rachel to take. "You've got some drool there, Rachel. Might want to clean that up."

"Ha. Ha. You're a bucket of laughs." Rachel snatched the wispy bit of paper out of Heather's hands, balled it up, and tossed it back at her friend. Not that Hailey was any better. She should have been jumping into the conversation, but her gaze had gone all waxy.

"Hello?" Waving a hand in front of Hailey, Rachel tried to snap her out of her trance. "Earth to Hailey."

"I'm sorry." Hailey blinked, glancing quickly between Heather's smirk and Rachel's scowl before offering up a tentative smile. "You were saying?"

"Oh, no." Rachel shook her head, not about to let Hailey off that easily. "You're not getting off that easy. Say it again, and try a little sincerity."

Sucking up a breath to bring her straight up in her seat, Hailey met Rachel's gaze. "I'm sorry, Rachel."

Rachel sniffed back a snort at that act. "No, you're not. But I forgive you nonetheless. I know that puppy-eyed disease anywhere."

"Don't start with me," Hailey growled, antagonizing Rachel into doing just that.

"You've got it bad."

"I do not."

"So bad," Heather echoed.

"*I do not.*" There went Hailey's ears, bright red and a clear sign she had lied.

"You're a stone's throw away from being like Marie down at the grocery store." Rachel's gaze cut to Heather. Both women gave a dramatic sigh as they fell back, speaking in unison.

"*Oh, Kyle.*"

"Oh." Hailey's head hit the table as she whined into the wooden surface. "I don't want to have it this bad. Not if he doesn't have it this bad."

"Oh, honey, he does." Heather patted her on the back. "It's just he's a Cattleman. Their whole thing is to control their wants."

Rolling her chin to the side, she gave Heather a one-eyed glare. "That really doesn't help."

Rachel snickered, completely understanding Hailey's position. "Nothing helps. Take it from me, Hailey, resist."

"Rachel," Heather snapped at her, shooting her one of those disapproving looks she'd mastered on her son. She really hated that expression. It made her squirm even though Heather wasn't her mom.

"I'm just saying," Rachel muttered. "We're fighting a war here. Look at me. I'm trying to establish my career as creditable reporter, and I have a man at home who thinks the most dangerous thing I should do with my life is bake cookies."

Actually, Killian probably wouldn't want her to have too many cookies. They contained too much sugar. It was like dating a nutritionist, only Killian didn't practice what he preached. Neither deputy did. They wanted her to content herself with stories about beauty pageants while they went out every night and worked one of the most dangerous jobs she could think of.

The hypocrisy infuriated Rachel, but it was somewhat all her fault. She'd let them have control from the beginning. That had been a bad move. "You see, it's all my fault. I didn't run the bonfire story, and now they think they can just boss me all around. Well, I don't think so. I'm getting smart, and I'm not telling those bullies anything about my next project."

"Well, that's a mighty fine tantrum in the making." Heather saluted her with her glass. "'Course, I don't think that's going to help you when they find out what you and Kitty have been up to these past couple of weeks."

"I don't know what you're talking about. Kitty and I have barely spoken in over a week." Rachel could have left it there, but if she couldn't be honest with her friends, who could she talk to? "It's kind of hard to get the time to see Kitty when Killian and Adam don't *approve* of her."

At least Rachel had timed that confession right, catching Heather in mid-gulp. Coughing into her cup, Heather struggled to breathe as she bent over the table. It took her a moment, but Rachel waited through it, sure that Heather had a comeback burning in her throat.

"Finally," Heather straightened up, "something I agree with your boyfriends on."

"Will you stop calling them that?" God, Heather could be so aggravating. "They're not my boyfriends."

"But they are right," Heather shot back. "Or is Kitty not pressuring you to go along with her idiotic scheme to go undercover in a whorehouse?"

"I don't feel pressured." That was the truth. Rachel was tempted by the idea all on her own. Not the undercover part, that kind of scared her, but the idea of breaking that kind of story... "At least not by Kitty. Adam and Killian, now that's another story."

"How's that?" Heather asked. "I didn't even think they knew the real details of Kitty's idea."

"Of course not," she said, but it had been a close. Fortunately, staying away from the sheriff and keeping her investigation quiet, as in completely silent, had fooled the two deputies into thinking the matter had been settled.

"Why are you smiling like that?" Heather studied her for a moment and then broke into her own grin. "Oh, don't tell me. You've already started pursuing this crazy investigation. I thought you decided on your birthday to let it go."

Then the next morning, after reading their Cattlemen files, Rachel had changed her mind. Reading the details of their sordid pasts had hurt as much as she known it would, but it had also stiffened up her spine. Those pages had confirmed what her gut had told her these past few weeks. Her men needed variety.

They didn't have a type or a specification when it came to requesting pets, except that they never repeated themselves. Asian, African, white, Latina, short, tall, big boobs, heavy set, or shy, they'd gotten so desperate for diversity that Killian had actually put in a request to pick by state. Killian wanted to nail all fifty, while Adam appeared to be working on the alphabet.

Rachel guessed they could check off Alabama and the letter R now. Soon they'd be onto Georgia and the letter S. They'd move on, and she'd be left devastated but not destroyed. Rachel wouldn't let them have total control over her life.

"A woman has to do what a woman has to do."

Heather snorted at that piece of bullshitted wisdom. "And does that include hiding your research into a prostitution ring?"

"Well, duh." Rachel snorted, about to tack on something more obnoxious, but Hailey cut her off.

"And just how long do you think you can hide your investigation into a prostitution ring?" Rachel hadn't even thought Hailey was listening given her googly gaze had been stuck on Kyle. Apparently, she'd picked up enough to smirk over Rachel's predicament. "Hmm?"

"Long enough to get my story," Rachel shot back, feeling hounded. She knew she was treading into dangerous waters, but that's where journalists went. "Besides, I have a little help."

"Kitty Anne isn't going to save you from Killian and Adam." Heather snorted.

"I'm not talking about Kitty Anne." Rachel couldn't help that smug smile pulling at her lips. Being one step ahead of the pack fed her confidence. As long as she stayed there, she might be able to escape Killian and Adam's wrath.

Ideally, they'd break up with her first, so she could avoid whatever punishment they deemed fit for this deception. Of course, this kind of betrayal might very well be the thing that broke them up. Rachel had considered that before she contacted Deputy Watts over in Enterprise, but she wouldn't let it be a reason to stop her investigation.

She needed help. If they weren't willing to help her, then she had every right to find somebody who would. Besides, Deputy Watts was married with five kids, so neither Adam nor Killian could accuse her of anything other than maintaining a professional association with the man. If that bothered Adam and Killian, then so would her working at the newspaper, given half the staff was male.

All of those perfectly reasoned points didn't stop her stomach from tightening at Heather's snicker. Leaning to her side, she tapped Hailey on the shoulder before nodding at Rachel. "What do you think Killian and Adam are going to do to her when that story hits the paper?"

"I don't know." Hailey shook her head, going along with the game. "But I'm thinking we're not going to be seeing much of her after."

"What do you mean?"

"I mean Killian and Adam are cops, Rachel." Hailey grinned, unable to help the mirth that bubbled into her tone. "I'm thinking you're going to be wearing metal cuffs once they find out about your little project."

Hailey had no idea. Being cuffed would be the least of her problems if Killian and Adam decided to take the argument to the bedroom. Rachel knew that possibility existed, but it only angered her. She didn't like being manipulated with sex.

"And that's my point," she shot back. "What am I supposed to do? Just give over because they're bigger and stronger?"

"And there are two of them," Hailey tacked on. "At least I only have to deal with one."

That caught Rachel off guard, breaking her annoyance with the conversation as Hailey's stupidity hit her. Hailey talked as if Kyle didn't have a partner, but everybody knew he did. Cole Jackson wasn't the kind of man women forgot and certainly not the kind a wise one would dismiss. His reputation would have made Casanova jealous.

Rachel could have held back her laughter at Hailey's absurdity if Heather hadn't started chuckling. She was just about to thank Hailey for making her realize somebody had it worse when the main door shoved open with a shout.

Wild catcalls and howls rolled into the bar as a group of boys piled in, stumbling with the effects of obvious inebriation. Seven…eight…nine of them, Rachel could already imagine what Killian would have to say about this situation. Time to get out before she got in trouble.

"Well, ladies," Heather sighed, "I think that's the end of the night."

Chapter 26

"This is all your fault."

Adam snorted at that, not even bothering to look in Killian's direction. Thursday night and so far the shift had been dead quiet. Killian and he had pulled their cars into the little clearing that flattened out at the top of a rolling curve. Killian had his radar pointed south and Adam north.

Maybe they'd get lucky and a drunk driver would come along. That would give Killian something to do besides bitch at Adam. Lord knew if something didn't happen soon, Adam might just have to assault his partner just to distract him off his merry-go-round moaning.

"If you hadn't dragged her off to the bedroom then we would have had time to sit down to a proper dinner and hear about this idiot idea of hers before we had to run out the door."

Adam rolled his eyes at that. "You started it. I wasn't the one who burned the fries."

"And I would have finished it in the kitchen with enough time left for dinner," Killian retorted instantly, cocky and annoyed at the same time. He wasn't wrong, though. It shouldn't have taken Adam the half hour it did to find satisfaction.

Hell, he hadn't found any, anyway. A week and half of shallow releases had made him desperate and itchy to finally find ease. It was all Rachel's fault. The damn woman refused to say she loved him again. Instinctively, Adam knew that's what he needed, but no matter how hard he pushed her, the words never whispered out of her lips.

Adam didn't understand why she denied him. Rachel had said it before. She had said it and meant it because he'd felt it. For the first time in all of his life, Adam had felt loved. He had felt the warm perfection he'd always imagined, but what Adam hadn't counted on was how cold and empty the world would be without it.

"I'll tell you one thing, that woman better be at home, safe and sound, like I told her, or there is going to be hell to pay." Killian grunted before eyeing the laptop mounted on the console of his dash. "You know we could get one of those security systems installed. They have cameras now, so you can check on things through the net."

At least he wasn't the only one acting weird lately. "You want to spy on Rachel?"

"Don't be stupid." Killian shot him a glare. "We work a lot of nights, and it would be nice to know she was safe when we weren't around."

"Yeah, I don't think Rachel's going to buy that excuse."

Actually, Adam could see her getting a little annoyed with them. Hell, two weeks ago he'd have said that Rachel would have Killian's balls, but things had changed since her birthday. Instead of lashing out at Killian's ever-growing domination, Rachel meekly appeared to accept every new rule and edict.

That wasn't her and Adam knew it. What he didn't know was why she'd changed. He guessed that she might be worried about losing them, thinking she had to be just what they wanted to hold on to them. It worried him because he couldn't help but wonder if she was keeping back her confession of love for fear of scaring them off.

"Maybe we should go ahead and tell her we love her?"

"What?" Killian's head snapped around to take in Adam as if he expected to find a second head spontaneously growing out of Adam's shoulder. "Where the hell did that come from?"

"I'm just saying, if you tell her you love her, she might let you put a security system in." That sounded lame to even Adam's ears, but it was all he could think of in the pinch. He sure as hell couldn't admit to his real worries with Killian still looking at him like he'd just confessed to wanting to wear a dress.

"That is the stupidest thing I have ever heard. I'm really beginning to wonder about you, man." Killian shook his head shamefully at Adam. "After all that grief you gave me about the weak thing and now you're suggesting *this*?"

"'You make me weak' was a really dumbass thing to say at that moment." Adam would never back down on that point. "But now she's said it, so—"

"So what? You think because she said it it's now safe to say it ourselves? That's just dumb because you know what happens after you tell women those three little words. They change.

"Trust me, I've seen it more times than I can count. A woman does herself up all nice and plays it sweet with a man until she knows she has him trapped, and then she starts with her little comments about how you should do this or that. She begins to get picky about your friends and make plans for you without asking. She—"

"—treats a man the way you've been treating Rachel?"

That had Killian going real still, his tone dropping dangerously. "Are you calling me a woman?"

"You're acting like one."

"Fine then," Killian snapped. "Go on and tell the girl you love her. Just don't come whining to me when you screw everything up."

Not about to sit quietly in the face of that accusation, Adam gave as good as he was getting. "Why would I do that? So you can tell me how to make it worse?"

"Me?" Killian looked honestly taken aback. "Am I not the one who got the girl to say, 'I love you,' huh? Am I not the one who has been leading us toward domestic bliss? Isn't that what you wanted?"

"Domestic bliss?" Adam snorted at that phrase. "Why don't you go write a damn poem, because you might actually be better at that than wooing a woman."

"I'm not the one using the word 'woo.'" Killian snickered. "And I stand by what I said. My ideas are working."

"Oh, really?" Adam didn't know how his friend could be so dense at times, but Killian honestly thought everything was going well. Everything but one little issue and Adam latched on to it. "So you don't think your sudden need to dictate every little thing to her and control every moment of her life is the reason our woman suddenly has a hankering to go off to…what was it you said about the bar?"

"Bars can be a dangerous place for a woman without a man." Now Killian was lecturing him, but Adam didn't need a keeper. He didn't think Rachel did, either.

"Yeah, she could poke an eye out with a pool stick."

Adam's easily dismissal only had Killian digging in. "Dart accidents can be serious."

Adam couldn't argue that without bringing up one of Killian's favorite grudges—the time Adam had accidently stabbed his friend. Still, he wouldn't be cowed. "Or maybe that one beer she always drinks will go right to her head and she'll end up dancing on the tables naked."

He shouldn't have provided Killian with any more support for his paranoia because obviously his friend didn't get the joke. "Drinks left alone can lead to drugging and rape."

"She could be starting a bar fight right now."

"People *die* in bar fights, Adam."

"You're turning into a born-again prude," Adam complained. "Maybe Rachel just wants to have some fun."

"And you're *not* taking her out to the club, so don't even get that dirty idea started."

Killian must have had ESP because he'd blocked the direction Adam had intended to turn the conversation. It irked Adam that Killian wouldn't even talk about the idea because he knew once he had Rachel out there, he could get her to confess again. Better yet, this time the whole club would hear her. Then everybody would know and the damn itch in his gut would surely die down.

"I'm not kidding." Killian filled the silence, obviously worried over Adam's failure to agree. "You know damn well where that will lead."

"To hell of a lot of fun?" As far as Adam was concerned, having a girlfriend who would enjoy the Cattleman's Club benefits ranked as a miracle. Killian did not share his sentiment or Adam's sense of humor.

"Go on and laugh it up, funny man, but this is going to blow up all over us. See, she's just beginning, and you remember what it was like in the beginning. You can never get enough."

"Man, what a curse, a horny girlfriend who likes it rough. I'm going to write a complaint to Santa."

"See, it's that attitude," Killian leveled a finger over the gap between their cruisers, "that's going to ruin everything. Sure, you'll get your collar on her first, but how long do you think it's going to be before some buck tries to challenge that authority? And don't even *think* that's not going to happen."

Adam wouldn't fool himself into thinking Killian didn't have a point. He knew damn good and straight that they'd done the same thing in their single days to enough club members to have a long list of eager Cattlemen waiting to bring them down. Rachel could easily become very popular, but she wouldn't let herself.

While Killian obsessed over what they'd unleashed with her birthday surprise, Adam marveled at what he'd gained. Rachel wasn't a club girl. This wasn't just a wild fling or some experiential vacation for her. Like Killian had originally assured him, she was a good girl.

Good girls didn't give themselves that completely with total trust to men unless she'd already given them her heart. Adam just wished she'd admit it. If it took taking her out to the club to get his confession, then so be it.

"Rachel isn't going to stray. Any man who gets into her bed will be a man we put there."

"Don't even think about taking things to that level." Killian looked about as panicked as Adam ever had seen. "The last thing we need to be showing her is that one dick is as good as the next. What the hell do you think will happen then?"

"Then we take her home and show her that one man isn't as good as another." Because that's what it was really all about. Not that Adam was all that eager to let another man touch what was his, but it would be the ultimate show of trust, of love.

"Why can't we just be thankful that we steered her clear of the sheriff and that stupid prostitution thing? Then instead of focusing on how to ruin our good thing, we can try convincing her to stay at home when we have night patrol?"

"Then we can paint her a nice white picket fence and get her a little purse dog to carry around." Adam rolled his eyes. "You're the one that's going to ruin everything if you keep trying to make Rachel into something she's not."

"Me?" Killian growled. "I'm not the one who took a sweet, wholesome lady and turned her into an insatiable sex kitten."

Killian could cry on all he wanted. Adam knew he appreciated Rachel's more than healthy appetites. Adam would have loved to get a comeback in on that one, but the radio started squawking and their quiet Thursday began to show a little life.

* * * *

Nobody ever listened to him. Killian knew they all thought he was just some big, dumb redneck. So they dismissed his worries as extreme and laughed at him. Well, Adam wasn't laughing now. Hell, nobody was, except for Kyle Harding who danced around Killian like a puppy ready for action.

"Just tell her I'm too drunk to drive myself home." Kyle's eyebrows wiggled as he nodded enthusiastically over his own suggestion.

Killian ignored him, preferring to glare through the sea of flashing lights to where Rachel sat on the tail of the fire department's medical response truck. With half her jaw already swollen, she wasn't even able to smile without pain right now. Of course, if she'd listened to him, she'd be home, safe and sound, instead of having to answer whatever questions Brandon pestered her with.

That's where I told her to stay. He'd been an idiot to assume she'd listen to him, but he had told her anyway. Killian figured she'd been listening to everything these past couple of weeks. Why, though, went beyond him right then. Rachel had already been caught once keeping secrets. Now he had to wonder if she didn't have a few more tucked away.

"Come on, man, just do me this one favor." Kyle Harding's stupid face blocked out the sight of Mickey tending to Rachel and forced Killian to crane his neck to get the view back. "I promise you do this for me and I'll owe you whatever you name."

Killian growled, casting Kyle a dirty look for bothering him with his nonsense. Nothing but an eager smile and a pathetically hopeful gleam in his gaze. There would be no getting rid of him. At least not quick enough for Killian's patience.

"See, if you just do me—Hey, now!" Kyle hollered when Killian suddenly latched on to his elbow. "Watch it, buddy!"

Killian didn't know if it was a part of Kyle's act or if he was lodging a sincere complaint. He didn't care, either. Dragging Kyle behind him, Killian used his considerable bulk and foul disposition to send both Mickey and Brandon scattering. He wanted to have a private word with Rachel and even Hailey Mathews with her stubborn chin turned up at him wouldn't be getting in his way.

Killian thrust Kyle at her, not about to be intimidated by the tiny redheaded spitfire. "I think this belongs to you."

"Then maybe you shouldn't be doing too much thinking."

Killian almost didn't catch her sour mutter as Kyle talked right over, playing up the drunk thing with a wobble and a wide grin. "Hey, Hailey. You see me whoop that guy?"

"Yeah, I saw you step in unwanted and make an ass of yourself. What of it?"

Tuning out the couple as they bickered, Killian caught Rachel's eye. No upturned chin from her. With a bow of her head, she tried to appear submissive, but it was a lie.

"Touch me again and I'll whoop you myself right here, boy." Hailey's bark masked a retreat that only had Kyle stumbling after her.

At least I'm not trying to tame the feral. That cold comfort brought the first smirk to his features since arriving to find Rachel trapped in the middle of a bar fight. Whatever Kyle's game was, he obviously did need some help. Hell, if Kyle managed to leash Hailey, Rachel would be down one partner in crime.

"Well, don't hit him here," Killian finally spoke up, interrupting the couple as Hailey fought to keep Kyle's arm from her shoulder. "Then I'd have to arrest you for assault, so why don't you take him home and beat him in the privacy of his own house?"

"You heard the deputy, dumbass. Get. Lost."

Kyle's nose dipped until it bumped into Hailey's before he responded to her last two shouted words with his own smug ones. "Can't. Drive."

"Then walk."

"I could wander into the street and get hit by a car."

"I'd suggest you avoid the street then."

"Come on, Hailey." Killian lent the authority of his position to Kyle's cause. "I can't let a drunk wander off, and I can't let him drive. I'd appreciate if you drove him home. Otherwise, I'll have to drive him to the station."

"Yeah, Hailey, you don't want to piss off the already pissed off deputy."

It had only taken Kyle a second to make Killian regret even dragging him over in the first place. Of course, Hailey did a good job of annoying him with all her questions.

"If you can drive him to the station, why can't you drive him home?"

"Not allowed to have civilian passengers in the cruiser because of liability reasons. He gets in the car. He goes to the station." Killian paused, casting a look at the top of Rachel's head since she refused to look up and meet his gaze. "Besides, I have other things that need to be attended to."

That had Rachel's chin snapping up, showing off not only her narrowing gaze but her swollen cheek. "You better not be referring to me as a thing."

"I'm sure he was referring to the men we're hauling down to the station," Alex cut in smoothly.

The sheriff's sudden help didn't come across as sincere to Killian. Instead, his arrival only prickled Killian's nerves. Not that he could do a thing about it. The sheriff-deputy thing really got in the way. The rotten bastard used that to his advantage, stepping right in between Rachel and him.

"I'm going to need you to come down to the station to give a statement and swear out a warrant."

Before Killian could assure the sheriff he'd handle Rachel, Hailey perked up, all too eager to help. "I'll give a statement."

"You," Alex said, turning a scowl loose on the couple in front of him, "get that drunk ass out of here before I change my mind and have Killian haul him down to the station, too."

God, but the woman was beyond stubborn and ballsy, too. Instead of giving in to the inevitable, she just stood there glaring at the sheriff, silently refusing to obey that order. Killian was pretty sure Alex wouldn't be getting Hailey's vote in the next election.

"Come on, Hailey." Killian tried to coax her with a sincere tone. "He really did fail his sobriety test. We can't just let him go without knowing somebody is looking after him."

"Fine. I'll look after the sorry bastard." Hailey looked ready to bite Kyle as she held her hand out. "Give me your damn keys."

Kyle grinned, throwing his arm over her shoulders and using his weight to steer her away, no doubt before she changed her mind. She might if the boy didn't take it easy.

"They're right here in my pocket, darlin'. Wanna fish them out for me?"

Killian watched the couple go after each other as they headed toward Kyle's truck. It didn't take much intuition to figure out how their night would end. The only thing he couldn't figure out was where the hell Cole was.

Not that Killian really cared about the answer. He had his own, much bigger, problems to deal with—like getting rid of the sheriff. Alex met his gaze, and Killian could almost read the thoughts in the other man's mind. He wanted Killian gone.

"I think maybe it's best if you clock out for the night."

Son of a bitch. Killian wouldn't be taken out that easily. "And I think maybe I should be taking care of Rachel's statement, given that she is my girlfriend."

The corner of Alex's lip curled upward in such a smug twist Killian knew he'd stepped into some trap. The problem was he didn't know what he'd just done. Not that Alex would explain it. Rachel might if the way her look darkened was any indication.

"That's just why I need you to clock out. I can't have those boys' lawyer arguing anything improper happened, which he will the moment he finds out the responding officer's girlfriend was injured in the fight."

The cocky bastard had reason on his side. Not to mention the authority of his position. "Fine. I'm sure, though, that the lawyer couldn't complain that I was with her as her off-duty boyfriend."

"You and Adam?" Alex shook his head. "I'd hate to see some slimeball decide to try and convince a judge that Rachel likes to manipulate men into fighting over her, and you know how some defense lawyers love to rip into innocent victims."

"Oh, please," Rachel muttered. "Like this is even going to go to trial. Now the two of you stop it."

Killian didn't like the way she so easily dismissed the importance of this case, much less the way she spoke to them like they were children. He wasn't the idiot who had gotten himself into a bar fight. "Stop what? Stop caring that an innocent woman was injured in a fit of violence by a bunch of hot-heads trying to prove something?"

"I'm not really injured, Killian." There came that tone again, annoyed and condescending all at once. "The guy's fist barely glanced off me. Nothing is even broken."

Her complete dismissal of the danger made every one of Killian's muscles clench with frustration. "Well, it could have been. It could have been a hell of a lot worse than broken. You could have died. He could have hit you and you could have fallen over, cracked your head on the table or the floor, and died right there!"

Rachel snorted, not even bothering to respond to him.

"These things happen," Killian found himself insisting. "Tell her, Alex."

"They do, sometimes." Alex shrugged before proving why Killian really was the idiot in the group to ask for his help. "But obviously not tonight, and I think you've proven just why you need to go home and cool off. I can't have you near those boys in the state you're in."

Killian couldn't hit the sheriff, at least not here and now in front of Rachel. He certainly couldn't put her over his knee and paddle her as he itched to. All he could do was simmer and brood and wait until he had Rachel all to himself, alone in the privacy of their bedroom.

"Fine," Killian ground the word out despite how much it hurt him, "I guess I'll see you at home, then."

Turning, he didn't once look back as he stormed off toward his cruiser. He'd have made it there incident free if Adam hadn't come jogging out of the bar and into his path. Now there was somebody he could hit.

"Hey, man, where you headed?"

Killian flattened him with one good punch and kept on walking.

Chapter 27

"I cannot believe she got into a bar fight. *A bar fight.*"

Adam held the ice pack to his jaw and sighed back into the couch. What a long night it had been for so few hours to have passed. Real time didn't matter to his body. He was sore and tired and kind of cranky, given he'd been punched for no good reason.

"Did you see her cheek? It was all swollen and bruised. She could have broken her jaw, if not her damn head."

He could have, too, though Adam didn't think Killian would care much right then if he'd died. Adam could forgive Killian for his insensitivity, even his violent reaction. It wasn't like he approved of the girl getting herself hit or cared to sit around while the sheriff played hero to his lady. Still, Adam figured his night would be going about fifty percent better if Killian would just stop yelling at him.

"This is all your fault."

Adam didn't know how Killian had come to that conclusion. He hadn't gone all bossy on the girl. Nor had Adam lied about anything. As far as he could tell, this nightmare had resulted from both Rachel and Killian's inability to communicate.

"What's next? *What?*"

Adam didn't know, but he suspected it wouldn't be good. Even if Rachel shared some of the blame for this disaster of a night, now would probably not be a good time to go all commando on the girl. Tomorrow would be soon enough to get the ropes out and get down to another confession. That is, if Killian could wait.

Adam bet he couldn't. Instead, he had a feeling that Rachel would come in that door about as sore and annoyed as Adam felt right then.

With Killian's temper greeting her at the first step it would probably be like a spark to a powder keg.

"Well, I'm not going to wait to find out. No, sir. I'm going to paddle that ass so hard she wouldn't be able to leave this house for a week."

Killian was all blustered. Adam knew for certain that Killian wouldn't hit Rachel.

"Fuck that, it will take a whole month to talk some sense into that woman—"

No matter what he said.

"—not that the woman has much of that to start with. She should be damn happy to have us taking care of her. She should be home at night waiting on us, making our house right and our lives easier. Not out there, tearing up the town like some wanna-be teenager chasing after every stupid-ass idea that pops into her empty little head."

Of course, Rachel might hit Killian. Adam knew Killian didn't mean what he said, but he also knew Rachel wouldn't care. Some things couldn't be taken back and others could never be forgiven. Maybe it was actually time to try and cool Killian down because Rachel would be home soon.

"And to go off with the sheriff? The *sheriff*? That punk's making his move right now, acting all calm and reasonable, trying to make me look all insane and jealous. Like I would be."

"No, of course not. You're acting in a completely calm, reasonable, and sane fashion right now."

Adam lowered the icepack from his throbbing jaw to meet Killian's dark glare with his own pointed look. The staring match lasted a good minute and kept Killian grounded for all sixty seconds before he muttered an obscenity and turned back to his pacing. This time he kept his bitching under his breath, but Adam still caught pieces.

"…idiot started this in the first place…" Killian curved around the edge of the sofa, his voice fading out until he'd passed her desk and came back around the edge. "…my good girl and turned her into…"

Killian's good girl had returned, judging from the headlights flashing through the room. They must have sliced right through Killian's skin because the big man jumped. With the smooth, gracefulness of an ox, Killian managed to knock over a whole stack of papers piled on the side of her desk with his hurried motions.

"Way to go, slick."Adam chunked the ice pack onto the coffee table and pushed off to his feet.

Things would be bad enough once Rachel got a whiff of Killian's foul mood. They didn't need to be made worse by throwing her things all about or snooping through them. Adam intentionally bumped Killian, who had bent down to pick up the papers but gotten sidelined reading them.

Shuffling the rest on the floor, Adam felt compelled to pull on the stack Killian had curling in his fists when a car door slammed. "Come on, man, we got like—"

"What the hell is this?"

* * * *

Rachel stalled at the door, staring at it as dread mounted in her stomach. The sick sensation tightened, making it all the harder to reach out and turn the knob. Killian and Adam waited on the other side, and it didn't take a genius to guess what their moods would be.

Or where she'd be heading the moment she walked through the door—back to the bedroom. This time they'd probably be particularly brutal, especially Killian. Rachel had seen the darkness in his eyes, but the redness in his ears was what really worried her. When he got flushed, she knew somebody had really managed to piss him off.

Before tonight that somebody had never actually been her. Even on her birthday, Adam had played the heavy, and Killian had said she'd made him weak. Well, she'd probably return that favor tonight. Only, she was already feeling weak. Weak, tired, sore, and worse, guilty, Rachel didn't have a single bit of happiness to cling to right then.

It didn't matter that she hadn't technically lied to them about staying in tonight or that she was old enough to do as she pleased. Staring at the door, Rachel felt the dread of a teenager coming home to face an irate parent. Except that she was a woman returning to her lovers.

They weren't supposed to behave like fathers. That really irritated her, helping her to take one step forward and reach for the doorknob. Inhaling a deep breath, she twisted and pushed. She expected a full-on blasting the second the door creaked all the way open. What she hadn't expected was to be the one doing it.

"What the hell is this?" Rachel couldn't believe what her eyes showed. With Killian and Adam on their knees with her papers splayed out between them, it looked an awful lot like she'd caught them snooping.

At least Adam had the decency to act startled and try to defend himself. Shooting to his feet, he dropped the papers he'd been holding. They cascaded into a fine mess even as he tried to explain.

"It isn't what it—"

"I want to know what the hell you think you're doing." Adam couldn't speak fast enough to soothe her temper. Nor was he the one who she really wanted to talk to. Killian dominated her attention as he rose up, the papers clutched in his white-knuckled fists trembling. Pissed didn't even begin to describe his expression, but Rachel didn't care. She'd had enough.

Flinging her purse over the couch, she met him as he shoved Adam out of the way.

"I could ask you the same question. What are *these*?" Killian rattled the papers right in Rachel's face, causing her to snatch them out of his hands.

"They're my personal, *private* papers, so what are *you* doing with them?"

"How did you get these files? *They* are supposed to be *private*."

"What files?" Adam asked from the side.

Not that she paid him any attention. "Oh, please." Rachel snorted. "Like your preference for big-boobed redheads who like to suck cocks like lollipops is some great secret?"

"You aren't supposed to have these." The veins stuck right out of Killian's corded neck as he flushed so badly with his roar.

But she did, and where she'd gotten them, how many files she had, and just what kind of mischief she might be up to would all be questions they'd want answers to. Rachel tilted her chin up, deciding then and there that she wouldn't be giving any answers. *They're cops. They can figure it out their damn selves.*

"What are these?"

Ah, crap. She should have paid Adam more attention. Now she'd pay for that mistake because he'd scooped up some papers. They weren't Cattlemen files but something a whole lot worse. Not that they should be. Rachel had grown about sick of the argument she could feel coming.

It was stupid and dumb. She treated it as such, barely sparing Adam a glance as she shrugged. "They'd be my confidential files. You know, ones most cops would need a warrant—"

"Don't." Adam didn't need an incendiary bellow. All he needed was a whispered snarl to make her feel threatened. "I want to know what these are."

Not in any mood to indulge him no matter how much he growled at her, Rachel remained firm in her response. "They're my work notes and no concern of yours."

"No concern?" Adam repeated, only to be drowned out by Killian's impatience.

"I want to know who gave you these."

"Like I'm going to tell you my source," Rachel shot back at Killian before sharing her glare with Adam. "*Or you.*"

"Wanna bet?" Adam's drawl thickened, becoming deep and velvety. Rachel knew what followed that tone, but she wouldn't stand for it tonight. "You're going to start explaining why you've been lying to me and what you're planning to do with those notes, and then we're going to discuss your punishment."

That broke her. Before Rachel could think better of it, she snatched the papers out of Adam's hand. With one roll of her hand, she had a whacking stick that she made instant use of to pop Adam then Killian until they stumbled backward.

"I have had just about enough of *both* of you. With your snotty-ass commands and obnoxious-ass babbling about punishments. Well, let me tell you something, cowboy. If you don't stop pissing me off, I'm going throw both your arrogant asses out on the street."

Adam had danced all the way back to the dining room's arched opening, driven nearly into the other room by a relentless pelting of slaps to his shoulders. Growling over Rachel's rampage, he snatched the roll right out of her hand and took a brave step forward.

"I'd like to see you try."

"It won't be hard," Rachel assured him before taking the fight below the belt. "I'll just give Alex a call."

Adam reeled for a second like she'd actually dealt him a punch to the gut. She might as well have. She left him gasping for air, the papers crinkling into a ball as his fist went white around the knuckles. "That had better not be who's been helping you with this project because don't doubt, little lady, I can tell somebody has."

"So what of it?"

Adam jaw clenched so hard he had to strain to crack his lips open enough to form words. "You promised us—"

"Under duress, you really think that you can rely on a person to keep her word when you forced her to give it in the first place?" All the annoyance and frustration of the past couple of weeks had broken the dam. Rachel couldn't stop the flood of words pouring out her mouth.

"Obviously, I don't need your help because I already have it, which is actually part of my job, and I'm getting good and sick of having to hide things and justify everything to you two. I shouldn't have to because I'm a capable, independent woman and not some idiot child that needs the two of you to oversee every fucking thing in *my* life.

"So let's get everything straight right now." Turning on Killian, she lit into him in the rapid-fire manner of an auctioneer. "Those files were given to me by a source and, no, I'm not going to tell you now or ever who that was. But you can relax. I'm not using them for any story.

"And you," Rachel turned back to Adam. "I am researching my prostitution story. I am doing it my way. I don't care what you think about it. I don't even want to hear one damn word about it. Got it?"

"Then how about two? 'Hell' and 'no.'"

"Go fuck yourself, Killian, because you aren't sleeping in my bed tonight. Neither are you," Rachel shot at Adam a second before she brushed him aside and stormed out of the room. Slamming her bedroom door vented none of her anger.

Instead, it ballooned it into dread as she waited for the door to shove open. Nothing happened. Neither one of her men came after her but left her standing there trembling so badly she couldn't breathe. What had she done?

The way she had spoken to them burned inside her head, multiplying the misery as her conscience whispered they'd been right. She shouldn't have had their files, shouldn't have read them. She should have told them about her research. She should have done everything differently because everything had started to unravel.

Sucking in a squeal with a painful breath, Rachel rushed over to the bed, collapsing into it in time to smother her sob. The end had begun. It hurt even worse than she'd imagined. Her heart called her every type of fool because all she had to do was what they wanted. If she'd obey, she could hold on to them...*for a little longer.*

Delayed, that's all the pain could be. Nothing could stop this, her mind whispered back. Nothing but Killian or Adam. One of them could have come to her, checked on her. They didn't because they didn't love her. How could she change for men like that?

* * * *

Killian watched Rachel walk away, feeling a nearly uncontrollable need to race after her and make her heed his authority. A very small sliver of reason, all that he had left, assured him that wouldn't work. He had to be careful to play this smart. Smart meant giving her a little room and time to calm down, no matter how much it rankled him.

If Adam could do it, he could, too. Amazingly enough, the big dumbass actually stood his ground. Panting, making little snarly noises but nevertheless, Adam's feet stayed planted firmly to the floor. "This is all your fault."

"Me?"

It didn't matter if Adam had a point. Primed and ready for the fight Rachel had denied him, Killian would be glad to take out his aggression on his friend. Of course, tearing up Rachel's house wouldn't win them any warmth from their woman.

"I think we should finish this discussion outside."

"After you." Adam gestured toward the kitchen and the backdoor. As civilized as they could be under the circumstances, both men piled out into the backyard and politely removed watches along with shirts before squaring off.

This was how they always solved their big arguments. They fought it out. Once they drained all their energy then they might be able to get around to talking. That's how they'd used sex with Rachel for the past couple of weeks, but apparently that hadn't won them any golden stars. For her, Killian would take the beating.

"Okay, then." Killian clenched his fist as he raised them up, issuing Adam a warning in the process. "I'm not going to give you any free shots because of earlier, either."

"Wasn't expecting any," Adam retorted a split second before he threw his first punch.

For the next half hour, Killian ducked, rolled, punched, and kicked, and ended up bruised, scraped, and sore by the time they finished. The yard didn't fare much better, but they'd managed to keep things quiet enough not to draw Rachel outside or tempt any of the neighbors into calling the cops.

Still, Killian suspected Rachel wouldn't be thankful for either once she saw her trampled flower beds and squashed tomatoes. Killian had enough red goo smeared across his pants to make it look like he'd been through a blood bath.

He was bleeding, but only a few trickles from around his brow and lip and over his cracking knuckles. They were raw and red and would ache worse the coming morning, but it had all been worth it. Violence or sex, it all ended the same. When he got hot like that, Killian needed some kind of release. It all ended the same, with him feeling good.

"I need a beer." Or something to wash the coppery taste out of his mouth. "I think I might have bit my lip."

For some reason, that made Adam laugh. Turning his head to glance over the few wooden slats that separated him, he smirked at Killian. "You want me to go get you one?"

"Like you can stand." Killian snorted. If Adam got up, then he'd have to. Otherwise, it would be like admitting Adam won the fight. That would never happen.

"I could if I wanted to," Adam muttered, rolling his head back toward the stars. "Just don't feel like it now."

"I know what you mean." That would be a draw. Now they could both sit there and come to the realization that as good as the fight had been, they still had a problem on their hands. "So what are we going to do about Rachel?"

Adam inhaled an audible breath before letting it sigh out. "I really don't know."

"She lied to us about staying home tonight and about her researching the prostitution book." There was no heat left in Killian's tone as he listed Rachel's sins. He didn't have the energy to be mad right then. "Not to mention working with somebody else and getting herself into a bar fight. But what I really want to know is who the hell gave her those Cattlemen files."

Because if it was the sheriff, Killian wouldn't care if he lost his job or ended up in jail. The two of them would be having a conversation.

"Isn't it obvious?" Apparently, it was to Adam because he sounded very sure of himself. Only, he hadn't picked out the same culprit as Killian. "Rachel was at that bar tonight with Hailey Mathews. Her good friend Hailey Mathews."

By Adam's tone, Killian knew he should be getting a clue right about then, but he had nothing. "So?"

"Hailey Mathews's best friend is? Come on, Killian, you know the answer to that one."

He sure as hell did. Patton Jones, the Davis brothers' woman. The Davis brothers had stared the club. They owned and managed every aspect of the club, including maintaining all the records.

"Son of a bitch." Killian had never had a soft spot for Patton. Not like most men developed when they got a good look at the girl. She might be hot, but she also acted like a man. All bossy, demanding, and even combative, she was a damn feminist. Of course, it could be because she'd been raised in a house full of men.

Either way, Killian liked his women sweet, like Rachel was when she wasn't telling him to go fuck himself. "Hell, you don't think she's the one riling Rachel to act all bitchy tonight? Maybe it's Hailey, birds of a feather and all that. She didn't seem particularly sweet this evening and—"

"No." Adam squashed Killian's budding hope that the answer could be that simple. "Don't even try to blame that girl for your own screw-ups."

"My screw-ups?"

"Yes, yours," Adam repeated, only sounding more firm in his conviction. "You're the one who's been bossing that girl around for the past two weeks, treating her like a damn child."

Killian bristled at that accusation. He didn't think of Rachel as a child, but she was sweet and soft and didn't understand how hard and brutal the world could be. "I'm just trying to keep her safe. What do you want me to do? Encourage the girl to go off and interview pimps and whores?"

"Of course not," Adam snapped, "but that doesn't mean you have to take away the girl's coffee in the morning."

"She didn't object."

"And don't you find that odd?" Adam turned toward Killian. Straightening off the fence to face him head-on, he had to brace a hand on the ground to hold himself in position. "I mean, seriously, the girl's been way too complacent lately."

It hurt, but Killian managed to offer up a shrug at that observation. "She's settling down. It's what most women do."

"No she ain't." Adam scoffed. "If she were settling down, she wouldn't be going through our Cattlemen files or researching a book behind our backs, and she certainly wouldn't be using another cop to help or getting caught in *bar fights.*"

Killian hated to admit that Adam had a point, but the evidence couldn't be denied. "So what do you think it is?"

"I think she told us she loved us and we never said it back."

"Oh, God," Killian groaned. He'd rather give in on the club issue than this. Adam didn't understand, though. He thought those words actually meant something, but Killian had been hearing them all his life.

They were just words. What really counted were actions, and as far as he could see, Rachel didn't trust them, so how could she love them? He could have asked that question of Adam, but he didn't have it in his heart to hurt his friend that way.

Hell, he'd thought she'd meant it when she said it. If Killian hadn't discovered all her secrets tonight, he'd probably still believe Rachel's confession. Obviously, though, it had been a moment of passion, but that didn't mean it couldn't become real.

They just had to figure out how to get her to trust them.

"I say we tell her we love her, and then you back off on all your little dictates."

"I'm not telling her I love her." Not until she said it and meant it first. "But you might be right about the other. Maybe it's time to use a little subtlety."

Adam snorted. "Do you even know what that word means?"

Chapter 28

Friday, May 2nd

The tantalizing scents of strong coffee and delicious bacon roused Rachel from her fitful sleep the next morning. She didn't wake rested or happy, no matter how much sunshine flowed through the windows to greet her. The sheets were cool on either side of her and had been all night.

At least they hadn't left. She really hadn't wanted them to. A part of Rachel regretted last night, wishing she had stayed in. Then none of this would have happened. It didn't matter if reason argued that it would have happened eventually. Sleeping alone felt more miserable than she wanted to bear.

They were like the bacon that lured her from her bed, delicious and bad for her in every single way. Loving them shouldn't mean sacrificing everything she was for them, but it did. Her affection twisted her pride to the point where Rachel almost didn't care what it would cost her to become the woman they wanted, even if only for a moment.

Hell, wasn't the art of every relationship compromise? Then again, putting on a little makeup to look pretty wasn't the same thing as going to a doctor to have him mold her into a beauty. Rachel couldn't do it. That left her with no answer or defense prepared as she slipped into her robe and went to face the men who had put her in this untenable position.

Expecting something of a confrontation, Rachel stepped into the kitchen, braced for round two. They caught her off guard with their smiles, smiles that cracked already busted lips. Taking a double look at both men, Rachel was appalled to realize they both looked worse than her that morning.

She only had a faint bruise darkening her cheek, but they had bruises all over. Not that either appeared the least bit sore from what had obviously been a raging battle. Rachel could guess from their busted knuckles what the two of them had gotten into, but why, when, and where escaped her.

"Morning, darlin'." Busy at the stove, Adam nodded to her.

"Here." A big mug full of rich-smelling coffee floated in front of her nose. Killian handed over the cup before gesturing to the dining room table. "Go on and have a seat. Adam will have your breakfast up in a moment."

They were up to something, but Rachel didn't know what. It was too early and the coffee smelled too good for her to bother starting an argument. Accepting the coffee as a peace offering, she settled down at the table. Sure enough, a moment later, Adam lowered down a plate loaded with bacon, hash, and a perfectly prepared omelet.

Loaded with mushrooms and parmesan, the fluffy yellow offering turned out to be a trick because it was really hard to bitch at them with her mouth full of food.

Seating himself at her side, Adam began the conversation with a bit of politeness. "Is it good?"

"Mmm-hmm." Rachel nodded her head. "Very."

"I'm glad you like it." Adam smiled and then blew her hopes of just forgetting last night altogether. "You know, it's not that we don't want you to eat well or enjoy your life but—"

Adam shot a pointed look in Killian's direction in a clear signal for him to pick up on his own explanation. Clearing his throat and straightening up, he did. "But we want you to be healthy and safe."

Rachel glanced from Killian's serious expression to Adam's earnest one and recognized they were trying. To what end, she didn't know, but Rachel wanted this to work too much not to aid the effort.

Instead of coming back with a smartass comment about how dangerous coffee might be, she strived for a more mature attitude.

"I understand that." She did. Rachel wanted them to be both of those things all the time. As deputies, they couldn't promise her half of what she could promise them. "But I am healthy…enough and I don't exactly engage in risky behavior."

"You were in a bar fight last night."

It must have hurt Killian to say that without growling because he almost flinched over his words. The fact that it cost him so much to remain rational sounding made Rachel appreciate the attempt all the more.

"It wasn't like I went out looking for one or started it, Killian." Rachel couldn't help the slight pitch of annoyance lifting her tone as she pointed out those obvious facts. She tried to cover it up by talking on until her frustration mellowed out of her voice. "Anybody anywhere can run into trouble. Hell, I could be driving down a street and a tree could fall on my car and kill me, or a drunk driver—"

"Trust me," Killian cut in, impatience shading his words, "that's just all the more reason to take every precaution."

"I think what Killian is trying to say is that we want to minimize any risk you're exposed to." Adam's fast-paced interruption showed his rush to avoid what had started to become a tense conversation. "You know, something can be made safer by really thinking through the consequences and—"

"Are you trying to say I'm too stupid to know when something is dangerous?" Rachel didn't need to hear any more of Adam's fancy talk. She could read between the lines.

"Of course not." Adam flushed, shooting her annoyed glare. "You're trying to twist this conversation into an argument, and all we're trying to say is if you go to a bar with your friends, you should tell us."

"Because I'll be safer," Rachel concluded, appearing to appease Killian when he nodded.

"Absolutely."

"And exactly how is that?" Rachel glanced between the two men, who were scowling. "What are you two going to do? Go sit in front of the bar?"

There went Killian's ears, turning bright red and telling her she'd guessed right. Of course, he denied it. "No, but then we will know to check on you, give you a call and make sure you got home all right, and you can wipe that smirk off your face, girl. There isn't anything unusual about that. Lots of couples do it."

He might have a point, but Rachel couldn't help her suspicious nature. "So, if I told you, say…I'm going up to the county jail to do an interview, you'd just call and check to make sure I had a safe drive. Nothing else."

Of course not, and Killian didn't even bother to lie but automatically assumed her example to be real. "Why would you go to the county jail?"

"See, that's my point." Rachel paid his real question about as much attention as he had her implied one. "I don't have to explain or justify my actions to you, either of you. I'm not some idiot who needs you to do her thinking for her. To treat me that way tells me you don't have any respect for me."

"You want to cry on about how we don't respect you, but you know what, Rachel?" Killian paused, taking a moment to calm his tone down slightly before taking his best shot. "You don't respect us."

Rachel's jaw fell open and sputters came out, but she didn't actually have a response for that one.

"That's right." He didn't give her the time she needed to recover and blast him. Keeping her head spinning, he nodded over his own conclusion. "You think we're a couple of idiot men, unable to change or be reasoned with. In fact, you refused to even take our courtship seriously from the beginning, writing us off as incapable of being the kind of mature men that would be able to keep up with the likes of you. Well, you know what, honey?"

Rachel clicked her teeth shut, hating the way he drew out that endearment.

"We ain't the ones running around lying about things, keeping secrets behind *your* back. We've been open and honest with you from the beginning. Now I think it's time you started giving us equal measure."

As much as she really wanted to take on that fight, Rachel couldn't deny he had a point. She never really had given them a chance, always assuming she knew what their reactions would be. Even recognizing her bias didn't stop her from thinking she was right. Still, they did have a right to screw up before she got mad at them for it.

Adam must have sensed the weakness in her hesitation because he brought all his tender charm into play when he covered her hand with his. "Killian may be a bastard—"

"My parents were married, thank you."

"—but he isn't wrong. We wouldn't worry so much if we didn't care so much. I know you've probably thought this is all just a game to us, but it isn't, Rachel. We love you, and we want to build something here, but that's going to require trust and compromise on both parts."

Rachel blinked, staring at Adam with wonder. She couldn't believe he'd sunk so low. Those were the words her heart had been aching to hear, words that had been whispered to her in her dreams, but she'd never imagined he'd use them to get her to submit. This was worse than when he'd used sex against her because she had no defense.

No matter what her mind reasoned, her heart wouldn't listen. It had heard what it wanted and overruled any objections. Maybe he meant it. Maybe if she tried to trust them, they'd surprise her. Hope filled her, moving her to make the riskiest decision of her life.

"You're right." That appeared to stun both men, making them cast nervous glances at each other as they no doubt tried to figure out this unpredicted move. "This relationship isn't going to work without trust and compromise, so I'll make a deal with you. I will tell you everything, but you don't get to make my decisions for me, nor do you have the right to punish me for the ones I make that you don't like."

She'd trust, but they'd compromise. There could be no other way to move forward. Adam appeared to understand and didn't hesitate to agree. "I can do that."

They both turned to look at Killian, who glared back. True to his difficult nature, he needed clarifications. "Then what the hell do we get to punish you for?"

Rachel couldn't help but smile at the whine hidden in Killian's words. "I promise to give you ample reasons to go all He-Man on me, Killian."

"Okay." Killian didn't look appeased but determined. "Then answer me one other question. Do you regret reading our Cattlemen files?"

That caught Rachel off guard. She didn't have a clue how to answer. Her heart regretted because it had hurt, but her mind reveled because it had wanted to know. Either way, she couldn't guess which answer would appease Killian the most. The honest one revealed too much of her emotions. Despite Adam's confession or her agreement, Rachel wasn't ready to let the secret into the world.

"Because the way I see it," Killian continued on after giving her a moment, "is there isn't much difference between you reading our private files and us going through your private papers. Is there?"

Rachel hated being wrong, especially when she kept turning out that way this morning. "I guess."

"And since you punished us last night by kicking us out of your bed for our sins, don't you think we should get equal measure?"

He'd led her right to the water's edge, but Rachel refused to drink. "I guess that depends on whether or not you agree to my suggestion."

"I'll agree, but I want the file incident grandfathered in."

He should have been a lawyer or a union negotiator because more than being stubborn, Killian had a valid point. "Fine, but this is the last time you're using sex against me."

"Against you?" Killian snorted. "Don't even complain like that, Rachel. We know you loved every single second when we got you in those ropes."

She might have, but that didn't mean it didn't cost her the next morning when she realized the night had meant the same thing to them. "Just promise me."

"Fine. I promise. No more using sex *against* you."

Chapter 29

Wednesday, May 7th

Adam had interfered before the conversation soured after that crack by Killian. Still, with Killian sitting there glowering at her, Rachel hadn't been inspired to give their new agreement her full cooperation. Not that she could have.

It didn't matter if Patton hadn't asked for her loyalty, Rachel still couldn't rat her out to Killian and Adam. Thankfully, they hadn't pressed her for an answer. They had, however, made her hand over the files.

That along with a promise that she had no intention of writing a story about the Cattleman's Club had appeased them. An achievement that hadn't been as easy to attain when it came to their concerns about her research into prostitution. Now there had been a conversation fraught with tension.

Rachel had ducked and avoided the more sensational aspects of the truth. She'd even managed to answer their questions without directly lying. She'd simply glossed over the parts she'd known would upset them.

Killian and Adam weren't dumb, though. They'd already figured out that she had some professional help. While Rachel managed to keep Kitty's name out of the conversation, she hadn't been able to avoid mentioning Deputy Watts.

True to form, Killian and Adam had wanted to butt right in and take over, indignant that she was working with another cop. Rachel hadn't wasted her breath arguing with them. Instead, she'd tested their newfound truce and put her foot down.

Killian and Adam would not be involved in her research. There would be no more discussing that matter. Shockingly enough, there had been none. Suspiciously, though, Watts had become too busy to assist her.

Rachel wasn't dumb, either. She could put two plus two together, but lacking any real proof, she hadn't dared to make an outright accusation. Besides, she might just thank Killian and Adam for their interference. They'd helped provide the motivation she needed to do her own research.

That research had led her to Nick Dickles and the luxurious Camp D. Luxurious was actually an understatement for the well-appointed complex she discovered at the end of the narrow dirt road. Following the twisting drive to a secluded little parking lot, she tucked her car into a shaded spot.

A sign clearly directed visitors to the office, but the path led into a wandering maze of flower beds. Strolling into the Disney inspired fairy-land, Rachel quickly became lost but not concerned. Instead, she allowed herself to get lost in the pleasures of the massive garden.

Drugged by the sweet, flower-scented air and lost in the joyous music of the birds tweeting above, Rachel wandered right around a curved and smacked right into a brick wall. Only brick walls didn't grunt and stumble backward. Still, her nose throbbed like she'd rammed it straight into steel. Cupping it, she tried to throw off the sting while the man recovered his balance and offered her a hand.

"Are you all right?"

Rachel released her nose to wiggle about. It throbbed in response. "No piercing pain. No blood loss. No permanent damage."

The man laughed, drawing her eyes up until she almost stumbled backward. He had the most brilliant blue eyes. *Not even blue...they're like violet.*

"Are you wearing contacts?" The question just popped right out of her and almost instantly Rachel regretted it. "I'm sorry. I guess I must've done some damage after all."

"It's cool." The man's grin didn't dip an inch as he extended his hand. "I get that kind of response a lot and, no, these are my real eyes. I'm Seth Jones."

"Rachel. Rachel Adams." Rachel smiled as she took his hand. This man could be in the dictionary next to the word beautiful. Tall, solid, with the kind of smooth features that made his easy charm contagious. "And I really am sorry about the mow down. I was just looking for the office."

"Adams?" Seth's gaze narrowed slightly as he considered her. "You're the reporter for that paper down in Pittsview, right?"

"Did Mr. Dickles tell you I was coming?" Rachel asked, letting her question be her answer.

"Yeah, uh, I heard about it. Nick's up in the office." Seth nodded down the path. "You need some help finding it?"

"I guess I am a little lost," Rachel confessed, unable to shake the feeling of familiarity. There was something there, something she couldn't put her finger on. "But I don't want to keep you from anything."

Seth snorted at that as he turned to start leading the way. "Never too busy with work not to take a break. That's the best way to live life, now isn't it?"

Rachel couldn't help but smile at his words. Seth Jones had a charm about him that went deeper than dazzling eyes or a velvety drawl. "I guess that depends on whether you're the employer or the employee."

"Could also depend on who your employer is. Nick's a pretty laid back boss. Besides, he'd have my butt if I didn't help out a pretty young lady like yourself. Always got to be mannerly when a lady is around."

"Is that right?"

Nick Dickles was a legend through southern Alabama. Not because he'd managed to secure himself a full academic scholarship to some Ivy League school. It was the multi-million dollar prostitution ring he'd built and managed while attending college that had earned him notoriety.

The good ol' boys back home had reveled in knowing one of their own had conned all those proper rich girls into taking off their clothes for money. Unfortunately for Dickles, the IRS didn't share in local boys' sense of humor. That explained why he'd graduated with not only a diploma but also with a four-year, all-expenses-paid trip to a federal penitentiary.

Dickles's stint in the big-house had only added to his reputation. He was back now and working on his legend by helping disadvantaged youths. But if keeping a man as charming as Seth on the payroll was any indication, Dickles's good deeds still didn't make the man tame.

"Well, then," Rachel returned Seth's smile, "I'll be sure to tell Mr. Dickles you're his number one employee of the month."

"Trust me, he already knows." Seth winked at her as he led her around a tiny courtyard and under the shade of the cherry trees lining the walk. The landscaping really was beautiful, but as they walked Rachel began to realize that much of it was edible, too.

"If you don't mind me asking, Mr. Jones, what exactly do you do here?"

"It's Seth," he corrected her. "And I teach the auto shop class."

"So you're a mechanic." Rachel couldn't help but think of Hailey in that moment. Seth Jones might be a good distraction if she really wanted to escape Kyle Harding.

"That would be a charitable description. I actually used to run cars for a chop shop down in Louisiana. I picked up a few tricks before I got pinched." Seth spoke with no hint of shame for his colorful past but almost sounded amused. "I got shipped here and just never left."

"Well." Rachel looked for something positive to say. "That's quite a compliment, in a way. I mean that you would want to stick around and help out. You must really think a lot of the work Mr. Dickles is doing."

"Nick's cool." Seth shrugged. "And I ain't got nowhere to go."

That sounded sad to Rachel. "You don't have family?"

"Eh." Seth made a face as he paused outside a door bearing the words "Main Office." "My mom left my dad before I was born. Of course, I'm not sure where she is right about now. As for him, I hear he got killed not too long after she left."

"I'm sorry." Rachel could feel the heat in her cheeks, but this blush had nothing to do with her men. "I shouldn't have pried."

"It's cool. It's old news." He flashed her a quick smile. That's when it hit her. As the hinges on the door whined open, they heralded a revelation that left Rachel stupefied.

She'd seen eyes like that only on one person ever. That smile, too, the slightly perverse sense of humor and…*My daddy was murdered.* Davey Jones had been killed by his best friend, Mitch Davis, leaving Patton Jones orphaned because her mother had run off. Orphaned as in with no family of any kind, anywhere. *So who the hell is Seth Jones?*

"Well, it was nice to meet you, Miss Adams." Seth broke her stupor and the long silence with a nod past the door he still held. "I'm sure Nick's waiting on you."

His prod made her realize she'd been gawking. Feeling the heat of her flush fill her cheeks, Rachel offered up a quick smile and words that ran too fast together as she hoped he didn't realize the reason behind her staring. "It was nice to meet you, too, Mr. Jones, and thanks for the assistance. Maybe one day I'll have a chance to return the favor."

"Ah, don't sweat it. Between you and me, Nick's been in a great mood and I think partly because he's been having so many visitors. What with that deputy showing up yesterday and taking him down memory lane and your pretty face today, the boss is happy. That makes all our lives easier."

Rachel stalled out in mid-step, feeling everything inside her swirl for one dizzying moment. She didn't need to ask Seth to repeat himself. He'd spoken clear enough. A deputy had come to see Nick yesterday. Killian had been late, saying he had to pick up a few hours because he pissed the sheriff off.

She should have done the math then, but it had been a plausible excuse. Killian seemed to specialize in irritating Alex into giving him extra shifts. It could have been mere coincidence that she'd told him about her upcoming interview at lunch and he'd happened to be four hours late for dinner. It could have been, but it wasn't.

Now the only question was what had he done. The way to find the answer wouldn't be asking either Killian or Adam but going in there and seeing what kind of interview Dickles gave her. With that thought firming up her conviction, Rachel entered Dickles's office, ready to give him the roughest interview of his lifetime.

Try as she might, Nick didn't make it easy to be difficult. Just as Seth had commented, Dickles turned out to be as easygoing as the ocean's breeze. Between his quick smiles and disarming charm, it became quickly apparent how a man like Nick Dickles had ended up a pimp. He had a smoothness that, strangely enough, made a woman instinctively trust him.

It made it that much harder for her to tell if he were bullshitting her. On the surface, he appeared to answer her questions with a frankness that made her think she'd gotten an honest answer. Still, knowing Killian had interfered made Rachel certain she was being expertly led in the wrong direction. It frustrated her trying to figure it out. By the time Nick led her back to her car, Rachel gave up on trying and went with the blunt method.

"I wanted to thank you again for taking the time to answer my questions." Rachel paused in the shadow of the door Nick held open.

It was hard to look up into his smoky gray eyes and concentrate, but she managed.

"I always have time to help a lady in need," Nick responded with a natural graciousness that didn't come off as phony in the slightest.

"So I hear." She'd referenced Seth's comment, but Nick didn't know about her earlier conversation.

Lifting an eyebrow at her, he appeared more amused than curious when he asked, "And who's been telling you stories about me?"

"Killian." Rachel saw her chance and took it. "Killian Kregor. I believe you know him."

"Oh, yeah." There came that grin again. A slow, sexy lift of Nick's full lips, that smile had the power to make women go weak in the knees. "Killian and I go way back."

"As in yesterday." Rachel tried to match his amused tone, but the hurt inside her cut through, sharpening the words. Nick clearly heard the undertone in her voice, and it had him pausing for a second before responding.

"He didn't tell you he came up here."

"No." There seemed to be no point in lying about that one. "I figured it out all on my own."

"Then I guess you figured out you shouldn't be too thrilled by his unexpected visit," Nick concluded, strangely growing an even wider grin. "And you shouldn't be."

Nick couldn't have been clearer than that. His words wiped out her ability to smile, much less pretend to be anything other she was— pissed. She'd trusted them, and they'd made a fool of her. She should have known. Hell, she had known, but she had been stupid enough to hope for something different.

"I don't mean to be causing problems between you and yours," Nick's thumb lifted her chin up to meet his gaze again, "but you're a hell of a better reporter than he insinuated, and I didn't hold anything back."

Rachel sniffed back the pain and misery trying to overwhelm her and bring her to a screeching halt. She knew what she needed to do. First, though, she had to get back to Pittsview.

"Thanks." She tried to offer up a smile with that bit of gratitude. "Well, I'd better be going."

"Yeah." Nick stepped back as she slid into her car seat. He hesitated for a second to tell her to drive safely before slamming the door. She minded his advice all the way to the end of Camp D's drive, not wanting to run over any kids who might pop out of nowhere.

Once on the highway, though, she put the pedal down and did nearly twenty miles an hour over the posted speed limit. She wanted to get home, needed to get home as fast as possible because she'd had enough. Rachel couldn't delude herself and wouldn't any longer.

Watts hadn't backed down. He'd probably been intimidated. For all their sweetness and pledges of love, neither Adam nor Killian had changed. They might be doing it behind her back now, but they were still trying to control her. It hadn't even been a whole week since they'd pledged to do otherwise.

While she'd up held her end, they'd never intended to honor theirs. There could be no future in a relationship like that, and delaying the inevitable only made everything harder. The time had come to end it. Like a Band-Aid that needed to be ripped off, she'd do it quick and try to save herself the pain of some overdramatized scene.

* * * *

Killian stared at the clock and then glanced at the phone on his desk. As much as he hated being stuck in the station house, that wasn't what had him itchy today. Rachel's interview with Dickles should have been over. She should have called by now to tell them that she was on her way home.

It was one of their newly developed couple rituals. They called. She called. Everybody knew where everybody was at almost any moment of the day. The small shift that sort of familiar tradition made over the past few days had helped ease some of Killian's anxiety that Rachel was up to mischief, but hearing about her interview had put all the tension back in his gut.

"Stop staring," Adam muttered from his side of their conjoined desks. "It'll ring when it rings."

Killian didn't take Adam's advice but only glowered harder at the phone. "I should have gone with her."

"She wouldn't have allowed that," Adam retorted, the annoyance clear in his tone. Only Killian didn't know if Adam was pissed at him or himself.

"This is all your fault. Don't roll your eyes at me. I'm not the one who wanted to play it all nice and agree to let the girl allow or not allow things. That isn't the way the power should be balanced, and you know it."

Adam stiffened up in his seat at that accusation, never one to take blame. "And if Dickles actually presented a physical threat to Rachel, I'd have agreed with you. Short of telling Rachel just what the problem is with Dickles, how would you have possibly proved your case?"

He wouldn't have, but Killian didn't think he should have to. It should be enough for him to express his opinion and have her respect it. Respect, he'd grown to hate that word. Rachel wanted it, and Dickles thought they hadn't shown him any.

How one actually showed respect to an older brother before deflowering his younger sister, Killian didn't know. That was Dickles's axe to grind with them. Forget the fact that it should have rusted after all these years or that Deborah Dickles was, by all accounts, happily married with three kids. The bastard should have gotten over it by now. Then again, older brothers tended to hold grudges.

Technically, years back, that made sense. After all, Deborah had been a virgin, but she hadn't wanted to be. If Killian and Adam hadn't cured that problem for her, she'd have found somebody else. Besides, it wasn't like Nick didn't enjoy having sex. The jackass was just being sexist, but again, that's how older brothers tended to be.

Killian figured he'd gotten lucky by having a younger sister who was gay. It saved him from fulfilling a lot of older brother duties because he certainly couldn't go around threatening or beating up on women. He could threaten Nick, though, so he had.

"You should have seen him laughing yesterday. Said he heard we settled down and wanted to check out our woman for himself." Killian's knuckles went white with the memory.

He should have hit Nick then and there instead of just promising to hit him if he did anything other than look. Because of Rachel, he'd held back, knowing there would be more hell to pay at home if she found out about his impromptu visit to Camp D.

"Relax, Killian." Adam's advice didn't help when his own tone held so much tension. "Nick doesn't know how to hurt us. He probably figured Rachel knows our reputation."

She did, too. At least, she knew the half she'd read in their files, a fact that still irked Killian. Rachel shouldn't know the details of that side of his life. Hell, he didn't know about hers and didn't ask. Women, though, were always too nosey for their own good.

So now she knew about their insatiable appetites and the record number of women they'd funneled through their bed. Still, that didn't compare to what had come before the Cattleman's Club. At the club, the women were all willing and all knew the score. There wasn't any romance on anybody's part, so there weren't any delusions either.

That was a little different than it had been in the years stemming from high school through the military where they'd had to work at getting women in their bed. While they'd never promised any woman anything other than a good time, the very act of seduction sometimes led women to think things they shouldn't—like Killian would be there in the morning.

That's kind of what started Deborah crying and Nick chasing after them. Truth be told, Nick didn't stand in a line of one when it came to pissed off brothers wanting to beat Killian and Adam's asses. He didn't want Rachel to know anything about that hate club. Then she might start thinking they didn't take any of this seriously, or worse, that they shouldn't be taken seriously. Rachel didn't need any help in that department.

"It's almost three," Killian commented, not needing to glance at any clock to verify that information. He'd spent the last hour monitoring every click of the minute hand. "Maybe I should call her."

Adam sighed, barely looking up from his papers. "She'll call when she calls."

"What is your problem?" Killian had enough of Adam's dismissive, don't-give-a-shit attitude these past few days. "Don't you even care that she's late?"

"Sure," Adam shrugged, "but I'm not going to get worked up over it."

That only infuriated Killian's already raw temper. "Yeah, apparently you don't get worked up over anything these days. Not worth your time, I guess."

"What's the point?" Adam finally lifted his chin to pin Killian with a calm, almost remote look. "She either loves us or she doesn't. You can't make a person feel something when they don't. If she does, then she'll come to us first, not take the word of some man she just met."

That awfully grim view frustrated the crap out of him because he didn't know when or why Adam had come by it. Killian hoped to hell that it wasn't Adam's past coming to haunt them because he could only fight so many fronts at once. First, they had to settle things down with Rachel. Then, they could move on to Adam's emotional issues.

"Forget the whole notion of fighting for something you want, right?"

That obnoxious question had Adam focusing back in on his papers. "Some fights you just can't win."

Killian had a retort for that but forgot it as the lobby door pushed in. "Rachel."

He was on his feet at the front counter's edge in the next breath, so relieved to see her healthy and back that he didn't notice the stiff tension in her features until she responded.

"My key."

That was all she managed to grind out from her clenched jaw, but it didn't make sense to Killian. Neither did the hand she held out, but he could figure right then it wasn't good. Nick had done something. *That son of a bitch!*

"What did he say to you?" Killian demanded to know, uncaring that his question made as little sense as her demand.

"My house key," Rachel repeated, appearing completely uninterested in holding any kind of conversation. "Now. And yours, too."

Like Killian would obey that tone. He'd be dead before he gave in without a battle. "What the hell is this about? What did Nick say? What the hell are you doing?"

He directed that last one at Adam, who shocked him more than Rachel by silently whipping her key off his ring. Pausing to give Killian a dead stare, he dropped the key in Rachel's hand before turning and simply walking away.

"*Damnit*, Adam, get back here!"

"My key."

"I'm not giving you shit." Killian whipped around on Rachel, ready to do battle with the strength of two men if that's what it took. "Not until you tell me what the hell is going on."

"I packed your shit, put it in the driveway. I want It gone by the time I get home, and I never want to see you again. Now give me my key." Her tone never shifted up into a yell, but the sharp, crisp tempo boiled with anger. Rachel must have been beyond pissed because he'd never seen her this mad.

Before he could try to diffuse her or at least get her down to a simmer, Alex, that bastard, butted his nose into their business. "Give her the key, Deputy."

Turning to tell Alex what he could do with his commands, Killian realized now would not be the time or place as he saw every single eye in the station house watching him. She'd done this on purpose to give him no room to wiggle. Of that Killian had no doubt, but knowing it made him all the more itchy to rebel.

It took all his willpower to obey the wisdom of the moment and fish out his keys. He took his time removing hers from his ring, letting her suffer the scene she'd caused for an extra minute before plunking the key into her hand.

"This isn't over."

Rachel matched his lean across the counter. "You stay away from me, Killian."

That would never happen, but he'd let her walk out right now. Later, he'd be setting things back to right, but at that moment he had to go figure out what happened to his wingman. Adam had disappeared into the back. Killian didn't even spare a moment for the gawking gazes or beginning snickers as he stormed off to the locker room.

Sure enough, he found Adam washing his hands, calmer than before, if anything. That only ticked Killian into taking the issue up with his fist. Swooping in from his side, Killian caught Adam's shirt around the shoulders and used it to slam his partner against the wall.

"*What the hell are you doing?*"

"I could ask you the same thing," Adam shot back, finally showing some attitude as he shoved Killian away.

"I'm trying to figure out when you and Rachel did whatever drugs it is that have the two of you acting crazy all of a sudden," Killian roared, venting his frustration.

"No." Adam shook his shirt out before shooting Killian a hard look. "What you're doing is trying to make something work that obviously isn't. Rachel doesn't love us. She doesn't want us. End of story."

"Oh, the hell it is." Killian blocked Adam when he tried to walk away again. "Since when do you run from a fight?"

"Look," Adam's voice whispered out with an edge that spoke more of anguish than anger, "we told her we loved her. We did everything she asked. What more can we do? Trying to hang on, to make this fling into a relationship, I can't do it. I won't. I need somebody who also needs me. Now I'm going to go take care of our stuff."

Killian let Adam pass, watching him shrug through the locker room door with a growing sense of desperation. Given Adam's background, he had some right to be difficult at points. Rachel didn't. From everything she ever said, she'd been coddled and sheltered. Yet she acted as skittish and insane as Adam did.

He was stuck between two crazy people and damned tired of having to be the rational one. Perhaps if he went nuts they'd have to behave like adults. Killian certainly felt the lure of going berserk right then. Hell, Rachel had gotten her scene. Maybe it was time for him to cause one of his own.

Chapter 30

Rachel couldn't drive away from the station house fast enough, convinced that any second Killian and Adam's cruisers would be flashing lights at her. Taking corners like she'd just robbed a bank, she hightailed it over to Heather's.

Her friend wouldn't be home, but Rachel had a key and permission to use it. Explaining what had happened on the phone had nearly broken her control. The very words had trembled on her lips, but she'd held strong. There would be time enough to break down after it had actually ended.

She wouldn't fool herself into believing the scene she'd staged at the station would be the final word. Not with the heat that had flared in Killian's eyes. He'd want revenge, a totally expected response and the very reason she'd chosen to kick them out in public where the rest of the police department could make sure they obeyed.

If she'd tried to do it privately, it wouldn't have been done. Killian and Adam had shown a willingness to sink to any level to win. As weak as her love made her, she couldn't have resisted. So Rachel had chosen to do things the brutal way, the final way. Hopefully, in such a way that they wouldn't follow to tempt her with the fantasy she so desperately desired.

It had been clear from the second Killian had started yelling at her that he wouldn't be so easily dismissed. Adam…Rachel closed her eyes and tried not to let the despair wash over her as she remembered how cold his gaze had been.

Behind her, the clink of Heather's garage door helped to prod her into action. She couldn't think about her feelings or theirs. Not now when she needed all her focus on her next move just to keep from collapsing. She'd emptied her house, gotten her keys. Now came the ritual hiding.

The only problem with the plan was the silence. If she'd been home, Rachel would have crawled into bed and cried herself to sleep. She couldn't cry in Heather's empty house. She couldn't get comfortable enough.

Instead, the grim peace settled in every shadow of the house only appeared to taunt her with how vacant and empty her life was. The cold reminder twisted the sick feeling in her stomach until the hours piled up, almost too long for Rachel to bear.

When Hailey's phone call broke the tension, Rachel jumped at the chance to get out of the house. She couldn't be quiet right now. She needed the noise and chaos of the world to insulate her from the reality awaiting her at home.

There would be time enough for grieving. Right then she needed to catch her breath. Surely not even Killian would cause a scene at the Bread Box, especially during the dinner rush. It would be safe. There would be other deputies eating there. They would all have heard about the breakup by now, so they would know to keep their man in line.

Perhaps, she wanted to be caught, wanted to take back everything until nothing hurt anymore. That wouldn't happen, but she couldn't stop her heart from yearning. It dreamed of them showing up. Then they'd say…what? Rachel drew a blank because she couldn't think of anything that would fix this situation.

It frustrated her, leaving her feeling tired and in need of some escape. Maybe listening to Hailey's problems would do her some good, reminding her of the world that didn't revolve around her relationship with Killian and Adam. If not, then she'd at least have an ear to talk off and a whole deli full of sweets to stuff herself with.

She couldn't leave early, though. Having her car parked out in public would be a risk that she should minimize, so she waited until she could be sure Hailey would be there. What protection her friend could offer, Rachel didn't know, but she'd feel better not being on her own.

Her nerves made her driving a little risky as she sped toward the Bread Box. She managed to make it there without incident and in good time. Still, the deli's lot had overflowed and the only parking remained on the street. Maybe she should have gotten there earlier. Now she had to risk Heather's ire by blocking the dumpster and hoping it wasn't pick-up day.

Scurrying to the front, she kept her eyes wide, but the only deputies she saw as she shoved through the entrance were the ones already piled in at a booth. Their glances immediately turned her way before smiles starting kicking in. Doing things the way she had probably made Killian and Adam the joke of the day, but she didn't feel any sympathy.

They'd made her their joke. That reminder hardened her enough to walk past their looks to where Hailey sat slumped over a table. Coming around the edge to drop her purse on booth's bench seat, Rachel assured Hailey of the one thing she knew for certain.

"It can't be that bad."

Cracking an eye, Hailey frowned back. "At least, not as bad as it is for you today."

"I don't really want to talk about that," Rachel muttered as she slid into the booth.

Hailey rose up, her features softening into a sympathetic look right along with her tone. "You sure?"

"I'm not dying, Hailey." As wretched as she felt, Rachel didn't have the stamina to talk about it. Nor did she have the patience for pity. "We just broke up, happens all the time, all over the world. It's not any big news."

That didn't erase the concern from Hailey's gaze, but at least she tried to stiffen her lips into a smile. "Thank God there were no children, right?"

Rachel gave an unwilling laugh at that. "What's got you thinking procreation? Did Kyle finally manage to lasso you into his bed?" She'd expected an instant "no," but when Hailey glared back, beginning to slouch back over, Rachel's eyes went wide. "Oh, my God. You slept with him."

"It was only the once," Hailey snapped back as if she'd been accused of a crime. "Okay, maybe twice, but that's it. It's over."

"Uh-huh."

"Oh, don't use that tone on me," Hailey groused, flipping open her menu only to bitch at Rachel from behind it. "I did it. I got it out of my system. I'm moving on."

"Trust me, there is no moving on from a Cattleman. There is only being left broken in his dust." Rachel knew that too well.

Hailey peeked out from the top of her menu to cast Rachel another pitying glance. "I'm sorry about Killian and Adam. I know how much you liked them."

Liked? Try loved, but Rachel kept that response to herself. Instead, she shrugged it off. "They made their decisions. Nothing I can do about that."

Her cryptic comment caused Hailey to scowl, jumping to the wrong conclusion. "Did they cheat on you?"

Not that she knew. Given they kept too busy with her to stray, Rachel knew about almost every moment of their day. *Almost.* "I don't think so, but sex isn't all there is to a relationship. There also has to be respect and trust and not being bossed around all the time or having them go behind my back to arrange my life to suit them. I mean, seriously, I'm not some damn doll to be dressed and posed at their convenience."

"Thank you." Hailey's menu slapped down onto the table. "That's just what I was trying to tell Patton earlier, but she's so ruined by her men. With them wrapped around her little finger, she doesn't even know how hard it is for the rest of us."

"Hard?" Rachel snorted. "Try impossible."

"Absolutely impossible," Hailey repeated like Rachel had spoken from the gospel. "You know I try, try to get along, but does he? Not likely. He's always having to have things his way, trying to push me around my own damn shop and intimidating me, tempting me into all sorts of things, but we both know where that ends, don't we, Rachel?"

Rachel sure as hell did. "Collared and leashed, like a damn dog trained to their command."

"I'm not a dog."

Rachel was about to agree when the door to the Bread Box flew open enough to bring the tension back to her stomach. Expecting to see Killian storm in, she was caught off guard by Cole Jackson's sudden appearance. He might not be her problem, but he was trouble and heading their way fast.

"Uh, Hailey—"

Rachel didn't have to finish that warning. Cole delivered the rest of it when he slid right into their booth, doing as he pleased. The man kept going until a blink later, he had Hailey pinned up against the wall.

"Hey, Hailey, been a long time since I've seen you around here."

Rachel gave Cole two seconds with that drawl and cocky grin before Hailey gutted him right then and there. Except Hailey had gone white, looking as close to afraid as Rachel had ever seen her. It didn't last a second before Hailey flushed with anger, her gaze narrowing on the rude man.

"Cole."

"Hailey."

"Get out of my booth."

"I don't think so, darlin'."

Now Rachel would really like to see Hailey hit him, especially because Cole had actually tried to touch her. When Hailey only flinched back instead, snarling at him, Rachel began to realize how flustered her friend really was. At least she hid it well, snapping at Cole with a proper edge to her words.

"Don't touch me."

"But you like it when I touch you. Don't you? Just a little?"

"No."

"You're a liar, Hailey Mathews."

Rachel rolled her eyes at that response. How like a Cattleman to be so confident...and blunt.

"It's those hard, little nipples, darlin'. They give you away."

Rachel would have kicked him for Hailey, given her friend didn't seem in any condition to. Hailey sputtered, clearly overwhelmed.

"I think maybe you need to leave us alone, darlin'."

Now it was Rachel's turn to gasp at the man's audacity. Finally appearing to recognize her presence, he thought he could dismiss her? That she'd leave her friend to this predicament? The man must be on drugs. Either that or she had wax clogging her ears.

"Excuse me?"

"There is no excuse for him." Hailey recouped enough of her spirit to actually try shoving Cole back. Rachel really hoped he fell off the bench and busted his ass. He'd deserve the spanking.

"I'm beginning to see that."

"Now why do you two got to be so mean? Huh?" Cole Jackson should have been an actor. With those looks and that ability to fake indignation, he'd have made a million. "And you...you don't even know the story, but you're going to stick with Hailey just 'cause she's a woman, right? It don't matter at all that this little darlin' here almost got my ass beat. Three against one, that's the odds this little girl set me up against."

"You deserved it," Hailey retorted. "And you'd better get your ass out of my booth before I call up the Davis brothers and get them to issue another invitation to the dance."

Rachel laughed, a second from cheering her friend on when her world started to slide sideways. Without even giving her a chance to keep upright with the motion, Kyle Harding put his hard-ass hip into her side and pushed Rachel into the corner as he smacked down into the booth.

"Hey! I was sitting here." What the hell was she, a damn Beanie Baby to be tossed about? Not that anybody paid her any attention.

"I told you to leave Hailey alone."

Straightening up and matching Kyle's snarl, Cole squared off with the male interloper in a way that reminded Rachel of two feral dogs about to attack. "And since when do I take orders from you?"

"Do the two of you mind?" Hailey snapped. "I'm sitting right here."

"I haven't forgotten about you, darlin'." Cole curled in on her, brushing her ear with a whisper Rachel didn't catch. She heard Hailey's response as clear as day.

"I didn't issue—"

"I'm going to be putting my hands all over that sweet body, darlin', and you're going to be begging." That came out loud enough for Rachel's cheeks to flame in embarrassment for her friend. Hopefully, nobody else had caught that rude comment. Nobody but Kyle, and that was bad enough.

"Damn it, Cole," Kyle spat. Not that anybody paid him any mind.

The only person getting less attention was Rachel, who didn't even know what to say about the situation blooming around her. Perhaps she should have rethought that whole "nobody makes a scene in public" theory because obviously Cattlemen did.

Thankfully, it wasn't her scene. Hailey could handle it, as evidenced by her sharp retort. "Maybe you'll be the one that's begging."

Rachel would have advised against provocation right then, especially with Cole curling back in on Hailey with that no-good grin spreading across his face.

"Is that so, darlin'—*ahhh!*"

Hailey didn't give him a chance to finish that taunt or corner her. In a flash of motion, her hand shot out and latched onto Cole's shirt.

Correction, Cole's nipple, and Hailey twisted. Rachel gasped as Cole hollered. The man almost banged his head into the table he doubled over so fast.

"*And don't call me darlin'.*"

The only thing that could have shocked Rachel more was Cole's response. He didn't play fair but went for even, sending Hailey shrieking back as she smacked his hand away from her chest. Not to be left out of the drama, Kyle shoved the table hard at his friend and, inadvertently, Hailey.

"Damn it, Cole. I told you not to touch her."

"Why are you sitting next to my woman?"

It was as if hell itself had decided to consume Rachel because this day couldn't get any worse. Kyle didn't appear to realize that the devil himself had come to cast his shadow over the table. Kyle might not understand, but Rachel did. She was trapped in a booth, defended only by a fool against the very large, very pissed off deputy glaring down brimstone and fire on their heads.

"What?" Kyle really should have obeyed and not questioned.

"Get out of my way, Kyle. I need to have a word with *my woman.*"

Oh, the hell with it. Rachel had tried to do things the civilized way, but if Killian wanted a war, then by God, she'd use all her pain and anguish to fuel her rage and give him a battle that would go down in Pittsview's history forever.

"Don't you take that tone with me." Rachel shot that back at Killian over Kyle's head. "And don't you call me yours. I'm not a damn dog, Killian."

"Don't you worry, darlin', I'm going to get to you once this prick gets out of my way."

"Get to me?" Rachel could not believe her ears. The man couldn't think he'd be dragging her out of here to the nearest bed to be punished, but she had a sick feeling he did. "Listen up, you prehistoric baboon, there isn't going to be any getting to. I called *red light.*"

There went Killian's ears, turning bright red as his nostrils flared. "Don't start with that light shit again. You're going to shut up and listen to what I have to say, and when I'm done, you can apologize for being an irrational bitch."

Rachel shrieked, about ready to crawl over Kyle to get her hands on Killian. "*What did you call me?*"

"You heard me." At first, she thought he'd dared to bark at her, but a second later when Kyle went whipping out of the booth and stumbling across the floor, Rachel realized Killian had turned his focus onward. "*I said get away from my woman!*"

That did it. There could be no hope of escaping the gossip now. The diner had gone silent, and all eyes had turned toward them. Well, Rachel would give them a story to tell. Once she finished, the whole town would be talking about how Killian got his because Rachel would not be the one humiliated at the end of this day.

"Damn it, Killian! I ain't interested in Rachel." Kyle shoved himself free of the fist clenched in his shirt.

"And I'm not interested in *you*."

Rachel made sure everybody knew who she meant by giving Killian a hard shove in the back as she came out of the booth. He didn't budge an inch but whipped around fast on her, a snarl already falling from his lips.

"Don't even start with all that unimpressive whimpering," Rachel snapped back, leveling a finger at Killian's chest that actually did have him backing up. "I'm not going to take you back, no matter how much you beg or how big a tantrum you throw. You've been dismissed, *deputy*. Now find the damn door."

Mouth open, eyes wide, Killian stared back at her in such shock Rachel almost snickered. She'd finally rendered him speechless after all this time. Score one for her, or maybe not. Not when the click of Killian's jaw snapping shut was drowned out by the shuffle of too many feet across the tile floor. The deputies were rushing their way, and they wouldn't do that if she wasn't in a whole lot of trouble.

"You fucked Hailey Mathews, and *you didn't even share!*"

No, Rachel certainly hadn't, but Killian hadn't yelled that accusation. Cole had. Roaring like the first cannon blast of a battle, his shout heralded the sudden eruption of violence. Shoving Killian out of the way, Cole launched himself at Kyle in a full body tackle that had them falling back to crash through a table full of customers.

As absolute chaos consumed the diner, Killian paused long enough to lean in and growl a warning at her. "We're not done with this conversation, so you best stay put."

He really is out of his ever-loving mind. Rachel couldn't explain his behavior any other way. He couldn't appear to grasp the concept that she didn't want to see him. For some strange reason, that actually made her feel better.

Taking a deep breath, Rachel reminded herself that what she should feel was utter annoyance at his arrogance. Then the way he'd dismissed her to join the pile of deputies trying to separate the brawling friends could only be considered rude. He'd come in here and caused half these problems. Now he expected her to wait on him?

"Men," Rachel muttered in disgust.

Directing that comment at Hailey, she finally turned to find her friend in an apparent state of shock. White as paper, not even appearing to breathe, Hailey stared unblinkingly at the battle knocking down tables and scattering people everywhere. It dawned on Rachel right then what Cole had actually said, what he'd shouted out to the whole world.

With one hand, Rachel snatched up her purse and with the other, she latched on to Hailey. Not even sparing a second to worry over disobeying Killian's order, she began dragging her friend out of the building. There would be no point in hanging around. If the sheriff wanted a statement, he could come over to Hailey's and get it himself.

Chapter 31

"Sit down."

Killian helped Kyle follow that order by giving him a shove into his chair. He sounded too damn happy by Adam's reckoning. Since he'd shown up at the Bread Box to help lug Cole and Kyle back to the station house while Alex handled things with Heather, Killian had been full of nothing but swagger and bluster.

"Hey," Kyle objected, fumbling around in his seat. "Don't you think the cuffs are a little overkill, Killian?"

"It's Deputy Dog to you, scumbag." Killian matched that cocky response with an even more dramatic gesture. He whipped out his baton to slap it threateningly, but nobody seemed impressed.

"You know, Killian, I'm going to enjoy when it's your turn."

Unfortunately for Kyle, that time had come and now gone. Apparently, Killian should be told, too, because he didn't appear to have gotten Rachel's message in the slightest.

"Never gonna happen. 'Cause, you see, I already got my lady, and I don't plan on humiliating her by screaming out the intimate details of our sex life in a public building before engaging in yet a second brawl this week."

"Your woman?" Kyle asked with as much apparent doubt as echoed in Adam's head. "That little brunette that called you a prehistoric baboon? That one?"

"Yeah, she's *feisty*, ain't she?" Killian smirked. "'Course, it won't take me long to get her settled down, and then she'll be back to purring. I'm thinking naked, on her knees, and asking me how she can serve her master. You know, those kind of fantasies. The kind you won't be indulging in with Hailey anytime soon."

Kyle snorted at that. "Well, ain't your shit just all shiny and sweet smelling."

"Hey." Killian tilted Kyle's chin up with the end of his baton. "Consider this, you jackass. My girl is good friends with the girl you're trying to get with. You know what kind of position that puts me in?"

Kyle jerked back away from the hard wood under his chin and glared.

"That's right, buddy." Killian nodded, projecting an arrogance that could only be a cover.

That's all Adam could figure any of this show was. He'd heard about what Rachel had said. She'd dismissed Killian. There could be no worse blow to a Cattleman's ego. Killian must be overcompensating. Either that or grief had overwhelmed his sense and caused him to have a psychotic breakdown.

"You just remember that, and maybe if you sit here nice and quiet, I'll just be suggesting to the judge a little anger management therapy instead of suggesting to Hailey you've got serious issues."

Kyle stilled at that threat. "You wouldn't."

Nobody with any sense would tempt Killian with those two words. Killian never could resist a challenge. Adam knew that well enough.

"I'm talking psycho, dude. I'll have that woman convinced you're one twitch away from going all postal." Killian grinned, clearly enjoying his authority over Kyle. "Now sit there and be a good boy, okay?"

"That goes double for you, dumbass." Adam shoved Cole toward a seat, not bothering to pay attention to how he landed. He'd already forgotten about Cole in his rush to catch up to Killian. His partner had strutted off down the hall, no doubt to go wash up.

That's where most of the deputies from the Bread Box had gone. As Adam pushed in, their snickering gazes shifted to him from where Killian lurked over a sink. Adam shot them back a hard glare with the clear sign that they should leave before somebody got hurt. All five remained, gleefully tracking his every step until Adam paused out at the edge of the row of lockers.

"Is there something you wanted?"

"Nah," Brandon answered for the group, "we're cool."

That cheerily obnoxious answer had Adam turning. He didn't want to fight them, but if it came to it, he'd do it. "Then why don't you be *cool* elsewhere?"

"Come on, boys." Duncan nodded toward the door. "I think we were just dismissed."

They didn't save their laughter for the hallway but spilled out of the room, chuckling and throwing out more lines to amuse each other with. Adam didn't care what they said as long as they left him alone with Killian. He wanted to have a few words with his partner.

They started with, "What the hell do you think you were doing out there?"

"What?" Killian appeared honestly startled by Adam's intrusion. Looking over his shoulder as he pulled out a pile of paper towels from the dispenser, he shrugged. "Out there? Just having some fun. Same as Kyle and Cole would if things were reversed."

That wasn't what Adam had meant, but he let it go for the real question bugging him. "What are you smiling about? Unless you failed to grasp the situation, things are not good, Killian."

"No," he snorted, wiping down his arms, "they're better than. Did you hear what Rachel said? She dismissed me, and that, my friend, is a punishable offense. Just think of the possibilities."

Maybe he really had flipped his lid because Adam shouldn't have to explain the obvious. "You can't punish her, Killian. She's not ours to punish."

"Please." Showing the first signs of annoyance, Killian chunked the used towels into the waste basket with undo force. "Today's events are just a temporary setback."

"Not according to the three truckloads of stuff I had to haul back to our place."

That should have broken Killian's smile, not widened it. "Oh, another punishable offense. They're just stacking up now."

"Damnit!" Adam wheeled around as Killian shoved past him. "Why don't you get it? There aren't going to be anymore punishments or anything else. Rachel dumped us, kicked us to the curb, threw our stuff out on her drive, and then publicly dismissed us. It. Is. Over."

"No." Killian's smile did straighten out into as serious an expression as Adam had ever seen him wear. "It's you who aren't getting it. You never have, and maybe that's your mom's fault. See, you loved her, and she didn't love you back."

Adam flinched from the truth in Killian's words, but that didn't stop his friend from saying his piece. "Now you want to say fuck Rachel, I don't love her anymore, but it doesn't work that way. You love who you love, and no, it ain't easy, but that's the point of unconditional love.

"It makes you feel safe and secure because you know no matter what you do, you are loved." Killian paused for a bare second before offering up a little shrug. "The only way to get there is to give it."

Adam didn't have anything to say. He'd never been loved like that, but he wanted to be. How Killian could think a woman who had walked away from them could ever return that depth of emotion eluded Adam. More than anything, he wished he could be that blind, but all he could do was let his friend walk away without bursting his bubble.

Killian hesitated at the door. "No matter what, you know there's always a place for you by my side."

He didn't even bother to turn and see if Adam had a response for that but left him alone to consider everything Killian had said. One thing his partner had right, he couldn't stop loving Rachel just because he wanted to. The damn woman had worked her way into more than his heart. She managed to work her way into his very life.

Now, knowing she wouldn't be there tomorrow or the day after made his future feel bleak and pointless. He knew the feeling well enough from his childhood. It had passed, sort of. Killian had it right when he said Adam had never stopped loving his mom.

He'd certainly never stopped wishing at the most absurd moments that he could actually have a conversation with her, one where she acted like a mom. No matter how much Mums acted like a mother to him, that didn't stop him from wishing his mom would care. That's what it would be like from now on with Rachel.

There would never be another like her. No matter how many years passed or how many women filled them up, Adam knew that he'd never feel that moment of perfect peace again. But was that really worse than spending every day with a woman who didn't love him?

In Adam's book it was yes because he couldn't take that slow, painful torture. It wouldn't work. Eventually, his love would sour into bitterness. It would be better to be left yearning than to be hardened by rejection. At least with the first option, Rachel could have a chance to find somebody she could love.

Lifting off the bench he'd settled onto, Adam left that sickening thought behind him. Instead of focusing on what he couldn't stomach, he returned to work, letting the monotonous task of pushing paperwork consume his every thought. The mindless routine helped to buffer him from the voice trying to nag at him.

He couldn't let another man touch her. Adam would kill the son of a bitch who tried. Just what the hell he was supposed to do about that raging insanity, he didn't know. It all went to show that he was the one really being driven crazy.

The distraction of work helped him ignore that concern up until the phone rang. Brandon already had a call at the front desk, and the others had gone back into the booking room to hassle Killian, Cole, and Kyle. That left him to pick up line two, which Adam did without hesitation.

"Pittsview Sheriff's Department, Deputy Whendon." Adam paused, but nobody answered back. "Hello?"

Only the hollow echo of an open line echoed back. About ready to hang up, every single fiber of his being froze with a sudden, soul-deep chill as a voice whispered across the phone.

"Adam?"

Rachel. He couldn't breathe, couldn't think beyond the hope that maybe she'd called to apologize, to tell him she'd taken a heavy dose of drugs that afternoon and lost her mind or maybe aliens had—

"I just wanted...I'm at Hailey's, and I didn't know...What happened to Cole and Kyle?"

Rachel stumbled through her question, sounding nervous and hesitant. Each soft, breathless pause was like a lash from a flaming whip across his skin as every time he felt a slight lift of optimism that she might say something else. Of course she didn't because it was over.

"They've been arrested. Killian's booking them right now."

"Oh. Do you need us to come in and give a statement?"

"I guess that's up to the sheriff."

"Oh."

There came that pause, that awkward silence that he didn't know how to fill. Adam fought the urge to demand answers, to demand explanations, to argue with her conclusions, but what would be the point? Rachel had made herself clear.

"Well, you'll tell him we're here if he needs us?"

"That would be my job."

"Yeah." The word sighed across the line with such sorrow that Adam didn't understand, not until she spoke again. "I really am sorry about...everything. I didn't mean to hurt you. I just—"

"Whatever." The last thing Adam wanted to hear was all her pitying comments. He wasn't pathetic, nor was he hurt. By all the strength in his body, he wouldn't let himself be either of those things. "Hey, I've got work to do, so I'll talk to you later, or I guess not."

Not waiting for her to get in another dig, Adam simply hung up the phone. He couldn't deal with her right then. The very sound of her voice made his muscles twitch and itch with the need to do something, something violent to whoever stood too close. It took all his concentration and a few minutes for Adam to quell those urges until he had all his emotions locked down under tight control.

"See you, buddy."

Adam blinked as Cole went sauntering by. Locking on to his image, Adam stared in numb confusion as Cole waved out a farewell to Brandon and disappeared through the front door. The sound of a drawer being pulled open had Adam realizing Killian had returned.

"What was with that?" Adam asked, pointing to the door swinging closed behind Cole. "We just let people go now?"

"Sheriff's orders." Killian shrugged, snatching his keys out of the drawer and banging it closed with his thigh. "Didn't Brandon tell you? Alex called and said he'd settled everything up with Heather. Cole's going to pay for the damage, so we're to let them go."

That made sense. That's how Alex liked to run things. It saved them the paperwork, the taxpayers the money, and everybody the headache of dragging things out too long. In the end, the judge would have made Cole pay, so why go through all that effort?

Still, Adam looked around before casting Killian another confused look. "Them?"

"Cole's a generous man." Meaning he paid Killian to let him go first, probably to get a head start on his hunt for Hailey.

"Idiot." That had Killian hesitating long enough to shoot Adam a grin. "And he isn't the only one. Where do you think you're going?"

"Back on patrol."

Adam didn't believe that for a second. The last time Killian had patrolled, he'd conveniently run into Rachel, which proved that Cole wasn't the only fool around. "You're going to be the one Alex throws in jail if you don't back off Rachel."

"I ain't going to see Rachel," Killian informed him with enough snootiness to have Adam doubting him.

"Yeah, right. I'm not going to bail your ass out. You'll have to call your mom."

That threat should have wiped out Killian's smirk, but it only made the other deputy chuckle. "That's just who I'm going to see because it is time to go nuclear on Rachel's ass. We need help."

"There is no 'we' in this," Adam corrected him.

"Fine, then. Me, I. I need help, so I'll catch up with you later."

Adam watched Killian saunter out of the station with much of the same cockiness Cole had. "Idiot."

Whatever Killian thought he'd accomplished by bringing Mums into this disaster, Adam didn't know. All he knew was that he would save his pride and dignity and keep his ass seated. Rachel had made herself clear. He wouldn't be chasing after her like some fool because he got what Killian couldn't grasp.

He thought just loving the girl would be enough, but it wouldn't be. Adam had loved his mother, but that had never made her love him back. All his attempts had been nothing more than a waste of time and energy. Eventually, Killian would realize that's all his attempts would be.

Sitting there, trembling under the strain of staying seated, Adam listed every reason that he was right and Killian was wrong. All the reminders didn't make it any easier to hold back and not go racing off after Killian. The only thing that held him back was Rachel herself and the cold look she'd given him when she'd demanded her key back.

"Hey, Adam." Brandon broke his concentration, bringing back to life the noise and commotion of the station house around him. "Line three."

God help him, he hoped it wasn't Rachel again. He couldn't handle another round of her poor-little-Adam tones. Glaring down at the phone, he brewed a hard shell of anger before he snatched up the receiver.

"Deputy Whendon."

"Adam."

Not Rachel. "Nick Dickles."

"Hey, man," Nick sang out like they were actually friends. The gloating cheer in his tone warned Adam of what would come next. "I just wanted to call and offer my condolences. I heard a tale of your dismissal and wanted to lend you my sympathies."

He could have not laughed when he said the word, but Adam wouldn't have believed him no matter how sincere Nick sounded. "Is that all?"

"All?" A chuckle rumbled over the line, smooth, easy, and full of victory. "No, son. This is only the beginning. We'll call it all when Rachel's wearing a smile twice as big as any you put on her face."

"Touch her and I'll kill you."

"You'd rather I get a buddy to do it while I watch?"

Without thought, the need to hit Nick manifested itself into action. Adam slammed the phone down before he realized what he'd done. No longer trembling, he sat there shaking outright at his desk. He couldn't believe Rachel had listened to whatever crap that man had said.

She should have come to them, asked them, but Killian had it right. Rachel didn't trust them, didn't respect them. There could be no future in a relationship like that, but he'd never let Nick have her. Nobody would touch what was his.

"*Shit!*" Shoving away from his desk with that violent expletive, Adam snatched up his keys and went racing after Killian.

* * * *

Rachel stared at the phone, unable to shake the echo of Adam's voice. His tone had been beyond cold, sounding completely flat and lifeless. *Whatever.* That's about what his tone said with every word, but hearing him actually dismiss her had cut deep. He really didn't care.

A wheezing breath broke the silence in Hailey's kitchen, a warning of the storming sobs building inside her. Her hand clamped down over her mouth, fighting to hold back the tide. She wouldn't cry. Not now, not here, not ever. Not over men who didn't love her.

"Don't 'now Hailey' me!"

Hailey's roar fortified Rachel's control. It was easier to focus on the trashing her friend's life had taken tonight than the one Rachel would have to wake up and face in the morning. There would be time for tears, but right now tea sounded better.

Focusing on that small task, she kept an ear to the conversation floating back from the living room. Patton had started to calm Hailey down, which Rachel considered a minor miracle. She'd called Patton to give her the heads-up, only because there could be no two closer friends than Hailey and Patton.

Still, Rachel had honestly expected Patton to show up and make a bigger disaster out of the night given her predilection toward chaos. Then again, maybe she had reason to be concerned. As she carried the tea tray down the hall, their softer words started to define themselves.

"Well, this is going to be your game, Hailey, but you need help. The first thing I suggest is for you to figure out what Cole's weakness is."

Patton might have wound down Hailey's temper, but she'd done so to focus it on getting into mischief. That figured.

"He doesn't have any, Patton," Hailey groaned. "Don't you think I've already looked? The man doesn't care about anything beyond cars and fucking."

"Cars? Kind of like that rusted thing Kyle lured you in with?"

"Oh, great. Let's play copycat," Hailey snapped. "I'll go find a car Cole can't resist, and then what? What good does that do me?"

That sounded like Rachel's cue to interrupt and hopefully bring whatever insanity was brewing between the friends to an end.

"Well, I just got off the phone with Adam," Rachel declared over the tinkling clings of the cups on the tray. "I'm sure you'll be pleased to hear that Killian arrested both Cole and Kyle and is in the process of dragging them down to the station."

That should have triggered a conversation shift, but only silence greeted her. Silence and Hailey's trancelike stare as she watched Rachel lower the tray onto the coffee table. The only thing creepier than the way Hailey gazed at her was the way her words whispered out.

"Cole would give his left nut for Bavis's Fastback."

"What?" Rachel did not understand how that connected to anything, but when Hailey continued on, her voice growing stronger, she began to get a clue.

"Rachel and Kitty Anne are running an investigative story on a whorehouse down in Dothan."

"Why am I nervous at hearing my named mentioned?" And why were they smiling at her like that? The slow spread of Patton's grin wound the nervous tension in Rachel's stomach because she knew that look well.

"I think see a plan."

Chapter 32

Wednesday, May 21st

Two weeks later, Rachel still couldn't get over her shock at what Hailey and Patton had called a plan. She'd have called it a disaster, a convoluted, destined-to-fail mess. That first night she'd been too wrapped up in her own misery to reason through any argument that would have put the brakes on Hailey's wild scheme.

Not that logic really counted for much these days. Hailey seemed to have completely flipped her lid. Instead of calming down and considering the consequences to her crazy actions, she appeared to have thrown herself headfirst into an all-out affair with Kyle Harding and, Rachel suspected, Cole Jackson.

Patton never had any sense. Neither did Kitty, which explained why she'd eagerly jumped at the chance to join Hailey's game. All of them were gung-ho with Rachel trapped between them, a place she began to fear Killian had been right about.

Juggling crazy ladies, soon-to-be irate Cattlemen, prostitutes, and their madams, not to mention the police and one really miserable old man, this story had gotten dangerous. Strangely enough, Rachel didn't thrive on dangerous. It didn't make her excited but left her feeling sick and on edge.

All the tension and worry only added to the heavy weight of depression that crept into her life. That might be a mild description. Post-traumatic stress disorder probably came closer given she couldn't even sleep in her own bed.

Once upon a time, crisp, cool sheets had invited her to snuggle in and inhale the clean scent of her bed. Now all they looked was cold and sterile, lonely without the musky scent of men clinging to the cotton. It was all right. The couch felt comfortable enough, and with the pillows behind her, Rachel could almost delude herself into believing she wasn't alone.

Sleeping in the living room did have a disadvantage. Namely, she couldn't ignore the knocking on the front door. Whoever dared to come calling that early was lucky because Rachel really hadn't been asleep. She'd been faking.

Not having any sleep didn't make her any happier to be bothered. Irritation added to her rushed movements as she fumbled for her robe. It didn't hit her until her fingers closed over the cool latch on the deadbolt that she really shouldn't open the door. Killian and Adam could be lurking on the other side.

Well, maybe just Killian. Adam had disappeared, a fact that she tried to avoid noticing but couldn't stop from feeling every moment of every day. A part of her ached to catch just a glimpse of him, but then his cold dismissal would whisper through her head and warn her that seeing him might hurt more.

Adam didn't care, didn't love her. If he had, he wouldn't have given up. He'd have fought for her like Killian did. That one drove her insane with his pursuit. Sending her flowers, leaving her messages, Rachel had even heard the man had even tried to take an ad out in the paper. Killian's behavior explained why she got all those looks out in town. Hopefully, he got a lot of laughs for making them front and center in the summer's gossip column.

Everybody wanted to know if and when she'd take him back. Heather said the men were even betting on it. All the attention didn't make it any easier to stand her ground. Neither did knowing she was wrong about damn near everything. That pained her the most because it gave her heart leverage to argue its point.

So what if Heather was right and Dickles had some old score to settle with Killian and Adam? Killian could have told her about it instead of going out to Camp D and threatening the man. And even though Watts had said Killian had never threatened him, he had had Watts checked out.

When Watts had called the day after she'd dumped Killian and Adam, Rachel had half suspected they'd put him up to it. Her pride had to know, no matter the embarrassment in asking if her boyfriend had arranged Watts's co-operation. Rachel still didn't know if she trusted Watts's answer. After all, cops covered for each other.

None of it mattered, anyway, because Adam—

"Rachel?" Her name was followed by another round of banging, way too soft sounding to be one of her deputies' heavy fists. Neither Killian nor Adam sounded that high pitched, either.

"Patton?" Rachel asked the door before she opened it up to find her answer beaming at her from the porch.

Patton's grin only grew as she did a quick once over of Rachel's frumpy appearance. "My God, you look like hell."

"Good morning to you, too," Rachel snapped. She was in no mood for Patton's lively obnoxiousness or her bossy pushiness. Not that glaring at the other woman saved her.

"You need coffee."

Without even asking and acting like they were close enough friends to give her the right, Patton walked right past Rachel and started finding her own way toward the kitchen. Sighing at the realization that she didn't have what it took to intimidate dominant personalities, Rachel closed the door.

That's why it would never work out with Killian and Adam because she was too much of a wimp. They walked all over her. She didn't have a clue how to stop them, much less Patton Jones, who was tearing up her kitchen from the sound of it.

Sure enough, when Rachel wandered into her kitchen Patton had half the cupboard doors open. She had managed to find the coffee and start the maker but still rooted around in Rachel's pantry unit. It took her a moment to swing back around with a bag of sugar in her hands. The instant her gaze lit on Rachel, Paton went back to smiling.

"I figured you'd need the sugar."

"Yeah." Rachel reached down the counter and pulled the little bowl of the sweet stuff forward.

"Oh." Patton chuckled. Shrugging, she chunked the sugar back onto the shelf. "I guess maybe you'll get it from here, huh?"

"Perhaps that's best," Rachel agreed. "And while I'm at it, maybe you could tell me what the hell you are doing in my house at seven in the morning?"

Patton puckered up proudly at that question. "I'm here to help you."

"Is that right?" Rachel really hoped not because she knew what kind of help Patton offered.

"Now, I know we're not real close friends—"

"Not really."

That grumpy response didn't faze Patton in the slightest. "But I am moving back to town permanently, and I'd like to start setting roots down. So since I like you, I figure you could be my friend, and friends help each other out."

Rachel debated how to respond to that. She probably didn't want to know what Patton did, but getting her out of the house would be way too difficult. That would require energy. So she'd give Patton until the end of her first cup to say her piece. Rachel had conditions, though.

"If this has anything to do with Adam and some tramp he's taken up with at the club—"

"What?" Patton's confused expression gave Rachel a little reassurance this conversation wouldn't turn into a nightmare. "Adam hasn't been to the club in weeks. Not since you took him off the market…You don't really think he'd do that?"

"Why not?" Rachel shrugged, fishing out two mugs from the cabinet. "It's what men do, isn't it?"

"Only losers," Patton retorted with total disgust.

"Maybe in your world," Rachel said, because Patton lived in the world of beauty and privilege. "But down here with the normal people, it's a common enough occurrence. Men need variety. It's genetic."

"Variety? That's the best argument you've got?" Patton shook her head. "You know not all men are victims of their dicks and Cattlemen least of all. Hell, their whole thing is to be in charge, to control themselves."

"Patton," Rachel groaned out her name, "why are you even arguing with me on this? You're the one who gave me Killian's and Adam's files. You know I know how short-term their attention span is."

"You can't hold that against them." Patton gave her a look like she was the dumb one in the room. "Of course they didn't settle down with any of those women. They're club women. Nobody's there looking for happily ever after. They're just having some fun until they find it."

"Then how am I supposed to know if I'm just another stop on the happy train?" Rachel shot back because she didn't believe in converting bad boys. People were the way they were. Killian and Adam liked diversity.

"Well, you could start by taking note of the fact that Killian's making an absolute fool out of himself over you." Patton actually laughed. "That he's willing to make such an ass out of himself has to mean something."

"Yeah, that he doesn't like to lose."

The ding on the coffee maker chimed, giving Rachel the distraction of pouring out the cups. The minute delay in their conversation didn't stop Patton from latching back on to her point.

"He might not like to lose, but trust me, Cattlemen only place sure bets when it comes to women…Ah, I saw that look." Patton nodded as Rachel busied herself stirring in her sugar. "You're thinking that you are a sure bet because in the end, you don't think you can resist them. You know what that means?"

"Patton—"

"You're in love with them."

"I am not." Rachel began to try and explain that she wouldn't discuss this with Patton. Not that Patton gave her the chance.

"Wow, you really are butt-ass dumb."

Rachel's mouth fell open, shocked by Patton's blunt rudeness. "Excuse me?"

"You had it all, didn't you? All the happiness and pleasure and assurance that you belonged somewhere in this world, were irreplaceable to somebody, and you just tossed it out the nearest window." Patton paused to consider her own words. "That's a pretty damn dumb thing to do."

Patton's words really irritated her because Rachel had been carefully avoiding the fact that she'd brought all this misery down on her own head. She wasn't dumb. She was right. "I had my reasons."

"Yeah?" Patton cocked a brow. "Like what?"

"I don't have to explain any of this to you."

Patton snorted. "You ain't got shit. Hey! Give that back."

Patton reached for her cup, but Rachel took a step back, keeping it out of the other woman's range. With a pointed look and the coldest tone she had, Rachel ordered her, "Get out of my house."

"So that's the way it is, is it?" Patton settled back and shook her head. "You just throw everybody out and run away from the confrontation, too damn scared to fight. You're going to end up lonely if you aren't willing to fight for what you want."

"Out!"

"Fine. I'll go, but you remember one thing, Rachel. Nothing in this world will make you as happy as love. *Nothing.*" With that,

Patton twirled and sauntered out of Rachel's kitchen, leaving her stunned and amazed at the other woman's audacity. Scenes like this were why Rachel had always stayed clear of Patton. There was nothing wrong with that.

Rachel's parents had had a long and happy marriage. They hadn't found a need to shout and yell at each other. In fact, she couldn't remember any argument where her parents had shouted or cussed at each other. They'd raised her to be civilized and polite, a proper lady.

Damnit, she would not end up lonely because of that. Rachel stormed off to the bathroom, swearing that she'd be happy. She didn't need all the drama and craziness. What Rachel wanted was a nice, calm, easygoing man. One who didn't feel a need to try and control every detail of her life. More importantly, she'd find a man who loved her back.

It would just take a while to find that man. Hopefully, by then, the idea of being touched by anybody other than Killian and Adam wouldn't fill her with disgust and shame. Pausing by the couch to stare at her makeshift bed, Rachel had to admit to the depressing possibility that her repulsion might be a lifelong condition.

* * * *

"Okay, so I figured it all out."

Killian shoved Adam's breakfast out of the way to plop down his notebook. The arrogant gesture earned him a dark look from his partner, a harder look than normal given how little sleep Adam had gotten over the past two weeks. His friend's condition showed, but Killian didn't say boo about it given Adam's attitude of late.

The man had gone from outright cranky to a complete bastard. Killian knew what the cure was, but hell if Adam would listen to him and actually try to seduce his way back into Rachel's bed. Well, Killian didn't intend to wallow in his misery. One way or another, he was going to fix this.

"Dare I ask what you've figured out?" Adam grumbled, barely paying any attention to the flow chart Killian had painstakingly made.

"See," Killian said, pointing to the first item on the list before sliding his hand down the rest, "I thought since I tried all the polite civilized things Mom told me to do—"

"Mums said to woo the girl, not stalk her."

She'd also said to wait three weeks and give Rachel time to cool down. Killian didn't see any reason to delay, but Adam had taken Mums' advice and memorized it down to the letter. Now Killian basically had to listen to his damn mom all day. It really made him regret starting Adam down this annoying path.

"I'm not stalking," Killian shot back as he went rummaging for his own breakfast. "I sent her some flowers."

"Every other day."

"I left a few messages."

"About five hundred."

"Will you shut up?" Killian slammed the refrigerator door. There wasn't anything in it but beer, soda, and leftover takeout. "At least I'm trying. What are you doing but sitting around repeating what Mom says?"

"We're supposed to be giving her space and moving slowly," Adam repeated Mums' mantra, "not taking out humiliating ads in the paper."

Killian would give Adam that one. It had been kind of a lame idea, like eating cold pizza in the morning, but a man had to do what he had to. Opening the refrigerator to fish out the oversized box, Killian could take at least some comfort that nobody had seen how desperate he'd become.

"It's not like they ran it."

"Thank God for that," Adam muttered. "We don't need to be the biggest laughingstock ever."

"Is that what you're worried about?" Killian already knew the answer. Adam's hard and difficult childhood might have made him stronger than most, but it had also made him more sensitive. It made him somewhat of a ticking time bomb in Killian's eyes, one that could blow the situation up even worse. Adam's grin did not soothe Killian's worry.

"I want to get Rachel back." Adam paused before adding, "and then she's going to pay."

"Yeah?" Killian chunked he pizza box onto the counter. "Well, there isn't going to be any getting Rachel back unless she's willing to talk to us first. All those flowers? In the garbage can. Those messages, unreturned, and that damn ad never got run. We've been cut completely off."

That really pissed Killian off because he *still* didn't know what they'd done. He knew Dickles had done something, but he couldn't very well ask the man what. With Rachel not speaking to them, Killian was left completely in the dark.

With his mom handing out stupid advice like waiting for three weeks, Killian had been forced to shamefully turn to his last hope— the Internet. Boy, had he been shocked by what he'd learned online. Killian had always known the fairer sex tended to confuse things, but he'd never realized how twisted women tended to be. Of course, he couldn't use this newfound information if Rachel wouldn't talk to him.

"Which is why I've come up with this plan." Killian used the tip of his pizza to gesture to the outline he'd come up with last night. Adam glanced down, growing a scowl as he stared at Killian's scribbled handwriting.

"Abjunction?" Adam lifted the little notebook to glare even harder at the page. "You mean adjunction? No. That doesn't make any sense."

"Abduction, dude." Killian rolled his eyes. "Adjunction, I don't even know what the hell that is."

"It's when you join—Wait a minute!" Adam slapped the notebook down onto the counter. "Did you say 'abduction?' You're thinking of kidnapping Rachel?"

* * * *

Adam didn't know the number of a good shrink, but he intended to start looking for one because Killian needed medical attention now. His friend had obviously lost all reason right along with his sanity. Mums had given them very good advice. They wanted this thing to be serious, so they should take it seriously by moving slowly, taking their time, and not abducting Rachel in the process.

That argument should have sounded logical, but there Killian sat on the truck's bench seat, grinning. It made Adam's knuckles whiten over the steering wheel. They'd argued so long about Killian's new plan they'd be late for work. For all that, Adam suspected Killian still intended to harass Rachel.

Hopefully, though, he wouldn't be kidnapping her. Adam would so beat the crap out of Killian if he did. Adam had plans for Rachel and wouldn't be tolerating Killian screwing them up any more than he already had with all his pathetic begging.

That wouldn't win Rachel back. Adam had come to some honest revelations over the past two weeks. Rachel might not love him, but that didn't stop him from loving her. It put her in a position of power, though, that he wouldn't tolerate. If he had to endure being made weak and vulnerable by his emotions, then he'd make sure her addiction made her more so.

That's what she was, addicted to them, to the sex. Adam knew how to use that kind of power to get exactly what he wanted. What he wanted was Rachel in his bed, in his life, under his control. All things he could have if Killian didn't go and screw everything up with one of his crazy schemes.

Glancing over to where Killian grinned on like it was a shiny, happy morning when, in fact, it was overcast and miserable didn't fill Adam with much optimism. Maybe he really should send Killian to an asylum for a while, if for no other reason than to get his friend the serious help he needed.

Pulling into the station's back lot, Adam tucked the truck neatly under the shade of the azalea that grew out of control along the gravel lot's edge. At the jerk of the tires coming to a complete stop, Killian nodded and turned toward Adam.

"Okay," he commented as if they'd been holding some kind of conversation. Killian had slowly gone a little nuts as far as Adam could tell. "I'll hold off on snatching up the girl, but what do you think about some gifts? I mean really thoughtful gifts, because you remember how she was with Alex on her birthday."

"Somehow I don't think trying to buy Rachel's affection is going to work. That's not very respectful, and that's what we're trying to prove here, how much we respect her." Adam felt like a damn record. Every five minutes, he had to repeat something Mums had said. Not that he was a mama's boy, but the lady had made sense. "Remember, we're going slow this time."

Killian snorted, shoving open his door. He still managed to get in his favorite complaint. "Wasting time is more like it."

Rolling his eyes, Adam pushed out his own door. He wouldn't have wasted his breath in responding to that one, but even if he had wanted to respond, Adam wouldn't have gotten the chance. Before either of them could even close the door, Killian's name started to echo across the lot. A man jogged toward them, looking oddly familiar, though Adam knew he didn't know the guy.

"Deputy Killian Kregor?" Despite his run, the man didn't sound the least bit out of breath as he pulled up to a stop. He had a certain ex-military feel to him. Adam could almost peg him for being a cop but not from around these parts.

"Yeah?" Killian slammed his door. Apparently suffering from Adam's curiosity, he squinted at the guy. "Do I know you?"

"Officer Watts." The shorter, stockier man extended a beefy hand toward Killian before offering it to Adam as he came around the tailgate. "I'm sorry, I don't..."

"Deputy Whendon," Adam answered the leading comment with some hesitation. Not because he didn't want to but because now he had placed the man.

"My partner," Killian filled in. "So you're Watts, huh? You've been helping Rachel with her little project. And I'm going to assume the fact that you're now here looking for me isn't good news."

Killian said just what had Adam worried. Watts didn't make that sensation die down with guilty sigh. "I don't know if it's good or bad or whatever, but I heard you asked about me. The word is that Rachel used to be yours."

"Still is, thank you very much," Killian interjected, causing the officer to smile slightly.

"Yeah, I kind of heard it was like that with you, so I figured when I started to get worried, you might be inclined to do the same."

"And what does he have to be worried about?" Adam could already feel his muscles start to ache. Tensed and strained for two straight weeks, he didn't know if they had the energy left to take on any more worries. Hell, he might just snap.

"Well, you know she told me she was researching prostitution for a book, and so I was helping her out," Watts began slowly.

"You're not telling us anything we didn't know." Adam didn't even try to hide the implications lurking in his hard tone. It obviously gave Watts pause as he shot Adam a curious look. He didn't flinch under the scrutiny.

"So it's like that, huh?" Watts smirked again and shook his head. "I heard tales about you Pittsview boys but thought it was all just bragging."

"I don't really care what you heard about us," Adam shot back. "I'm still waiting to hear what you know about Rachel."

"Well, I know she's been feeding the Dothan police tips about a whorehouse being run through a motel out their way." Watts's words sank in like hot little bullets slicing through Adam's chest. It made it hard to breathe, but the shots just kept rolling out of Watts's mouth.

"According to my buddy, she knows things that only somebody on the inside would know." The officer paused to pin Adam with his piercingly light blue gaze. "And I mean on the actual inside of the building.

"When I heard that, it kind of put a set of bricks in my stomach," Watts confessed.

Adam knew what he meant. His gut filled with iron, though. Burning, red-hot rage boiled in the caldron that had become his stomach.

"I figured if you knew about it," Watts said as he shrugged, "well, you'd be in some kind of trouble with your boss, and if not then you might want to consider how much trouble your woman is digging herself into. Those boys out there are already working on their case and got their plans in place. It's going to be bad if Rachel gets caught in all of that."

"Don't worry," Killian assured him with such a chipper tone Adam's head rolled to stare at his friend in amazement. That fucking bastard was *still* smiling. He really had gone and lost it. "We'll handle Rachel. Thanks for the heads-up. If we can ever return the favor, you know where to find us."

"Yeah." Watts's puzzled look as he glanced from Killian to Adam and back confirmed that Adam wasn't the only one who thought Killian might be in need of a little time on the therapist's couch. "I'll remember that, and good luck with Rachel."

Adam would need it, stuck between a lunatic and a madwoman. What the hell could she possibly be thinking? Investigating a real prostitution ring was nowhere near the same thing as doing research for a book. The woman had completely lost control of her senses. The one thing Adam would not tolerate was her getting hurt.

"So," Killian said as he turned his fool's grin on Adam, "do I get to abduct her now?"

Chapter 33

It seemed strange to Rachel that a person could be so determined to be happy and still end up weighing twenty pounds extra at the end of the day from all the misery. The high point of her career had come to a stumbling stall these past two weeks. While she had the prostitution story in the works, Rachel didn't have the focus or concentration to take up anything else as intense.

So Rachel had spent her day interviewing Mary Sue Jennings about her Elvis-faced vegetable collection. Really, Mary Sue was quite sweet, and art was always a matter of interpretation, but Rachel didn't get it. The wife of an organic vegetable farmer, Mary Sue had collected over thirty different squashes, potatoes, even some bi-colored corn that kind of had a silhouette of a face, if that face happened to belong to Mr. Potato Head.

Rachel figured the readers would have to decide. She'd taken more than enough pictures to run with the article and expected some of the older townsfolk to get into a heated debate over what those faces really looked like. Of course, the article probably wouldn't be safe enough for Killian's approval. It was possible she could go out to the farm and get bitten by mosquitoes and end up dying of some rare tropical disease.

That made it easier for her to drop her purse on the coffee table and go listen to the message she knew awaited on her machine. Killian left one every other day right around six o'clock. It had become such a ritual that Rachel didn't answer her phone during the danger period.

The last thing she needed to deal with was a direct confrontation, no matter what Patton thought. What she really should have done was just erased them without listening, but she couldn't. A part of her clung to this one last remnant of their relationship and the warmth it gave her to hear Killian's voice.

Braced, she pressed the play button next to the flashing one, showing how many messages she had.

"You have one message...Six-oh-one pm...Rachel?"

She froze at the cold, hard sound of Adam's voice. It held no more emotion than the last time she'd heard it coming across the phone line. Only this time, there was a dark, determined undertone as he issued his warning.

"This is your last chance to do things the civilized way."

Every fiber of Rachel's being bristled in alarm as she went perfectly still, straining to hear something soft moving in the silence. Were they here? Already in her house? Or were they watching? Her gaze cut to the living room windows, curtains pulled back. Nothing moved out in the road, and she studied the bush line, fearful of what it might hide.

What the hell were they planning now?

Rachel started and shrieked at the shrill sound of the phone. Clamping a hand to her chest as if that would stop the pounding of her heart and let her catch a gasp of breath, she stared at the cordless unit as it let out another ear-piercing yelp.

She didn't recognize the number flashing in the caller ID screen, but it couldn't be Killian or Adam. The area code clearly came from out of the county. Still, she hesitated answering, not really in the mood to be distracted when she had to focus.

Adam had threatened her, which meant that he hadn't disappeared because he'd given up. He'd sulked off. From the sound of it, he'd brooded himself into a dark state. One where he obviously had detailed out a plan of retribution.

That should have terrified her because Rachel knew what Adam was capable of, but the fear fueling her blood was thick with arousal. It made her anticipate the coming attack instead of running from it as a wise woman would do.

The answering machine beeped, finally bringing an end to the obvious ringing. Rachel glanced down at it, snickering to herself as a velvety voice fairly purred out of the machine.

"Hey, Rachel, this is Nick. Nick Dickles. I was thinking about your story the other day, and I might be able to give you a little more help. There's this—"

Rachel hit the mute button, not caring to hear the rest. The man must have thought she was as bright as Patton did. Of course, if Rachel had followed Patton's advice, she'd have picked up the phone and given the man his due. There really wasn't any point in starting that argument. The man was an ass. She knew it. That's all that needed to be said.

Clicking the ringer off, Rachel sighed and surveyed her living room and dining room. She'd been standing here and so far nothing had happened, so it seemed unlikely that her deputies lurked in any of the corners. Still, to be on the safe side, Rachel searched the whole house, doubling-checking every window and both doors before drawing all the curtains closed and hiding herself away.

They'd come. Rachel couldn't afford to fool herself into thinking they wouldn't. Nor could she deny that after the past two lonely weeks, she would submit to a full-on seduction. The real question was what they planned to do after.

Or what she would do. As irritating as Patton had been, their conversation had plagued Rachel all day, making her question just why she didn't trust Killian and Adam. She obviously didn't because she remained morbidly convinced that she couldn't hold on to them. What she didn't know is where that conviction came from.

Certainly not from them because neither Killian nor Adam had ever done anything in the slightest to make any of her fears legitimate.

Just the opposite, they'd been the ones focused and pushing, outright clinging to her. If actions spoke louder than words, then theirs clearly said how much they cared for her, worried over her.

So why didn't that count? Why didn't it calm her fears instead of riling them up? Patton had it right. There would never be another man in her life whom she trusted half as much as she did Killian or Adam. That should be enough to take the risk and call them back, but it wasn't because a part of Rachel couldn't believe that they'd ever love her.

Realizing how sick she was didn't make her day any better. Nor did the sight of her empty bed, but she couldn't take another night on the couch. What the hell would be the point, anyway? It wasn't like she slept anymore.

Not that she would spend her night obsessing over whatever Killian and Adam planned. It would be better to be a victim of their seduction than seeking out her own destruction. That way when it was done, she could blame them. It would make a good defense if she got hurt.

* * * *

She decided to ignore Adam's threat, which turned out to be as hard as Rachel imagined. The fact that they'd decided to wait didn't make it easier. Thursday came and went without any flowers or other surprises. The most unexpected event had been Brandon's invitation to his and Duncan's ritual barbeque on Saturday.

Since Rachel had publicly dismissed Killian, a growing number of Cattlemen had started to issue her invitations. As with all the others, she'd been polite in her rejection, but the practice had started to wear thin. Being suddenly popular hadn't made the last two weeks any more bearable.

It actually made everything a little worse because she knew they only wanted her because Killian and Adam did, if that were even true. Rachel had begun to wonder just what they were really up to.

She kept her eyes peeled all of Friday for the slightest signal of her oncoming fate, but nothing out of the ordinary happened. The waiting began to drive her nuts. That evening, she finally snapped.

Unable to take it anymore, Rachel changed out of her sweats and went to tempt the beasts into the open by leaving the sanctuary of her house. She even decided to go over to the Bread Box for the first time since the day she'd dumped them. If they were watching her, then they'd read her actions as a silent challenge. Of that, Rachel was sure.

It still felt creepy leaving her house. The neighborhood was strangely quiet, the streets still and uncluttered. Brandon must have canceled his party because Duncan's and his house sat dark and deserted. It was how the whole town felt as she drove through it. Even the diner's parking lot was strangely vacant for the dinner rush hour.

There was a quite hush to the building as she entered, nothing like its normal chaos of conversation. Only a few patrons filled in along the booths, mostly families and elderly couples. Only one long-limbed figure sulked alone at the bar, the sheriff, and he couldn't have better timing because there was no way Killian and Adam could see her talking to him and maintain their patience.

It was a low, dirty trick, but Rachel felt like they'd come to the gloves off part of their battle. Everybody knew she'd be losing in the end, anyway, so she might as well go down fighting. Patton had it right in some respects. Cattlemen only placed sure bets.

That meant they didn't really need to chase because they knew they could have her whenever they wanted. Maybe that was why she was afraid to trust them. They had all the power. They controlled everything except for one thing.

Plopping her purse down the bar, Rachel beamed a wide grin at the sheriff. "Hey, sheriff, mind if I join you?"

Since she already had, it would have been polite for him to say yes, but Alex shot her a guarded look, issuing a cautious warning. "I don't know if that's wise tonight, Miss Adams."

"Miss Adams?" Rachel cocked a brow. "What happened to Rachel?"

"What happened to my deputies?" Alex shot back. "You know, Killian and Adam aren't the easiest of men to work with under normal circumstances, but at least they're good at their jobs. Or they were.

"Now I've got Adam running around giving eighty-eight-year-old Mrs. Porter a ticket for doing three miles over the speed limit. And Killian spends more time in a day plotting whatever crazy-ass idea that's fascinating him at the moment than actually bothering to issue tickets." Alex pointed his coffee-dipped spoon right at her. "I don't need this headache, Rachel."

Somehow, some way, Alex's rapid paced complaint actually lightened Rachel's mood. It felt good to be around somebody just as miserable as she was, driven there by the same two exasperating men. "So you want me to take them back to make your life easier?"

"Yes." Alex nodded. "Thank you."

Rachel really did laugh at that, settling back in her stool. As the mirth died off, a question remained that she couldn't resist asking. "So, they've been missing me?"

Alex snorted over the edge of his coffee cup. "Hell, I've seriously been considering pulling them off patrol and sending them to a shrink's office to see if they can be saved."

"Well," Rachel said, pausing to straighten out her silverware, "that's good to hear."

Alex choked on his coffee. She imagined he had a response for her flippancy, but Heather cut him off, appearing to flip over Rachel's mug and start filling it with coffee. "You want your usual?"

"That sounds good." Rachel's stomach grumbled, thinking about the fried chicken to come.

That normally would have ended their conversation, but Heather hesitated. "You, uh, wanna eat in back and keep me company?"

Rachel got the pointed message in Heather's glance at the sheriff. Then Rachel smiled at the silent warning. "No, I think I'll stay out here and keep the sheriff company."

"Are you sure?"

"Geez, Heather." Alex cocked his head to send her a smirk. "You know, some women actually find my company pleasurable."

Since Rachel knew he hadn't said that for her benefit, she had to wonder why he'd bothered for Heather's. Her friend certainly didn't jump to his bait. At least not directly. Instead, she focused her attention on Rachel. Resting her arms on the table, Heather slid in close to whisper, "You look around, Rachel. Look good and hard and consider what is missing." After issuing that cryptic warning, Heather shot Alex a dirty look. "And remember, some sheriffs consider when they want to know what they know."

"I have no idea what you're talking about," Alex retorted, sounding outright bored.

"Of course not."

"Well, I'd like to know what you're both talking about," Rachel interjected. Whatever was going on between Heather and the sheriff, Rachel didn't want to be in the middle of it. Not with Killian and Adam prowling around in the shadows. Maybe coming out hadn't been such a good idea.

"I don't really know," Heather shrugged. "All I can tell you is what my eyes aren't seeing."

That was Heather's second reference to vision. It had Rachel scowling as she turned around to study the diner. Besides the patrons, what was missing? Nothing but the men who normally filled—Rachel eyes widened in alarm as she spun around on her stool, but Heather had already disappeared. That left Alex, calmly chewing on a Danish.

"Where are they?"

"Huh?"

She'd give the sheriff his due for being a good actor and projecting the perfect expression of innocent confusion, except Rachel wasn't in the mood for games. Not anymore.

"The Cattlemen, where are they?"

"The who?"

"Drop the act, Alex. I know you know what I'm talking about."

"You're a reporter, Rachel." Alex smirked. "And I'm an elected official."

Rachel narrowed her gaze on that obnoxious response. "Off the record, Alex."

"Off the record?" He appeared to consider that for a moment before shrugging. "They're all gathered at the club. Got a big night's entertainment planned."

Rachel had a sick feeling she was the entertainment, even if that seemed an extreme conclusion. One thing she knew was Killian and Adam wouldn't be passing her around to all those men, so if they had planned something, the most they'd let any other man do was watch. The very second the idea hit her, Rachel felt her stomach fall away.

"So," the sheriff said, shoving back his empty plate, "you want to come home with me tonight?"

"What?" The very suggestion startled Rachel.

"Or," Alex offered with a smile, "you going to go out there alone?"

He knew, and he was offering her an escape. Only a crazy woman wouldn't leap at the chance to avoid her fate. The thing about fate was it caught up to everybody eventually. Rachel hesitated to think of what Killian and Adam would up the ante to if she hid behind Alex.

Or maybe it would decimate them, be the final blow that finally had them admitting defeat. Then she could go home to her comfortable couch for the rest of her miserable life.

"I think I'll be fine on my own."

"Suit yourself." Alex slid from his stool to fish his wallet out of his back pocket. "Just remember, they're only acting so crazy because you drove them to it. If you'd just settle down, they would, too."

Rachel glared at Alex's back as he sauntered out of the deli. Now the sheriff was giving her relationship advice. She'd hit a new low. If so many people thought she'd messed up, one had to question if they didn't have a point.

Her dinner ruined, Rachel barely picked at her chicken, obsessing over what would come after she left the diner. She could wait until close and escape to Heather's. Killian and Adam couldn't get overwrought about her hiding behind a female friend.

Still, when Heather offered her a lifeline with the check, Rachel shook her head.

"Want to hang out?" Heather glanced up at the front windows, now gone dark with the night. "You could come over to my place after."

"Nah."

"You know they're probably out there, waiting."

"Yeah." Rachel sighed and offered Heather a small smile. "But hiding for the night won't change the fact that they'll still be out there, waiting."

Heather gave her one of those concerned mother looks. "Do you want to go out there?"

"I want them to love me," Rachel whispered, finally admitting to it aloud. "I want them to promise me forever and then actually give it to me."

"Well, then," Heather said, giving the windows another bleak glance, "I guess you're going to have to go out there because you're not going to find either of those things in here."

Rachel would, in a moment, once she got her nerve up. "Patton said I should fight for them."

"Patton's half-cocked," Heather retorted instantly. "She's already got you, Hailey, and Kitty in enough trouble. This isn't some kind of game, Rachel. We both know you love those men, despite all reason.

"Now, the question is, are you willing to give this relationship a chance." Heather held up one hand before raising her second. "Or are you still intent on crashing it headfirst into a brick wall. And don't for a minute think that your decision is going to bring you happiness or misery for the rest of your life."

She paused to offer Rachel a small smile. "I'm sorry, honey. Everybody's future holds both."

Except that hers could be weighted to one side or the other, all depending on what decision she made now. Ultimately, she had nothing to lose. If she took a risk and they crushed her, that wouldn't be any worse than the past two weeks.

"I guess it's time I settled down then, huh?" Rachel offered up as a weak joke.

"It's time to make your decision and stick with it."

Chapter 34

Rachel stepped out of the diner, feeling like she was walking out into the set of a movie. There was something surreal about the lacy rays of moonlight brightening the darkest of shadows into a hazy gray. A plump, full moon filled the sky, appearing too close to be real. At any moment, Gene Kelly would appear to go singing and dancing down the street.

Except that if her life was a musical, the *Jaws* song would be playing. Her heartbeat mimicked the song that whispered through her head. The steady thump kept her braced and ready to fly into a full gallop at the least sign of danger, a possibility of which existed in every car she passed and every shadow that shifted in the night's cool breeze.

Strung up on anticipation, Rachel twitched and shied her way around the edge of the Bread Box and into the most treacherous part of her path. She really should have parked on the street. Of course, when she'd arrived, Rachel had hoped to bait Killian and Adam into action. Boy, had that been a dumb idea.

Score one for Patton. Actually, score two because it had been her voice nagging at Rachel into action. This is what came from listening to Patton. Now she crept down the parking lot's drive, staying dead center and well away from any shadow, probably making a complete fool of herself in the process.

They were just men, after all. Killian and Adam weren't some mythic warriors with magical powers allowing them to shape-shift through the night to sneak up right on her heels and...Rachel spun around, half expecting to see Adam smiling down at her, but the only thing looking at her was a vacant parking lot.

She really had to calm down, Rachel told herself. Killian and Adam didn't scare her. They never could. The only thing frightening about them was what she felt for them. That existed whether or not they stalked her through the night or ignored her existence. In the end, she couldn't escape, which was why she'd stepped out of the Bread Box alone in the first place.

The pep talk worked at lifting her chin, straightening her shoulders, and getting her feet to move forward in a brisk, determined pace. Rachel didn't even fumble with her key when she got to her car door. It popped open, banging her in the stomach as she stepped back into a hard wall of unforgiving muscle. An arm as solid as any tree branch shot out from around her to slam the door back closed.

Adam. She'd know him by his scent alone. His appearance didn't scare her at all. Just the opposite, Rachel found her first real smile in days. "I knew you were out here."

She'd meant to turn with that comment and confront him directly, but Adam apparently had other plans. The hand he'd slapped back the car door with lifted to clamp over her mouth at the same moment his other hand plowed into her back. With the speed and efficiency of a well-trained cop, he bent her right into the car, cuffing her hands behind her before Rachel's mind could register his actions.

By the time it hit her what Adam had done, it was too late. He levered her back onto her feet, continuing to hold her hostage with his hand pressing her head back into his chest. The world went black even as the sound of a truck engine shattered the night's silence.

It rumbled over the gravel, the heavy tread vibrating through the ground beneath her feet, but Rachel couldn't see the headlights around the blindfold Adam had lassoed over her head. No piece of rolled-up fabric tonight, Adam used a proper blindfold.

This one bunched her hair as he tightened down the strap, making her wince slightly and finally issue an objection from behind the tight grip of his fingers. Adam's only response was to begin dragging her back over the gravel toward the growing growl of the truck.

He had to release her to heft her up into the bench seat, but as Rachel's butt hit the long, smooth cushion, she didn't bother to offer any more complaints. Nor did she waste any efforts on fighting. She had lied to Patton when she'd said she didn't see any point in it. If she hadn't wanted to be here, then she could have ducked out the back and gone home with Heather.

Instead, she was back to her favorite spot, tied up and pinned between Killian's long length and Adam's hard heat. It could only be better if they were naked, but Rachel suspected that would be next on the agenda. That and making a show out of her for all the Cattlemen. That made her womb melt instead of putting the vigor back into her spine like it should have.

It did a little as it dawned on her that if they planned on only revenge, they'd be doing what they were doing right then and staying silent. It wouldn't work that way because Rachel needed this to be something more. That meant they had to have a conversation before she agreed to Killian and Adam's payback.

With the truck bumping over the road and speeding fast into the night, Rachel figured she didn't have much time. So, in the spirit of compromise, she began.

"Don't you two think this is a little much?" Rachel asked to neither one of the deputies in particular. "I mean, I know what you're planning to do."

She waited but nothing happened, not even a slight shift in the men bordering her. Sighing over their stubbornness, Rachel decided to prove a point. Turning her head, she leaned over slightly to press her nose against the soft cotton of a T-shirt and inhale the clean, fresh scent.

"You're Killian. And that makes you," Rachel guessed, leaning in the opposite direction to take a sniff of the man to her right, "Adam. Now that you've kidnapped me, which, by the way, was a completely overdramatic statement so I have to figure that it was Killian's idea, you're taking me to the Cattleman Club to fuck me in front of all your friends, which has to be Adam's brainchild for as deviant—"

Rachel choked on the bolt of cloth that was shoved in her mouth, effectively ending her attempt at reconciliation, right along with her tolerant mood. It didn't help that Adam tied the gag as tight as he had the blindfold, pinching her in the process. This time, Rachel did fight, or at least squirmed, trying to rub the gag off along with the blindfold.

With such big men taking up all the space, she didn't have much room to twist about in. Every time she managed to get her cheek to rub against her shoulder, Killian would jerk the truck and send her flying sideways, plowing her head into either his or Adam's lap. Rachel bet the big lug was grinning, too.

That had her ignoring the gag to shout out obscenities that might have been muffled but still came through as angry, aggressive noise. He jerked the truck hard again, this time making enough of a curve that they had to have turned into or onto something. The sudden rotation had her falling into Adam's lap before her head started to roll down into the floorboards.

She'd have ended completely upside down in her seat if one of them hadn't caught her. A big hand fisted in the back of her dress, curling around the elastic edge of her panties to hold her pinned in position as the massive truck came to a screeching halt.

The sudden stop jerked the whole vehicle. Rachel was thankful for the hand keeping her from slamming into the dash, even if it hurt to be dragged back onto the seat by her underwear. The discomfort distracted her for a moment as she wiggled around, trying to smooth out her bunched panties. Not embarrassed and not silent, Rachel gave Killian hell through her gag for pulling such a juvenile stunt.

Her tirade came to a squeaking halt when Killian's hands clamped onto her arms. Pinning them tight to her side despite the cuffs, he held her still as he waited for something. Not knowing what only made

Rachel more nervous as her mind jumped from one outlandish idea to another.

Anything was possible because she was pretty damn sure they'd arrived at the club. Her wildly perverted musings did not prepare her for the simple brush of cool metal against her neck. It snaked around her, Adam's fingers brushing like heated leather against her flesh as he worked to clasp the two ends.

Rachel didn't need her eyes, didn't need to see, to know that Adam had collared her. What she needed was to have her hands free so she could rip the damn choker back off. He would not be leading her around all his obnoxious buddies naked and directed by a damn leash. She might not be able to pull it off and lasso his damn neck with the chain, but Rachel could still throw a hell of a tantrum.

As the crank and creak of a gate opening whined through the air, Rachel went into a frenzy, thrashing about in her seat and managing to stomp her feet and dig her heels into their shins. The revelry was short lived, brought to an end by Adam smashing Rachel's face into Killian's heavily muscled lap. It had grown a new one, a big one that pressed his zipper out and into her cheek.

Rachel snarled back at the penis flexing for her benefit and jerked hard to free herself of Adam's hold. Even one-handed, he managed to keep her pinned while his other hand jerked her legs up and into his own lap. She'd have loved to have bent a knee and done some damage to the other erection now rubbing against her thigh.

They didn't give her the opportunity as one of Killian's hands came to keep her face pressed into his crotch, freeing up Adam to hold her legs stiff and steady across his lap. Unable to do more than ground out a few obscenities that came out sounding more like moans, Rachel found herself stuck, stretched flat across the bench seat on her tummy, her shoes lost somewhere in the floorboard.

The truck rumbled and jerked forward, moving at a slower pace now. Rachel knew they'd passed through the massive entrance that protected the Cattleman's Club from unwanted visitors. She might not be unwanted, but Rachel didn't know if the sentiment was fully returned.

For as much as their arrogant and rough antics aroused her, they also stirred a panicky sensation that made it hard to breathe. Her heart and body might pulse with the anticipation of what came next, but a part of her seethed with the knowledge. It wanted to rally and fight, but not having those options made it harden into bitterness.

Nothing would ever change. It would always be like this, with them trying to control her every move and her pulling back because she needed some amount of independence. Her love didn't matter. Even if they loved her in return, this constant tension could only lead to disaster.

That solemn thought kept her still and quiet as the truck wound its way into the darkness. At the silence, Rachel's ears perked up, straining for some tinkling of glasses or murmuring of conversation when the truck's engine finally died out. They'd arrived. Rachel knew that throngs of men awaited this moment, but as Killian pulled her from the truck all that greeted her was the noisy hum of crickets and the guttural thrills of frogs croaking all around.

They had to be at the club, but there was no way so many men could be so silent. Their scent certainly would have no place to hide, but no hint of smoke or must tickled her nose. Only the rich, drugging odor that was Killian's alone penetrated the fresh air to warm her from the inside. It was a comfort when his hard shoulder was not.

Being carried around like a sack of feed gave her some satisfaction that Killian knew better than to walk her like a dog at the end of some damn leash. Mostly, it made her stomach object to the hard bone digging into it.

Rachel squirmed and whined behind her gag in a clear signal that she wanted to be shifted. If not to her feet then at least to his arms, but Killian only responded with a pat on her ass as another gate cried over being opened.

This one they walked through into a garden judging from the crunch beneath Killian and Adam's footfalls. Perhaps even an alleyway made of shrubs because she could feel the occasional scrape and scratch of stiff, brittle leaves brushing past.

They lingered, appearing to pass endlessly by until Rachel wondered if her mind hadn't shut down for a moment. Perhaps it couldn't handle everything this time and had simply forgotten to track time because it felt they'd wandered for over five minutes before another gate groaned on its hinges.

However far they'd walked, wherever they'd carried her, they'd arrived at their destination. Rachel knew that for a fact when her feet touched the ground. The soft grass caressed her toes, leaving her no doubt that they remained outside, still surrounded by the happy murmurings of nature…and the soft babbling of flowing water.

Rachel strained to hear more, knowing they hadn't dumped her in the middle of a field. Her mind, though, hadn't fathomed the decadent beauty that greeted her eyes as the blindfold lifted. Rachel turned, taking in her lush surroundings as Killian went to work on untying her gag.

Stacked stone walls encircled the small patio, bordered on either end by wrought iron gates nearly overgrown with rose vines. Above, leaves fanned out across slender tree limbs that grew over the edges of the wall to form a natural canopy. It diffused the moonlight, letting it rain down in soft slivers that shifted and danced with the breeze.

Everything grew so full and thick but was tailored to give the little oasis a sense of civilized nature. Or perhaps not. Rachel reconsidered her opinion as her gaze fell over the altar-like structure erected in the very center of the circle.

She could make out the shadow of drawers lining the sides, thick and big. Rachel could well imagine what lay hidden beneath the padded top. The rings cemented into each corner gave the not-so-subtle function of the altar.

"So," she breathed out evenly, trying to sound nonchalant, "this is where you sacrifice you virgins, huh?"

That earned her a slight smile from Adam before his voice purred out with a promise that made her shiver. "You're not wrong."

He flicked a switch, and suddenly the rock walls glowed to life with the gentle umber of the glass lanterns. Bathing the whole area in a seductive warmth, the light revealed that the Cattlemen had more than civilized their garden. They'd modernized it. From the wide stretch of the black screen embedded in the wall to the little kitchenette built into its side, they'd made their garden of Eden a place to relax and enjoy a good show.

Rachel's eyes glanced up, and sure enough cameras were mounted, discretely but pointedly, along the entire perimeter. Easy to be forgotten in the moment, they were sure to leave a woman tingling over the memory for years. The moment had really come, and she couldn't help but glance at the gates.

"You'll never make it," Adam warned her in that velvety tone that made her breath catch. He was prowling, watching her with a gaze feral enough to make her start to truly worry. She'd never seen him this pissed or this hungry.

"So you're going to tie me up to that altar and have your way." Rachel silently cursed at the way her voice trembled, betraying both her fear and her desire. "Is that going to make it all better?"

He came to a stop with his boots brushing against her toes, and he split into a true, double-dimpled grin. More intimidating than an angry Adam, the happy one had her breath catching as he leaned down close to whisper in her ear.

"Oh, honey, you're not getting off that easy."

Then he bumped her, brushed right past and banged her backward into Killian in the process, like a shark would challenge something it was considering eating. Rachel turned with the jarring motion, unnerved in the extreme by his attitude as much as his words. Killian got in her way. Instead of catching her, Adam moseyed off, too, leaving her to ram her nose hard into the bulge of his arm.

"Watch yourself now, darlin'. Don't want to hurt yourself."

Rachel stared up into Killian's laughing eyes and told herself she had it right. Killian was about as giddy as a five-year-old rushing down to see what Santa had left for him. The big deputy might be even more excited than that, given he knew what present awaited him.

He never seemed to take anything seriously, which was probably why she loved him so damn much. The man had a way of charming the good sense right out of her head with vivacious enthusiasm. Not tonight, though.

Tonight she stared up at him, wondering if he even understood how important this moment was. They could either destroy her or heal her, but they couldn't laugh at her. Not tonight.

* * * *

Killian watched the tension fade in her gaze as her eyes clouded over with thoughts. The flush on her cheeks receded as her whole face seemed to swell with sadness. The pensive look made him groan, forcing her back around so he could undo the cuffs and avoid looking at that serious face.

"You're thinking again, darlin'. Ain't you figured out that's what gets you in all this trouble in the first place?"

"Is that what I'm in?" Rachel whispered back, not sounding angry but cold enough to make Killian scowl. "Because I don't really think you have the right to punish me for breaking up with you, but I certainly have the right to leave if I want to."

He snapped the second cufflink free and stepped around to address that one. "Yes, I do, and no, you don't. It all depends on whether you broke up with us for a good reason or some stupid-ass one."

That brought the frown back to her brow and the glare back to her gaze. "Why did I even think we could have an honest conversation?"

"Oh, honey," Killian shook his head at her, "we're not here to have a conversation."

"I figured that out." Rachel snorted.

"This is the part where you shut up and listen." Killian smiled at the way his blunt words had her cheeks flaming again. He'd really missed messing with his Rachel. She always jumped to every scrap piece of bait.

"No," she snapped back instantly. "This is the part where you take this damn collar off and point me in the exit because I've had enough of these games."

Killian didn't think that was true in the slightest. In fact, she appeared to be doing everything she could to rally them into action. Adam didn't need any encouragement. He'd been straining on the end of his patience since Wednesday.

It hadn't helped that Rachel had turned down Brandon's offer and blown Adam's plans for a seductive dinner to smithereens. Killian had always thought that one was stupid, but it had been the last straw for Adam.

The very last thread came undone when Rachel's hands lifted to tug at the clasp of the choker Adam had given her. The defiant gesture snapped Adam into action. He caught her wrists in his hands, pulling her arms straight up until she had to go on her tip-toes.

The position brought her ear level with Adam's lips. Killian watched as her hair danced when he growled. "The games don't begin until you run through one of those gates. Do you want to flee now?"

Adam took a nibble at her neck, blurring her words into a breathy whimper. "Adam—"

He released her so quickly she stumbled right into Killian's chest and his waiting arms. Catching her, Killian offered her confused expression a helpful grin. "I told you to watch yourself, darlin', or you really are going to get hurt."

That snapped her features back into a look of annoyance as she jerked back. "Nobody likes an—"

"Best you shut up and listen to him," Adam warned her. "Otherwise, I'll be taking *my turn* first."

That snapped Rachel's jaw closed as she cast a dirty look in Adam's direction. His partner didn't flinch but held her gaze until she folded. Glancing up at Killian, he could see that her sass had turned to a sulk. While the tempting pout of her lips distracted some parts of him, Killian managed to remain focused on the current mission.

They'd get to fucking their brains out once he had an assurance that it wouldn't be a one night thing but an every night thing. Somebody had to remember the point of all this because Killian knew Adam didn't right then. Adam wanted Rachel too bad and she'd pissed him off too much for the man to be thinking straight.

So Killian was left to play the gracious host and hope that his partner didn't make anything worse. With that in mind, he offered Rachel's wary look a big smile and gestured to the plush bench behind her.

"Why don't you have a seat?"

Chapter 35

Rachel glanced nervously at Adam, not completely convinced he'd retreated, even if he had paced into the shadowed corner of the patio. She didn't know what he'd meant by that "flee" comment, but she had a strong feeling he actually intended to run her to ground like honest-to-God prey.

Between Adam's restless aggression and Killian's Cheshire cat grin, she certainly felt like the mouse about to be feasted on. It had her hesitating to do anything Killian commanded, even if he masked the order as a cordial suggestion.

"I think I'd rather stand." Rachel lifted her chin at Killian, letting him know she wouldn't be cowed. She might feel skittish and pretty damn aroused with Adam's kiss still tingling down her neck, but she could still be just as strong as them and control herself.

"Suit yourself." Killian let her attitude slide, not even dimming his grin. "Maybe I could offer you some soda or a beer. The refrigerator is fully—"

"You did not kidnap me and drag me all the way out here to play host," Rachel snapped, not in the mood to be toyed with. "So why don't you say what you have to say and let's get this over with."

"That anxious to start the game?" Adam murmured as he brushed past her, giving her a heated look that left a trail of fire in his wake.

Rachel steeled herself against the effects of that smoky tone. She would not be caught off guard tonight by their good cop, bad cop routine. They would not wind her all in circles and make her about crazy as she tried to figure out if she were too damn pissed or too damn horny for her own good.

"Why don't you sit before you fall over?" Killian did more than suggest this time. He used his hands on her shoulders to back her up until she toppled onto the bench. "Those knees are shaking, darlin'. You itching to run, then?"

"Maybe she's itching to spread," Adam growled from the shadows, making her jerk back to her feet.

Shoving Killian aside, she glared at the man circling her slowly at a distance. "Why don't you just keep your mouth shut, Adam? Killian has something to say."

Killian snorted out a chuckle. "Actually, darlin', it's you that have something you should have told us well before now."

It took her a moment before she figured out that comment. With Killian patiently waiting for an answer and Adam shifting through the shadows, Rachel forgave herself for being a little dense. "You want to know why."

Killian nodded. "It is the question I've been asking your answering machine every other day. Are you ready to answer now?"

Rachel owed him one. It would be the first good step in trying to sort out this disaster of a relationship, if there was one left. "When I went to see Dickles, he kind of implied that you'd stopped by to see him, and you left him with the impression you didn't think much of me as a reporter."

She hesitated for a moment, giving them the opportunity to attack her for that admission. When Killian only waited expectantly and Adam didn't bother to crawl back out of the shadows, Rachel forged on ahead, thinking she knew what they wanted.

"I've since learned that he probably lied and did so to settle some score with you two." It took all her strength and a deep breath to get the rest out. "I was wrong."

It was time for them to gloat, but neither man jumped at that tempting piece of bait. Killian only nodded and prodded her along. "And?"

"And?" Rachel glanced around before shrugging. "I'm sorry?"

That irritated Killian. She caught the slight flash in his gaze before his smile tightened into a sardonic twist. "Sorry that you didn't come to us like a mature woman would? Sorry that you believed in a man you'd known for a couple of hours over the men who'd been sharing your bed for over a month? Sorry that you don't have the barest idea about of trust or respect for us to give us a chance to tell you our side? Just what exactly are you sorry for, darlin'?"

"I don't know. All of that sounds good." She was baiting them, and Rachel knew it. Only it didn't make any sense. She'd wanted to have a conversation to set everything right between them. Maybe it was because the sex was safer. No matter how kinky or perverse they got, they couldn't scare her on that front. This one, though, had started to make her itchy.

Killian seemed to understand. With a gentle touch, he cupped her cheek and lifted her eyes past his grin to where his gaze had hardened. "You're not going to tempt Adam off his leash. You know better than that. The angrier you make him the more controlled he becomes."

"And the more detailed my plans become," Adam whispered right over her shoulder. He pressed in close behind her, letting her feel his heat and hardness as his erection bulged out to rub against her ass. "The longer you make this take, the more pain I suffer, the more retribution I will demand."

Rachel licked her lips and swallowed, not daring to turn around and confront the lust she knew would be simmering in his eyes. It was hard enough to get the words out as she stared up into Killian's molten gaze.

"Fine. I'm sorry about all of it but…" She couldn't hold Killian's look and dropped her head to whisper out the rest. "I wasn't wrong to let you go."

"Now see, darlin', that's the part that don't make any sense." Killian chuckled and shook his head. "It's been bothering me, trying to figure out just why you're so screwed up."

"Excuse me?" That had Rachel bristling with enough indignation to step free of Adam's strength. "I'm not screwed up!"

"Sure you are," Killian argued with her. "But don't take it personally. It's just 'cause you're a woman."

That had Rachel choking. At the snorted laughter behind her, she found herself more than capable of turning to give Adam a dirty look. He might have sounded amused, but that mirth didn't make it to the hard eyes trying to hypnotize and paralyze her. Rachel wouldn't fall victim to his seduction so easily.

"Do you mind?"

He didn't answer that snapped question but to bump her as he shouldered past. This time, Rachel shoved back, about damn tired of being intimidated by him. She didn't have the strength to topple him, and the only reason he turned was because he wanted to.

Like the shark she'd considered him a minute ago, Adam decided to finally take a bite and see if his prey was ready to be eaten. Devoured, because that's what it felt like to go from angrily glaring at him to dangling from his arms.

Before she could even think to pry herself free, his lips broke over the tip of the breast he'd lifted up for his feasting. The thin cotton of her sundress offered no real protection against the liquid heat of his kiss. Always exciting but comfortingly familiar, his tongue wound over her tit, flicking and circling the sensitive nub until he bit down and sent a shower of sparkling pleasure erupting out of her chest.

Rachel gave herself over to the brilliant sensation, letting it drench her parched senses. So hot, his kiss flamed across her skin, branding her flesh as his again. His always. She could never deny him or this. The will to even consider such a thing didn't exist in her body, nor did the strength.

Melting into his embrace, Rachel arched, offering more of her swollen breast up for his tasting. Adam ignored the silent plea, almost seemed to punish her for it when his lips tightened over her trapped nipple and began sucking with such greediness Rachel couldn't hold back the moans anymore.

Losing herself to the rapid winds of rapture howling through her body, Rachel gave herself over to the rhythm of his swirling tongue. Her hips lifted, rolling with a sensual beat that built steadily upward until she couldn't stop from crying out.

"Adam, please!"

She didn't know what she asked for. Only knew that she wanted what he obviously didn't intend to give her that easily. With a snarl, he dropped her, letting her stumble backward on legs too weak to hold her sudden weight. Rachel couldn't catch her balance or grasp what had happened, but slamming onto her ass helped to rectify both conditions.

Rachel could have said, "Message received. Don't push Adam," but being so quickly discarded made it all the more tempting to chase after him and do something like kick him. He wouldn't see her coming with his back to her, but the steady, angry march of his feet warned her that violence wouldn't earn her an orgasm.

"See, women got to convolute everything," Killian commented as if their conversation had never been interrupted.

The bastard still sounded as chipper as ever, which earned him a dark look from Rachel before she lifted herself. At least he reminded her that she hadn't come here for the pleasure…well, not solely because of it. Getting what she really wanted appeared even harder to come by with Killian carrying on with his obnoxious comments.

"When a man makes a decision, he makes it and it's done. Now a woman," Killian gestured toward her, causing Rachel to pause in the act of dusting off her dress to await his pearl of wisdom, "she makes her decision and two days later has to rethink it, and about a week later has to reassess it, and maybe a month later she's got to review it."

"Yeah, I'm reassessing some things right now," Rachel assured him as she stiffened up.

Her hard tone didn't even dent Killian's grin. "A man, he can make a commitment, but a woman comes up with all sorts of excuses. Trust me, honey, I know. I've been doing some research."

"Is that right?" Rachel smirked.

"Oh yeah." Killian nodded. "I read this study about how something like sixty percent of men want to be married but only around thirty percent of women want to. Apparently, most women think they got to take care of men, and so I figure that's what you're all in a twist about. You think we're like kids or something that's kind of beneath you, and while you like the fun, you really don't want to be encumbered in the long run. Right?"

He had it so wrong, so backward that Rachel could only stare at him for a second in blind shock. What amazed her more than Killian's twisted conclusion was the very fact that he hadn't lied. Obviously, he had done some kind of research.

"No." Her quiet denial finally penetrated his happy glow, leaving him with a growing scowl. "That doesn't have anything to do with anything, Killian."

"Okay." It took less than a second for his grin to pop back. "I've got another theory."

"Why don't you just save us all the time, darlin', and just tell him what's wrong?" Adam had circled back around to her. The warmth of his breath teasing over her flushed nape didn't have her teeth grinding half as much as the hand he slipped around to press over her mound. "Then we can get onto the game, and you know you want to get there. Don't you, pet?"

Rachel's response choked on her gasp as Adam's fingers spread out, pressing down into her dress until he found the seam of her pussy through her panties. One thick finger slid down into her slick folds of her sex, discovering her heat. The flimsy material of her clothes couldn't hide the truth from him, and Rachel didn't even try when her hips began to match the slow undulations of his finger rubbing over her clit.

"You're wet."

"Yes, I am," she agreed, but she wouldn't be played again. It took all her strength to jerk free of his hold. From a safe distance, she turned to confront the man staring back at her with a predatory hunger that made her take another quick step back. "Wanting you isn't the problem, Adam. I'll always want you."

"See, now. That's confused." Killian leapt onto her comment. "How does it make any rational sense to want something that you're denying yourself? If you want us, why not just be with us?"

"Because," Rachel explained, turning so that she could still keep an eye on Adam while addressing Killian, "wanting something doesn't make it good for you."

"We're not good for you?" From his hesitant tone, Rachel knew she'd hurt him. That wasn't what she wanted to do.

"No...I'm not saying this right." Rachel sighed. "I meant...the relationship. It wasn't exactly a healthy one."

Killian's sulky expression tightened into a pissed one in an instant. "In what kind of way wasn't it?"

"You..." Rachel faltered, really wishing she had something more solid to defend herself with. "You tried to control me to the point where you were checking up on me and going through my papers."

"First off, we didn't go through your papers," Killian shot back, like a commander reprimanding an immature private. "I accidentally knocked them over and caught a glimpse of something that drew my attention. Of course, you never did ask about that.

"You just assumed you knew we were up to no good, and if you were so damned worried about us snooping, you should've put your shit in a drawer." Killian's temper was lit now. All the surface show of happiness had pinched out under the tirade raging out of him. "And second off, once you made yourself clear about us over-involving ourselves in your professional activities, we backed off.

"We actually did the mature thing and listened to you, but still you don't hesitate even a moment to think the worst of us. But we ain't done anything wrong. I defy you to tell me how *we* screwed up this relationship."

"You went to see Dickles," Rachel shot back instantly, not ready to take all the blame yet.

"So?" Killian didn't concede even a bit of indignation to her accusation. "The words I wanted to have were with that bastard, not with you. Why would I talk to you? I know you can hold your own against a man like him, but that don't mean he couldn't make things difficult or uncomfortable for you. That's something I had to address with him because it would be my fault if my past messed up your research."

"What about Watts?" Rachel could have argued the Dickles thing, but she backed off, seeing she wouldn't be winning on that score. "You looked into Meeks."

"Yes, I did," Killian told her proudly. "I'm a cop. You're my woman. I'm going to keep you safe, no matter what. The first thing I need to know is who you are associating with, because trust me, honey, nobody will get you into trouble faster than a friend."

Rachel cringed at that last comment, her mind immediately jumping to Hailey and Patton's wild scheme. If Killian knew about that, they wouldn't be standing around having a nice conversation. They'd have already moved onto Adam's game.

"So?" Killian goaded her, taking her silence for defeat. "I'm still waiting to hear what it is we did."

"You would have left anyway." Licking her lips, Rachel lifted her chin and decided to go for broke. There really wasn't any point in hiding anymore. Not with all the extremes they'd gone to have this conversation. "We all know it. I just...did things on my timeline. I'm sorry if that was a little faster than yours, but it's still the same ending you would have wanted at some point."

She'd opened up her heart and bared her soul to him, only to have Killian snort and roll his eyes. "See, now that's just screwed up."

"Oh, go fuck yourself, Killian." Rachel didn't need to hear anything more.

"Trust me, darlin', you're going to be doing that for me in just a bit, but first I'm going to have my say."

"I don't want to hear what you have to say." She'd already gotten the message. Hopefully, her heart had, too, because knowing that he didn't care would only make tomorrow worse. She really should have hidden at Heather's.

"Do you want to be cuffed and gagged for this?"

He could and would. That only made her hate him more right then. "Fine. Get everything off your chest, Killian, because this is the last time I'm ever going to bother listening to you."

"You never listen anyway," Killian shot back. "Or didn't you hear what I said? Men want a commitment, and I know you're smart enough to read between the lines and get my point, but since you want to play it dense, I'll just say it.

"Adam and I want a commitment. One of those until-death-do-you-part kind of things. Hell, dumb-shit over there," Killian said, waving at where Adam paced in the shadows, "he already told you he loved you. That's the problem, isn't it?

"Now you know you've got us by the short and curlies, so you think you can run all around, acting crazy and free and we'll be chasing after you because we got no choice. Well, I got news for you, missy. It ain't going to work like that.

"After tonight, we're going to lay out the rules, and we're all going to obey them. Unless it is unanimously agreed that somebody broke the rules, nobody gets to leave the relationship. Got that?"

Rachel blinked and then blinked again, trying to figure out what the hell she felt. Part of her thought she should be angry if for no other reason than he'd yelled at her. His words, though, didn't give her any motivation but to stare.

What he said only made sense if she was wrong about one thing. The very thing she'd never doubted in all the weeks. "Adam only said he loved me because I was pissed at you two. He didn't mean it."

"Are you calling me a liar?"

Rachel jumped well over a foot as that growl came, low and threatening, right over her shoulder. She shouldn't have turned, though, because catching sight of the unholy fire burning in his eyes and tensing his muscles to stone only made her too nervous to answer honestly.

"No."

"Yes, you are." He took a step forward, and she immediately matched it with one backward.

"I'm just saying, that's kind of like a man's notion of a get-out-of-jail-free card." Another step forward and another backward.

"Yeah, sort of how it's like a woman to scream it when she's orgasming harder than any other lover she's known made her." Rachel banged into Killian, coming to a forced stop while Adam caged her in from the front. "So tell me, sweet Rachel, did you lie?"

Chapter 36

Adam waited, feeling the air burning his lungs with the need to escape. He couldn't let go over the breath. He couldn't even feel the beat of his heart until it contracted painfully with the dipping of her chin. In that moment, he was so sure the answer was yes that he couldn't even hear the one she whispered a moment later.

"No."

Rachel shifted slightly, a silent demand to be released that Adam ignored. He wouldn't release her now, not after all the weeks of loneliness and doubt. She'd gotten halfway to where he wanted her to be, more than enough for the pain to recede beneath the avalanche of lust fueling his suddenly racing heart. All she needed now was to give him those three little words and he'd be flying.

"It doesn't matter, though." Rachel's eyes lifted to give him a sorrowful look from under her lashes. "I might love you, and you might love me, but that doesn't change anything."

Oh, the hell it didn't. It changed everything, but Killian would be better at explaining that. With a pointed look at his partner, Adam stepped back to step around the couple. He couldn't stand still, couldn't be that close to Rachel for too long without breaking.

Never before had he fought so hard to control the primitive urges to take and ravage. Knowing what came next didn't help soothe the ache in his balls. If they didn't get to it soon, he might very well explode in his damn jeans. That certainly was not how he planned to end this night.

"And why not?"

Adam cast Killian a glance, wondering how his friend could sound so chipper when his own voice seemed to scrape out of his throat, rough and dry. Killian, though, had insanity on his side, which made him more than qualified to handle Rachel.

She proved his assessment right by going from sad looking to pissed in a blink of an eye. Adam suspected Killian's overly happy façade irritated her as much as it did him.

"Because this isn't a movie." She stated it like they didn't already know that obvious fact. "This is real life, and sometimes, love isn't enough. There are still problems."

"Like what?"

Adam would like to know that answer, too. Pausing by the kitchenette, he waited for Rachel's answer while considering he might need to pour himself a drink if she took too much longer with all her drama.

"Like the fact that I'm going to get fat...ter."

"What?!"

Adam seconded Killian's outraged response by flipping open the refrigerator and reaching for one of the many miniature liquor bottles. He didn't care what and didn't need a glass. All he needed was something to smother the fire raging in his groin because he really wanted to punish Rachel for that answer.

"And my boobs...already starting to sag."

"I have no earthly idea of what you are babbling on about."

"Oh, come on, Killian." Rachel had worked herself up into a fit now, all flashing eyes and flushed cheeks—ripe for the picking. "You don't think I don't remember what those amazons at the bonfire looked like. That I didn't read your file. I'm short, fat, and frumpy, and you're used to dating swimsuit model lookalikes."

"Okay, first off, you're not short. You're dainty," Killian shot back, looking every inch as pissed as Rachel. "Second off, you're not fat, you're plush and soft and rounded just like I like. Third off, I don't care what you wear as long as you're naked when you get into my bed at night."

The drink didn't help. He couldn't stay away from her, needing to be close enough to touch, taste, or just drown in her sweet scent. Adam prowled forward, gaze locked on his Rachel even as she roared back at Killian.

"Don't even start that charming bullshit. You know what I mean."

"Yeah," Adam agreed, because he surely did. "You mean to say that my love is so shallow as to be based on nothing more than appearance."

The way she started made the aggression prowling in his spirit claw that much harder to be released. The primal man inside wanted very desperately to shed his decency and civility, to be released to hunt, capture, devour. He'd start with those trembling, pouty fuck-me lips.

"No...I..."

"Yes." Adam nodded, aroused by the way she stuttered and shifted away from him. The scent of feminine arousal mixed with her look of wariness triggered all of Adam's primal urges. He pursued her, cornering her not only with his body but his words.

"Yes. It doesn't matter to you that we've fucked dozens of gorgeous women and were never once motivated to say 'I love you' to them. Never say it to any woman." Adam pressed her right into Killian, not once releasing her wide-eyed gaze. "I'm going to tan your ass for that later."

"Adam—"

"If you tell me I don't love you, I'll beat that pussy, too."

She looked so sad, so scared that her worry reached right down to his soul. Adam couldn't bear feeling her pain, much less hearing it as it whispered out of her. "You know you'll get bored of me eventually."

She almost broke him. A hairsbreadth from giving her all his tenderness and comfort, Adam about folded, but Killian's boisterous interruption broke the spell her honey gaze had wrapped him in.

"Ah-ha!"

Like a triumphant detective solving the greatest mystery of all time, Killian beamed over Rachel's head with a pride that almost made Adam smile. He could do that now because he knew it would all work out. Rachel loved them, and what fear she had would just take time to lose. As long as the outcome wasn't in doubt, Adam could give her that.

He'd even put all his efforts into sweetly seducing the worry out of her head, but not tonight. Tonight, the little darling still owed him big-time for the past two weeks of hell. Adam intended to collect. He figured that moment was just about on them. Time to start preparing. That began with the painful task of releasing Rachel.

"See? Didn't I tell you my plan would work?" Killian gloated as Adam passed by. He spared a dirty look for his partner for taking all the credit.

"I don't remember you ever being agreeable about bringing her out here."

"Yeah, but once I got onboard, I transformed your stupid idea into brilliance." Killian smirked, seeming to have forgotten the argument that had nearly brought them to blows for a second time in two weeks.

* * * *

"I don't know why the two of you are acting all victorious," Rachel snapped, earning her an annoyed look from both men. "Just because I said I love you doesn't mean I'm taking you back."

Free to breathe the fresh air, she'd gotten her vigor and sass back. So she'd crumbled completely, confessed all to them, and now they were gloating over her and their plan. It still irritated her, even if she'd begun to realize she had actually won.

The hardening realization that they loved her didn't fill Rachel with bulbous joy. Instead, it worried her because now she really had something to lose. Perhaps she was as screwed up as Killian accused her of being because she should be happy. So why wasn't she?

"Ah, honey," Killian crooned to her. His big hand cupped her cheek in its rough, warm grip. With gentle pressure, he forced her gaze up to meet his shining one. No fake smile tipped his lips up. This time, they curled with slight hint of a true smile. "I know you like to worry everything to death, but I don't get why.

"Adam," he said, jerking his head to where Adam lurked in the shadows, "I get his issues and I know he hasn't talked to you about them. It's hard for him, you see, because his family didn't know how to love. He grew up with all sorts of insecurities—"

"Hey!" Adam barked from the sidelines, clearly insulted by that. It didn't stop Killian, who remained fully focused on her.

"—so I get why he's a mess, but you I don't get it."

Rachel had come too far, revealed too much to back down now. This last bit, it didn't come easy. For most of her life, she preferred to ignore her own self-doubts, but that didn't get rid of them. It didn't make it feel any less silly as she tried to explain.

"I was never picked first."

"What?" Obviously, Killian needed more than that.

"I never got picked first for anything. I was never a teacher's pet or a playground darling. My yearbooks were filled with 'have a nice summer' because nobody knew me well enough to write anything else." Just talking about it brought up all the old depressed feelings of always being on the outside socially. "I never had more than two friends through school. Never got asked to the dance or the prom. Nobody ever seemed to notice me.

"And you," Rachel whispered, looking up hopelessly at Killian, "you're like the A-crowd and I'm way back in C-land."

If he laughed at her, Rachel really might hit him. Killian wanted to. She could see it shining in his eyes, but he managed to surprise her. Instead of telling her how dumb she sounded or even arguing her point, he showed that he actually understood.

"And that's why you're always running off, isn't it?" His thumb brushed over her cheek, making her gaze dip for a moment as she savored the small touch. "You like it when we chase. It makes you feel wanted."

"Maybe." Thinking back to the very first time she'd met Killian at the police station all the way until now, Rachel couldn't deny it. "It makes me feel…special."

"And you are, sweetheart. You are our heart and soul. Without you, we're empty," Killian assured her with such depth of emotion, Rachel could have sighed right into him. She would have if his lips hadn't kicked up in a new, wicked direction. "That's just why Adam and I have devised a way for you to run without having to throw us out."

Rachel couldn't help but to return his smile, finally feeling the lightness of euphoria sinking in with the realization this would work out. "I take it the game is about to begin?"

"Oh, yeah, darlin'." He savored the words with such joy that Rachel could tell he looked forward to what came next. "Take a look at the screen."

Rachel rolled her head in the direction he nodded to find Adam had turned on the TV. Leaning back against the altar with a remote in hand, he studied the movie playing out before him. She barely glanced at it before throwing Killian smirk.

"We're beginning with porn?" That sounded old hat to her. At least this one was a ménage— "Oh, my God. That's the sheriff!"

Before she could focus on the man helping Alex screw some blonde, the screen flipped to an image of a vacant bed. One lonely bed after another flipped through the monitor while Adam scanned the channels and Rachel tried to understand what the hell was going on.

That hadn't just been a tape of Alex. That had to have been live-action footage because he'd been wearing the exact same shirt not a couple of hours ago. That made this closed-circuit TV. Rachel's eyes glanced at the cameras overhead. Her fear was confirmed when Adam glanced back at Killian to offer him a smirk.

"Looks like nobody's busy. I guess they're all in the ballroom, waiting for the action to start."

"What does that mean?" Adam didn't even look her way, making her eyes dart to Killian. "*What does that mean?*"

"It means," Adam finally answered her, "that the next time you want to handle private business, you should do so in *private*."

Translated, that meant he intended revenge for being publicly humiliated by airing her apology to all his perverted friends. They'd turned the camera lens on her. That should have had her heart racing but not to pump molten lust through her body. Rachel stood there vibrating, deathly afraid and horribly aroused by what they planned next.

"See," Killian purred in a voice soft enough to keep her transfixed on the new images flashing through the screen. Each one showed nothing but empty paths lined with towering, perfectly-groomed bushes. "Sometimes, when a filly is too wild to tame, we bring her out here and give her this one chance to escape.

"All you have to is make it through the maze. Find the exit and we'll take you home to love you sweet and tender all through the night. No punishments. Fail and—"

The screen came alive with the image of a sea of moving people. There had to be hundreds, men and women.

"—we're going to put on a show, teach those punks how it's done."

"Killian, I—" Hell, she didn't know what she had to say to that.

"Are you going to call red-light now?"

Part of her wanted to, but she couldn't. The wanton need gripping her from the inside wouldn't let her chicken out. It didn't care what they did or who saw as long as they were touching her. With their touch she could forget anything and just feel.

"No." Rachel looked up at him and, with all sincerity, told him her honest position. "I intend to find that exit."

"Well, then." Killian broke into a grin, looking strangely satisfied despite the hunger flaring in his gaze. He glanced over at Adam, taking Rachel's gaze with him. For as dangerous as he'd looked all night, before her eyes Rachel could have sworn he'd grown new muscles just to capture her with.

Over his shoulder, the mirrored image of the patio caught her attention. Rachel knew then they'd gone live, but she didn't doubt or wonder if they'd opened up their previous conversation to the masses. They'd kept the true intimacy private.

"I guess you better run, darlin'."

Killian's helpful suggestion had her gazing up at him with the realization now meant exactly that. Still, she stood there staring at him, trying to figure out if any of this was actually real. It felt real, seemed real, but somehow she couldn't escape the sudden worry she was actually dreaming.

If she was, then things were about to get very heated. Killian made that point with another silent glance at Adam. Damn if he hadn't gotten bigger. He appeared to be growing, or she was shrinking. That must be it because Rachel could almost feel her body trying to will itself into invisibility, just like all prey did when the predator had focused in on them.

"Run."

Chapter 37

Rachel didn't have to be told twice. She didn't even know if one of them had or if that thought had manifested itself, forcing itself through the anticipation to finally snap her into action. It all happened way too fast for her to catch more than the flash of Adam's legs as he leapt over the altar, the brush of Killian's fingertips as she barely managed to dodge his grasp.

All Rachel knew was she went from standing in the middle of the patio to slamming through the cold bars of garden's gate. It slammed closed behind her, catching one of the men with a grunt. Then she was simply lost.

Fear and adrenaline kept her rushing forward, turning right at every intersection until finally the pound of her own heart pained enough for her to nearly topple over, gasping for breath. Clamping a hand over her mouth, she tried to restrain the heaving sounds even as she strained to listen for the crash of oncoming men.

Only silence, crickets, and frogs echoed down the moonlit corridors. It painted the leaves of the upright bushes with a pale, waxy sheen. The ethereal glow wrapped the night in its seductive embrace, trying to mask the menace lurking the speckled shadows. They waited out there for her.

Rachel straightened up, glancing either way down the narrow alley she'd stalled out in. They should have been here. She hadn't honestly outrun them. She couldn't. That meant they let her escape, that they had something more in mind than catching her and ravishing her right on the ground.

Glancing up at the camera mounted overhead, she wondered how hard all those people would laugh if she started burrowing her way right through the walls of this maze until she found her escape. The answer didn't matter, not given the consequences of failure.

Failure and several scrapes from the pointed leaves of the bushes were all that greeted her attempt. Buried behind the wall of shrubs, caught between spindly arms of the bushes, the bastards had run a chain link fence. No doubt to assure nobody cheated at this game.

With no option to go through or over the walls, she had to make her decision—left or right. What did it matter because they'd probably already surrounded her. For no other reason than a desperate need to keep moving, Rachel chose to go forward instead of backward. This time she didn't run, panting down the aisle, but crept along, keeping a careful eye on the darkness surrounding her.

Nothing stirred around her as she came to another decision point. Right or left, the fork stalled her out as she studied both options. Both passes curved quickly, blocking her view and making it impossible to know what lay beyond.

"You know, if you turn right every time, you're never going to get out of here."

Halfway to stepping in that direction, Killian's smooth comment startled Rachel so badly she actually screamed in fright. She shouldn't have turned. She should've run, but some primitive instinct made her confront him.

From the smug smile tugging on his lips to his relaxed slouch against archway she'd just come through, Killian looked down right amused. Strung high on fear and anticipation, Rachel snapped under the provocation of his slow chuckle.

"And if you let me make my own decisions, we might not be in this mess to begin with."

Perhaps she shouldn't have said anything at all. That was the last thought that occurred to her before Killian made her forget every damn thing with his kiss. In one second, she went from standing on her own two feet to being plastered against his hot, corded length.

Literally sweeping her off her feet to capture her lips with his, Killian's broad hand flattened like a heated brand over her ass as he ground her pelvis against his mouthwatering erection. He humped her right there, through their clothes, as his warm lips moved against her own with torrid intent.

He tasted like beer and man, penetrating her with his intoxicatingly addictive flavor until her tongue tangled with his in the endless dance of desire that had her hips flexing in time with his. The blatant intimidation of his possessive embrace made her ache to feel him flesh-to-flesh, softness rubbing into hardness, heated palms and rough grips that clung, gripped, bit...oh, God, she wanted him to bite her and then pin her down and ride her until they dripped with sweat.

It wouldn't be enough. It would never be enough no matter how hard, how long they fucked. The fires searing through her stomach would always smolder. That's what scared Rachel. There would be no line she wouldn't cross with this man. Nothing she wouldn't let him do.

"Ah, baby, you're all wet," Killian groaned, his hand curving around her ass to dip in between her legs.

His touch seared through the layers of fabric as he cupped her mound and began rubbing her panties over her slit. Swollen with lust, her clit blossomed out from her folds, getting caught and teased by the hard brush of such soft cotton.

The unbelievable pleasure only left her aching for more. Arching into his touch, Rachel's fingers dug into Killian shoulders, using his strength as leverage to grind her pussy back into his palm.

"All wet and ready to ride," Killian chuckled, "but I think these boys were hoping to see more than just you pinned up against the shrubs with your skirt around your waist, don't you?"

"I don't really give a damn what they want to see," Rachel ground out, not about to let him ruin her moment with irritating worries.

She'd gone too long without his touch to bother with modesty or decency right then.

"Yeah?" Killian pressed one thick finger between her puckered lips to trap her clit beneath its toying caress. "Maybe this location can work. They might like seeing you naked, being ridden on all fours. Hell, we could do the wheel barrel. You'll be the bucket, your spread legs the handles, and my cock can be the hitch. What do you say, darlin'? Want me to take you for a walk?"

Rachel blinked at the very idea he planted in her mind. He had to be kidding, but the thing about Killian was she could never tell. Time to flee and wonder later. Of course, getting free to escape would require some deception, like smiling down at him and cooing.

"Let me slip out of my dress."

He knew. The bastard knew she intended to run, which made Rachel almost sure he had been joking. Still, if she didn't run, he might feel honor bound to go through with his threat. Either way, Rachel didn't linger once her feet touched the ground.

Giving him a shove that never would topple him over, she took off as fast as she could down the right path. If he didn't want her taking all the right turns, then he shouldn't have said not to. Convinced that she must have discovered the hidden secret, she ran for nearly five minutes straight, certain that freedom awaited around every corner until she ran right into a dead-end.

Well, shit. Now she had to go backward, but that way felt dangerous, looked darker than it had when she'd come tearing down the aisles. Perhaps if she made nothing but left turns she could end up back at the patio. Then maybe she could lock them out.

Or maybe she should come up with a good idea because Killian and Adam could easily come over those gates. Hell, they could probably come right through them if properly motivated. She had to stop panicking and think. *The stars.*

Rachel glanced up at the heavens, not recognizing a single thing in the sky, but that didn't matter. All she needed to do was pick one and always walk toward it as best as she could, and eventually it would have to lead her to the edge of this maze. It seemed wise to pick the brightest one, that way she couldn't lose it in the glimmering sea of millions of stars.

This time, she moved forward, concentrating on keeping to the shadows, staying as quite as possible. At every turn she glanced up, making her choice based on the direction of her star. Things felt like they progressed more quickly. Now that she had a plan, Rachel felt more in control, more confident as she moved along the paths.

Using her intellect and reason, she'd find her way out of this maze. Then Killian and Adam could take her home to celebrate in private. It could work. After all, man hadn't climbed to the top of the food chain by brute strength alone. Intelligence, that's where true power lay. These Cattlemen had probably never had to deal with prey armed with that kind of weapon.

No. She was a new breed of woman to them and…she was totally fucked. Rachel froze in the middle of another Y-intersection. With her eyes shifting down from her star, she caught the slightest glimmer from the shadows. A hint of reflected light there and then gone. It had her gaze narrowing in on the darkest part of the path to the right until slowly the blacker shape of a man became visible.

He shifted forward, barely moving into the light, leaving most of his face clouded in darkness but for that feral gaze glinting with full focus in her direction. Adam. From the crunch of a heavy footstep not but a few feet behind her, Rachel knew Killian had come in to block her escape. That left her one option. Without pausing to take a breath, she took it and fled down the path to the left.

This time, she could hear them chasing after her. Not crashing in from behind, but circling all around her. For a moment, she could have sworn one of them raced right past her, just on the other side of the bushes. Clearly, they knew this maze well, too well, because as they appeared in every turn, Rachel began to realize they were controlling her decisions, chasing her toward something.

The only way to escape would be to go through one of them. The only way to win would be to disable one of them completely. She couldn't do it, or didn't think so, until the dim glow of electric light brightened the sky over the hedge line.

She could hear the babble of water. That had to be freedom because they were trying to block her from it. Every time she tried to turn toward the small sign of civilization, one of them appeared to force her back into the maze.

Somehow, she had to break their line. Rachel bet Killian would be an easier choice than Adam. He didn't appear to have half as much pent-up aggression as Adam did tonight. Whatever trauma lay in his childhood, he'd never told her about it. That didn't mean Rachel couldn't sense the depth of hurt masked by his anger and lust.

What fueled him tonight would make for a hell of an explosion if he caught her. That made Killian her obvious choice, but she had to wait through two more turns before he appeared as the shadow in the bend trying to force her in the opposite direction. With Adam bearing down hard behind her, Rachel didn't have any time to question her decision but threw herself in a full throttle run at Killian.

He lunged, and she ducked, shockingly clearing past him to sprint in an all-out dash for the light at the end of the alley. Feeling them pounding over the ground and swearing their heated breath brushed over her nape, Rachel threw everything she had into making it to the lit archway to freedom.

Racing beneath its blossoming canopy, she welcomed the warmth of the light and the soft granules of sand beneath her feet…Pulling up hard, she skidded through the dirt, nearly stumbling into the tailored stream that surrounded not her victory but her defeat.

She knew this place. She'd seen it flash by on the television as Adam had flipped through the channels earlier. All those differently styled beds and they'd chosen this one for her.

She took in the sight of the thatched roof cabana buried in the lush and the tropical foliage that grew thick on the other side of the rocked lined pond encircling the little oasis. No amount of elegant lighting or decadent looking bedding could disguise the savage purposes of the little hut.

The danger glinted in the sheen of the metal rings encircling each of the wooden posts. It whispered out in the soft whoosh of the sway of the metal bars that spanned their distance and had nothing to do with support. At least not for the cabana, but as she studied the bed stretching the entire length and filling the full width, Rachel realized it hung off the ground by several feet, suspended almost like a large swing.

Similar to the patio, the small hut stood as the altar in the center of the rock enwalled garden. The stacked stones crumbled artfully into the waterfall and grew out the other side to enclose the back of the garden with all the modern conveniences, including more cameras.

"Custom made of a prehistoric baboon," Killian drawled from the archway behind her. "What do you think?"

Rachel had to hand it to the good old boys, they'd done things right and spared no expense. Despite the rapid chase, ending up corralled into an exotic garden obviously designed for luxury and excess didn't exactly put terror into her stomach.

"It's a little too romantic looking for that." She offered him a smirk over her shoulder, catching sight of Adam prowling determinedly closer. She ignored him to turn back and inspect the location they'd picked to ravish her.

"More like Tarzan's honeymoon hideaway. Tell me, are those vines real or used for something else?" Rachel nodded at the thick, woodsy branches curling around the edge of the roof and falling down nearly to the sides of the bed.

"Metal reinforced." Adam's words washed across her shoulder with the sultry heat of a promise. "Why don't you take a closer look?"

With one hand he might have gestured, matching the politeness of his request. His other, though, pressed into the small of her back, forcing her to obey when she hesitated. Once she crossed over the small arch of wood bridging the two sides of the pond, there would be no escaping the unblinking eyes of the cameras.

There would be no escaping anyway, not with Adam prodding her forward. As much as she wanted to play it calm and cool, fear nibbled away at her arousal, making her all too aware of the spies in the sky. She tried to focus on something else, like the cool breeze whispering around her ankles and tickling up her sides.

The obviously artificial cold distracted her, giving her sanity a much-needed break as her mind began to obsess over its origins. The vents she found artfully cut into the cabana's post made her smile with both triumph and wonder.

"An air conditioned gazebo?" Rachel arched a brow at Adam, who only shrugged.

"Gotta keep things cool when you're getting sweaty."

Rachel rolled her eyes at that but couldn't help the smile that tugged at her lips. Despite the coiled tension keeping him stiff as he angled her closer to the bed, there had been a hint of true humor in Adam's tone. It quelled the chattering nerves in her belly and sent Rachel a few more steps into her doom.

Still, that didn't carry her far when her gaze caught the stretch of blackness against the far wall. The sight of the television stood as a grim reminder of everything she'd been trying not to think about. Appearing to catch the direction of her thoughts, or possibly her gaze, Adam growled beside her.

"Don't worry about them, Rachel." Deep and husky, Adam's words rumbled through her head to sink their warmth and assurance into her quivering stomach. "There ain't anybody here tonight but you, me, and Killian. That's the way it's always going to be, just the three of us, and who really cares what the rest of the world knows of it? Thinks of it?"

The rough edges wore on her panicked nerves, melting them until she rested against the hard wall of his chest. He smelled like alcohol and musk, sexy as hell. The scent drugged her, making her muscles go limp beneath the soft brush of his lips along her nape. The slow, sensual slide sent shivers racing down her spine until his kiss paused at the edge of her dress's strap.

"You have the softest skin." The rough sprout of whiskers along his cheek both tickled and scratched as he rubbed his chin along her shoulder. The sharp, almost jagged shards of pleasure had her flinching slightly, shrinking back just enough to let him nudge the strap out of the way.

"There's nothing like grinding into all your plush, silky curves, darlin'. It's a small taste of heaven that I've been aching for these past two weeks. Wanting you awake, asleep, always." The words peppered out across the sensitive dip in her nape as he strung them, kiss by kiss, across her shoulders until his lips rested at her other strap.

"I want to feel you like that again, sweetheart, all naked and wet, hear you moaning my name and begging me for all your pleasure. I need to have you my way, Rachel. At my mercy, mine to please and to demand my pleasure from."

Rachel shivered, trapped not in his arms but by the very heat of his words. They slipped out with such longing and echoing the very pain she'd carried for the past few weeks that Rachel couldn't deny him.

"Let me have you," Adam pleaded in a whisper no louder than the soft swoosh of her strap being nudged over the rounded edge of her shoulder. "And I promise to take very good care of you."

He already was. Rachel couldn't stop the whimper that slipped from her lips as Adam's rough palm scraped up her arm. The small touch sparked fissures of electricity through her. The tingles tightened her nipples, puckering them to points that caught the edge of her dress as Adam slid the second strap down. It clung there for a moment before dropping to a puddle at her feet.

"My sweet Rachel, you're not wearing a bra." Wrapped in the strength of his arms, Rachel sucked a breath in and arched as his hands slid around to cup her breasts. Already puckered with need, her nipples sent out spasms of pleasure as his thumbs rolled over their pebbled tips.

"You really shouldn't go about not properly dressed," Adam warned her. "It puts all sorts of ideas into a man's head. Doesn't it, Killian?"

Chapter 38

"Mmm-hmm." That soft savory sound tickled over her stomach, making Rachel's eyes flutter open. Somewhere along the way, the slow, rolling wave of liquid heat Adam's tone had whirled to life inside her had slid her lashes down. She'd let go of the rest of the world to drift in that sensual tide.

Knelt at her feet in the puddle of her dress, Killian's gaze gleamed up at her with undisguised hunger. Her breath caught in the back of her throat as his chin dipped to press a small kiss over her quivering muscles. His tongue lapped out to twirl over her belly button before sliding straight up to where Adam held her tit captive for him.

Heat sizzled through her veins as his velvety tongue curled around her nipple and drew her into the liquid suction of his kiss. The sensual pull unleashed a torrent of molten need sliding down skin already flushed by the rough rub of Killian's clothed body.

Cocooned in the comforting scent of her men, Rachel let herself melt into them and gave over to their will. Slowly, her body began to roll and grind, matching the smooth, easy rhythm of Killian's mouth as he loved on her…and he did love her.

Those big, callused hands caressing up her sides to chase Adam's from her breast held her in a slightly possessive grip. Even though they were both hers, they warred over who got to enjoy what. Adam admitted defeat with a soft growl.

As his hands slid down to her waist, Killian celebrated with a nip that jolted her into a sudden arch. The small assault sent sharp bolts of pleasure straight down to her pussy, which had started to grow warm under the heat of Adam's palm.

Thick fingers slipped under the band of her panties, pushing the lacy fabric out of his way until they sighed down her thighs. Then he was touching her, the edge of his palm pressing down over her mound, those magical fingers slipping between her swollen folds. Rachel moaned, needing this too much to let them deny her. That small fear that they might stop at any moment had her hand curling into Killian's silky hair to hold him fast to her breast while her other covered Adam's fingers in a silent demand.

"You want to show us how you like it?" Adam growled, lacing his fingers through hers.

"Please, Adam," Rachel begged with the press of her palm against his.

Miraculously, he obeyed, letting her grind his hand over her clit. The hard rub set her tender bud vibrating with a frequency so pleasurable Rachel's entire pussy started to pulse in wanton demand to join the party. Adam took over, whipping her sensitized nub into a frenzy that Killian matched with his tongue whirling over her nipple.

They knew her too well, loved her enough to have learned every single thing that drove her insane. Giving herself over to the pleasure, Rachel dropped her head back against Adam's shoulder as she gave him one final direction. Curling her fingers over his, she plunged them into her pussy and moaned out as the rapture started to engulf her.

It's been too long... "Too long." *Missed this every day...* "Every damn day." *Dreamt of fucking you...*"Every damn night...All damn day...The things you did to me...Adam!"

Rachel babbled through the whispers swirling through her head, ending in a screech as Adam's fingers picked up tempo. As his fingers pumped into her hard and fast, her hips slammed her up and down as she strained for the final explosion. Only one thought remained.

"Not enough," Rachel whined, arching her whole body as she tried to make his fingers long enough, thick enough to fill her the way she needed. "Please...oh, God. It's not enough."

"Well, maybe this is, darlin'."

Like that, Killian was there to save her. Rachel didn't know when he'd released her breasts or straightened up, but she didn't care as the thick, bulbous head of his cock tried to stretch open her opening enough to fit alongside Adam's fingers.

Again they warred, making her mew and squeal as they fought over who had the right to fuck her. Killian won, surging in harder and thicker than she remembered. He filled her to perfection, making her gasp as the world faded into nothing but blurs and pleasure.

"Greedily little bastard." Adam growled, clearly annoyed to be on the losing end again. The rumble of his words sent a thrill through Rachel, leaving her smiling around the pants Killian fucked out of her.

"Shut up, Adam."

"Watch it now, wench," he warned her, bringing that threat through with a twist of her nipple. The small pain got magnified by the pulsing waves of splendor radiating through her. The sharp contrast had her twisting on a moan that only tempted him to do it again.

"*Adam.*"

"That's right, darlin'." Adam treated her other nipple to the same rough caress. "Soon it's going to be my cock tunneling through that tight pussy. You're going to wish you'd been nicer to me then."

"Shut up, Adam," Killian seconded her command then caught the giggle that rolled her lips in a kiss.

Behind her, Adam muttered a few choice insults at this partner but held her steady for him as Killian drove her one thrust at time into the heavens. Dazzling prisms of exploding light flared behind her eyes, and with a snap, she catapulted right into the most amazing orgasm she'd ever had. It took her to a fairy land where everything was bright and happy.

Slowly, she floated back to the musky, sweaty embrace of men. It still felt like heaven. She smiled dreamily, thinking they'd only started to play. What came next had her lashes lifting, but with her head lying limp on Adam's shoulder, the first thing she saw was the dark gaze of the camera staring back at her.

A second later, Killian stepped back, leaving her naked, used, and exposed. For some reason, that only made Rachel feel sexy. Maybe tomorrow, when she came down from this high, she'd reconsider the matter, but right then her smile only grew as she turned her gaze on her stallion.

With his hair curling around his forehead in sweaty clumps and his features drawn tight, Killian looked more like a war horse ready for battle than a stud that had already won the race. Her gaze flirted over his shirt to where his jeans hung open. Glistening with her cream, his cock still stood rock hard and ready for action.

Rachel knew Killian could go a couple of turns in a row, but not like that. That came from holding back. A smile tried to tug at his lips, nearly cracking his clenched jaw in the process. The effort warmed Rachel as did Killian's gentle touch.

Reaching out to cup her chin, he made her melt all over with his sweet words.

"This night is for you, honey. All for you, and we're going to give you all the pleasure you deserve." Killian swiped a finger over her trembling lips, closing them when they went slack beneath his thumb. "There aren't going to be any more punishments by denial because you deserve better, because you deserve to be pleased, and we live to pleasure you."

"Of course, after the seventh orgasm, the eighth might feel like punishment." Adam's tone didn't sound the slightest bit tender but more like downright amused, as if the idea of driving her insane with climaxes almost made him laugh.

"Only eight?" Rachel tipped her head to the side so she could share her own smile. "Really, Adam, I thought you were good for more than that."

He tensed immediately at that taunt. His fingers tightened their grip on her hip, pulling her back into the large erection he kept holstered in his jeans. "Are you sure you want to be challenging me right now?"

"Oh, come on, Adam," Killian cajoled. "You know our little Rachel likes to play. So what do you say, darlin'? Ready to step up to the bat?"

Rachel eyed the blindfold he'd pulled from his back pocket. They might think being blinded would intimidate her, but it would only help her escape this reality to live in the one they created with their touch. Not that she could help tweaking Killian's smirk with a lofty tone.

"Really, Killian? A blindfold? Aren't you boys ever going to come up with something original?"

* * * *

Every possessive instinct, every dominating desire hardened Adam's body as he watched Rachel take a hold of the blindfold. It wasn't enough to have her naked at their mercy with that sweetly creaming cunt scenting the air. Adam thrilled to watch her accept her position, to claim it as her own as she blinded herself and gave herself completely over to their control.

She didn't have to tell him she loved him. Adam didn't need the words when her actions spoke so clearly. He knew she didn't trust any other men enough to let them do this to her. Needing to touch, to feel her compliance, Adam ran his fingertips down the graceful arc of her spine.

With a murmur of desire, she followed his touch. As his fingers flared over her hip and curved around the plush slope of her ass, Rachel moaned and shifted forward to rest her chest against Killian. Anchored in his partner's arms, her back arched and her legs parted, silently presenting him with the shadowed access to her pink folds. Adam gazed at the fruit she so willingly offered him.

He would be feasting on that sweet flesh, but first he wanted her complete submission. Meeting Killian's gaze, Adam smirked slightly. It didn't pain him in the slightest to help Killian arrange her on the bed. Their jealous actions earlier had been solely for Rachel's benefit, an assurance that they desired her that much.

From the sexy little moans she made as they tied her into place to the glistening trickle of desire slicking the inside of her thighs, Adam knew their plan had worked. From Killian's idea to run her to ground to Adam's conviction that they torment her with the idea that they were being watched, they'd staged the whole night with one sole purpose—to seduce Rachel.

With Rachel flushed and panting already, Adam figured they'd achieved their goals. There could be no hiding the evidence of her desire with her stretched out and bound to the bed. Rachel was a thing of sensual beauty, catching him between the need to stare and the equally consuming urge to dip down deep into her pearly cunt and forage for heaven.

It was just a shame that Rachel couldn't see how very sexy she looked. Then maybe she wouldn't doubt that it was Killian and him who had gotten lucky. Next time, maybe, they'd leave the blindfold off and she could watch as he pressed his head between her pinned and trembling thighs to lap at her swollen folds.

She tasted like sex, rich, addictive sex. The flavor stirred the blood in his veins to a boil, intoxicating him, addicting him to the delicious flavor. He couldn't stop, and with the demand pounding in his balls, Adam couldn't be gentle.

Whipping her clit with his tongue, he delighted in the shrieking twist that ripped through her body. With the binds holding her in place, she couldn't escape him as he feasted on her pussy. Forcing her to a hard, furious climax, he rode her swollen bud straight through it with his kiss until she stiffened a second time. Screeching as her thighs clamped tight around his head, her cunt pulsed with wave after wave of thick cream.

Feeling driven by a primitive instinct that only increased as he drowned in the flavor of her release, Adam tormented her clit as he relentlessly drove her from one screaming orgasm to another until he'd counted seven climaxes in a row. The thighs that had once gripped his head now spasmed and jerked as she sobbed his name.

Finally, he paused, lifting up to cover her sweaty, quivering frame with his own. It took several moments for her breathing to stutter down to a more normal pace and even more for her to stop mewing with every breath. Only when he knew she'd hear did Adam bother to tease.

"So, wench, are you ready for that eighth one now?"

Her head had flopped to the side, limp and weary. Now it tilted, her chin rising slightly as she turned blindly toward him. He couldn't believe she had the energy left to smile, albeit a small one.

"Well, if you're feeling generous, I'll take seven more."

Adam growled, both pleased and provoked by her flippant answer. "Brave words for a woman whose heart is trying to beat right out of her chest."

"And hollow ones from the man whose dick is veined with the imprint of his zipper," Rachel shot back. "Tell me, Adam, can you really last seven more, yourself?"

No, and if he said yes, he'd be made a liar of soon enough. Not that he'd admit defeat so easily. "What if I give you the next seven on the end of that pole, darlin'? You think you can take that ride?"

"I don't know," Rachel admitted, her smile never dipping. "But I'd sure like to find out."

Ah, hell. Why did she have to go there? Adam had planned all sorts of fun and games, but he'd failed to take into account his own urgency. She wasn't wrong about his zipper. Since hearing that greenlight Adam was having a hard time keeping his cock leash anymore.

It was coming out whether or not it had to bust his jeans open its damn self. Adam placed all the blame for the pain and difficulty of getting himself free on Rachel's head. If she'd just been docile for once instead of driving him completely bonkers, he would have had a chance at completing at least some of his things on his to-do-to-her list.

Later, maybe tomorrow, he'd get to them. Now he had to get his zipper down without doing too much damage. Rachel didn't help, whispering his name in that breathy way that heated every primitive instinct Adam possessed. It gave him the strength to rip the zipper nearly clean off, popping the tab free to assure it would never zip up again.

Adam didn't care. Not when after two straight weeks of hell, he was finally back to kissing heaven. The engorged head of his cock sizzled against the cool, creamy welcome of her cunt. Slick and swollen, her pussy parted easily as he ground his way past her tight entrance. With narrowed eyes, Adam watched as her pussy swelled with his girth, stretching wide and clenching tight as her cunt sucked him right into its heavenly embrace.

His little wench moaned and bucked, trying to drive him deeper, but Adam wouldn't be rushed. Gripping her hips to hold her still, he pressed forward even slower, savoring the delicious feel of her muscles clamping and pulsing all down his sensitive length. Then he was there, balls-deep, back where he belonged.

Pausing to hold on to the moment strained his control. His lungs began to bellow out air in great ragged gasps as he fought the need growing to a ferocious level. Beneath him, Rachel twisted in an endless sway of smooth curves and soft skin, moist with sweat and slick with desire. *His woman.*

But not his alone. Adam knew Killian waited at the sides. The moment Adam had penetrated Rachel, Killian had gone to work on her binds. Adapting to the new plan, he hadn't released her so she could curl her arms around Adam's neck or her legs around his waist.

No, Killian wanted something different. Adam didn't deny him. Wrapping his arms around her and holding her flush and tight to his chest, Adam rolled until she sprawled over him. Rachel knew this position well. Her anticipation showed in the sudden clench of her muscles.

Trapped inside her tight heat, Adam groaned over the sweet constriction. It made it all that much harder to stay still and wait for Killian to join them. As his partner's knee sank into the mattress and his weight shifted forward the, bed swung slightly, jarring Adam up against the velvety walls of her pussy and making his control slip ever so slightly.

He couldn't stop himself from rolling his hips, making Rachel squirm and amplify the glorious spasms that raced down her cunt's walls. Adam felt every one like a blazing kiss that sucked straight down his cock. The searing pleasure tempted him into another flex that had Killian grunting out obscenities as he climbed the rest of the way into the bed.

"Damnit, man. Will you hold still?"

"I'm trying," Adam retorted, his voice strained with the effort. The bed had started a slow easy rocking motion that made Rachel shift in the most delightful ways. "Maybe you should just hurry the fuck up?"

"Maybe you shouldn't wait on him," Rachel murmured against his neck before licking a spot clean to take a bite.

"*Damnit!*"

Killian snarled as Adam jerked. He didn't have it in him right then to punish Rachel's insolence, but he made a note to get to it later. Much later, maybe tomorrow or the day after, Adam reconsidered as Rachel nibbled her way up to his ear and began whispering all sorts of dirty, encouraging things.

Or maybe he'd let her come up with her own punishment because the things she said made his cock swell too painfully to stay still. Feeling Killian's thickness compress her tight channel into a form-fitting sheath didn't help other than to make Rachel's words dribble into a moan. She twitched and panted as Killian settled his full length into her.

"Now let's hear you give us some sass, wench," Killian growled over Rachel's shoulders, pumping his hips enough to make Adam match the sound.

God, he wanted to move, but with Killian holding Rachel still by the waist, Adam didn't even get the pleasure of her motions. All he got was stuck in a molten heaven quickly turning to hell without the sweet friction of fucking to save him.

"Nothing to say, huh?" How Killian could gloat so cheerfully while Adam lay there burning with need, he did not know. What he did know was if Killian didn't get to moving, Adam would rip Rachel out of his grasp and take care of things himself.

"I love you, Adam, and trust me when I say I'll make you suffer in ways you can't imagine if you ever leave me for another woman. You belong to me."

Rachel snapped the thread of his composure with the wild passiveness of her words. He couldn't hold on any longer. His hips shifted, making sweat gather and bead down his back as he suffered the exquisite pull of her pussy when he slid almost completely free. The coiled tension in his muscles snapped as he drove back into her warmth.

Behind her, Killian grunted out a curse and returned Adam's favor with his own full-length thrust. Then it was on. Trapped between them, Rachel writhed in screaming ecstasy as Adam raced Killian, fucking their woman with the savage need that had built over the past two weeks.

Swollen and already straining toward release, his balls flared brightly with pure rapture at forcing his cock back through the clenched muscles of her tight pussy, harder, faster, never being able to fulfill the demand for more. Even when all he knew of the world was the sweet suck of her cunt clamping down and trying to milk the seed right from his balls, Adam's lust only grew.

He didn't want to give in to that pleasure. Not yet. Not when it was so much more fun to make her scream even louder as her torso flushed and glistened with sweat. She'd turned into a creature of pure wanton demand, moans and inarticulate pleas falling from between grunts as she bucked between him and Killian, chasing after her own release.

Then her teeth sank into her lower lip and he knew she'd arrived. Only then did Adam finally give into the bliss searing right down his spine until his cock pulsed with endless waves of rapture. Stiffening under the impact, his fingers gripped down on Rachel's hips as she followed him in the ride through the sun.

Blinded and consumed by his release, it took Adam several minutes to crack his eyes and return to the world around him. He didn't even have the strength to groan at finding himself flattened under the pile of bodies. Nor did he have the energy to do anything about the fact that he remained hard, despite having blown through the greatest climax of his life.

A fact Rachel apparently couldn't help teasing him about as she wiggled. "One down, six to go."

Either her motions or her words caused Killian to finally rouse, answering her with a grumpy tone before Adam could. "We put her down, Adam, but we didn't put her out. How do you think that's going to look to the boys back at the club house?"

The pointed reminder to the cameras should have had Rachel showing some amount of apprehension or at least reservation. She didn't know that it was all an illusion, that nobody was really watching them. Apparently, it wouldn't have mattered if they had given the boys back in the ballroom a good show.

"I think it means you two are going to have to work very hard to impress anybody this night."

"Oh, baby," Adam whispered. "You really shouldn't have said that."

Epilogue

Monday, May 26th

"And it better not be stale. You're not passing any heat-lamp warmed pie off on me, young lady."

Heather smiled in the face of Mr. Bavis's dour comments. The man had becoming into the Bread Box long enough to know they didn't even have any heat lamps. That didn't stop him from ending his order with the same warning every Monday morning when he showed up for his ritual slice of rhubarb pie.

"I'll make sure you get the freshest slice." That was Heather's traditional rejoinder, along with a wink that she knew irritated the crabby geezer. "Along with coffee from the top of the pot."

Bavis's jaw clicked closed as Heather managed to get her response in before he could offer up his warning about bottom of the pot coffee. The way his gaze narrowed at her near flippancy only made Heather's grin grow. It still didn't beat the smile Rachel wore as she shoved in the front door.

That kind of glowing happiness would have Bavis griping more than usual if he got wind of it. Hoping to avoid any unpleasantness, Heather nodded toward the back in a silent signal for Rachel to meet her in the kitchen. It didn't take but a minute to get Bavis's pie ready.

Serving it to him with a large glop of whip cream and a steaming cup of coffee, she paused, giving him the opportunity to warn her about canned whip cream. Then Heather assured him she'd whipped it by hand just that morning. Once all the traditions in their preprogrammed conversation had been observed, Heather turned to head back toward the kitchen, leaving Tina to keep Bavis's cup full.

"Well, I can already tell you had a good weekend. Let me take a guess, you're back together with Bevis and Butthead." Heather didn't even wait for Rachel to start in as she shoved through the kitchen's double doors.

That dimmed Rachel's smile as her gaze sharpened on Heather. "Don't call them that."

"Why not?" Heather asked. "You'll be calling them that by the end of the week when they do whatever it is that will piss you off."

"Boy, you're cranky today," Rachel grouched. She'd settled down on the stool Heather kept right next to the racks of cooling cookies just for Rachel. "Let me take a guess, you still haven't found a replacement for GD."

Heather shot Rachel a dirty look for that crack. "Are we going to argue today?"

Rachel appeared to consider that option before her eyes suddenly lit up on the tray of chocolate chunk cookies within arm's reach. "Of course not. I'm a kind and sensitive person. I wouldn't torment you with the details of just how fantastic it is to have two men totally worship you and dedicate hours to your personal pleasure.

"Why it would be rude to rattle on about how Killian goes off like a stallion in heat every time I tell him I love him. And I am not a rude person." With that assurance given, Rachel popped a cookie into her mouth and still managed to grin while chewing.

"No, of course not." Heather rolled her eyes before turning toward the warming oven filled with rising dough. "So did Killian go off like a stallion in heat when you told him you'd helped set up one of his best friends to be busted visiting a whore house you've been investigating behind their backs? Or did you just skip the confessions and cave completely into the sex?"

"We talked," Rachel retorted, pausing with a cookie halfway to her mouth to return the hard look Heather shot her. "*We did.* We actually sat down and wrote out a list of rules."

"Rules?" Heather almost laughed at that. Starting to turn the dough out onto the table to be kneaded, she cast Rachel another look. "We're not talking about sex again, are we?"

"Like there are any rules to sex," Rachel snorted, waving the idea away. "No, I'm talking about relationship rules, like they won't smoother me at every turn and I'll be more open and honest with them."

"Honest? So you did confessed all?" Heather asked in disbelief.

"No, I didn't tell them about Hailey's game," Rachel shot back indignantly before pausing to kind of shrug. "But you know, they love me and they're just worried I might get hurt. That does kind of give them some rights to interfere when they believe I might be in trouble. I can't really get mad at them for that, now can I?"

"It's your life," Heather responded evenly, though she wouldn't have put up with that kind of arrogant behavior from a man.

Thankfully for her, she didn't have to because there wasn't a man around Pittsview who wanted to get bossy over a woman with a kid. Get busy with, sure. There were way too many of those types cluttering up Pittsview, which was just why Heather needed GD.

"Yes, it is," Rachel answered, drawing Heather's attention from her grim thoughts back to her suddenly righteous friend. "Killian and Adam love me, and I love them. We might have our issues and our friction but love—"

"Conquers all?" Heather asked, smirking at Rachel's naïve sermon.

"Yes, it does." Rachel had to know how she sounded, but that didn't stop her from lifting her chin.

"Well," Heather turned back to her dough, "I know who will be getting conquered once those two deputies realize what you got going on with Kitty and Hailey. You want to take a guess on how they'll react?"

"No. I'm just waiting to experience it," Rachel murmured way too smugly.

That tone had Heather pausing again to study her friend. "What did you do?"

Heather knew Rachel had done something. The truth was there in the flush that flashed across her cheeks. Going still, Rachel blinked, looking guilty as hell and searching for a good lie to cover her tracks. The best she apparently could come up with was a simple, one word retort.

"Nothing."

"Rachel?"

"*Nothing!*"

That was a bold-faced lie that Heather could see right through. "You didn't tell them anything?"

"I would never betray a friend." There was enough indignation in that retort for Heather to believe Rachel. "You know me better than that."

"Yeah, I do," Heather agreed. "You might not squeal, but you would make sure everybody got caught. So what did you do? Leave some notes conveniently lying about the place?"

"I don't know what you are talking about." There went Rachel's chin, up and out. It was a clear indication that she was not only affronted but guilty as hell. A truly offended Rachel would have gotten pissed and not gone cold, but Heather didn't call her on it.

As far as she was concerned Hailey, Kitty, Patton, and even Rachel deserved what they got for playing stupid games with those Cattlemen. Not that she felt any great sympathy for Cole Jackson. Cole had too much charm and not enough substance in Heather's book.

He probably did deserve the hell Hailey wanted to rain down on him. Still, that didn't excuse Hailey's behavior. She'd gotten involved with the cocky Cattleman and knew what she was getting into. As far as Heather saw it, Hailey didn't have much right be complaining now.

"Besides," Rachel pointedly turned the conversation, "I have a new, more interesting case to pursue. If I'm right, this is going to be the story of a lifetime."

Before Heather could jump at that juicy bit of bait, Tina stuck her head in the door and called out, "Heather, Konor Dale is out here asking for you. I think he wants to put in a special order."

"Konor Dale," Rachel fairly purred, her grin growing big again. "Now there's an option you should consider, given GD's busy and all."

"Don't even," Heather warned Rachel. Konor Dale might be a hottie in most women's book, but Heather only saw his one tragic flaw.

"He's a Cattleman."

Make that two, Heather corrected herself at Rachel's reminder of the other reason she would never be ordering up any of Konor's special services.

"And partnered with the sheriff."

Which was the very reason why Heather wouldn't have said yes if Konor even asked her to dance. That pervert, Alex Krane, had gotten to see all he was ever going to see of her naked body.

THE END

http://www.jennypenn.com

ABOUT THE AUTHOR

I live near Charleston, SC with my biggie, my dog. I have had a slightly unconventional life. Moving almost every three years, I've had a range of day jobs that included everything from working for one of the world's largest banks as an auditor to turning wrenches as an outboard repair mechanic. I've always regretted that we only get one life and have tried to cram as much as I can into this one.

Throughout it all, I've always read books, feeding my need to dream and fantasize about what could be. An avid reader since childhood, and as a latchkey kid, I'd spend hours at the library earning those shiny stars the librarian would paste up on the board after my name.

I credit my grandmother's yearly visits as the beginning of my obsession with romances. When she'd come, she'd bring stacks of romance books, the old fashion kind that didn't have sex in them. Imagine my shock when I went to the used bookstore and found out what really could be in a romance novel.

I've worked on my own stories for years and have found a particular love of erotic romances. In this genre, women are no longer confined to a stereotype and plots are no longer constrained to the rational. I love the 'anything goes' mentality and letting my imagination run wild.

I hope you enjoyed running with me and will consider picking up another book and coming along for another adventure.

Also by Jenny Penn

Ménage Amour: Cattleman's Club 1: *Patton's Way*
Ménage Everlasting: Cattleman's Club 2: *Hailey's Game*
Ménage Amour: The Cowboys' Curse: *Sweet Dreams*
Siren Classic: Sea Island Wolves 1: *Mating Claire*
Ménage Amour: Sea Island Wolves 2: *Taming Samantha*
Ménage Amour: Sea Island Wolves 3: Tasty Treats 3: *Claiming Kristin*
Ménage Amour*: Deception*
Ménage Everlasting*:* The Jenny Penn Collection: *Tanners' Angel*
Ménage Everlasting*:* The Jenny Penn Collection: *Jamie's Revenge*
Ménage Everlasting*:* The Jenny Penn Collection: *Kansas Heat*

Available at
BOOKSTRAND.COM

Siren Publishing, Inc.
www.SirenPublishing.com

Lightning Source UK Ltd.
Milton Keynes UK
UKHW02f2348120218
317766UK00006B/1018/P